Black Empire

Black Empire

George S. Schuyler

MINT EDITIONS

Black Empire was first published between 1936–1938.

This edition published by Mint Editions 2023.

ISBN 9781513136127 | E-ISBN 9781513136370

Published by Mint Editions®

 MINT
EDITIONS

minteditionbooks.com

Publishing Director: Jennifer Newens
Design & Production: Rachel Lopez Metzger
Project Manager: Micaela Clark
Typesetting: Westchester Publishing Services

Contents

PART I

THE BLACK INTERNATIONALE

STORY OF BLACK GENIUS AGAINST
THE WORLD

I

New York Reporter Sees a Murder, Then Gets Taken for a "Ride"

They say curiosity killed a cat. Well, it certainly got me into something destined to shake the whole world. We had just put the *Harlem Blade* to bed. I was dog-tired and before turning in I stopped by the Pelican to have a drink and a bite to eat. As I gave my order to the waitress, the front door opened. A charming, young, blonde white girl swathed in a gorgeous fur coat entered the cafe, followed by a very tall, stern-visaged black man dressed entirely in dark gray and carrying a gold-handled cane in his gloved hand. The waitress showed them a table exactly across from me.

The girl was like dozens one sees in the better parts of New York City but seldom sees in Harlem. She was not an actress or entertainer, I gathered. Rather, someone of consequence. The man was something else again. His perfect white teeth contrasted sharply with his smooth, almost black skin. Although obviously a settled individual, there were no discernable lines on his face, no pouches or bags, those telltale marks of self-indulgence. He never smiled more than in a perfunctory manner nor revealed in anyway the slightest interest in his mate. Instead, he sat almost impassive, looking thoughtfully out of the plate glass window as she animatedly talked.

I could not understand what she was saying because she spoke in undertones and was talking at a great rate. The black man continued impassively gazing across the street. She placed one bejeweled lily-like hand on his coat sleeve affectionately, almost reverently, as she changed to a begging, imploring mood. I could see the supplicant in her whole manner, could even see her lips quiver and tremble as she pleaded with him. He shook off her hand and, turning a stern and frowning face toward her, growled, "So you have failed. I cannot tolerate failure." His voice was cultured but deep and cruel. She recoiled, beaten, frightened.

"Who is that man?" I whispered to the waitress.

"I'm not sure but I think he's Dr. Belsidus. They say he lives downtown. He comes up here occasionally and he's always with some pretty white girl but I've never seen him with the same one twice. He's very refined and he tips out of this world."

This information merely quickened my interest. I wanted to know more about this mysterious doctor. As familiar as I am with Harlem and everybody who is anybody, I had neither seen nor heard of him before. When the couple finally rose, I was so consumed with curiosity that I decided to follow them. I wanted to know more about this majestic, handsome black man.

I watched him tip the waitress, then gallantly assist the pretty girl with her coat. It was after midnight when they left. They walked up Seventh Avenue to 144th Street. They were evidently engaged in deep conversation. Occasionally I could hear his booming negatives and the whimper of her pleading voice as I kept a respectable distance behind.

At 144th Street, they turned toward Lenox Avenue. I was following them on the downtown side, was indeed almost opposite them, keeping as much in the shadow as possible. Suddenly I saw the man glance up and down the street over the woman's head. Then he quickly stepped into a darkened doorway, yanking the woman with him. He placed his hand over her mouth but not before I heard a little agonized squeal. With his other hand he grabbed her throat. Then he held her tightly. Her struggles grew less and less violent. Finally, she sagged and he let her drop like a sack of oats.

Frozen to the spot by this drama, it had not occurred to me before to make any move or say anything. It had all been so sudden and unexpected. Now, as he deposited the limp body on the hall floor and turned to go, I impulsively shouted. "Hey, you. Stop! What are you doing to that girl?" I should have kept quiet and followed him, of course, but one doesn't think about such things until afterward.

He stopped in his tracks and whirled. Never have I seen such a look of trapped cruelty and sheer animal ferocity on a man's face. In his hand was clutched a wicked blue steel automatic, with a silencer on it.

"Come with me, young man," he commanded in a low gruff voice. "You have seen too much for your own good. Walk ahead of me now and walk very quickly. I shall not hesitate to kill you. You noticed, I imagine, that this gun is equipped with a silencer. The shot that kills you will make no sound."

I walked rapidly toward Lenox Avenue, cursing myself for getting into such a mess. As we got to the corner a Broadway-Columbus Avenue bus was approaching. "Hail it!! my captor growled. "I'll pay the fare. No foolishness now or I'll kill you and everybody on the bus." I knew he meant it, too.

I got on ahead of him and sat down in the first seat. He sat behind me. One hand was in his gray overcoat pocket. I knew what was in that hand. I'm not kidding when I tell you I was frightened. Suppose the man were insane? Gooseflesh grew on me at that thought.

At 125th Street he pulled the cord, whispered a gruff "get out!" and we stepped down to the curb. The bus buzzed away, leaving us practically alone. Minutes passed, how many I don't know but certainly not more than ten. Occasionally I would steal a glance at my captor and was always confused to find those deep, stern eyes drilling me through.

At last a long black limousine, with curtains drawn, drew up to the curb. A giant black man in chauffeur's uniform was at the wheel. "Get in!" the doctor ordered, prodding me with the gun. I hastened to obey. He stepped in beside me and closed the door with a bang. In the second that the light flashed on I noticed that the car was luxurious in its appointments.

When we were seated, the limousine shot down Lenox Avenue. I tried to follow its direction. Dr. Belsidus must have noticed my preoccupation and in some uncanny way divined my purpose. He snapped on a light. "Open that cabinet," he commanded, pointing to a cleverly built-in cabinet in front of us. I obeyed with alacrity and saw before me an array of bottles and whiskey and wine glasses. Dr. Belsidus tapped with his fingers on the window in front of him. The car slowed up.

"You see that black bottle?" he asked. I nodded, "Well, fill one of those whiskey glasses half full, no more, and fill it the rest of the way. with the contents of that brown bottle. Come, make haste!"

"What is it?" I asked, frightened anew at the suspicion of poison.

"Hush, and make haste!" he growled, glowering at me, irritation written in his tones. There seemed no other alternative. With sinking heart I opened the black bottle and immediately my nostrils were struck by a strange, oriental odor of unusual pungency. With trembling hand, I poured a half glassful of the stuff. It was syrupy stuff, bright green in color. The limousine had almost stopped now.

I had a premonition of something terrible, some impending tragedy. I hesitated and then glanced appealingly at the stern, silent man, who was watching me intently.

"Well, go on," he growled, frowning.

Out of the three-sided little brown bottle I poured a jet-black watery liquid that smelled like good brandy. As it mixed with the hall glass of green syrup it formed a strange coalescence, a weird agate-like pattern. I watched it hypnotically, wondering with fear and trembling what it might be.

"Drink it!" commanded Dr. Belsidus.

I took the glass in my right hand and brought it slowly to my lips. What was this strange liquid? Was it a drug or was it a poison? Who was this cold-blooded, murderous Dr. Belsidus, who so impassively sent people to their death? Even as I felt that I might be breathing my last, my curiosity of a news hound was all-consuming.

"Will this kill me?" I asked, hesitating, before I drank.

"Drink!" commanded Dr. Belsidus.

With an unspoken prayer, I tossed down the concoction. It burned my throat like raw corn liquor. I was suddenly faint with nausea. My head whirled. The man beside me became a giant striding across the skyscrapers of Manhattan. And then, in a trice he was a gnome teetering on the edge of the whiskey glass. Then he assumed his natural shape. I noted just the trace of a malevolent smirk distorting his shiny black face.

Then there was a whirling of limbs. I felt my feet walking on the ceiling of the limousine. There was nothing left of my body but a humming feeling. The air seemed filled with vague perfume. The glass fell from my hand and seemed to take a century to reach the carpeted floor. When it struck, the sound seemed almost to burst my eardrums. I tried to fight my way back to consciousness but without avail. And yet it could hardly be said that I was unconscious. I could feel, see and experience, but what I saw was strange, uncanny, unthinkable, utterly mad.

I felt as if my head had been turned by 180 degrees. My abdomen became a soft, fluid mass, my face acquired giant dimensions, my lips swelled, my arms became wooden, my feet turned into spirals and scrolls, my jaw was like a hook and my chest seemed to melt away.

Suddenly, to my great surprise I found that I had no head but in its place a sheet of ground-glass like a camera screen. Then my brain went dead and I remembered nothing more.

GEORGE S. SCHUYLER

II

REPORTER IS URGED TO ACT AS SECRETARY:
"DOCTOR" BARES PLANS

Hours, days, weeks seemed to have passed. I felt a great weight on my eyes, a weight that pressed down upon the eyeballs. Slowly, very slowly, the weight lifted, to my infinite relief. It was my own arm!

The arm was stiff, almost paralyzed. I raised my heavy eyelids. All was blackness! Was I blind? I sat up panicky, yet, even though blind, thankful that I was at least alive. I looked hastily about. Everything was blackness, silent, awesome blackness. Horrible blackness.

I felt about me. There was the touch of linen. I sat up and felt further about me. I was in bed, a great, wide, soft bed. Gradually it seemed that once more I had legs and feet. I moved them almost gratefully and luxuriated in the soft caress of the bedclothing. I had on silk pajamas.

Where was I? What had happened? Then I remembered the drink and the strange, unbelievable phantasmagoria that had whirled through my brain before everything went blank. Again I asked myself, where was I?

I lay there for hours in that black silent room, or at least it seemed hours. Then very faintly and at great distance I heard the faint honk of an auto horn. It seemed like the embrace of a long-lost mistress. I sat up eagerly in bed and my heart sang. Then everything fell silent again and I drifted off into sleep.

How long I slept that second time I do not know, I was awakened by the feel of something cold and clammy on my forehead. I jumped with a shiver. I opened my eyes. A blaze of light blinded me. Now I rejoiced that I could see, after all. I looked up, then shrank back startled and frightened. The cold, clammy object on my forehead was the hand of the chauffeur of Dr. Belsidus. So I was still in their power, then? He was a very ugly black man with bloodshot eyes and bulbous lips. He was watching me intently. Looking about, I saw that I was in a large modernistic bedroom done entirely in aluminum and black. The bed was ebony inlaid with ivory, as were the other pieces of furniture. The walls were black and aluminum. The velvet drapes were dead white. The windows were closed with black shutters which I suspected to be steel,

The lighting was indirect, shedding a soft glow. It was a rich but awe-some boudoir, like the last resting place of some long-dead Egyptian Pharaoh.

"Where am I?" I asked.

The black giant shook his head solemnly and placed an index finger to his lips. He turned and pointed me to the long ebony and ivory bench in front of the dressing table. There, neatly folded, were my clothes. The black giant nodded his head as he pointed.

"What's the matter with you?" I asked. "Can't you talk?"

He shook his head sorrowfully. He pointed again to his mouth. Then he opened it. There was nothing but a great, red cavity surrounded by fine white teeth. His tongue was gone!

I shuddered and, rising from the white linen sheets and black pillow, I walked unsteadily, almost groggily, over to my clothing and began putting it on. When I had on my underwear, socks and trousers, the dumb chauffeur clapped his hands sharply together. I started at the sound. He grinned broadly. It was in such marked contrast to the mysterious solemnity of the whole procedure that I had to smile myself.

The door of the room opened silently. A colored maid, neatly uniformed in black dress and white apron and cap, entered with a wash basin full of water, a bar of soap and a fleecy white towel. She sat them down and without a word turned and disappeared the way she had come. The dummy pointed to them and grunted, indicating that I should perform my ablutions. I wondered if they didn't have a bathroom in the place.

Finally, I was ready. I was conscious of a great emptiness in my stomach and the pangs of hunger began to assail me. The chauffeur tapped me on the shoulder and pointed to the door. I went to it, opened it and walked out of the bedroom to find myself in a long corridor hung with heavy black velvet. The door was closed silently behind me. Down the indirectly lighted corridor, I walked for perhaps fifteen paces followed closely by the dummy. At last there was break in the velvet drapes. My guard tapped me on my shoulder again and pointed to the door in the opening.

I turned the aluminum knob and pushed the door open to find my very breath taken away by the exotic magnificence of a stately dining room. The motif was green and rose and gold. The heavily piled rug was rose. The walls were a modernistic design of green and gold. Rose draperies hung from the steel-shuttered windows. Soft yellow

GEORGE S. SCHUYLER

lights from golden wall fixtures flooded the place with a gentle aura of illumination. On the walls were three beautiful murals invitingly showing all manner of exotic fruits and foods. In the center of the room was a great, long table spread with pea-green cloth. But most striking of all was the service with which the table was spread. The cutlery without exception was either golden or gold-plated. The great filigreed fruit dish, laden with huge oranges, apples, peaches and plums, was certainly golden. The cups, plates, the same precious material, eggshell thin.

I hesitated, nonplussed by such regal splendor. The door closed behind me. I turned around only to find myself again alone. I tiptoed over to the table and examined the marvelous service. Yes, it was indeed gold. Each piece carried the bold monogram "B" surmounted by at three-pointed crown. I stepped back with a little awe before such a treasure. Then I had a feeling that I was not alone; that someone was staring at me, studying me. I glanced up and down the room, puzzled. Then I turned around. There, standing silently and regarding me with a coldly amused intensity, stood tall, stern-visaged Dr. Belsidus.

"Goodmorning. Mr. Slater," he said. "I hope you slept well."

"Why, yes, I guess so. But where am I? What time is it? I've got to get back on the job."

"So you can write about what you saw last night and this morning?" he inquired sarcastically, with a slight sardonic smirk.

"Well, I'm a newspaper man," I said defiantly, "and you can't expect a newspaper man to keep quiet about murders in cold blood, drugging and all that sort of thing, can you?"

"But you will keep quiet, Carl Slater," he warned softly. "And you're not going back to that job. You are through working for the *Harlem Blade* or anybody else except Dr. Henry Belsidus."

"What do you mean?" I inquired, startled by his tone.

"You are working for me now, Slater, that's all." he said a little roughly in the tone of a man who must not be crossed. "I have spared your life because I need a competent young fellow like you as a secretary."

"How do you know I'm competent?" I countered.

"I know about every Negro intellectual in the world," he said calmly. "That is my vocation. Medicine is merely my avocation. I have been intending for sometime to bring you into my organization. Now you come by accident. I need loyal race-conscious youngsters to help me. You are that type. Slater. You can do much to aid the cause of Negro liberation, not only in America, but throughout the world. White world supremacy must be destroyed, my lad and it will be destroyed. I, Dr. Henry Belsidus, will destroy it with the aid of my loyal assistants in all parts of the world."

I couldn't help but smile at this grandiose scheme. He noted my amusement.

"It sounds mad, doesn't it?" he said.

"Yes, rather Garveyistic. I'd say."

"My son," he continued gravely, "all great schemes appear mad in the beginning Christians, Communists, Fascists and Nazis were at first called scary. Success made them sane. With brains, courage and wealth even the most fantastic scheme can become a reality. I have dedicated my life. Slater, to destroying white world supremacy. My ideal and objective is very frankly to cast down the Caucasians and elevate the colored people in their places. I plan to do this by every means within my power. I intend to stop at nothing. Slater, whether right or wrong. Indeed, in a plan such as this there can be no talk of right or wrong. Right is success. Wrong is failure. I will not fail because I am ruthless. Those who fail are the men who get sentimental, who weaken, who balk at a little bloodshed. Such vermin deserve to fail. Every great movement the world has ever seen has collapsed because it grew weak. I shall never become weak, nor shall I ever tolerate weakness around me. Weakness means failure. Slater, and I do not intend to fail."

"But how can you succeed?" I asked, eager to learn as much as possible. "Haven't white people got all the power, all the industry, all the money?"

"They have now," he admitted. "but they not have it long. I and my comrades shall destroy them or make them destroy themselves. We have brain, the best brains in the Negro race. We have science of which the white man has not dreamed in our possession. We have courage. And we are absolutely ruthless."

"I noticed that last night," I said, significantly.

"You mean that white woman?" he asked. "Bah! I use their women to aid in their destruction. As long as they succeed in carrying out my mission. I spare them. When they fail. I destroy them. That girl failed to obtain a valuable secret I desired, so I destroyed her. Otherwise, she might have talked. You know, I do not trust white people. I just use them."

"But that's murder," I objected. "Cold-blooded murder."

"Of course it's murder," he said, smirking sardonically. "What of it? What are a few paltry lives compared to the goal we seek? Murder. Hah!

"Haven't they murdered millions of black people? If we murdered one of them everyday, it would take us several centuries to catch up, Slater."

"But come," he said, changing tone and gesturing toward the table, "let us have breakfast and then we can go into the details of your work."

"I haven't said yet that I want to have anything to do with this," I said boldly. "It sounds crazy to me. It sounds too much like jail."

I realized a moment after I had spoken that I should not have said what I did. Dr. Belsidus's face grew wooden and his deep-set eyes smoldered like twin volcanoes. He whirled and confronted me with upraised index finger, but when he spoke his voice was as soft as a purring leopard's. He half smiled.

"You remember the drink I had you take last night, Slater? That was Teyoth, a Hindu drug that induces temporary insanity. I did not want you to know where you were going. You knew nothing until you awoke this morning. No one saw you enter here. If I cannot persuade you to join me, young man, no one will see you leave. Indeed, in that case, you will never leave. Understand?"

I nodded slowly and with sinking heart. I had no alternative but to accept. I was in the power either of a madman or a genius.

"You are a sensible youngster," he said, smiling broadly for the first time. "After breakfast I shall tell you about The Black Internationale."

III

Dr. Belsidus Reveals Source of His Secret Wealth to Secretary

My first morning in the mysterious mansion of Dr. Belsidu was the most interesting and revealing I had ever spent. We dallied long over the breakfast table as he told me of his plans for Negro control of the world. As he spun out this strange, almost insane scheme, a malevolent, satanic smirk played about his stern mouth and his deep-set eyes glowed like coals in a cavern. With a golden spoon he traced geometric designs on the green linen cloth as he outlined the most amazing conspiracy in history. His voice was deep, alternately cruel and insinuating.

"Doubtless you wonder at all this," he said, a sardonic smile fastening down the corners of his determined mouth. He indicated with a wave the ornate dining room and let his glance linger on the dozens of solid gold dishes on the table. "Perhaps it seems rather garish and unnecessary, something like the extravagances of the newly rich. But I am no Trimalchio, my lad. There is method in what you might call my madness,"

I said nothing, preferring to listen and learn.

"Take these golden dishes and cutlery," he continued. These are not kept for purposes of ostentatious display, my boy. They are kept so that I may, in the oriental manner, always have a supply of wealth which the white man's government will not molest. Since no one is permitted to keep gold bars, gold coins or gold certificates, I have converted my gold into these articles and works of supposed art. I have millions of dollars worth of gold and jewels in this house and elsewhere in the world. Come, I'll show you." He rose and went over to a large red and gold and green closet whose sloping top almost reached the ceiling. He produced a small key, unlocked the doors and threw them open. What I saw left me breathless. There were eight shelves. On each shelf were stacked scores of large golden dinner plates, golden soup plates, golden candlesticks, and dozens of knives, forks and spoons made of that precious metal. They reflected in dull yellow beams the light from the room. He evidently enjoyed my amazement.

"Come," he said. "There is much more you must see, Slater. I want you to know everything. You are to be my secretary. I must have one with more than the ordinary intelligence whom I can trust. I think you fit the bill."

"But how do you *know*, Doctor?"

"I'll show you," he said, striding ahead of me across the dining room to a wide door. He pressed a button in the wall. We waited for perhaps ten seconds. Then the door opened in the middle swiftly and silently and we were facing what appeared to be a small closet. We went in and then I realized that we were in a small residential elevator. My host pressed a button and we descended perhaps ten feet. When the door opened in obedience to the pressure on a button, we entered a room quite as large as the dining room but fitted out elaborately as an office.

Two large windows with panes of frosted glass were at each end of the room. Across from the elevator was another door which I surmised opened on a corridor similar to that on the upper floor. In the center of the floor between the windows were arranged about ten mahogany desks, each with a noiseless typewriter on a moveable shelf. Along the wall were filing cases of fireproof steel that reached almost to the ceiling.

"Look here," he directed, going to one of the files and pulling out a drawer. It was packed with hundreds of large cards. He fished out one and handed it to me.

To my astonishment it read:

SLATER, CARL, b. Richmond. Va., May 25, 1910. Carl Slater. Mother: Thelma Slater. Came to New York with parents, April 19, 1916. Graduated from New York public schools, June, 1927. Valedictorian Active in school sports. Outstanding in football and track. Editor-in-Chief of high school paper. Entered Columbia University, October, 1927, specializing in literature and journalism. Worked as a Pullman porter every summer. Graduated with high honors June, 1931, Unemployed that summer. Did reporting from 1931, for out-of-town Negro weeklies Went to work for the *Harlem Blade*, January. 1932. Single. Parents living. Does not gamble or dissipate. Drinks moderately. Sex life normal but somewhat promiscuous. Apparently no steady girl. No political affiliation but seems to be intensely race conscious and familiar with the history of his people. Dark brown, 5 feet, 6 inches, 150 pounds.

"But how did you get all this?" Its amazing accuracy almost scared me.

"That is part of our work, Slater," he said nonchalantly, placing the card back in the file. "We keep track of every Negro of promise to our cause. Sooner or later I would have recruited you. As it is, you walked right into my hands at the right time."

"What do you mean—the right time?"

"Well, it's quite a story. You see, my last secretary was a rather clever man about your age. Yes, too clever." He smirked diabolically and stroked his smooth black cheek.

"What happened to him?" I asked, apprehensively.

"Oh, he was so indiscreet as to say things he should not have said. He discussed my business with others, and, of course, then we had to do away with all concerned. We can't have any talking out of turn, Slater. All of us understand that."

"Do you mean to say you murdered him?"

"A very ugly word, Slater, a very ugly word. We prefer euphemisms, but, if you choose, then, yes, we murdered him. Oh, nothing mussy. you understand. It is done quite quickly with a needle. In a minute it's over."

He must have noticed my revulsion because he smiled reassuringly.

"We must get used to bloodshed, Slater. We must be hard. We must be cruel. We must be unrelenting, neither giving nor asking quarter, until either we or the white race is definitely subjugated, or even exterminated. There is no other way. Softness is weakness. Compromise is disastrous. Tolerance is fatal."

His voice was cruel and bitter now, his face stern, his eyes smouldering with hatred.

"We must disobey all laws that hinder our plan, for all laws here are laws of the white man, designed to keep us in subjugation and perpetuate his rule. All the means of education and information, from nursery to college, from newspaper to book, are mobilized to perpetuate white supremacy, to enslave and degrade the darker peoples. No student of the race problem, Slater, can escape that conclusion. The problem cannot be solved by compromise, by cooperation, by tolerance. As well talk of cooperation and compromise between a hungry lion and a bleating lamb. As well talk of the fish tolerating the worm. No, we who have been on the bottom so long must now come to the top. We who have created the wealth of the world must now enjoy it."

GEORGE S. SCHUYLER

"But how?" I asked, frankly puzzled. "You know very well that white people have all the wealth and all the power, and that our people are not only poor but in the main ignorant."

"Quite true, Slater, quite true," he agreed, beaming benevolently. "But white people haven't got all the brains. We are going to out-think and out-scheme the white people, my boy. I have the organization already, Slater, scattered all over the world; young Negroes like yourself: intellectuals, scientists, engineers. They are mentally the equal of the whites. They possess superior energy, superior vitality, they have superior, or perhaps I should say, more intense, hatred and resentment, that fuel which operates the juggernaut of conquest. All they need is money, instruments, new weapons of science. I have the money, my boy. Yes, I have the wealth, and I am getting more daily. You will see in your time a great Negro nation in Africa, all-powerful, dictating to the white world."

"But how have you accumulated the money?" I inquired. "Has it come from your practice?"

"Partly, yes. Most of my patients are wealthy white women. I have great magnetism, great skill, Slater. I am unscrupulous. Whatever they want done, legal or otherwise. I do it if they have the money to pay me or can get it. I use them in many ways. When they are no longer useful, I either drop them or destroy them. Some I pretend to love. They are intrigued by the idea of a black lover, a man of culture and refinement superior to their husbands and orthodox sweethearts. I give them exotic surroundings, liquor, drugs. When I need them no longer I dismiss them."

"Or murder them," I added.

"Or murder them," he repeated calmly. "What difference does it make? They have murdered millions of black men, women and children, and indirectly destroyed millions more by impoverishment, discrimination, segregation, cruel and inhuman treatment. They haven't been very squeamish about it, have they, Slater? No, so why should I be? Well, my other wealth is derived in the following illegal manner. Illegal, that is, from the dominant white man's point of view, my boy, not from mine. Sit down and keep silent." He waved me to a chair.

I obeyed.

He clapped his hands twice. The office door flew open. The gigantic chauffeur stood at attention before us.

"Jim," commanded Dr. Belsidus, "tell Mr. Fortune to report on the night's work." The dummy disappeared. "A most trustworthy man," observed the Doctor. "He hates white people worse than I do, which is saying a whole lot. They burned off his tongue with a poker one day in Georgia about eight years ago. How he escaped is more than I can imagine but he outran the mob somehow or other. If I should command it, he would wring your neck without changing expression. You know, Slater, one must have loyal followers. Now I'll show you how we get much of our other wealth."

There came a tap on the door. "Come on in, Fortune," Dr. Belsidus called.

The door opened. A short, plump man, reddish brown with gray eyes, entered pushing a rubber-tired cart somewhat resembling a tea wagon. On it was heaped an amazing collection of jewelry: rings, ear rings, necklaces, bracelets, necktie pins, watches, brooches and tiaras. The short man looked at me suspiciously.

"Fortune, this is a new brother, Carl Slater. He's on probation but I think he'll do alright. Slater, this is Alton Fortune, mechanical engineer, and a good one. Our good white folks won't let him work at his profession, so we're letting him work on them until we are ready to use his skill otherwise."

"Glad to know you, Slater," said Fortune, gripping my hand and pumping it energetically. I thought I detected in his eye something of the fanaticism that occasionally glowed in those of Dr. Belsidus. mumbled something.

"So this is the night's haul, eh?" said the Doctor, fingering the hoard with satisfaction.

"Yes, the boys did some good work, Chief, and nobody caught."

"Is this stuff stolen?" I couldn't help but ask.

"A very ugly word, Slater, observed the physician, smiling sardonically, "a very ugly word. We don't use it here. This is wealth to finance the revolution. It is gathered by some of our nervy young men whom white civilization denies a chance, from wealthy men who have entirely too much."

"But the police. I objected, "suppose. . ."

"Ah, yes, I know what you are thinking. Follow me into the basement and I'll show you what we do with this stuff."

Dr. Belsidus nodded to Fortune and led the way into the elevator.

IV

SLATER LEARNS SECRET SOURCE OF BELSIDUS'S FAST-GROWING FORTUNE

We went down two flights in the little elevator. Fortune opened the door and wheeled his jewel-laden wagon into the basement, I followed and Dr. Belsidus brought up the rear. We walked along a whitewashed corridor until we came to a steel door. The physician knocked twice in a peculiar manner. The door rolled upward. Beyond was a small room, whitewashed and prison-like. At the far end blazed an electric furnace. In front of it were several clay moulds. On a large oaken table nearby sat several golden vases, platinum vanity cases. golden plates and platters, goblets and chafing dishes of silver. Presiding over this chamber of Vulcan was a wavy-haired brown man who must either have had Hindu or Indian ancestry. He was dressed entirely in white with a pair of green goggles perched on his head.

"Hello, Chief," he said. "Got some more stuff there?"

"Yes, Sam, a very good haul this time," the Doctor replied. "By the way, Sam, I want you to meet my new secretary, Carl Slater. Carl, meet Sam Hamilton, one of the outstanding chemists in the United States. Sam graduated from some of the best scientific schools in the country. The white people won't give him a break. But he'll show them a thing or two when we get our plant going, eh Sam?"

We shook hands. Then we all stood around while he went to work on the jewelry. Deftly, with delicate tools, he took jewels from their settings and after inspecting the baubles through an eyeglass he would place them in a little silver box which stood at his elbow. The settings he would toss into three different fire clay containers, for gold, silver and aluminum. These he thrust into the orange glowing furnace. When reduced to molten form, he poured them into clay moulds candlesticks, dinner plates, saucers, etc.

"You see," Belsidus boasted. "We have thought of everything."

"But what about the jewels? How do you get rid of them?"

"Ah," he wagged his head mysteriously, "there are ways."

It was nearly ten days before Dr. Belsidus would let me leave the house during that period I supervised the office staff, consisting of ten colored men, wrote his personal letters, which were numerous, and generally familiarized myself with the work. The ramifications of his organization were amazing, and as I learned more and more about it, my respect for the bloodthirsty, fanatical revolutionist grew.

Once outside the house I was surprised to find that it was a large private residence in the Seventies between Park and Madison Avenues. From the outside it seemed very austere and respectable. A simple brass plate on the door read "Dr. Henry Belsidus."

I hurried uptown to see my folks. Imagine my surprise when I learned that they had received letters every day signed with an excellent lorgery of my signature saying that I was on an assignment and would be back shortly. At the *Harlem Blade* office I learned they had received a letter of resignation, also over my forged signature.

It impressed, but at the same time, depressed me. Suppose I should sometime want to get away from Dr. Belsidus? With such an organization of spies and agents as he undoubtedly had, how could I hope to escape? Looking at the last number of the *Harlem Blade*, I noticed that the police had sought in vain to find out something concerning the murder of the young white woman on 144th Street. She had been killed by some deadly poison unknown to the police, killed instantaneously. How much I could have told them if I had dared!

With each successful haul, Al Fortune widened his operations. There were mornings when both shelves of the rubber-tired cart were loaded down with valuable baubles destined for the furnace and to assume an endirely dillerem shape and form. He told me one morning that he had a corps of forty young working on percentage, i.e. twenty-five percent of the value of all they stole. I was eager to learn more about the details of this lucrative business which the police seemed unable to stop.

Al finally consented to take me one night. We left the house afoot and boarded the Madison Avenue bus going uptown. At 110th Street we got off and caught a taxicab. He gave an address on St. Nicholas Place.

"I never call any taxis to the house," Al explained. "and I never leave that district twice in the same sort of conveyance. We've got everything down pretty fine but there's no use taking chances."

We stopped in front of a gray stone residence with stone balustrades that sat behind a tiny hedge and flower bed. Fortune led the way. In response to his ring a brown maid in uniform opened the door.

"Is Mrs. Harris in?" he asked, lowering the lid of one eye significantly.

The maid quickly stood to one side.

"You'll find her in the sitting room," she said. Fortune walked in and I followed behind.

THE CURTAINS WERE DRAWN AND there was no light. When our eyes got accustomed to the darkness, I noticed for the first time an enormous black woman, certainly all of three hundred pounds, sitting in the center of a red plush sofa. She said nothing but studied us curiously like a great fat spider gloating over its prey. It was embarrassing to me. I glanced at Al Fortune questioningly. Then I looked more closely. Nothing seemed to move about the woman except her eyes and her mountainous breasts. She was garbed in a tent-like blue velvet dress edged with lace around the collar and sleeves. For one so large her shoes seemed incredibly tiny. Her little roaming, too-close-together eyes sparkled in the darkness like two beads on a black hat. A faint odor of perfumed perspiration rose from her.

Suddenly, she spoke in a voice that rumbled from some lower depth far in the recesses of the earth.

"Who's your friend, Mr. Fortune?"

"New secretary to the Chief, Mag. Come on, let's go."

"Well, okeh. she rumbled. She shifted one of her enormous arms and reached behind the back of the sofa. To my astonishment the red plush sofa began to move sidewise, slowly and noiselessly, Farther and farther it moved until it was some six feet to our left and where the grotesque woman had sat was only an empty expanse of parquet flooring. I looked at Al Fortune. He was watching the bare space as a bacteriologist might gaze through a microscope, alert, expectant.

Now a square of the bare flooring moved downward and away from us, disclosing a light collapsible steel staircase descending into a dimly lighted cellar. Without a word Fortune went down the steps with me dose behind him. At the bottom I turned around and looked back. The collapsible staircase was already moving upward into a recess and the trap door was closed.

"Pretty neat," I observed.

"We take no chances," he observed gruffly. "Come on."

I followed him to the rear of the cellar. We stood facing the stone wall. There was no stairway, no door, nothing but the wall. I looked at him, puzzled by all these maneuvers. He was listening intently, his head inclined to one side. At last he stepped forward close to the wall.

He touched the middle finger of his right hand against a small stone. It sank forward. At once a section of the wall, four feet wide and about six feet high, swung noiselessly on a pivot. Fortune stepped forward with me at his heels. We were in a wooden closet about six feet square. The wall behind us closed silently.

Now, whispering to me to keep absolutely silent. Fortune pushed aside an eyehole in the wooden wall in front of each of us. We were looking into a low room with cement floor, poured cement walls and whitewashed ceiling. About five feet in front of us an iron grill, through which one might reach, extended from floor to ceiling and surrounded the three sides of our closet. Otherwise, the room was completely bare. At the far end was a steel door.

Fortune pressed a button somewhere. The door at the far end opened. A flashily dressed Negro in spats, black form-fitting overcoat and pearl-gray fedora entered and walked briskly to the grill. Fortune disguised his voice with a sepulchral tone. "What have you tonight, Sanderson?"

"This," said the man. He drew from his inside overcoat pocket a long, beautiful pearl necklace.

"Put it in the box. The man reached through the grill and deposited the necklace in a box on the floor in front of the closet.

"Is that all, Sanderson?"

"Yes, sir. That's pretty good, ain't it?

"You are sure you were careful, Sanderson?" Fortune asked, ignoring the man's question.

"Oh, yes, sir. You know I'm th' cat."

"You may go, Sanderson." The man turned and hurried out. Man after man followed him. Yeggs, pickpockets, highwaymen, a motley file out of Harlem's criminals came one by one and deposited their loot in the box. At intervals and while the room was empty Fortune would unlatch the little door at our feet and swing the treasure box inward. He would quickly empty its contents into a large velvet bag. Then, opening the wall into the cellar through which we had come, he would place it alongside the wall in there.

"That's just in case," he explained. "No telling what might happen."

He seemed highly elated with the evening's business. The box had to be emptied many times. I counted altogether thirty-eight men. It appeared that two had been caught.

"We get them the best lawyer the town affords," he explained. "And if they can't beat the rap, well, most of them are the kind that can take it."

"Suppose one of them should squeal?" I asked.

"Well," he observed. "I don't know where he could go and stay alive. Our men and women are everywhere, and these rats all know it. But we only need a few more hauls and we'll be ready to get down to business in earnest."

I didn't know what he meant, but I found out the very next week.

V

BELSIDUS BARES HIS PLANS FOR
CONFERENCE OF BLACKS OF THE WORLD

No one coming to the office of Dr. Belsidus for treatment would have suspected what was going on above and below that main floor. His fashionable white patients saw only the well-appointed office of a wealthy physician, an immaculate office done in soft tones, with gleaming equipment, two smiling brownskin nurses and the handsome assistant of Dr. Belsidus, young Dr. Matson. The doors leading to the stairways going to the upper floors and the basement were always locked. They were camouflaged steel doors. Only Dr. Belsidus and Jim possessed keys.

I was struck by the number of Dr. Belsidus's patients. All day from ten in the morning until three in the afternoon the gleaming limousines and town cars paused in front of our door. Mostly, the patients were female. Girls, young women, middle-aged women, old women, but always white women and always wealthy women. I learned from the nurse who kept the accounts that they paid fabulous fees.

The sinister physician was the very soul of courtesy and consideration. He bowed low, smiled occasionally, made witty remarks that kept his fair patients giggling, and worked with a swiftness and sureness that inspired confidence. At three o'clock sharp he retired to the upper floors.

It was the day following my trip with Alton Fortune to the mysterious basement under the house of Mag Harris on St. Nicholas Place that the tinle green light on top of my desk flashed twice and I knew that the Chief wanted me. I grabbed my stenographic pad and, taking the private clevator, went to the top floor.

The Doctor must have spent $25,000 furnishing that top floor apartment. It was strictly late Egyptian. As one left the elevator, one stepped immediately into a vast room at least fifteen feet high and extending to the left and right the full length of the house. Directly in front of the elevator, but across the room from it, was the bed. It was ten feet wide and slightly longer, not over a foot high and hung with a gorgeous. canopy of royal purple edged with golden fringe. Inside the canopy was a great French mirror so arranged that it could be slightly

GEORGE S. SCHUYLER

tilted by the pressure on a small lever at whatever angle the occupant of the bed wished.

The walls were of sandstone. Extending all around the room were the most exotic murals in vivid greens and crimsons, rich chocolates and yellows depicting scenes of the wildest passionate abandon. Nymphs, Satyrs, cupids, angels and devils were depicted in the most suggestive and provocative poses. They poured red wine and lost themselves in nameless excesses of which common folk never dreamed in their wildest nightmares.

The dark red glass floor that clearly reflected every figure that crossed it was strewn with leopard and tiger skins. At intervals here and there were low Egyptian chairs and divans of dark red wood inlaid with gold. The four great windows, two at each end, were hung with royal purple drapes fringed with gold. Each window was equipped with a fine steel rolling curtain painted a deceptive green. These, with the steel doors, made the place impregnable.

Between the rear windows in a concave, softly lighted recess stood an amazingly life-like male phallic symbol made of translucent porcelain and fully six feet in height. In a similar recess between the two front windows stood a statue of three nude young women in the full bloom and vigor of life with their arms on each other's shoulders. They were obviously made of the same porcelain. One was a Caucasian, one an African and the other a Mongolian.

To the right and left of the elevator shaft were twin lavatories with sunken marble bathtubs, entered through embossed bronze doors. On the same side of the room and near the front was the door leading to the stairway to the third floor. The whole scene was suffused with a soft rose light from shielded fixtures imbedded at intervals in the sandstone walls. No one could long remain in the place without one's mind dwelling on soft flesh, rounded forms, perfumed breaths, libidinous movements and all the intimate lecheries the fertile mind of love has invented down through the countless ages of man's earthly sojourn.

In his usual position on the low upholstered bench at the foot of the bed lay Ben, the Doctor's trained leopard. As I entered, he opened his wicked eyes, frowned, and rose up threateningly. I stood still, a little frightened, as he moved toward me with a slinking crouch. I remembered what Al Fortune had told me about his daily diet of fresh raw meat and his almost insane ferocity. His yellow eyes glowed ominously.

"Ben!" At the sound of the Doctor's voice, the leopard returned sheepishly to his position, curling his tail about him as he closed his eyes. "Frightened you, didn't he?" said Dr. Belsidus, chuckling mirthlessly.

I turned to confront the physician, who, clad in grass-green silk pajamas and brocaded robe of the same color, was standing in the door leading to the front bathroom.

"Yes, he did frighten me." I admitted. "It's the first time I've ever faced one of those big cats."

"Never enter unless I am here." he cautioned. "or unless Jim is with you. Ben is friendly only with us. Others he promptly kills. I got him as a cub and trained him that way."

He strolled over to the bed, crawled between the pink linen sheets and lay back with his hands cupped under his head. I waited respectfully until he was settled, then I pulled one of the curved-back Egyptian chairs up close to him.

"I suppose you're wondering why I'm going to bed at four-thirty the afternoon, aren't you, Slater?"

"Well, pardon me, but it does seem a little unusual."

"That's because you haven't been here very long. Slater. Whenever you see me retire at this hour, you know that I am not going to sleep." The corners of his mouth lowered in a sardonic smirk. "A middle-aged patient who has a million times more money than she has brains has succumbed to my wiles, Slater. Her check, which will be forthcoming in the course of time, will pay for our convention."

"What convention, Doctor?"

"That's right," he mused more to himself than to me. "I have not told you, have I? Well, take this message: Upon debarkation proceed immediately by taxicab to place designated. Sign it 'World.'"

"To whom shall I send it. Doctor?"

"Look in File Number One in the office. There you will find a typewritten list of names. Send the same message to each of the fifty persons on the list. Some you will notice are en route on the *Queen Mary*. Others are coming on the *Normandie*. A few are coming in on West Indian steamers. These men, fifty of them, will arrive tomorrow. They are delegates to our first convention of the Black Internationale, coming from wherever black men live, at my command and at my expense."

He paused a minute, eyeing me to see that the significance of what he was divulging was sinking in. "Now," he said, rising on one arm and frowning slightly as he concentrated, "you tell Al to tell Mag that as soon as they arrive at her place at St. Nicholas Avenue–that's where they're going from the dock–she is to send them downstairs, see that they have refreshments and everything. Al is to have two of our buses in front of the cabaret tomorrow night. He will ride in the second. Promptly at eight o'clock he is to lead the delegates from Mag's cellars into the cabaret cellar and on out into the street."

"Then where are we going?"

"To a place where we may confer without interruption interference," he snapped. "To my mountain place in Green County. Al knows the way. Remember, there must be no slip-up. Many of these men have taken their lives in their hands in making this journey. Most of them have been spotted as dangerous by colonial governments. They expect to be protected. They must and will be protected. Understand?"

"Yes, sir," I mumbled.

"Well, you may go then, Slater. Tell Jim to show the lady up when she arrives."

I followed directions exactly. The *Queen Mary* docked early the next morning, the Columbian Line boat came in round eleven o'clock. The *Normandie* got to the wharf at noon.

Following Dr. Belsidus's later instructions, I watched the passengers disembark. As each black or brown man went through customs. He promptly got his baggage together and hailed a taxicab. Each gave the same address. 151 St. Nicholas Place.

When the last man had gone uptown. I followed. Arrived at Mag's. I went down the steel steps into her basement. The fifty delegates from all over the world were sitting around talking, drinking and eating the buffet lunch Mag's cook had prepared. Although they came from all over the world, I was surprised to find all of them spoke English. Alton Fortune explained: "It was the Chief's orders, that they learn English. He says the Negroes can never be united as long as their leaders speak different languages and can't understand each other. After all, he has given them a year to prepare themselves."

Not long afterward Al gave the signal and we filed through the revolving stone door into the basement of the cabaret where Dr. Beldus's thieves came to surrender their loot. Thence to the darkness of St. Nicholas Avenue. Two big buses were quickly filled. At another signal from Al, they lumbered forward up to the George Washington Bridge and through the night to the wilds of the Catskill Mountains.

VI

Delegates of Black Nations Go to Secret Rendezvous for Confab

It was well past midnight when the buses halted in a high well wooded valley two or three miles off the road. The big headlights cut four holes in the black darkness. We were pulled up close to a large wooden building which had once been a country hotel or a sanitarium. Al Fortune got out and I followed suit. The fifty delegates piled out after us. The little plump fellow led the way up the steps to the broad verandah and we entered the building.

"Everybody sit down," Fortune invited, and the waiters will serve you."

As he said it we were standing in a completely darkened hall which made his advice the more incongruous. Suddenly there was a click and the whole building was flooded with light. The broad entrance hall where we hung up our wraps opened into a large lobby beautifully carpeted and strewn with easy chairs, sofas and ottomans upholstered in red leather At a large hotel desk stood two brownskin clerks waiting smugly for our registration. Uniformed anendants stood rigidly by.

"Some dump, Al," I remarked, while the foreign Negroes looked about them in mingled amazement and growing respect. "Must have set the Doctor back something, didn't it?"

"Perhaps," he replied lacurically, "I never asked him. We don't ask so many questions, Slater."

My curiosity rebuffed, I turned to study the strange group of Negroes Belsidus had summoned from the ends of the earth and who now sat around chatting in strongly accented English. Some were tall, hawk faced and reddish brown. Others were short stocky and black as midnight. Some were brawny, others were slight and scholarly in appearance. While a few showed little trace of racial admixture, others were obviously possessed of some Caucasian or Mongolian ancestry. All seemed just a little puzzled, a little uncertain, certainly somewhat awed by these efficient preparations. While they laughed and chatted in a normal fashion, I could detect in their tones some slight trace of uneasiness, outward evidence of inner preoccupation with the object for which they had traveled over jungle, desert, mountain and sea to this house hidden in the Catskills.

I noticed the ample rotund form of my gray-eyed friend, Al Fortune, moving among the delegates, dropping a word here and there, shaking hands as he introduced himself and was introduced. It was more talking than I had seen him do before. Yet his affability, I thought, was afflicted. There was a shiftiness in those deep gray eyes, a hard monotonous character to that voice that somehow always struck me unpleasantly, although our relations had been most cordial and friendly. What seemed singular was the light of recognition that illuminated the face of Momodu, the tall, slender, cadaverous black delegate from Gambia when Al approached him for a few words.

Supposedly, Al had never met nor corresponded with any of the delegates. Everyone present was a stranger, more or less, to everyone else. Only Dr. Belsidus knew them all. He alone had corresponded with them and had their photographs in his personal files. And yet here were Al Fortune and this Momodu meeting like people who had met before.

Now, I do not mean to say that their actions were obvious or sustained. Nothing of the sort. Indeed, Al talked no longer with Momodu than he did with the others. It was, rather, their manner that struck me as strange. Even though at the time I felt my suspicion to be foolish and was just a little ashamed of myself. I decided to keep my mouth shut and my eyes open. After all, I was the Doctor's secretary, and I felt that he trusted me and expected me to look after his interests during his absence.

We had been sitting in the lobby for upwards of an hour when one of the uniformed attendants wended his way through the chattens throng and came up to me.

"Mister Slater?" he inquired, courteously.

"Yes, what is it?"

"The Doctor says the time has arrived. You are to follow me. The others are to follow you. You move up the stairway to the second floor thence to the ballroom door. When it is thrown open, you are to move down the hall and stand behind the first chair alongside that of the Doctor. The others will form around the table in order. There must be absolute silence. You are to wait for any command before seating your self. The others are to do as you do. Understand. Mister Slater? Those are the orders of Dr. Belsidus."

"Yes," I replied, "I understand." He stepped back. I clapped my hands to attract attention. When all was quiet and the delegates were eyeing me with expectation, I said, "Dr. Belsidus wishes us to assemble above. Please follow me in silence."

The attendant made for the stairway with slow and measured steps. I followed a few paces behind him. Up the stairs I went, followed by the sound of feet treading in unison. At the head of the stairs we turned to the right. I looked back down the stairs. The fifty delegates were ascending in single file, their faces grave and expectant.

The attendant stepped aside. I moved forward to the closed double doors which he indicated and halted. One minute, perhaps a minute and a half, I waited. I could hear the breathing of the others behind me. I could feel something of their suppressed excitement—the same excitement that was making my own heart beat loud.

Suddenly the doors opened inward as if by some mysterious force. The arrangement of the ballroom was certainly impressive, to say the least. Straight down the center of the highly polished floor ran a long wide table covered with green baize cloth. Along each side were comfortable mahogany arm chairs. In front of each chair was a large blotter, a well-filled ink well, paper and pencils. At the head of the table stood, a great, black, high-backed chair, elaborately carved and seemingly in laid with silver. Behind this chair, but on the little stage, was a huge map of the world indirectly lighted. Otherwise the room was absolutely bare.

I walked in as I had been instructed, wondering where Dr. Belsidus might be. The others took places, each behind a chair, and stood in silence. We all turned as if by command to the empty chair.

"The gentlemen will please be seated," came the voice of the attendant from the doorway.

With less clatter than you would have imagined, the delegates seated themselves. The attendant stepped out into the hall. The double doors swung closed. The delegates looked questioningly at each other but none broke the silence. Looking down the table, I noted that Al Forune and Momodu were seated side by side close to the door.

What was detaining the Doctor? The same thought must have been in other minds, for I noticed many a puzzled expression.

Somewhere a gong sounded. There was another sound of the gong and then every light in the ballroom was extinguished. I could hear the swift intake of breath that indicated everyone's surprise. The gong sounded a third time. The lights came on again as bright as before.

There had been no sound beyond that of the gong, and yet, seated in the black high-backed chair at the head of the table was Dr. Henry Belsidus, garbed, as ever, in faultless and appropriate attire. The corners of his cruel mouth were drawn in a sardonic smile.

The fall of a feather would have been audible in that vast room as the delegates gaped wide-eyed at the tall black man who had appeared so mysteriously, so noiselessly from nowhere. He looked at each man in turn as though he were reading their minds in succession as one might read a succession of billboards. It was just a little awkward, being stared at in this manner. It was as if one were a guinea pig. He had not spoken a word and we were constrained to silence.

There was something awesome and eery about the whole thing. How had he got up here before us? How had he been able to enter the ballroom in the two seconds the lights were extinguished and seat himself without making a sound? Why didn't he start the proceedings? Yet, he sit there, tapping quietly on the blotter in front of him with his long, cruel, devilish fingers, his eyes half closed in sinister calculation.

The place was as still as death. Only the soft tap-tap of the physician's lingers broke the terrible silence or withdrew attention momentarily from his penetrating scrutiny. It was maddening. I thought I should scream. Then he lifted his head and in an even tone announced:

"Gentlemen, before we begin we must rid ourselves of spies. Three of you must not leave here alive!"

VII

Belsidus Does Away with the Three Spies and the Meeting Proceeds

The announcement electrified the gathering. There was a swift intake of breath, a hasty glancing up and down the long table. I looked at Al Fortune and Momodu, the delegate from Gambia. The engineer was tapping silently on the green baize cloth, apparently lost in contemplation of his fingers' tips, his face an inscrutable mask. I thought I detected a small light of consternation in the narrow eyes of the Gambian. The room became as silent as the desert at midnight. All eyes studied the stern visage of the Chief. Fully a minute passed before Dr. Belsidus spoke again. Then in clear, measured tones he began:

"Gentlemen, I am Dr. Belsidus. Most of you have never seen me. Many of you will never see me again. But you will get my commands. You have sworn to carry them out. You will carry them out to the letter.

"I have brought you all here at great expense that you may receive your instructions personally and meet your colleagues. It is unnecessary for me to dwell at great length on our program. You know what it is. It can be summed up in a few words: for four hundred years our race has been in eclipse. For four hundred years we have been victims of superior forces. For four hundred years we have seen our civilizations crushed and controlled one after the other by the white man. We have suffered every degradation his fertile mind could invent. We have not only been enslaved in body, but in spirit and mind as well. We have been demoralized.

"Gentlemen, this must end. It is the business of the Black Internationale to end it. All revolutions are started by minorities who use majorities to do their bidding. All successful revolutions must be conducted along dictatorial lines by a minority obedient to one man. I am the man.

I have the responsibility of directing this revolution. To direct it successfully I must be obeyed implicitly. Disobedience simply means death. Treason means death. Cowardice means death. Victory is certain if my directions are followed.

"We have been subdued by ruthlessness. Now we shall triumph by ruthlessness. The white man has not hesitated to use any and every means to degrade the Negro and keep him demoralized. We shall not hesitate to use any and every means at our disposal to degrade and demoralize the white man.

"We shall run him out of Africa, out of India, out of the West Indies, out of the South Seas. We shall elevate the Negro people to the proud estate they once occupied four hundred years ago. And those who help to bring about this revolution will not have reason to regret their allegiance to me."

His voice fell to silence and the vast room was still. Sitting close to the Doctor as I was, I could study his face. There was in it the sternness of fanaticism, the canniness of the fox, the savagery of the wolf. He tapped lightly upon his perfectly manicured fingers and looked about him, up and down the long table.

"Mr. Fortune," he said, and my heart almost stopped as I glanced quickly at my friend, the engineer, "please get rid of the three spies so that we may proceed. Our time is limited."

The wide-eyed delegates turned as if by command to see what was about to happen. If Al Fortune felt that his task was an unpleasant one, he gave no indication of it. His reddish brown face was a mask as he rose and swept the upturned faces with an all-inclusive glance.

"Every colonial government," said Dr. Belsidus, breaking in before Al could say or do anything, "is quite naturally opposed to any such organization as we have effected. Each one has a certain number of colored or Negro police agents to spy on such gatherings and conferences to find out what our people are doing or planning to do. In this way, and also by selling out, the Negro has been betrayed as often by his own people as by the white man. It is doubtful if we should have been degraded as we have if it had not been for certain of our own people.

"Hereafter all such Negroes must die wherever and whenever discovered. Such men and women cannot be reformed or reconditioned. Once a rat always a rat. I want everyone here to watch closely what takes place and take it as a warning. Very well, Mr. Fortune, you may go on."

Al moved back his chair and then, turning, he walked almost to the end of the table. He stopped behind the chair of a very light Negro with Negroid features, half-closed eyes and a square British face. Al glanced significantly at Dr. Belsidus.

"Henry Pilkington," said the Chief, "you will have no opportunity to tell what you have seen and heard to the British Colonial Office. The

English have an efficient spy service, Pilkington, but our service is just as efficient."

"It's a dirty lie!" cried the delegate from Jamaica, jumping up, red faced and excited. Before he could say more. Al grabbed his head with his left arm and, bringing up his right hand in wide arc, he touched the struggling man's throat just as I had seen Dr. Belsidus touch the throat of the white girl some weeks before. With a hoarse cry, Pilkington's struggles grew weaker and weaker. Finally he collapsed back in his chair. It was only then that I noticed a black thorn sticking out of the neck of the unfortunate Jamaican. Like me, the horrified audience watched it with fascination.

Al walked around the end of the table and started down the other side. About three paces from me he halted again behind the chair of a slight brown man with mustache and goatee, pointed face and large, long-lashed eyes. Again he glanced at Dr. Belsidus. "Jules Constant," the Doctor began, "it is unfortunate that you will never see St. Louis, Senegal, again, but our plans and the lives of our revolutionaries are more important than your miserable existence. Mr. Fortune, please proceed."

The little man's eyes were filled with terror. He seemed helpless slumped there in his chair. Al reached for his head. Quickly and with great agility, Constant tipped his chair backward, throwing Al off balance. Then he sped toward the nearest heavily-draped window before Al could regain his feet, and yanking the drapes aside would doubtless have jumped to the ground, but instead of finding himself confronted with glass, he was faced with great steel shutters.

Al raced after him. Constant turned and whipped out a German Luger. I gasped. The others sat frozen to their seats, Constant's automatic came up, but before he could fire I heard a sound alongside me like the shaking of a spring from a window sash. The Senegalese dropped his Luger and dropped on the floor, a neat red hole drilled in his skull. I turned to Dr. Belsidus. He was holding in his long slender hands an automatic equipped with a silencer. That was the swishing sound I had heard. I watched the delegates. There was awe, horror and fear in their faces. Some of them shifted uneasily.

"The French Surete General will miss Jules Constant," observed the Doctor dryly. "He was a good operative. Very well, Mr. Fortune, you may proceed."

Quite unruffled, Al moved around the end of the table, passing behind the Chief's chair and moving back to his place. Who could the third man be? I wondered. The others must have been speculating about the same thing. Al was almost to his place now. The air was tense with expectancy. Al paused, then halted behind the chair of the delegate from Gambia with whom he had seemed to be on such good terms. just a few minutes before. Momodu's cadaverous visage grew ashen.

"Hasha Momodu," said Dr. Belsidus, "you served the British Colonial office, so I suppose you are willing to die for it."

"But there must be some mistake, Doctor. There must be some mistake," cried Momodu. "You cannot do this. I am innocent."

"You are a liar, a fool, and a traitor, Momodu," the Doctor hissed. He looked at Fortune.

The engineer plunged a thorn deep into the neck of the Senegalese.

There was a struggle, but it was soon over. The virulent poison with which the thorn was evidently smeared worked speedily as soon as it entered the bloodstream. The Gambian collapsed like an empty sack.

Dr. Belsidus clapped his hands twice. Two uniformed attendants entered. One of them was the man who had led me to the conference. hall. They were pushing a rubber-tired, three-tiered cart similar to the type used to transfer food in hospitals and army mess halls. Working swiftly, the two uniformed men lifted each corpse and placed it on a shelf of the cart. It was wheeled to a position two or three paces behind the Doctor and almost alongside the small stage.

Dr. Belsidus clapped his hands again. The room was plunged into darkness. Perhaps ten seconds passed. The Doctor clapped his hands again. The lights came on. The two attendants and the cart with its gruesome burden had disappeared. I looked quickly and questioningly at the Chief. Just the suspicion of a smile pulled down the corners of his mouth. I knew he was amused by the amazement of the others.

"Now," he said with evident relief, "let us proceed. Afterward I shall show you our acid tank where we rid ourselves of the corpus delection certain occasions. Very handy to have. Before you return to your homes, Mr. Hamilton, our chemist, will show you how the acid bath is prepared. But now, let us consider our immediate plans." The delegates leaned forward attentively to drink in every word.

VIII

Dr. Belsidus Explains His Plan of Action to Redeem the Black Race

S peaking softly, but in a voice that carried his words clearly to each of the dusky delegates, Dr. Belsidus spoke.

"Previous efforts of the colored peoples to emancipate themselves from white supremacy have failed because we were not prepared to emancipate ourselves. Every nation of people is destroyed first from within. It must organize itself within if it is to triumph without.

"Why was Africa subjugated? Why were India and Malaysia subjugated? Why do the dark peoples in South America, the West Indies and the United States remain in bondage?

"You all know the answer. First, there was lack of unity. Secondly, there was lack of knowledge of the resources of the white man and of how to properly organize and exploit our own resources. Thirdly, we were spiritually enslaved, and still are. Our religion is that of the white man. Our so-called education is one long praise and glorification of the white man. Our sources of information are controlled by the white man. Therefore, we have the minds of white men. And so long as we have the minds of white men, we cannot free black men. In order to triumph it is necessary for us to believe that we are superior and invincible.

"Thus, it would be unwise to either challenge or attack the white man at this time. Embarrass the white man, disorganize the white man, disunite the white man, disturb the white man, but do not attack the white man except secretly and with skill and intelligence."

"But Doctor," objected the delegate from Sierra Leone, "what then shall we do? Why have a Black Internationale at all if we are not to strike blows for our freedom? I and my little group in Freetown are ready to die for the race. My comrades would not understand a policy that negatived attack."

Several of the delegates nodded in approval, especially Corda, the delegate from South Africa, and Monu, the delegate from Grand Bassam, Ivory Coast, who, I had learned, had suffered severe persecution for their efforts to bring about racial solidarity.

GEORGE S. SCHUYLER

"It is your business, Joseph Kalanga," retorted Belsidus in a stern, hard voice, "to make your comrades understand my policy. Blows in plenty will be struck but we must first be prepared to strike them. Ignorance never won anything except poverty, disease and death. Still, I am glad you put the question because it will help to clarify our program in the minds of the delegates.

"Now," he continued, "who controls the Christian Church to which all the literate Negroes in Sierra Leone belong?"

"The white man."

"Very well," commented the Doctor, indulging a faint smile, "and who prints the books, magazines and newspapers you read?"

"Mostly the white man."

"And who dominates in the control of stores and trading stations?"

"The white man."

"And who are the engineers, chemists, architects, technicians and others of that type such as you have?"

"White men."

"If I am correctly informed," pursued the Doctor, apparently more amused, "your minority of educated Negroes are physicians and school teachers."

"That is true, Doctor."

"Then how can you hope to successfully attack a great mechanical civilization with great mills, mines, factories, fleets, and above all the thousands and thousands of skilled technicians necessary for the conduct of modern warfare as well as the perpetuation of machine civilization? It is quite impossible, is it not? Have you forgotten Abdel Krim, Haile Selassie and numerous other chieftains from Fuzzy Wuzzy to Cetawayo who threw themselves against the machines of white civilization and failed? We must never forget those facts, my men. We must always face them realistically. No, we are not yet ready for open attack. Today the white man is our superior in industry and commerce, and therefore is our superior in everything else because everything in our civilization is predicated upon industry and commerce.

"Our business is to prepare; to bring about unity among the colored peoples to rid them of that deeply ingrained inferiority complex, especially those who have been most exposed to the white man's influence to train technicians and to obtain the money to do all this. We shall wherever possible, use the resources and money of the white man to bring this about.

"It is easier to control and regiment literate than illiterate people. The latter usually believe only what they see or hear by word of mouth, while the former will believe anything they read. One of our first tasks for our fifty cells will be to teach the colored world how to read and write. It is easy, and any adult of normal intelligence can be taught to read and write in a week or more. Moreover, by the method we have perfected, it is possible to teach four or five hundred people at once. You will receive detailed instructions concerning this new method tomorrow. Before you leave, each of you will receive, in addition, a moving picture projector, several rolls of film, portable screen, and later you will be sent a gasoline engine, motor, and other accessories. With the aid of this equipment you will be able to show the people the white man's world and what Negroes are doing, you will be able to teach them something about the forces of nature and how to control them You will be able to do it freely because there is nothing in any of the films with which white officials might quarrel. In fact, you will be commended for your zeal."

An expression of great craftiness came over his face as he said that. He stroked his smooth chin and then proceeded.

"But people cannot be held merely by education. Most people, white or black, really do not wish to learn. It is necessary to reach them through their emotions. Therefore we must have a new religion, a religion designed for suppressed colored people. We must have a church which will supersede the white churches and the colored church, which are based on the white man's religion. Tomorrow you will meet Rev. Samson Binks, the head of the Negro Church. It is something spectacular and colorful, with gorgeous raiment, pageantry and music, all based on Negro motifs and psychology. It is as religion is supposed to be. Nothing like it has been seen since the days of Egypt. One temple at least will immediately be erected by each cell. This will serve as a meeting place under the guise of religion, it will serve as a center for educational work just like the missionary schools. It will serve also as a center for propaganda. This much of the program will be completed before the end of 1937. In these temples of the Negro Church we shall gather the people, tell them what we want them to hear and show them what we want them to see. We shall have a first-class radio receiving set in each temple, and there shall be frequent distributions of free food, free shoes, free clothing and free tools to all those who join us. By this means we shall build up a fanatical loyalty."

GEORGE S. SCHUYLER

"But Doctor." inquired Corda, the South African, "where shall we ever get the means to do all of this? How can we buy powerful radios, moving picture projectors and food, clothing, shoes and tools? How shall we build temples? All these things will cost millions. How can we get all that money and complete the program in just one year? I do not doubt your ability, for you have accomplished marvels, but I frankly cannot see how it can be done."

"You are all here at my expense, at the cost of $50,000. You haven't spent a penny and will not have to spend a penny. You follow my instructions. You will receive everything I say or the money with which to purchase it." There was a trace of irritation in the Doctor's voice but also great assurance. And certainly he had a right to be sure of himself. "Meantime, you will immediately select one young man and one young woman who have finished secondary school with honors and send them to America immediately for technical education. In July you will select ten young women who have completed grammar school and send them here to be sent to American trade schools for six months."

There was absolute silence as the Doctor paused. All gazed at him, some in wonderment, others in awe, others with unsuppressed enthusiasm gleaming in their eyes.

As my pencil raced over that paper, taking down in shorthand his every word, a little doubt crept over me. How could he do what he said? Then I recalled his store of gold, Al Fortune's robber band and the hints of astonishing developments in other parts of the country which the Doctor had let drop from time to time. Yes, he might do it after all. Certainly he had thought the program out well.

"And now, gentlemen." said Dr. Belsidus, smiling and rising, followed quickly by the others, "we shall descend to the acid bath and see what has happened to our erstwhile visitors. And then, perhaps, to bed There is much to do tomorrow."

IX

The Secret Conference Disbands, Then Carl Meets a Pretty Girl

Dr. Belsidus leaned down and pressed a button under the arm of his chair. Before our startled gaze a large section of the floor swung slowly downward, one end reaching to the floor below and constituting a ramp. I understood now how the cart of the three bodies of the three spies had disappeared so quickly.

At the physician's command we trooped down the ramp into a small room from which a similar ramp led into the basement. As we left each ramp, it moved slowly back into place.

In a six-foot pool at the far end, the nude bodies of the three spies lay in a heap. In the calm manner of a professor instructing a class, Dr. Belsidus explained the procedure followed in disposing of cadavers.

"Observe," he began, "that the pool is lined with black tile. Some such material is needed. The bodies are placed in the pool as you see them. Then they are covered with this corrosive acid made by our Mr. Hamilton. Alright, boys." This last to two attendants who stood obediently at hand.

The two men rolled big carboys of the acid to the edge of the tank and emptied their contents. Other than the gurgling sound, the basement was as still as a tomb. A sharp, offensive odor pervaded the air. In the pool a rapid bubbling began.

"Watch closely, gentlemen," the doctor cautioned. The bubbling. hissing acid was omnivorously devouring the flesh before our eyes. Two more carboys were now emptied into the pool. The activity increased. Slowly the bodies began to disintegrate. The things that had once been living, breathing men were now reduced to lumps of flesh, to pulp. Bones liquified, hair merged and lost itself in the mass.

"Stir it!" commanded Dr. Belsidus. The two attendants seized long steel rods and aided the disintegration by stirring the bubbling, hissing, evil-smelling mess. It had now become a ghastly pudding which no one would ever have guessed had once been men. Gradually the devilish commotion died down. In ten minutes only an even scum, dark green and odiferous, remained.

"Get rid of it!" ordered the physician. One of the attendants walked to the stone wall and pulled a chain. Immediately the contents of the pool began to empty. Down, down it sank, while the awed delegates craned their necks to see. Soon there was a sucking, gurgling sound. In another fifteen seconds the pool was empty.

"In our work," observed Dr. Belsidus blandly, walking toward the other end of the basement surrounded by the others, "it frequently becomes advisable to kill. It is safer, in view of the acumen of the police, to leave no traces. Mr. Hamilton, our chemist, hit upon this very excellent method. You will all receive the formula for this acid before you leave. It will come in handy, I assure you."

He said all this in a calm, matter-of-fact tone that made the cold chills run down my back. Somehow or other he seemed not quite human. Rather, he was a cold, cruel, fanatically determined machine. Each day I realized more and more that the man would stop at nothing to gain his ends.

AFTER THREE DAYS OF CONFERENCES and following receipt of detailed instructions, the delegates began to depart for their homes. I was rather glad to see them go, for the gathering had meant a lot of work for me. It had been part of my job to purchase motion picture projectors, films, portable screens, motors and gasoline engines. Dr. Belsidus had had special films made which in a very simple manner but quite effectively showed Negro progress in the United States. Others revealed the methods of producing various products such as plows, rifles, automobiles, and so forth. It was evident that he intended his followers to understand the background of the white man's supremacy. One set of files that particularly interested me was that used in teaching reading and writing Exceedingly ingenuous it was, and I could readily understand how even the most stupid person might be taught in a few days to read and write simple words. Some of the sets were in English, others in French, Belgian. Dutch, Spanish and Portuguese, depending on the country to which they were destined.

While the routine at the mansion of Dr. Belsidus was unpredictable, I had thought things would go on much as they had before. But here I was mistaken. The very day following the departure of the Brazilian delegate, the last to leave, Dr. Belsidus summoned me to his suite, I promptly seized my pencil and pad and ascended in the automatic elevator.

When the doors flew open and I started to enter the exotic Egyptian setting, a sight met my eyes that made me gasp and stop short. Facing me, and talking to Dr. Belsidus across a small table on which two half emptied cocktail glasses stood, sat the prettiest colored girl I've ever seen. She had the color of a pale Indian with the softness of feature of the Negro, and wore with trim and easy grace a modish dark green, business suit. Perched on one side of her head was one of those cute modernistic hats.

Although she seemed perfectly proportioned, it was her face that held one spellbound. It was absolutely symmetrical, with lips not large but sensuously full, rather high cheekbones, and large, wide-spaced eyes like limpid pools under the moonlight on a tropic plain. Her general expression was one of unbelievable innocence and sweetness. It was this contrast between her and the sinister physician that so startled me. I recovered my poise, finally. There was just trace of tolerant amusement on the Doctor's face as he noted my perturbation.

"Slater," he said, rising. "I want you to know Miss Patricia Givens. Patricia, this is Carl Slater, my secretary, of whom I've been telling you."

"I'm so glad to know you, Mister Slater." she said, revealing two rows of glistening, white, even teeth in an infectious smile, and offering a tiny gloved hand. I stammered out the usual thing while trying vainly to keep my eyes away from her hypnotic orbs. "Henry has been telling me how shocked you've been since joining us."

Then she was in it, too! I didn't know just what to say. I was frankly ill at ease, for I did not yet know what her relations were to Dr. Belsidus and she seemed more desirable to me than any woman I had ever seen. I dropped my eyes with difficulty and waited for the Doctor's orders.

"Sit down, Slater." he said, "and have a cocktail." He clapped his hands. The colored maid in black dress and white apron and cap hurried across the gleaming floor, a cocktail for me on her golden tray.

"Now, Slater," the physician began, pursing his lips and stroking his smooth black jowls. "Miss Givens is making a tour of our various enterprises, going as far as Mississippi. I want you to go with her and learn all there is at first hand about our resources. None of our staff can hope to serve efficiently without a detailed understanding of our work. You can't get that sitting around here. I suppose it will take you about a week, won't it Patricia?"

"Just about," she said. She seemed to be just a little amused at my dazed expression. I've always been a sap for pretty girls, and I don't think there's ever been one to out-rank Patricia Givens.

GEORGE S. SCHUYLER

"And when do we leave?" I managed to say. "What train?"

They both smiled at that.

"Miss Givens travels everywhere by airplane," said Dr. Belsidus.

"We leave at daylight," she announced in a matter-of-fact tone. "Jim will drive us to the field."

"Just we two?" I asked, aquiver with excitement at the prospect of having this angel's company for an entire week.

"Just we two," she echoed, smiling mischievously. "You're not frightened are you, Mr. Slater?"

I passed it off with a confused laugh while a dozen questions tortured me. Who was she? What was her background? What interest did she have in this bloody movement? What was she to Belsidus?

X

Carl Slater Learns Patricia Givens Is Head of Air Force

It was still dark when Jim awakened me. I shaved and dressed quickly, grabbed my travelling bag and ran down to the car, the mute giant in my wake. It was the long black limousine with which I was all too familiar. I stepped in. Miss Givens was already there. "Alright, Jim!" she ordered. The long car cruised over to Fifth Avenue and turned north toward Harlem. Then she turned to me with that dazzling smile. "Well, we're on our way," she said. "You're going to see something, Mr. Slater, before you get back."

"Yes," I remarked dreamily. I was studying her at close range now, and the nearer one got to her, the prettier she seemed. This morning, she was in green leather pilot's cap and jacket, green riding breeches, and cordovan boots. It was a becoming costume.

We turned over to Seventh Avenue, sped to 155th Street, crossed the viaduct, followed the Harlem Speedway and so wended our way into the Bronx and Westchester County. Jim was losing no time. There was little traffic as yet and on some stretches we made great, if silent, speed. About eight-thirty we ran up a side road for a mile or two and stopped at what appeared at first to be a country club.

"Well, here we are, Mr. Slater," she said. "Let's get out."

"What place is this?"

"This is our air school. The boys live in this building. The hangars and workshops are away over there. You probably thought they were big greenhouses. They do look like greenhouses, don't they?"

"Yes," I answered, although I confess I was more interested in the girl than I was in the hangars. She was just perfect.

"We put in glass roofs so the boys would have more light," she explained. Then, turning to Jim, she said, "Alright, Jim. You can go on back to town."

We walked into the long, low, rambling stone building with its wide verandah. A uniformed attendant probably the steward, met us and showed us all through, although Miss Givens was apparently no stranger there. There were two beds to a room and about thirty rooms

GEORGE S. SCHUYLER

A huge modern kitchen, an attractive dining hall and a well-equipped recreation room completed the picture.

"Come on," she said. "Our plane's waiting but I want you to see the workshops before we go."

We walked for about a half mile before we reached the hangars and workshops. The flying field was clear of weeds, well marked and lighted in accordance with government regulations. I have never seen a better ordered place. In the two big machine shops, more than a score of young colored men and women were working over engines, doping wings and otherwise engaged in the making and repairing of aircraft. In the five big hangars I counted a total of twenty planes. Most of them were built for high speed but several were huge transport planes capable of long journeys or carrying huge payloads.

Miss Givens was studying my reactions, a little smile playing about her pretty mouth. In the air overhead two of the small speedy ships were performing the most hair-raising stunts, dipping, sliding, slipping, banking, spinning: every gyration I had ever seen. "Those are our two latest productions," she observed.

"But what's to be done with all these planes?" I asked, for I was frankly puzzled, yet impressed, by the place.

"Oh, we'll use them," she said, lowering her voice. "The time will come when we won't have nearly enough. We finish one every ten days or so. It's excellent training for our young mechanics and pilots. I have to keep them busy, you know?"

"You keep them busy?" I was really surprised by her remark. "What have you got to do with this?"

"Oh," she said, laughing a little proudly, "I guess I didn't tell you that I'm in charge of the Doctor's air force."

"You don't mean to say that you're in charge of the manufacture of these planes?"

"Of course. Why, don't you think a woman can do things like this?"

"Well. . . yes," I stumbled, awed now by her brains as well as her beauty, "but it's so unusual, you know. It sort of took my breath away. Let me congratulate you."

"Not me," she replied soberly. "Congratulate Dr. Belsidus. It was he who made it possible for me to study three years in France and learn the business from the ground up. He is the most brilliant man in the world today."

The tone of reverence with which she said this somehow irritated me, and then, ashamed, I realized for the first time that I was in love with this girl and jealous of the sinister physician, master of both of us. Afraid of betraying my emotion, I remained silent.

"Don't you think so?" she asked, gazing straight into my eyes.

"Of course he is a remarkable man," I managed. And then, anxious to change the subject, I asked: "Who is in charge when you are away? I mean, who heads the highly technical work on engines and instruments? Surely you don't leave that in the hands of students?"

"Certainly not. She turned and called back toward the largest shop: "Juan! Juan! Come here a minute."

A voice answered her from the building. Then in a minute a giant of a man, dull black, with powerful muscles and flashing white teeth, came striding toward us, grimy overalls flapping.

"Yes. Mees Geevens," he said. "What ees eet?"

"Juan, I want you to meet Mr. Carl Slater, the Doctor's new secretary. Mr. Slater, this is Juan Torlier, our chief aeronautical engineer." We smiled and shook hands heartily. After a pleasant exchange, he turned and went back to the workshop.

"There's a real story for you," she exclaimed. "I met him two years ago in Barcelona. He was working in an airplane factory there where they turned out some of the finest engines in Europe, and he was the foreman in charge of production. He comes originally from the Muni River Settlements, you know, Spanish Guinea. Some colonial official took a liking to him, sent him to Spain to be schooled, but he'd seen enough of their misrule in Africa for it to rankle in his heart. So it wasn't hard to get him into the organization."

What a group this Dr. Belsidus had assembled! The more I saw of it and its work, the more I began to lose my skepticism about the possibilities of success.

We walked out on the field where a small black and gold autogiro was standing, its engine running. The rotor blades were extended. All was ready for flight.

"Everything okeh, Sam?" she asked the mechanic.

"It's alright, Miss Givens," he said.

I got in beside her. She gave it the gun and after a very short run, much shorter than would been required for a regular airplane, we rose quickly and were off over the tree tops.

I couldn't get over this girl's sureness, her nonchalance. She handled the autogiro as I would an automobile. We followed the Hudson to a point past Poughkeepsie, then we turned slightly to the east and flew toward a cloud of gray dust that rose from behind a hill around which railroad spur ran.

Miss Givens brought the machine down in a large open space before a huge gray building near the hill. Not far from it was a gang of men engaged in quarrying limestone which little cars carried to the nearby crusher.

"Well, here we are," she said, shutting off the engine. "This is our No. 1 cement mill. Come on, I want you to meet Bennie Simpson."

We walked over to the great building coated with cement. There the short, plump light mulatto with wavy hair, gray eyes and slightly freckled face who was in charge, took us through the place. We saw the hard limestone ground dry and mixed with the dried and ground clay. Then we saw the mixture dried and burned at a clinkering temperature, and finally the light gray powder being bagged. In a nearby warehouse were thousands upon thousands of bags of cement piled to the tool. A considerable number of Negroes were employed. The little houses in which they lived were not far from the mill.

"We're turning out fifty tons of cement a week." Simpson boasted. We've been running to capacity for almost a year now. If Doc don't start building pretty soon we won't have any room left to store this stuff."

"What building is he going to do?" I asked, puzzled, turning to Miss Givens. She smiled indulgently and her eyes sparkled. "I'll tell you all about it when we get going." she said. "Come on. We've got to reach our Jersey farm before dark."

We bade Simpson and his cement mill adieu and were soon again awing back down the Hudson. Frankly, my admiration and respect for Dr. Belsidus grew apace. There more I thought of him and his elaborate preparations, the more I wondered what, if anything, Patricia Givens was to him. She had spoken so worshipfully of him. Was she in love with him? If so, what chance had I? The thought was depressing and looked down idly as we passed over the Ramapo Hills. But inevitably my eyes came back to this brilliant, beautiful girl, and I wondered rather hopelessly whether and how I might win her affection. Then laughed at myself when I realized that I had scarcely known her twenty-four hours.

XI

Carl Sees Greatest Farm in World, With Science at Controls

"Why all that cement?" I asked, as we tore through the dying afternoon toward our destination.

"You've heard of Rev. Samson Binks, haven't you?"

"Yes, I heard Belsidus mention him in connection with some new Negro religion."

"Correct. And that cement is for the temples. Oh, we're going about it thoroughly, make no mistake about that."

"You seem very sure about the success of this Black Internationale program," I observed. She turned toward me, eyes shining fanatically.

"Yes, I'm sure," she shouted above the hum of the motor.

"And what makes you so sure?"

"Because we're using the weapons and knowledge of the white man against him. In the past, subject peoples have tried to match primitive weapons against the latest instruments of warfare. Either that or they have been ill-prepared or unprepared with the industrial organization incident and necessary to the manufacture of such instruments. It is the skilled technician, the scientist, who wins modern wars, and we are mobilizing the black scientists of the world. Our professors, our orators, our politicians have failed us. Our technicians will not. Everyday sees another trained young colored man or woman, sometimes both, added to our group."

"And the masses—what about them? Will they follow you as fanatically as your technicians?" I asked, chiefly to hear what she would say. "Can you depend upon their loyalty as you can that of Bennie Simpson, Juan Torlier, Ransom Just, Al Fortune and yourself?"

"We're not worried about the masses," she replied, airily, with a toss of her green helmet. "The masses always believe what they are told often and loud enough. We will recondition the Negro masses in accordance with the most approved behavioristic methods. The church will hold them spiritually. Our economic organization will keep control of those who shape their views. Our secret service will take care of dissenters. Our propaganda bureau will tell them what to think and believe. That's the way to build revolutions, Mr. Slater."

GEORGE S. SCHUYLER

I loved the faint flush on her checks which the bright green helmet and jacket only accentuated, and I couldn't help but admire the expertness with which she piloted the plane. Would she be interested in love. I wondered–this beauty who superintended an aircraft factory, piloted planes across country and talked of conditioning the masses, world revolution and such things.

"Listen." I shouted, "don't call me Mr. Slater, call me Carl."

She turned quickly, and smiled. "It is silly, our being so formal, isn't it?" she said. And then, "I suppose you might as well call me Pat, too." The friendliness in her tone made my heart skip a little. Just like a young fellow, I began wondering about the future.

I noted in the distance what appeared to be a small swamp lake, yet it was perfectly square and was criss-crossed by what seemed to be paths. On one side of it were a number of barns and silos, a large farm house with a lawn of several acres in front of it.

"That's our New Jersey farm," she shouted, jerking her head toward it.

"I can't see any farm," I replied. "There's nothing but some farm buildings."

"You just wait and see," she said, smiling knowingly. This is Sam Hamilton's first experiment."

WE CAME ON FAST. PAT banked the plane. Our shoulders touched and I found myself thrilling like some school kid. Then we came down and, after a surprisingly short run, stopped almost directly in front of the farmhouse. It was colonial in style but quite new: so were the barns and silos. The vast lawn on which we had landed was clipped short and looked like green velvet.

The sun was quite low now. I noticed that there were signal lights for night landing and a sleeve for wind direction on a nearby red and white steel-frame tower. We got out and approached the verandah. Pat rang the bell. Shortly, a uniformed servant admitted us.

"Come in and meet Sam," said Pat. "He'll show us something before dark."

"I thought he was in New York," I said, remembering that the day before I had seen him in the subterranean smeltery melting down precious ornaments and plates that had once graced the bodies and tables of rich white people.

"He always comes out once a day," she explained. "We're only about a hundred miles from New York, you know."

Sam strode out to meet us almost as soon as we had taken seats. Gone were the white clothing and green goggles he always wore in front of his furnace. Today he was dressed in a neat blue serge suit, a fitting contrast to his exotic, Hindu-like countenance.

"Glad to see you out here," he told me. "This is where the really big thing is going on. Of course we're not making any money yet, but pretty soon we'll knock 'em dead with our stuff."

"What are you doing out here on a farm?" I asked half seriously. "A chemist's place is in the laboratory."

"That's all you know about it," he laughed. "We chemists are soon going to put the farmers out of business. Come on out and I'll show you."

We followed him through the house and out the back door toward the lake. It was the most surprising, astounding lake I've ever seen. One can best describe it by calling it a mile-square rectangle of cement, gridironed by cement dikes a hundred yards apart. These gridirons converted the artificial lake or reservoir into contiguous pools, each about two acres in extent. Each pool was about four feet deep and half filled with greenish water in which plants were growing in serried rows. At intervals of about two feet, slender concrete posts were spaced across the pools and connected by ordinary fence wire. On to these the plants clung. The dikes were about ten feet wide, easily permitting a large car or truck to pass over them.

"This is our farm," announced Sam, a little proudly. "Only one of its kind in this country on a big scale. I understand there are some in Russia and Germany, though."

"Farm?" I echoed. "Where is it? Why, the whole place is under water."

Pat audibly snickered.

"Sure," explained Sam, "it's supposed to be. I had it built like this. We don't use any dirt at all, so soil erosion will never bother us. See those pipes down in the bottom of that pool? Well, they run along the bottom of everyone of the three hundred and twenty-four two-acre pools in this farm. When the water falls below a certain temperature, the steam is turned on to heat it up. In this time of year, the winter, it is on most of the time, although it doesn't stay so cold down here in South Jersey."

"But vegetables won't grow in clear water," I argued, although they manifestly *were* growing.

"That's what you think," he said, smiling, "but we supply each pool with liquid chemical food, the same elements vegetables extract from the soil. Sunshine does the rest. Not a thing is left to chance, my boy. There is no plant disease, no poor distribution of food elements, no excess or lack of light. Our plants grow quickly and the quality of the vegetables is better. Our tomato plants grow fifteen to twenty-five feet tall, and others in proportion. Soil culture produces about twelve tons of vegetables an acre. Our yield is two hundred tons an acre. Each pool will produce four hundred tons of produce, and it is ready for market long before products raised in the soil."

He reached down and pulled up a vine. It was loaded with strawberries, but such strawberries as I had never seen, nor anybody else for that matter. They were fully as large as full-grown plums, bright red and as luscious a sight as I've ever witnessed.

"White folks can't equal that," he boasted. "We're sending a crop to market in New York and Philadelphia tomorrow. They'll sell easily for fifteen cents a quart. Imagine the money we'll make! Why, the winter strawberries from the South and California won't be able to sell at all, except to the poor. We'll take all the quality trade, not only for strawberries but everything else."

"And the pretty part about it," added Pat, taking a big bite out of one of the strawberries with her strong white teeth, "is that they'll be carried to market throughout the East on B.I. trucks driven by Negroes."

"But isn't your overhead enormous?" I asked, a little weakly, somewhat subdued by this miracle of modern chemistry. "It must cost a tremendous amount of money to steam-heat a mile of water two feet deep. Where is your powerhouse?"

"I can imagine you'll be surprised to learn." observed Sam, somewhat mysteriously, "that neither our steam or electric power costs us a cent. Tomorrow I'm going to show you a source of power, hitherto practically neglected, that is inexhaustible. Negro brains, in other words, your old friend Al Fortune, have harnessed it and put it to work to serve our ends." So Al worked here, too, eh?

He walked over to the pool to our left, reached well down and tugged at a vine. In the gathering dusk I could scarcely credit my vision. For there in his hand was a bright red tomato as big as a full-size grapefruit. It completely silenced me. I could only look on in unabashed awe.

"I told you so, didn't I?" gloated Pat, amused at my expression.

"We're using the weapons and knowledge of the white man against him."

"Shucks," observed Sam, as we turned back toward the house. "We are way past white science already. Wait until you see our steam and electric plant tomorrow. We'll soon be able to turn every wheel in America."

XII

Carl Is Shown the Remarkable Powerhouse in New Jersey

I had been amazed by the Black Internationale's airplane factory and cement factory: the liquid chemical farm frankly astounded me. I could now scarcely wait to see the steam and electric plant invented by Al Fortune and which cost nothing operate. After a good dinner and a tour through the vast refrigerated storehouses where vegetables of astounding sizes were stored in bins from floor to ceiling, we turned in for the night, but I slept only fitfully.

I lay awake for a long time thinking about Dr. Belsidus and the Black Internationale, about the brilliant colored men and women he had assembled about him, about his spy system, his criminal acts, his fanatical plans for an international race war. But chiefly I thought about Pat. And with her face before me I fell to sleep.

It must have been two hours later when a noise of voices and coughing motors outside awakened me. I ran to the window, which looked out over the artificial lake. To my surprise the whole expanse was flood-lighted from above and also from below. Each pool of the three hundred and twenty-four that comprised the "farm" was brilliantly lighted. In the chemically treated water hundreds of colored men swarmed gathering the miraculously grown crop. On the dikes between the pools scores of black and gold B.I. trucks and hundreds of crates awaited their loads. As the trucks were loaded they chugged off and disappeared into the darkness, either to the city markets or to the storehouses.

I stepped out on the back verandah to see better this remarkable sight destined to revolutionize truck gardening. So engrossed was I in the spectacle, that I had been watching for perhaps five minutes when I felt the presence of someone else, and, turning, confronted Pat gorgeously arrayed in flowing pink negligee.

"So it got you up too, eh?" she remarked, smiling. Then she exclaimed ecstatically. "Isn't it marvelous! Isn't it perfectly unbelievable?" My pounding heart sealed my lips as I feasted my eyes.

She was like a vision, something ethereal, a flimsy pink fairy out of the ages of folk imagination, an exotic shimmering flower. The faint scent of gardenia came from her rich robes and luxuriously titillated my nostrils.

"Don't you think so?" she asked, coming closer, a slight challenge in her tone, the light of enthusiasm in her large brown eyes.

"Why. . . why. . . yes," I stuttered. Then, unable to restrain myself or to longer conceal my emotion, I blurted out, "But not as marvelous as you are, Pat. Oh. forgive me, will you? But I can't help it. I had to say it because I feel it, feel it overpoweringly."

The flush deepened in her cheeks. She drew back and I thought some of the sparkle left her eyes to be replaced by a misty light. Instinctively she wrapped her negligee closer about her.

I'm so sorry, Carl," she murmured, suppressing her emotion with difficulty. "We mustn't speak of such things. There's too much to be done. Please. . . please, excuse me." She turned quickly and hastened into her room.

I stood there unwitting of the spectacle before me, gazing straight ahead. Then, suddenly aware of the chill night air, I also repaired to my room, my thoughts dwelling not on Sam Hamilton's liquid chemical farm and the effect of flooding the markets of the East with huge fruits and vegetables, but on Patricia Givens, my sudden infatuation for her, and the possibility of her reciprocating my feeling.

The room telephone bell awakened me much sooner than I would have liked. The dull gray of daybreak had not been yet dispersed by the sun.

"It's Sam," came the voice on the phone. "We'll have to get out early because I've got to run back to town to work in the laboratory, and I want to show you our power plant before I leave. Hurry down and we'll have a bit to eat."

I hustled through my shower and shave, dressed and joined Sam and Pat at the breakfast table. I glanced at her and caught her eyes. She lowered them quickly and studied the piece of toast in her hand as her cheeks turned a dull red. It made my pulse leap. Then she had *not* forgotten last night! Perhaps. . . I wondered.

"I wish Al were here to show you this," said Sam as we strolled across the closely clipped lawn to the long line of buildings, "but I guess I can substitute for him. I'll have to. He'll probably be out this afternoon, but you'll be miles away by then."

He led the way to a long building about two stories high with a flat roof. We entered and climbed two flights of winding iron stairways to

GEORGE S. SCHUYLER

a penthouse opening on the roof which was about three hundred feet long and all of a hundred feet wide. The roof was almost completely covered with some sort of machinery covered with canvas suspended by cable from tall steel poles placed at intervals at both sides of the roof.

Sam went around to the side of the building and immediately pulleys began to squeak, the steel cable grew taut and the great canvas began to roll away from the objects it covered. It was quite ingeniously at ranged. The canvas ended up rolled tightly and lying along the edge of the roof. Now the sun had come out brightly from the East.

Disclosed were a great number of strange contraptions, possibly a hundred or more. At first glance they resembled a great battery of glass anti-aircraft guns or telescopes. They were glass–or aluminum–lined troughs set at an angle of forty-five degrees on a steel framework. In back of the higher end was what appeared to be a cylindrical water pump, at the other end a small engine. From the engine, iron pipes ran down into the building.

"This is Al's famous sun engine," Sam explained, "probably the most revolutionary invention in the past thousand years. Men have been trying for a century to invent a cheap sun-harnesser which will cheapen sun power below the cost of coal power. Now, a Negro has done it. There have been other solar engines but this surpasses them all. It only costs a hundred dollars to make and it seems to last indefinitely. Of course, bigger units will cost more.

"It stores up electric power," he continued, "and also stores up power for other purposes. Our silos over there are insulated with the new glass wool and are full of sand. They store up heat to extremely high temperatures and retain the heat virtually without loss for years. You see, we can only use these engines about nine hours a day at this time of the year and twelve or fourteen hours a day in summer, but we need power all the time to keep our farm at an even temperature and to make electricity. Heat, of course, makes power.

"Now, here's the way it works," he went on, leading us over to the nearest machine. "The sunlight is caught on the surface of the highly polished aluminum mirrors, which are six feet long and two feet wide. You notice they're curved in such a way as to focus the rays on that long tube you see that looks like a thermos bottle resting in the bottom of the trough. It rests in a sort of cradle which can be turned to catch the full force of the sun's rays at anytime of the day.

"The thermos bottle arrangement," he continued, "consists of three tubes, one inside the other. The outer tube is made of pyrex glass, six feet long, with an outside diameter of one and one-half inch and an inside diameter of one and one-quarter inch. This outer tube is known as the focus tube. Within the focus tube is a miniature 'flash boiler' of the type used in the old-fashioned steam automobiles, like the old Stanley Steamer. This miniature flash boiler is a steel tube one-half inch in diameter, made of the latest high-grade steel, thin-walled, but strong enough to resist a pressure of steam up to two hundred pounds per square inch. This steel tube slips into the pyrex glass focus tube, which is jacketed by a vacuum.

"The steel tube," Sam explained further, "is painted with lampblack so as to absorb eighty-five percent of the sun's rays that fall upon it after passing through the focus tube.

"Within the steel tube," he went on, warming to the subject as be noted our intense interest, "is a third tube, known as the water tube. This is only one-eighth of an inch in diameter, and is joined along t entire length by four copper wings, well soldered with high-melting point solder, to the inside of the steel tube. A supply of water automatically regulated by that meter you see in the rear passes through the inner tube at the proper rate to burst into steam at the desired pressure of one hundred seventy-five pounds to the square inch.

"As the four copper wings are such fine conductors of heat," Sam explained, "that heat produced by the absorption of solar rays in the lampblack on the outer surface of the steel tube penetrates with the utmost facility to vaporize the water. Thus, our heat and power here cost us nothing. The white man cannot successfully compete with any industry we may enter because he has no such machine as this. We have a distinct advantage of starting with something as far in advance of his industrial methods as steam was in advance of hand power."

Although Pat had seen it all before, she was trembling with excitement, her brown eyes sparkling like polished jewels. Involuntarily, quite unthinking, I know, her hand clasped mine and my heart jumped, although I knew her mind was only on the wonder before us. I forcibly banished thought of her and struggled to concentrate on Sam's scholarly explanation.

"Each of these units is only two horsepower," he was saying, "but there are a hundred units on this roof alone. A similar battery is on the roof of everyone of our ten storage barns or warehouses. This engine is capable of converting the sunlight falling on an area of one square mile into seventy thousand horsepower on a cloudless day. Imagine what that will mean when we set up these batteries in the tropics? Why, the sunshine falling on the State of New Mexico alone furnishes a hundred times as much energy per year as the total of all coal, oil and water power used per year in the United States."

Pat turned to me smiling, triumph in her eyes. "Now do you doubt that we can win?" she challenged. I smiled back and nodded a negative.

"Well," she continued, "you haven't seen half."

XIII

CARL RETURNS TO NEW YORK;
"INTERNATIONALE" MOVES INTO HIGH GEAR

The following week was like a dream, like traveling in some strange world. Down through Maryland, Virginia, the Carolinas and the lower South we sped, visiting truck farms, poultry farms, plantations and other enterprises until we were well into central Texas. Each establishment was equipped with its well-appointed private airfield and usually located some distance from a city. Each was headed by some bright young colored man or woman.

More marvelous than these economic enterprises, however, was the company of Patricia Givens. I hadn't summoned up the courage to tell her again what was uppermost in my thoughts. Her initial repulse had made me timid. So now I contented myself with feasting my eyes upon her beauty as she piloted the autogiro over the country with faultless precision. And although I had received no encouragement whatever, it was with considerable regret that I learned that we had reached the end of our journey and would now fly back to New York.

WE WALKED THROUGH THE PLOTS of tomato plants fifteen and twenty feet high while the plane was being gassed. I wanted to touch her and to stroll arm in arm, but one glance at her face inhibited me. Whether or not she sensed my mood I do not know. We went on in silence save for a prosaic comment on the enormous vegetables that rose out of the chemically treated water and hung invitingly from the wire fencing.

"You're rather cold, aren't you?" I asked finally, with something of my suppressed feelings betrayed in my tone.

She turned suddenly, a dark flush under her clear skin. "Why do you say that?" she inquired. And by the way she asked it, I knew that she knew what I meant.

"Well," I said, a little confused by her abruptness, "you don't seem to think of anything except the Black Internationale. After all, you're a pretty girl. . . I'd. . . Well. . . I've told you how I feel."

"Sorry, Carl, but there isn't much time for romance. There's too much to be done, and such a short time in which to do it. Romance can wait. Forget about it. There's plenty of time for that in the future."

"But you can't deny love." I insisted. "You can't dismiss it like that. After all, you are human just like I am."

"Yes," she said a little coldly, "and for that reason, I keep a good grip on myself."

"Do you love anyone?" I persisted, thinking of Dr. Belsidus. She smiled mysteriously. "Maybe," was all she said.

JIM WAS WAITING FOR US at the Westchester airport when we came in and he drove us down to New York City. At dinner that evening in the green, gold and rose room, off the precious service, Dr. Belsidus, stern-visaged as usual, sat at the head of the table. Others present were Sam Hamilton, Patricia, Al Fortune, Ransom Just. Rev. Samson Binks, Dr. Andrew Matson, Bennie Simpson and myself. We were more than halfway through the meal when the door opened and the silent Jim admitted a tall, hatchet-faced brown man with long, acquisitive nose, deep-set, calculating eyes and gray hair and mustache. I had never seen him before.

"Carl," said Belsidus, "shake hands with Alex Fletcher. Fletcher, this is Carl Slater, my secretary. He's been looking over our enterprises. Sort of familiarizing himself with things."

"A good idea," observed the newcomer, eying me shrewdly.

"Sit down," commanded Belsidus. Then, turning to me, he explained, "Alex is our business expert, and a damned good one, too. But, like the rest of us, he soon discovered that race and color definitely limited him. He's handling our marketing and transportation now. How are things going, Alex?"

"Very good," he replied, clipping his words off short. "We're taking the strawberry and tomato market. The other dealers are squawking. There'll be even a bigger squawk when our crops from the South are sent into market. It'll take them a year or two to meet our competition."

*Suppose they use force?" suggested Sam. "You know these crackers won't take it lying down."

Dr. Belsidus's eyes glowed cruelly. "Just let them try," he said. "I know a few tricks, too. Don't forget that." Then he turned to Rev. Binks, a short, brown man with silver-rimmed spectacles, a head of graying hair that badly needed cutting, a scraggly mustache and a studious expression. He was a slovenly fellow, almost ill-kempt, but the wisdom that shone from his eyes compensated for all his shortcomings.

"How is your first temple going Binks?" asked the Doctor.

"It will be completed in another month, Doctor." The clergyman spoke with deliberation.

"Everything?"

"Yes, everything."

"Good! We can't get started too soon. We want a temple in every Negro community before the end of six months. Our produce sales ought to swing that, don't you think, Alex?"

"Yes, Chief, if everything goes well."

"It's got to go well," grated Belsidus. "We must be in a position strike by the end of this year. We can't have any delays. The international situation is ripe. We can capitalize on the present uncertainty, but first we must get the Negroes organized. That will be your job, Binks."

"I will do my part," said the preacher, quietly. There was much to the same effect. The whole conspiracy was taking a definite head. The seriousness of the others, the earnestness of their expressions all conveyed that impression. I am sure we all walked away from that momentous conference quite a-tingle with expectancy.

In the next month, every effort was definitely speeded up. Cement and structural steel took form in a hundred cities and towns, and one by one the Rev. Binks's Temples of Love rose majestically out of disorder to architectural beauty.

Pat and I attended the opening of the first one in Harlem. It was a huge building closely resembling an Egyptian temple, and in the form of a truncated pyramid. It was a cement and steel shell, gray trimmed with blue and pink. A massive door was the only entrance and exit Long and very narrow windows were spaced at intervals of fifteen or twenty feet down each side. Their panes were of colored glass, each window being guarded by a wrought-iron grill. Once one entered the front door, one crossed a wide flagged court to the temple proper. In the center of the court was an alabaster fountain. The temple proper was in semi-darkness, indirectly lighted by electricity, but along the tiled walls great candles flickered in huge candlesticks.

The most surprising thing about it, however, was the fact that there were no benches, chairs or other provisions for seating communicants, and that at the far end, its figure indirectly lighted and so standing out clearly from the semi-darkness, was a huge statue of a nude Negro standing with legs apart, gazing sardonically downward with arms crossed. It was all of 50 feet high and every part of the body was clearly depicted. In front of the idol was a great semi-circular platform. In front of that was a small altar, evidently for the priest. When our eyes got used to the semi-darkness, we noticed that there were a large number of camp chairs on the large platform.

"Rather awesome, eh?" I remarked to Pat. "Do you think the Negroes will fall for it?"

"Binks is no fool, Carl. He's going to give the masses of Negroes the sort of religion they want but haven't been able to get. Music and dancing, no collections, plenty of pageantry, keeping things down to earth with enough sex to make everything interesting. They can come here and get everything they need. Let's go downstairs."

We stepped out into the entrance court and, turning to one side, descended two flights of stairs to the basement. Here we noted in succession a restaurant, a grocery store, a drug store, a hair parlor, a gymnasium with a swimming pool, a clothing store and a bank, all opening off an arcade.

"Why, if this thing clicks." I observed, "the Black Internationale will virtually control the economic life of colored America."

"Yes, of course. That's our intention. Binks is making the church what it was to ancient times. . . a center of everyday life and activity, of amusement and instruction, conforming to, yet shaping, society."

XIV

Wherein a Session in the "Church of Love" Is Described

I do not wish to burden you with uninteresting details, but so impressed was I with the first service at the Church of Love and so widespread did its influence finally become that I deem it necessary to describe it to you.

When Pat and I came up from inspecting the economic units in the basement, we found the great temple slowly filling with Negroes, entering between a double rank of tall men in priestly robes of black and gold. We followed the crowd into the vast auditorium. As we passed inside we were each handed a round straw cushion by a pretty girl. We were directed by an equally comely usher in black and gold uniform to a place on the floor. We noticed that the audience was being seated in rows as in a theatre but with about a dozen aisles leading down to the platform. Around the hall at intervals of about ten feet stood tall black Negroes with flowing golden garments, golden ribbons about their beads and black and gold sandals on their feet. They bore long, highly polished brass trumpets that almost reached their shoulders from the floor. The trumpeters stood motionless, glancing neither to the right left.

Soon the auditorium was completely filled. The many ushers hurried on soft-slippered feet to all parts of the room, cautioning against the slightest whisper. The people looked wonderingly at each other, plainly puzzled and no little awed by these proceedings. Most of them wereobviously curiosity seekers wondering what it was all about. They wanted to chatter but the alert and pretty ushers discouraged them.

Five minutes passed. The silence was oppressive. Suddenly, strong ghts blazed toward the seated audience, almost blinding us. We could se nothing at the other end of the temple. The lights went off. Looking quickly, I noticed that the semi-circular platform had disappeared, leasing a great black void.

Now the trumpeters around the wall, as if by command, moved the mouthpieces of their trumpets to their lips. Somewhere a light flashed momentarily. The trumpets let out a throaty, musical blast. Now a thousand hidden lights illuminated the semi-darkness of the place with every color of the spectrum.

The far end of the church almost leaped out to meet us. The a platform began to rise from the void, silently, impressively. Seated on it in concentric circles facing us were at least one hundred and fifty Negro musicians in black tailcoats faced with gold. The conductor, his back to us, stood with arms upraised. As the ascending platform stopped on a level slightly above us, he brought down his baton and a crash of majestic great music filled the place. Its strong African theme was indeed stirring.

Now emerged from either side of the platform a single line of fifty brown girls, young, shapely, almost all of a cocoa brown tint and garbed in flowing, multi-colored tunics, many pointed and diaphanous, which fluttered as they walked. Gracefully they formed a single line in front of the platform, a line that stretched almost clear across the temple, un dulating with the beat of the music.

Behind them on each side came fifty women in pale yellow tunics that reached to the floor. These grouped themselves in a knot near each end of the line of dancers and stood motionless.

The orchestra music died almost to a whisper. Now the two groups of yellow-gowned women began to chant, softly at first, then slowly, louder and louder until the great symphony orchestra was almost drowned out. Then the orchestra grew louder itself. The chorus and instruments seemed to vie with each other. Then the orchestra waned again. Soon only the powerful chanting of the women could be heard. Then toward the end the orchestra joined in. The trumpeters with muted instruments added their brassy tones.

I have never heard anything like it. The people sat tense, absorbed transfixed. Par's hand was gripping mine almost painfully. As the hymn ended we all relaxed as if by command, but I noticed that Pat's hand still held mine. Then suddenly she noticed it, colored, and removed it in confusion; a self-conscious grin was wreathing her pretty face.

Another blast from the encircling trumpets. Orchestra and chorus took up the theme. The graceful dancing beauties moved like wisps, forming beautiful figures, leaping, pirouetting swooping in perfect rhythm while varied colored lights from a cyclorama played upon them. No ballet could have been more perfectly trained.

Then an amazing thing happened. A great bell tolled from somewhere. A stentorian voice boomed, "Rise, All Ye Within! Rise, All

Ye within! Rise and worship the God of Love. Ruler of black men and women. Rise to greet Him!" The dancers stopped, transfixed.

All the lights seemed to die or concentrate themselves in one great spotlight, and this shone upon the huge fifty-foot statue of the nude Negro.

"Rise" boomed the voice again. The multitude scrambled to its collective feet, Pat and I along with them.

"Gaze upon Him!" boomed the voice again. We all looked upward. The music had ceased now. Only the low chanting of the chorus relieved this awed silence.

Now the great arms which had been folded slowly unfolded and stretched out full length. The great breast began to rise and fall. The huge eyes became luminous and the great head began slowly to nod up and down. It was awesome indeed. The singing ended. The eyes continued to blaze. The great head moved up and down.

One could hear the hard breathing. I saw fear in many of those eyes that stared hypnotically at the great image moving like a living thing.

Suddenly, a woman screamed. Then another, and then another. They were piteous, agonizing screams, and a body fell to the tile floor.

"Cast down thy eyes!" boomed the voice, Obediently we looked toward the floor. I knew it was hokum. I knew Binks had rigged up this robot and I knew approximately just how it worked, and yet for the life of me I could not but enter into the spirit of the thing and obey the commands of the voice, I, too, looked downward.

A full minute passed. A great blast from the trumpeter startled us to attention. Two thousand pairs of eyes looked upward to the huge Image It stood cold and silent as before, the arms folded, the eyes dead, the chest still. Gone was every evidence of life that had so startled us.

"Be seated!" boomed the hidden voice. Like automations, we returned to our cushions.

The great symphony orchestra, joined again by the chorus, produced blood-stirring music. The long line of girls danced like mad laines was difficult to restrain one's self from participating.

Dozens of pretty ushers now passed between the rows, bearing large trays loaded with tiny glasses. "Take one and drink!" they commanded pleasantly. Pat and I obeyed along with the rest. It was a dark red, fery liquor with a strong but pleasant odor. The usher paused until we had drained the tiny glasses and returned them to her tray. It was all done quickly and efficiently. In less than five minutes the vast assemblage had been served.

"Wonder what this is?" Pat whispered. "It tasted good."

Before I could answer, I felt a sharp pain in my chest. My head swam. Strange lights floated before my eyes. One moment the music was miles away. The next moment it almost burst my eardrums. The people about me were like hundreds of great corkscrews and Pat became a pane of brown glass. My hand weighed a ton. The top of my skull floated off into space.

As I fought against this strange drug, the music grew wilder and wilder. Bach and Sibelius gave way to evil, blood-stirring rhythms born in the steamy swamps of the Congo. From somewhere a crescendo of tom toms rent the air with their sizzling syncopation, and moaning minor chords tore the heartstrings.

"Dance! Dance! Move the Cushions to the walls, and Dance!" came again the command from somewhere.

Automatically, like zombies we obeyed, carrying the cushions to the sides of the temple, staggering under the effects of the drug, knowing nothing except to obey.

"Dance! Dance! Dance for Love!" commanded the voice. The eyes of the image again grew luminous. They held one with hypnotic intensity. As the music screamed louder, more insistently, I seized Pat and we whirled madly, insanely, drunkenly, like the others, in lunatic, erotic, passionate, frenzied embrace, as the women of the chorus and the beautiful balles girls joined in the shameless orgy.

Gone was all restraint, gone all inhibitions as the throbbing drums and sensuous, pulsating music tore asunder and subjugated our conscious beings. The inner man, the subconscious mind, the primeval urges born in the Mesozoic ooze, completely controlled us, dominated us motivated us.

And above the ordered din, the ecstatic screams and yells, boomed the hidden voice chanting, "Dance," while the luminous eyes of the gigantic God of Love looked down in hypnotic scrutiny. Then my brain went completely blank, and I knew nothing.

XV

Rev. Binks's Sermon in Church of Love Sounds Keynote of Movement

I do not know how long a time elapsed or what we did. I only know that suddenly my reason returned and I was lying stretched out on the tile floor. I looked around. The temple was again in semi-darkness. Only a light here and there and the flickering candles relieved the blackness. But there was sufficient illumination for me to rise up on my elbow and scan the strange sight.

The entire surface of the floor was covered with sprawling bodies of men and women in every conceivable recumbent pose, as though all at the same time had been stricken down by some lethal gas. Beside me, her clothing disordered and her eyelids just flickering back to consciousness, lay Pat, more beautiful and inviting than I had ever seen her. The trumpeters all stood in their places along the wall, but the ballet and the chorus were gone. On the platform the men of the symphony or chestra sat at ease, the conductor leaning on his lectern. But, singularly enough, the great ebony image of the God of Love had disappeared.

I leaned over guiltily and kissed Pat, unable to resist the temptation of her beautiful lips. She opened her eyes with a start, looking wildly about like one awakening from a nightmare in a strange place. Then reason returned to her. Shamefacedly she arranged her clothing, permitting herself the while a sickly smile. Now all around us the others were stirring, rising, standing around, discussing in low tones what had happened.

"Well, Binks really put it on strong, didn't he?" Pat observed, putting her hair back into place. "If Harlem doesn't fall for this. I don't know my people at all."

"It's a solid sender, alright," I agreed. "That drink really takes away your will and about everything else. It acted just like that broth, the East Indian drug Belsidus gave me the night I got into this outfit. You know it induces temporary insanity. This was a lighter dose, though, or we'd be asleep for hours. As it is, we couldn't have been out of our heads more than ten or fifteen minutes."

"Well, I'd like to know what happened during that ten or fifteen minutes," she remarked, looking at me as if I might know. I could see a light of suspicion in her eyes.

"Whatever happened," I observed, reassuringly. "I'm feeling swell. Just as light as a feather. Really buoyant."

"So do I, she admitted. "That's why I have a dark suspicion in the back of my mind. The last thing I remember you and I were dancing wildly together."

There was no opportunity to pursue the matter further. The buzz of conversation all around us was rudely interrupted by a blast from the trumpets. The great voice boomed, "Get Your Cushions! Get Your Cushions! Good People, Get Your Cushions! Return and Be Seated! Return and Be Seated!" We all did as we were bidden and soon the vast assemblage was seated approximately as before.

There was a long quiet pause until the last rustle and whisper had died. Then the great orchestra came to light at the tap of the conductor's baton and soothing music swept through the vast auditorium. In about ten minutes it ended. The pretty ushers now cautioned everyone to maintain the utmost quiet.

Slowly the platform on which the orchestra sat sank out of sight be low the level of the floor. The great orange-colored curtain that covered the back wall parted and a large silver screen was extended to view. From some hidden place rose the majestic peals of a pipe organ. Again the great hidden voice boomed out, "All Stand!"

Now down the central aisle from the great door at our backs moved a colorful procession. Marching four abreast came first a troop of twenty young boys dressed in long black and gold gowns and carrying three-foot black candles. As they proceeded down the aisle they shrilly chanted. Following them was a troop of tiny black dancing girls not one of whom could have been over eight years old. They wore ballet skirts of rose, purple and yellow. Behind them marched four giant trumpeters whose music accompanied that from the pipe organ. They in turn were followed by eight men bearing a golden throne on their shoulders. On each side of the throne strode a giant Negro in gold and black tunic bearing a huge ostrich feather fan which gently kept the air in motion. Seated on the throne, dressed in gold and black robes stiff with jewels, was Rev. Samson Binks, looking benign and papal.

THE COLORFUL PROCESSION MOVED DOWN to the front of the temple. The platform had now been returned to its former position. The candle bearers ranged themselves at equal intervals before it. The tiny dancing girls disappeared into the wings. The throne-bearers moved on to the platform and lowered their burden to the floor. Rev. Binks put out his hand One of the bearers grasped it and helped him out. With the trumpeters ranged on each side, the clergyman walked to the small golden altar, the lan-bearers following close behind. Mounting the three or four steps to the canopied altar, he rested one hand on the lectern and lifting the other he blessed the vast assemblage. The singing of the youthful choristers died. The pipe organ was still.

"My people," he began, "today you have seen and experienced that of which there is no counterpart in the world. You have taken part in our services in honor of the God of Love. You will henceforward be ruled and commanded by love. You will realize that black people can only become great, black people can only become prosperous, black people can only become powerful by loving one another. It must be a wholehearted, unashamed, literal love which black people have from henceforth for one another. Loving each other, my people, we must therefore help each other. We must not quarrel or contend with each other. Our love must include all black people, all brown people, all yellow people, for together these colored people are soon to rule the earth.

"That is the meaning of this church, that is the meaning of this religion, that is the meaning of this God of Love which only a short time ago greeted you, that is the meaning of the great Black Internationale which dominates and will control all black people and will soon control world civilization.

"Follow the Black Internationale. Obey its commands and all the world will be given unto you. From an inferior you will become superior. Now despised, you will come to be honored and feared. From a people cursed by poverty, discrimination and segregation you will be great in the councils of nations.

"Those that oppose the Black Internationale will perish. The God of

Love will strike down all those who sin against His injunction to black people to Love One Another.

"Leave your so-called Christian churches. Force them to close their doors. Christianity is a religion for slaves. You are no longer slaves. You are free men. You are warriors. You are rulers. You no longer serve the white man. You no longer bow down to the white man. You no longer take the white man's leavings. You no longer turn the other cheek when smitten. You no longer forgive your enemies. You no longer grin in the face of him who despises you. You stand with head high and shoulders square. A free man once more as were your ancestors in Africa.

"My people: This is the first temple. Hundreds are in course of construction. Thousands of young priests, choristers and dancers are being trained. We are making of organized religion something of color and beauty appealing to all the senses. This is religion as the temples of Egypt and Babylon knew it long ago. We have resurrected it so the church may again be the center of the people's lives and activities. So that the Negro may spiritually live again.

"All this, everything without exception, is the work of the Black Internationale. Through it you and yours will come to man's estate at last after centuries of servitude and inferiority.

"My people, I have spoken. Watch! See the power of the Black Internationale!"

Every light was extinguished. Only the line of candles flickered fitfully. Then a square of light leapt out of the darkness to the silver screen. In the half light Rev. Binks could be seen descending from the altar. Slowly the procession assembled, marched off to one side and disappeared.

Now followed an hour of talking from the altar. Slowly the reverend's lieutenants read propaganda charts and messages. Others showed factories, farms and powerhouses and all the far-flung enterprises presided over by Dr. Belsidus. But strangely enough the picture of that master plotter did not appear, nor were any of his able lieutenants like Sam Hamilton, Al Fortune, Pat and the others shown.

At the end, after a great world map depicting locations of the various Black Internationale cells had been shown, the long services were ended. The pipe organ burst forth with peals of majestic music. The trumpeters joined in. Ushers showed the way to the several exits. These all led to corridors surrounding the auditorium which, in turn, led back to the great front foyer. There other ushers guided the people downstairs to the economic center where the restaurant, grocery store, drug store, clothing store, beauty parlor and gymnasium awaited them.

Pat and I went out and were about to hail a cab when I was tapped on the shoulder.

XVI

BLACK INTERNATIONALE AVENGES LYNCHING IN MISSISSIPPI; THEN. . .

I turned quickly. It was Jim, dark and grim as ever. He pointed to the familiar Belsidus limousine parked at the curb. Then he opened the door and bade us enter. I surmised that Dr. Belsidus wanted us. Jim got up front and soon we were moving as quickly as possible through the congested Harlem streets.

When we arrived at Dr. Belsidus's house, Jim pointed to the door and nodded insistently. "I wonder what's up," Pat murmured as we entered.

Dr. Belsidus met us in the foyer. I could see that he was unusually grim today. "I want to talk to you two," he said curtly. He led the way back to the elevator. In a few seconds we were seated around his desk in the office upstairs. What was he planning now? Why this sudden all? We didn't have long to wait. He produced a U.S. map.

"Yesterday," he began. "there was a burning of a Negro in Mississippi, in some little town called Newton. Our cell in Meridian has investigated the lynching and reports that the man was absolutely innocent of the rape with which he was charged. Innocent or not, the Black Internationale is going to put a stop to lynching. That's final."

"But what are we to do about it, Chief?"

"We're going to strike," he growled. "We're going to make them pay in the only way they understand. The South and those who rule it understand only one thing: force. That country lives and dies by violence. Therefore we shall repay violence with violence, burning with burning death with death. Furthermore, we shall let them know why." His deep-set eyes glowed ominously, almost fanatically.

Pat looked somewhat uneasy and drummed on the table with her finger tips. I was wondering myself just what he had in mind. Then he spoke again.

"Of course," he began, a crafty smile playing around the corners of his stern mouth, "we shall neither say nor do anything that might imperil the Black Internationale program. We are not yet ready for open conflict with the whites."

"Then how is it to be done, Chief?" I asked, glancing hastily at Pat who seemed to be as puzzled as I.

"You and Pat will do the job," he announced, challenge in his eyes. "You need the experience and Pat needs to test her skill. You leave the airport at ten o'clock sharp. You do your work at three o'clock sharp Pat, you know what ship to take to get there in time. You should be back at the airport by eight o'clock without fail. Use the No. 1 thermite bombs. Here's your map, Pat, and here's a bundle of leaflets to toss overboard after the job is completed. That's all. Good luck. Remember, I want this done perfectly." He rose.

I confess that I was a little taken aback. I had not bargained for anything like this. To be associated with cold-blooded murder was bad enough to commit it was worse. But here we were being ordered to murder human beings, many of whom were entirely innocent of any participation in the brutal burning of the Negro, Lester Peters, in Newton, Mississippi, the day before.

Dr. Belsidus must have detected my indecision. When he spoke again his voice was hard and threatening "I need not remind you again," he grated, "that I will not tolerate failure. There'll be a lot more blood shed than this before we win our objectives. When you think of what the black people have endured and suffered at the hands of white people, Slater, a job like this must be a keen pleasure. I really envy you this opportunity to strike the first real mass blow for Negro freedom."

IT WAS A BEAUTIFULLY CLEAR March night. The ceiling was limitless. There was a slight breeze from the South, but not enough to make any difference in our speed. At nine-forty-five the great doors swung outward. Two mechanics and Juan Torlier, his white teeth flashing against his dull black skin, wheeled a huge, black, low-winged bomber out on the field and began warming up its motor. The engine was carefully gine over. Then the six hundred-pound No. 1 thermite bombs were placed in their racks while Juan explained the method of releasing them.

At ten o'clock sharp, according to the chief's directions, we started the long run down the field and were soon winging our way west southwest to our destination. Flying at six thousand feet and thundering along at two hundred miles an hour, we passed in quick succession Newark, Philadelphia. Wilmington, and Baltimore. Shortly after eleven o'clock we passed over Washington.

Pat was flying with more than her usual care. It was not the first time we had flown at night, but the first time she had ever undertaken such a mission. She was grim and tense, and silent.

As we tore over Charlotte, I thought of the package of leaflets Dr. Belsidus had handed me. Curious, I tore open the package, extracted one of the sheets and perused it by the light from the instrument board. It read as follows:

PEOPLE OF NEWTON

This is Your Punishment By Command of THE HOLY FATHER
You Burned to Death an Innocent Colored Man.
Now you, too, are Scourged by Flames.
Henceforth Live According to the Holy Scriptures and
Do Unto Others as You Would Have Others Do Unto You.
The Mother Church Will No Longer Tolerate
the Persecution of Black People
Contrary to the Teachings of Jesus Christ.
It Must Be An Eye for An Eye,
a Tooth for a Tooth, a Burning for a Burning.
The Catholic Church Stands with and for
the Oppressed and Persecuted Everywhere.

Signed: THE SONS OF CHRIST.

At the end was a large cross. Frankly, I was puzzled. What was the meaning of this jargon? What was the point in involving the Catholic Church? What deep-dyed, villainous scheme was Dr. Besidus now concocting?

I passed the leaflet over to Pat. She hastily scanned it, then grinned cruelly, that same hall-maniacal grimace that almost all the Black Internationale staff seemed to have developed for occasions such as this.

"Pretty clever, eh?" she shouted above the roar of the motor.

"Maybe, but I don't exactly get the idea. What have the Catholics to do with it?"

"You'll see," she said, smiling knowingly. "It'll help bring things to a head. Doc is a wise egg."

Columbia, Augusta and Macon in succession leaped out of the darkness below glowing, with mazda phosphorescence only to disappear as we fled onward toward our goal. At last we swept over Montgomery and in a few minutes the lights of Meridian leaped over the horizon to meet us. In a short time we were over the dark hills of that city. It was exactly two-forty-five.

Pat and I exchanged significant glances. Nothing more was necessary. In ten minutes, I knew, we would be over our target. I opened the door in the floor of the plane. Par shut off her wing lights and increased altitude until the thinness of the air was dizzying.

Now I could see the lights of Newton. Just a few there were. A water tower stood clear in the moonlight. Pat slowed down. I tossed out the bundle of leaflets and watched them flutter to the four winds. Pat nodded to me as she turned the nose of the ship down toward the courthouse roof. I grabbed the lever to release the deadly incendiary bombs.

Down, down, down we came, to seven thousand, to six thousand, to five thousand, to four thousand. I released two of the gleaming metal cylinders. Almost side by side they sped to their mark. There was a resounding crash. Streams of blinding fire ran in all directions, igniting everything in their path. In quick succession I released the remaining four thermite bombs.

Flames swept everywhere. The town became a raging inferno. Pat grinned triumphantly and I wondered what sort of woman she was, for there was no compassion in her face. I closed the trap door. Pat swung the big ship around and climbing rapidly headed for home. Through my night glasses I could see the victims below running for their lives as dozens of blazes burned briskly. Then, suddenly and unexpectedly, the giant plane lurched sidewise and began to fall.

XVII

Pat in Forced Landing; Repairs the Plane; Flies Back to Headquarters

Pat's face was as grim as death. She tugged at levers and turned wheels as the ship lurched sickeningly from side to side.

"What's the matter?"

She shook her head. We were losing altitude rapidly. I thought of our big load of gasoline. If we fell with that we'd be burned up even though the ship wasn't damaged very much.

"Why not jump?" I yelled, thinking of our parachutes on which we were sitting.

"No!" she shouted. "We stay with the ship!" There gleamed in her eyes that same fanatical light I had seen before as she tugged away grimly, watching the swiftly approaching ground with anxiety.

I was not to be outdone by the girl I loved. I killed my impulse to push open the door and jump to safety. Heroically she toiled away as I watched, helpless but fascinated.

We were down to fifteen hundred feet. It wouldn't be long now. Just a matter of seconds. Only for Pat's consummate skill we would have struck before. I comforted myself with the knowledge that if we survived we would still be out of Mississippi, for we had again passed over Meridian just before something went wrong.

A million flashing thoughts. Discovery of the plane would connect the Black Internationale with the burning of Newton... Race war would result before the organization was ready... So much accomplished, perhaps all to be lost... How did it feel to crash? ... How brave she was!

"We're landing!" she shouted. "Hold on!"

She cut the motor. We were wobbling sickeningly. With the most skillful piloting I've ever seen, she leveled the machine just before we struck.

I closed my eyes and gritted my teeth. There was a sharp bump and a lurch to one side. Pat was thrown against me. The shock had not been as great as I anticipated.

Then came peal after peal of hysterical laughter, wild, insane, maniacal laughter. I looked up in astonishment. With tears streaming down her pretty cheeks, Pat was sitting bolt upright in her seat, her hand still closed on the stick, her eyes staring forward and she was screaming with laughter, It was the strangest nervous reaction I've ever seen after a tense ordeal.

I placed one arm about her and drew her unprotesting form to me. As I held her in my arms she sobbed silently, the while she trembled as with the ague.

"Pat! Pat!" I called finally, "let's get out of here. We're not in New York, you know. We're in Alabama and mighty close to Mississippi."

"Yes, Carl, I know," she whispered, sobbing less violently. Despite the danger. I could not help but enjoy the exquisite pleasure of holding this gorgeous creature closely to me. At least five minutes passed. Then she must suddenly have realized where she was and what was going on. She straightened up a little shamedly, and gave her helmet an unconscious feminine pat.

IT WAS BRIGHT MOONLIGHT. WE were in a freshly plowed field. The nearest house loomed out of the shadows a half mile away. We bailed out. The big bomber towered over us as we walked around it to note the damage.

Singularly enough, the damage was slight, one wing tip being a trifle bent. Otherwise the plane was apparently as good as when we left the B.I. airport. Pat hustled around with her flashlight.

Soon I heard her curse softly from the rear compartment and she came out holding a curved wrench.

"That's the culprit," she announced, smiling with the joy she must have felt. "It got jammed back there. It's a miracle I didn't lose control. Boy, what a close shave! Come on, we've got to get out of here. These farmers rise early, you know."

"You telling me?" I Harlemed. "But how are we going to get a run in this muck?"

"Humph!" she exclaimed. "As bad as I feel after that narrow shave. I could get out of a teacup."

She walked over near the house across the field, looked around and then came running back.

There's a wide dirt road just about six hundred yards over there," she announced. "It's quite straight and will make a good runway once we get on it."

GEORGE S. SCHUYLER

"Suppose we meet a car or a truck?"

"We'll just have to take that chance. And that's nothing compared to what we've just come through. Get in!" She jumped in and started the motor. Its roar must have carried for miles through the still moonlit early morning.

The big ship lurched over the newly broken ground toward the road. Luckily, the ground was not wet, or we should certainly have come a cropper. Slowly we approached the house and the road, wings dipping from side to side as we jogged across the deep black furrows. I noticed a light in one of the farmhouse windows. Pat saw it, too, but she could send us forward no faster in safety. The road was about fifty yards away now.

Then we both noticed the three-strand barbwire fence.

"Get the cutters and cut that fence," Pat cried. "Quick! Some of those damned farmers are coming!"

It was true. The door of the house had opened and two figures with shotguns stood silhouetted in the rectangle of yellow light.

I got the cutters, jumped to the ground and rushed for the fence. Moving swiftly, I made the six snips close to the two posts. This left sufficient space for our under-carriage to go between. Our wings were high enough to clear them.

The farmers, two men, were now running toward us, preceded by a hound. Pat sent the bomber through the space between the posts and gained the road.

"Hey! Hey! Hey tha!" yelled one of the men, now less than fifty feet behind us. "You gotta pay for that fence!" Pat swung the ship around. There was a shot and fragments of glass from a broken window pane tinkled to the cabin floor.

Involuntarily I ducked. Pat shot the juice to the ship. We roared down the road, picking up speed at every yard. Up a gentle rise we tore, then down a hill which helped us off the ground. We were still flying low when a pine woods loomed straight ahead.

Pat cursed and bared her teeth. It was exasperating, coming just at the time when our troubles were almost over. We were up fifty feet, now sixty, now seventy, but the trees were almost upon us.

With one last supreme effort, Pat shot the ship over the trees, the tops grazing our landing gear. It seemed as though I could have reached out and touched them.

Lighter now than we were on the trip down, we made remarkable time, doing always better than two hundred and twenty miles an hour at an altitude of over a mile. At eight o'clock we sighted the Hudson River and shortly after ward Pat made a beautiful three-point landing on our field and taxied over to the hangar where Juan stood waiting. It was exactly eight fifteen.

We ate breakfast with Juan and the boys in the attractive dining room and then took the train into New York.

Already the extras were on the streets, their screaming headlines telling of the catastrophe: "FLAMES SWEEP LYNCH TOWN' EQUALITY CULT BLAMED!"... "TWO HUNDRED DIE IN FLAMES AS FIRE GUTS CITY"..."FIRE LYNCH TOWN IN REPRISAL, TWO HUNDRED PERISH"... One of the stories read:

MERIDIAN, Miss., Mar. 5—

Mysterious explosions followed by leaping flames wiped out the entire business section of Newton and many homes early this morning. The identified dead number two hundred, with many missing. Fire departments from this and neighboring cities finally subdued the flames but the town is a ruin. The Negro quarter was untouched.

Officials are agreed that the fire was of incendiary origin, a view strengthened by the finding of numerous leaflets scattered around the immediate countryside warning of reprisals for the lynching of Ed Lovett, Negro farmhand, Wednesday afternoon, signed THE SONS OF CHRIST and claiming to be a Catholic organization.

Catholic officials vigorously denied knowledge of any such organization and strongly denounced the outrage. Several Negro suspects are being held in the local jail for questioning.

Farther down was this item:

INTERCOURSE, Ala. Mar. 5—

A huge airplane landed on the farm of Jed Nixon about 3 A.M. today and left shortly afterward. Nixon claims occupants cut a section of his wire fence in order to get the big shop out on the nearby road, from which it new off in the vicinity of Montgomery. Although fired upon by both Nixon and his son-in-law, Alf Rackett, the plane refused to halt.

It is believed the mysterious visitor might have had some connection with the incendiary fire at Newton. Miss., sixty miles west.

Dr. Belsidus turned the patient he was attending over to Dr. Matson as soon as we came in and joined us in the upper office.

"Well, Chief," I reported. "we succeeded."

"You only half succeeded." he growled. "I've read the extras. You bungled things by coming down on that farm. Then you bungled them again by not killing those damn farmers. Remember, Slater, dead men tell no tales. You're too squeamish. You must be hard. Understand? We don't want excuses, we want accomplishment. You can't have an omelet without breaking eggs. . . Now you two get some rest. I'll see you at four in my apartment. We've got to work fast now."

XVIII

Belsidus Prepares to Wipe Out Two "Crackers" Who Know Too Much

I don't know how long I had been sleeping when a heavy hand. fell on my shoulder. I woke with difficulty. Jim was standing over me. As soon as I gathered my wits together I asked what was the matter. He silently pointed to the ceiling. Then he went out. I knew what he meant: Dr. Belsidus wanted me.

I dressed quickly and hurried to the ornate dining room of green and rose and gold. Places were set for twelve. The goldenware gleamed dully. reflecting the green and rose of the furnishings.

But there was no time to ogle this magnificence. I hurried to the elevator. In a few seconds I stepped out in the Chief's apartment, Ben, the Doctor's leopard, rose up threateningly from his place at the foot of the bed. I hesitated. The apartment was empty and I knew that not even the Doctor's secretary dared enter under such circumstances. Ben would see to that. He was starting to walk slowly, suspiciously toward me, eyeing me all the time, making no sound on the polished, rug strewn floor with his padded feet.

I was in a dilemma. What should I do? Ben would not permit me to stay. There was murderous menace in those narrow bloodshot eyes. Why wasn't Dr. Belsidus there? Was something wrong?

Well, better get in the elevator and go downstairs. I stepped backward, keeping my eyes on those of Ben. He was ready to leap, I knew. There was that tenseness of the rear leg muscles that signaled his intention. Well, one more step and I'd be inside the elevator. Then, pressing a button would close the door between me and the beast.

I moved my right foot back slowly for the last step into the elevator. my eyes still staring into those of the big cat. Then my heel struck the wall! I reached backward fearfully with my hand. The door was closed! Somebody had called the car. I was alone with Ben!

The big cat paused now, getting down closer to the floor, getting down until his belly almost touched. He spat ominously. Without any weapon, unable to move fast enough to avoid his leap. I was scared stiff. Cold sweat dampened my forehead and the palms of my hands. For some strange reason I took out my watch. Singular that Dr. Belsidus should have called me so early when he had announced the meeting for four o'clock. It was now only three. Ben came creeping ominously forward. I nervously dropped the watch but caught it by the chain on my vest. The movement probably saved my life. Ben's eyes rounded with astonishment. He gazed at the dangling watch in fascination, forgetting for the moment his mission. Lives and kingdoms, jobs and meals are lost, to say nothing of girls, by hesitation, by delay, by procrastination.

The door behind me flew open.

"Ben!" snapped Dr. Belsidus, coming out of the elevator past me. "Get back, boy!" The cat underwent an amazing metamorphosis. In a flash, the murder fled from his evil eyes to be replaced by the friendliness of the tame tabby. He turned about and ambled back to his place. I leaned weakly against the wall, struggling to regain my composure.

"You wanted me, Doctor?" I said feebly.

"Yes," he snapped. "Come here with your pad." He sat down in an easy chair by the table, pressing the buzzer at the same time I sat across from him. He leaned back and closed his eyes. The stern face lost some of its hardness. I waited in silence.

"Did you ring, Doctor?" came a voice from the small screen in the center of the table.

"Yes, bring me a bottle of John Jameson and some club sodas, glasses for three, please." Why three glasses, I wondered.

"Yes, sir," came the voice of the maid.

Dr. Belsidus leaned back again and closed his eyes. Then, he suddenly straightened up, as if he had been pondering deeply and just that minute made up his mind. He looked sharply at me. Then a cunning expression came over his face and his deep-set eyes grew smaller.

"Take this telegram for the Montgomery, Alabama, cell," he dictated grimly. "Eliminate Intercourse farmers immediately without fail, You know this code. Don't send it over the telephone. Carry it downtown yourself, probably to the office in the Grand Central terminal. After dinner will be ample time. Sign it Mr. Black."

I looked at him questioningly. A sardonic smile toyed with the corner of his mouth as he read my query in my eyes. "Yes," he said, as though I had asked the question, "we've got to do away with those two cracker farmers. They've talked too much already. We're not ready for our identity to be known."

"But they didn't see us, Doctor," I protested. "They couldn't tell whether we were white or colored."

"They might have seen you better than you know," he replied quietly. "They certainly saw the plane in the moonlight. An error has been made, Slater. And when an error has been made it must be eliminated."

*But it seems like useless murder," I objected.

"Even so," he continued amiably, "I shall feel better with them out of the picture. It is the little things that wreck big movements. Come, let's not worry about two cracker farmers in Alabama who have probably helped in many a lynching. There's more wheels to be set going. Send this telegram in code to all State commanders: White Americans Heavy. Signed Mr. Black. Get that off after dinner, too. I want that distribution made by morning all over the country."

"But, I don't understand, Chief. What does it mean?"

"The White Americans," he explained slowly, "is an organization I have invented to oppose the Sons of Christ. It is anti-Catholic, anti-Jew and anti-Communist, composed of native white Protestants. We already have several thousand members, but I have been keeping them quiet until I was ready."

"It's too complicated for me," I admitted. "Here you have the Black Internationale, an organization working for black supremacy with a new religion, and at the same time you are sponsoring an anti-Negro and also a supposedly pro-Catholic organization. Just what is the point, Chief?"

"Slater," he said, smiling indulgently and passing a well-manicured hand over his smoothly shaven jaw, "have you ever heard of the British Imperialistic policy of 'Divide and Rule'?"

"Yes, of course. But what has that to do with all this?"

Before he could answer the elevator door flew open and the maid came in with the Irish whiskey and soda.

"Shall I pour them, Doctor?" she asked, putting down her golden tray and standing poised over the table.

"Pour two, please," he directed.

When she had retired again, he turned to answer my question.

"The Saxons conquered England," he said, "by dividing the Angles. They helped one king eliminate the others. The British did the same in India. The whites rule Africa because they used the same tactics. People are always more suspicious of each other, always hate each other more when they are neighbors or kin. No war is as violent as civil war." He took a long drink, leaned back and then shortly resumed.

"I am using the same tactics against the whites. There are definite cleavages in the white population of which it would be foolish not to take advantage. Anti-Semitism is strong in the East where Jews are numerous and powerful. Anti-Catholicism is strong in the South, Middlewest and far West. There is almost everywhere a strong feeling against aliens, as one may gather from the anti-Communist propaganda. Where this hatred and prejudice is somnolent, we shall fan the smoldering embers into flames. We shall use force wherever it will further our ends. Our ends are to keep white people so busy fighting each other that we can carry out as much of our program as possible without their opposition, which, in the beginning, might well prove fatal. We're not yet ready to show our hand. We have generals and colonels aplenty, but too few competent captains and sergeants. Even when we come out openly against white imperialism, we can turn the rivalries and hatreds within the white race to good account. Today, it is generally believed among the ignorant white people in the Deep South that Newton, Miss, was burned by Catholics. Our White American Society's handbills will be distributed in two hundred cities and towns, wherever we have of the Black Internationale, before daybreak tomorrow by house-to-house distribution. I am particularly proud of those handbills." He prosed and chuckled. "I designed them, you know, a long time ago."

"What will that accomplish?"

"It will bring in hundreds of thousands of new members into the White American Society," he replied, his deep eyes glowing "Other things I have in mind will alarm and stiffen the opposition of the Catholics and Jews. The head of the White Americans will tell you all about himself tonight."

"You don't mean to say he's coming here?"

"Yes of course. He'll be here for our staff dinner. He's done fine work. But his work has just started. He'll stir up plenty of trouble. And while the white folks are fighting each other, we'll be consolidating our position unnoticed."

XIX

Pretty White Woman Brings Belsidus "Tips" as B.I. Idea Grows

S end cables to all international units as follows, continued Dr. Belsidus. "Select twenty candidates immediately. Planes where feasible."

"That will cost a lot of money," I observed, "a thousand students."

"Naturally," he snapped. "But we must start their instruction at once. The situation is tightening. We've got to get them in technical schools *now*. We've got to have trained men and women. We mustn't make the mistake of Russia and try to work without brains and skill."

I did not pursue the subject further. I knew it would be futile. Besides, the Chief had demonstrated that he had thought out everything.

"Telephone Alex Fletcher to be sure and be at dinner this evening. We must know just how our businesses are progressing. Do that immediately. Then return at once. Tell Pat I won't see her now. It really isn't necessary. But she must be at dinner this evening. Tell Jim to bring the lady up when she comes. He'll know who."

I obeyed quickly and was back at the Doctor's exotic apartment in about five minutes.

"Take a record of all my visitor says, Carl," the physician commanded as I took my seat. "She will be here in a moment. Do not leave us alone unless I say to. I have no time for love."

He had scarcely stopped speaking when the elevator doors opened and a pretty white girl swathed in expensive furs hurried out toward us. I guessed she was in her early thirties and a real thoroughbred.

Dr. Belsidus rose with his usual courteous aloofness and kissed her beautifully manicured tapering fingers. He introduced her as Miss Gas in and helped her with her queenly wrap. Then he offered her a drink. She swallowed it eagerly and promptly took another. She was obviously agitated.

"God, Henry," she exclaimed, "I certainly needed that. I'm worn out. My Lord! The things a woman will do for love." She looked at him softly and pushed back a fugitive hair that had escaped from the golden wealth upon her head.

"Did you get the information I told you to get?" asked Belsidus.

"Of course, darling," she exclaimed enthusiastically. "He was hard to track down but I finally made him. Talked like a phonograph after the fourth Scotch. Here, it's all written down here, just as he told me, dear."

"Good work," boomed the Doctor. "I'll take advantage of it."

There was an awkward silence. I knew she was anxious to be alone with him. I could see it in her eyes. I could also see that having got the information he desired, Dr. Belsidus did not want to be bothered with her. Smiling a little apologetically, she took a third drink. The color rose higher in her cheeks. She looked at him appealingly, as if to hypnotize him.

"Henry, can't we be alone?" she pleaded.

"Some other time." he replied abruptly. He rose to signify that the interview was concluded.

"Tomorrow? Oh, please, Henry!" There were eager tears in her blue eyes.

"Perhaps," he said, leading the way to the elevator. "I'm busy now,"

At the door the cast aside her reserve and, throwing her arms about his neck, kissed him passionately, one foot kicked back in her excitement.

"An excellent worker," he exclaimed when she had gone, "but I suppose I'll have to get rid of her. You know, Slater, women work best for you when they are in love with you. They are most dangerous to you when they find that you are not in love with them. This woman, Martha Gaskin, knows Wall Street like a book and is thoroughly at home in the stock and bond market. She gets valuable tips that help us tremendously. She just brought in some inside stuff on the market. Last week through her tips we cleaned up over a half million dollars. But inevitably she will find out that I care nothing for her except to get this information. Then, Slater, she will be dangerous. And, of course, she will have to be removed."

"You mean killed?" I asked, amazed by his callousness.

"Dead women, Slater, are no more articulate than dead men. Miss Gaskin knows nothing about the Black Internationale nor our other activities, but there's no telling how much trouble a woman may cause when she feels that she's spurned."

Events happened so swiftly after that afternoon that I am able only to touch upon them briefly in order to give you some idea of the magnitude of the national crisis which the Black Internationale precipitated.

At dinner that evening were: Dr. Belsidus, Sam Hamilton, Rev. Samson Binks, Ransom Just, Bennie Simpson, Patricia Givens, Alex Fletcher, Juan Torlier, Gaston Nucklett, Sanford Mates and myself.

Each reported on the progress of his work. It was a meeting that would have gladdened the heart of any real Negro. Sanford Mates, the architect, told of the great progress in erecting Church of Love temples. Dr. Binks spoke briefly on the amazing reaction of black America to the new religion. Alex Fletcher related the manner in which our vegetables were capturing the public's fancy, and told how angry the farmers were becoming because of loss of markets. Sam Hamilton described how acre-production of potatoes had been jumped from four hundred bushels to one thousand bushels by cultivation in chemically treated water. Bennie Simpson was equally enthusiastic about increased production of cement and deliveries of cement and the manner in which Fletcher had cooperate with in making deliveries to Mates in B.I. trucks. Gaston Nucklett, a white Negro from Atlanta who looked exactly like a sandhill cracker, told with many a chuckle how he had organized the White American Society and was busy furthering strife within the white race in his publication *White America,* which attacked Jews, aliens and Catholics. Pat and Juan Torlier reported on the completion of additional bombers and pursuit ships and how ten more pilots had been licensed by the government.

But the most exciting things happened in the forty-eight hours we had finished that memorable dinner.

First, about nine o'clock. I telephoned the Montgomery. Ala., cell in code, then I sent the second telegram in code to the two hundred other cells of the Black Internationale in as many cities, and the cables to our half hundred national cells in Europe, Asia, Africa, South America and the West Indies.

Afterward I took a little run up to Mag's place with Al Fortune to watch his nightly collection. I was back at the headquarters looking over the midnight edition of the morning papers when a telegram came addressed to me. It read, "Please Thank the Doctor for His Double Invitation, and was signed, "Montgomery Black." I knew without consulting the code book that the two white farmers of Intercourse. Ala., who had seen too much were dead. It was deadly, uncanny efficiency.

Next morning the papers were full of it. Not only had the two men been killed, but everybody in the house, by a terrific explosion that had rocked the countryside. Nearby were found SONS OF CHRIST leaflets. During the night in over two hundred cities, anti-Catholic leaflets had been thickly distributed through residential districts. It had been done quickly and efficiently.

The afternoon papers told of the mysterious explosions in Catholic churches in Boston, Buffalo, Baltimore, New Orleans, Cincinnati and Detroit. In each case leaflets had been distributed nearby preaching anti-Semitism and anti-Catholicism.

One incendiary act after another was reported hourly. They increased day after day. Newspapers were full of them. Editorials deplored the arson and murder, warning that civil war would be the result. Dr. Belsidus chuckled in demoniacal satisfaction.

Meantime, using the market tips secured by the white girl, Dr. Belsidus cleaned up over two million on the stock market. Taking advantage of the Bear movement which Miss Gaskin had accurately predicted and which had forced certain key stocks down from ten to fifteen points, he threw almost all his resources into a giant purchasing move. This, coupled with the even greater buying of the clique whose secrets the girls had learned, forced these stocks sky high. Just before they reached the point where he knew the others planned to get out from under and leave the "suckers" holding the bag, he sold everything.

The situation meanwhile grew more grim. Membership in Gaston Nucklett's White American Society grew by the thousands daily, Catholics were at the same time clamoring to join the militant Sons of Christ whose leaflets they had been reading but which only existed in the fertile mind of Dr. Henry Belsidus.

Within ten days there were clashes between Catholics and Protestants in over a dozen cities. Dead and wounded were reported hourly, Jewish synagogues were smeared with painted crosses or burned. Many beautiful Protestant and Catholic edifices were in ruins. Cells of the Black Internationale busied themselves further fomenting strife by acts of vandalism. In every part of the country each side was appealing to Negroes for their aid, but in the B.I. temples black people were being told to mind their own business.

By the time the thousand colored young men and women began to arrive in New York from various parts of the world and enroll in trade schools, civil strife was in full swing in America. Hatred having been stimulated through the Doctor's machinations, it was now rolling along under its own momentum. Business and finance felt the effect of the civil strife and the Black Internationale prospered. We were rapidly taking over the produce business with our giant tomatoes, potatoes, strawberries and other products. Our temples, now numbering a hundred or more, were filled every night. We had virtually captured the retail trade of sixty Negro districts through our temple basement stores and were rapidly monopolizing the amusement business. Alex Fletcher had purchased two cotton mills in Georgia and was negotiating for a shoe factory in Massachusetts.

Then, one evening at dinner, Dr. Belsidus announced dramatically but quietly, "Now we are going to have a *real* headquarters, a country of our own from which to direct our activities. Now is the time to get while white people are fighting each other."

"And how are we to get it, Doctor?" asked Pat.

"We're going to take it," he announced grimly.

XX

Belsidus Explains Details of His Plans to Conquer Africa

D r. Belsidus was a man of action, speedy action, but carefully thought-out action. All next day he pondered alone in his apartment, letting no one enter. Finally, around five o'clock he called for me.

"Notify all executives to be here for a dinner conference this evening," he ordered, "without fail. You'd better make it eight o'clock so as to give Nucklett time to get here. I understand he's addressing a big mass meeting of the White American Society in Richmond this afternoon. He's right on the job, Nucklett is. He's got these crackers steaming."

"Yes, sir," I agreed. "The morning papers were full of that bloody fight between white Catholics and Protestants in Indianapolis, and several of Nucklett's White Americans were jailed. And, of course, Chief, I know you've heard about those bombings of Jewish synagogues in Syracuse. Also, Nucklett's last report gave him three hundred fifty thousand members in his outfit."

"Good!" The Doctor rubbed his hands together in satisfaction and his deep eyes glowed. "By the way, tell Fletcher to bring Barton McNeel with him."

"But he's not an executive, Chief. He's just Fletcher's director of transportation."

"Send for him, I tell you," he snapped, frowning. "I know what I'm doing. McNeel distinguished himself in the Argonne during the World War. He was a captain in the 368th infantry, and was decorated by the American and French governments. He played a part, an important part in the Chicago riot. I've kept track of him through the years. The Depression had him down and out when I put him under Fletcher to direct our transportation. He'll do a good job in Africa. Besides, we need an experienced military man to advise us."

"Then you were quite serious the other night about the conquest of Africa?

"Of course I was serious, Slater, I'm always serious."

It was five minutes after eight when Gaston Nucklett walked into the dining room. The soup had not yet been served. The table was a symphony of green, rose and gold. Bowls of multi-colored blooms graced the center of the long gold-laden table, while a row of slender, tapering black candles in golden sticks shed a romantically flickering light. At the head of the table sat Dr. Belsidus. I sat next to him, my pad on my up in readiness to take down what was said. Around the table were Ransom Just, Patricia Givens, Juan Torlier, Bennie Simpson, Sanford Mates Alex Fletcher, Gaston Nucklett and Capt. Barton McNeel.

The dinner was the usual Belsidus culinary triumph, interspersed with rare wines: Rhine wine with the fish, sparkling burgundy with the fowl, champagne with the meat, Oporto port with the dessert and then with the demi tasse, a liqueur, half Benedictine, half gin. The uniformed waiters moved noiselessly, efficiently, courteously. I found myself marveling again at the remarkable discipline Dr. Belsidus had established.

At long last the dinner came to its inevitable end. Cigars and cigarettes were passed around and a blue haze soon hung over the heads of the executives. Dr. Belsidus leaned back in his chair and regarded them through partially closed eyelids. Finally he cleared his throat. At this signal conversation ceased. Silence ensued. He clapped his well-manicured hands twice. The door flew open and the giant Jim hastened to the Doctor's side.

"Has Gustave Linke arrived yet, Jim?"

The dummy nodded his head in assent, then pointed downstairs.

"Bring him in as soon as he freshens up."

Jim saluted, turned and disappeared. The others looked at each other. I knew they were wondering who Gustave Linke might be. They were not to be kept wondering long.

"Gentlemen," said the Doctor, finally, "we are now about to enter the second phase of our program for the liberation of the black world. Our first objective was to get money and to organize the brains of the Negro race. We have succeeded in doing that. Since our international conference, each of our fifty foreign units has sent us a young man and a young woman, one hundred young Negroes in all, who are now enrolled at technological institutions in various parts of the country. Each unit has also sent us ten young men and ten young women, total of one thousand in all, who are now in attendance at trade schools here in New York, in Pittsburgh, in Milwaukee, in Chicago and is Cleveland, taking six-month courses. In addition to these foreign students, we have two hundred American Negro men and women in institutes of technology and one thousand in trade schools.

"We have ten plantations from New Jersey to Texas, each with the latest equipment and methods of agricultural science. At each plantation we have an airfield. Our airport and airplane factory in Westchester County has trained five hundred colored pilots, men and women and manufactured one hundred pursuit planes and fifty bombing planes since we started the work under the expert direction of Miss Givens and Juan Torlier.

"We have Sam Hamilton to thank for our agricultural progress, and Al Fortune to thank not only for his sun-power plants which have saved us so much money, but also for his able direction of our association of criminals which is responsible for bringing ten million dollars into our treasury in the past year.

"Rev. Binks has made his idea of a new religion for Negroes a reality I had some misgivings about it at first. No one can have any now. Rev. Binks has brought in tens of thousands of fanatically loyal Negroes, the kind who are not afraid of being black and are willing to die for their beliefs. He has reported the erection of over one hundred Temples of Love in the United States and one hundred seventy-five under the jurisdiction of our foreign units in the West Indies and Africa. Alex Fletcher, who has done such a good job directing our business affairs and finances, reports that in each of the two hundred and seventy-five temples there are economic units: stores, beauty parlors, etc., just as in Harlem, which not only have the loyal patronage of our organization people but other Negroes as well, and doing a two-million-a-week business.

"Bentle Simpson," he continued, "has built and operated our cement plant most effectively, and established four more in various parts of the country. Our Gaston Nucklett, who is sacrificing much by living and working around white people, has done and is doing remarkable work in disrupting the white population, promoting civil strife and otherwise keeping attention focused away from us. It is a fine work and will continue on a larger scale. And, of course, excellent work has been done by Ransom Just in establishing powerful, secret radio stations, by Dr. Matson in the establishing of B.I. hospitals in Mississippi, Alabama, South Carolina, Georgia and Louisiana; by Sanford Mates in designing our various structures; and by Juan Torlier for his valuable work with Miss Givens as head of our aircraft factory. And, incidentally, I have made a couple million dollars myself on the stock market with the aid of my white girlfriend good enough to bring me tips. Altogether, I should say that we have done our first job well."

The others nodded assent. It was an impressive record of things accomplished. I knew of many other things which he might have mentioned, such as the two-million membership which the Black Internanonale now boasted.

"Now," continued the Chief, "as I told you the other evening, the period of conquest has begun. Listen carefully to your orders. I want no mistakes. We must not fail." His deep serious eyes ran over the group.

"McNeel," the tall distinguished man with gray hair looked up as his name was called, "you will be in charge of our expeditionary force of five thousand men. These men are to be physically fit, loyal and preferably with military experience because we haven't much time to spend on training. Fletcher has purchased fifteen thousand acres in South Texas. Mates has erected the barracks, six huge airplane hangars. The place will be used later as an airport. The whole thing is practically ready. Get the men from Rev. Binks. He has kept track of all his devotees with military training. The rest you can find in your motor transport division.

"There will be no uniforms. You will drill your men in the early morning just to be on the safe side, although you are forty miles from the railroad and five miles from the nearest road. However, Mates has constructed a good dirt road from the hangars to the main road. Fletcher is taking care of the food and equipment. You'll need plenty of small as practice, bayonet exercise, grenade throwing and machine gunning. Mr. Just will supply you with radio equipment and instructors. Dr. Matson will send you doctors. Fletcher will arrange for truck and plane transportation to and from the camp. You must be ready to leave here in ninety days for West Africa."

XXI

Belsidus Trains Five Thousand Soldiers in Texas and Sends Them to Africa

I confess that I was skeptical about the success of this latest venture. Dr. Belsidus had so far attained all his objectives with practically no opposition. Characteristically, he attributed this to his ruthlessness and to the fact that he had not advertised what he was doing.

"Slater," he said one afternoon while the expeditionary force was being secretly transported to the Texas coast, "one of the great mistakes made by minority leaders in the past has been ballyhoo. Therefore we have established no newspapers or magazines, given no talks over the radio, staged no parades or demonstrations. Consequently the enemy has no inkling of what we are doing. They associate our various enterprises with no central organization. Because they do not appreciate the magnitude of our work, Slater, they are unable to cope with it. What we do travels fast enough among Negroes without the aid of publication. If we had a newspaper and boasted in it about our far-flung efforts, white people would know all about it and crush us before we were ready."

"But, Chief," I objected, "you can't expect to train five thousand men in Texas and the white people not know about it. You can't expect to have Al Fortune's criminal corps keep on rifling the homes and stores of the country without white people eventually finding out. You can't expect to corner the produce business of the country and to corral all the Negroes in the Church of Love without white people knowing something about it."

He smiled indulgently and stroked his clean-shaven, militant chin His deep-set eyes sparkled and glowed as he listened tolerantly.

"You are quite right, my boy," he agreed. "The white people will eventually find out what we have been up to, but by that time I'll not care because we shall have accomplished so much they'll not be able to stop us. Al Fortune's work is over so far as the criminal branch is concerned. We've stolen millions and gotten away with it. Now I'm going to use Al's engineering ability in Africa, where it will be needed. There will be stiffening opposition, of course, to our produce business and our other enterprises, but that opposition is being nullified by my policy of divide and conquer the white people. While they fight among themselves, they leave Negroes alone, and that's what we want. We have nothing to fear for a long time, my boy."

LATER THAT DAY I DROVE down to our Jersey plantation with Sam Hamilton. On the way passed fifteen or twenty truckloads of Negroes going in the same direction. When we arrived a little after dark, the place was a beehive of activity. Great floodlights made the airfield as light as day. At one end were several rows of great bombing planes drawn up with propellers whirring. As each truck stopped, the men in it got down and, forming to a group of ten, marched over to one of the planes and piled aboard. Once loaded, the plane's door was closed, the portable step wheeled aside and, at a signal from a starter with a check and flag it would roar down the runway and soon disappear into the darkness.

"They'll be in Texas before daybreak," Sam observed, as he stopped his roadster in front of the farm headquarters. "Each plane carries ten men and enough gasoline and oil to get to our mobilization point. With fifty bombers we're sending five hundred men a day from here. Within ten days our entire force will be mobilized. It's good experience for the aviators. We've got a bunch of relief pilots at the other end. They bring these planes back tomorrow. The Chief chose this as a mobilization point because the presence of a whole lot of Negroes here arouses no comment. We're servicing the planes at the Westchester field when they return each trip."

We watched the proceedings for about fifteen minutes. Finally the field was empty. The last of the trucks had gone to the garages when familiar black and gold autogiro dropped out of the sky and rolled to Sup on the lighted field.

I recognized Par's familiar green garb as she stepped down out of the cockpit and spoke to a greasy mechanic who had run out on the field. She came over to where we were.

It was a happy culmination of a busy day. I always felt buoyant when Pat was around, even though she gave me no encouragement. Since the day at the temple, though, she had seemed to be avoiding me seemed self-conscious in my presence.

"What brings you down here?" I asked by way of saying something although I knew she had to be there with all of her big planes hopping off with their human cargoes.

"You're coming back to New York with me," she announced "Doctor's orders. An important conference, I believe."

"It'll be a pleasure to go back," I replied gallantly, "if you're going to fly me back." I put all that she meant to me in the glance that I gave her.

"That's why I came down." she replied indifferently. "We'd better go right back. The Chief is waiting."

We walked together over to the waiting autogiro. In a few moments we were soaring over the countryside toward the towers of Manhattan.

THE TWELVE WEEKS OF TRAINING and preparation were almost finished when Dr. Belsidus and I visited the Texas estate for the first time. Pat flew us down. A vast stretch of and land facing the Gulf of Mexico about seventy miles above Brownsville, it was ideally suited for our purpose. The great hangars were camouflaged to make them almost in visible a mile away. The edge of the estate was five miles from the nearest road and almost forty miles from the railroad. The most prominent landmark was a water tower and twin radio towers. East of the estate was the Laguna de la Madre and the great barrier reef that barred the way to the Gulf of Mexico. A half mile off the reef, six freighters awaited their cargo.

McNeel drove up in his car as we landed. "Well, Mac, is everything ready?" Dr. Belsidus eyed him questioningly.

"Everything is ready, Doctor," he replied quietly. "Food, small arms, ammunition and field equipment are already aboard."

"Crackers give you any trouble?"

"No sir. Those who have stopped by here think this is a big CCC camp laying out an airfield. But in the main we haven't had many visitors. This place is mighty far off the beaten path, you know."

"Yes, that's why we located here."

We got in McNeel's car. He drove us several miles across the estate until we came to the lagoon. A number of small wharves had been built and on these there was great activity, men moving goods of all kinds into barges towed by busy tugs across the lagoon. There, a channel just aske cough to accommodate the barges had been cut through the reef. They passed carefully through this channel out into the open sea and to the waiting ships, Altogether, the whole trip was seven miles.

"We embark tomorrow at daybreak," McNeel announced. Dr. Belsidus nodded approvingly.

We drove back to McNeel's quarters for dinner. There were the Doctor, McNeel, Pat, Hamilton, Just, Al Fortune and Juan Torlier gathered around the board. We were all in gay spirits. A difficult job was almost finished. We had trained five thousand Negroes and were embarking them for Africa, and white America knew nothing about it. Perhaps in the whole history of the Negro in America nothing had ever been accomplished so efficiently and so quietly. I observed as much to Pat just before we went in to eat.

"You're right, Carl," she replied, "but there's one little efficiency you don't know about. McNeel tells me that he had to remove about plenty of those Negroes who persisted in talking. You know Negroes, some Negroes, have just *got* to tell what they know. And of course that's against our rules."

I knew what that "remove" meant. I must have revealed something my revulsion because she looked at me sharply, even a little disapprovingly. We joined the others without any further exchange. I kept thinking throughout the elaborate dinner what a cold-blooded young woman she was. And yet how much I wanted her.

Dr. Belsidus had purchased the six freighters in New York, loaded them very lightly with cement and cleared them for the West Coast of Africa. Secret instructions were for them to stop en route and pick up the B.I. expeditionary force. This was accomplished according to schedule and without incident or accident.

We stayed around all day until the last man was aboard the tossing freighters. The six captains met Dr. Belsidus, General Barton McNeel, Pat Givens and I in the cabin of the S.S. *Bessie Coleman* for final instructions. I had not previously met the black skippers whom the chief had secured from the West Indies, Venezuela and Senegal. They were fine, standing black fellows, serious and capable.

"Captain Jorre," said Dr. Belsidus. "I place you in charge of the fleet. You will proceed in the SS. *Samory* direct to the coast of Liberia. You'd better keep your ships about fifty or sixty miles apart, I don't want you to follow the usual shipping lanes, but I want you to be off Monrovia exactly three weeks from today. The others will take positions as follows: Capt. Campbell's S.S. *Nat Turner* off Robertsport. Capt. Williams's S.S.

GEORGE S. SCHUYLER

Fred Douglass, off Cape Palmas, Capt. Sinclair's S.S. *Sojourner Truth* off Sinoe, Capt. Sanchez's S.S. *Bessie Coleman* off Nanna Kru while Capt. Bossona in the *Phyllis Wheatley* will stand off Monrovia with the SS. *Samory*. You are to be ready at your stations on the afternoon of the twenty-second day. You will receive landing instructions from General McNeel who will be aboard the S.S. *Samory* with his staff. You will each associate yourself with the colonel in charge of the troops ab oard your ship. The men will be absolutely under his charge.

"McNeel," he continued, turning to the gray-haired general. "you have my instructions. Kalanga, the head of our Sierra Leone cell, and Ralph Farley of our Liberian cell will supply the necessary guides. We confer with them about a week before your ships arrive."

He appeared amused at our expressions of surprise.

"Oh yes" he said quietly. "I shall be there. Slater and Pat and I are flying to Freetown by way of Brazil. Well, that's all. Remember, men. there must be no failure. This is the greatest venture black men have embarked upon in centuries. There must be no failure."

XXII

Dr. Belsidus Arrives in Africa to Start His Big Offensive

We fled up the Atlantic Coast with a helping wind behind us. The Chief sat brooding over a large map of Liberia as the black night hurried by. I was in front with Pat. She was intent on her task, watching her instruments, picking up radio weather reports. We cut across the Gulf to New Orleans and then made a bee line for New York. All through the night the silent man behind us marked up the map, made notes in his memorandum book, dictated into the machine, sometimes in succession, sometimes, it seemed, all at once. I have never seen anyone who could so lose himself in his work as Dr. Belsidus, and yet with no difficulty whatever take up consideration of any question submitted to him.

Pat and I exchanged a few, but very few, words. Somehow I had been imagining recently that she was becoming more distant. wasn't anything she said, particularly, but certain little looks and movements that indicated a growing indifference. To be sure, she had never indicated that she cared anything for me beyond the comradeship of a man and a woman engaged in a hazardous, adventurous enterprise. She had even told me that there was too much to be done for the race for her. to be bothered with love. And yet it somehow felt that she should be mine and I couldn't look at her radiant, intelligent brown beauty without my heart skipping a beat. I wanted to tell her of the passion that was consuming me, yet I quailed before the anticipation of her coolness, before the thought of rebuff.

Why was it, I wondered to myself, that courtship and romance often so difficult these days and yet is more simple than in the past. The days of chaperons and "for men only" are gone. Men and women are on a plane of equality, Social and economic differences between the sexes have become a thing of the past. We vote and work and socialize and even go to war together these days. And yet this sexual democracy, this fraternization, this single standard has too often accentuated hidden irritations and antagonisms and clashing ambitions to the point where barriers arise between the sexes which sadly inhibit the normal urges and desires once so easily consummated.

Of course, I realized, it is largely psychological. We have to become conditioned to our changed environment almost overnight, historically speaking. Physically, we live in the twentieth century; psychologically, we live many thousands of years ago. We come into this world made for a life as huntsman or herdsman and find ourselves in an environment of whirling machines, confusion upon confusion for the sake of order, complications and responsibilities and temptations that try the hardiest souls and often leave them balanced precariously on the precipice of insanity. Life has been made too complex, and man was intended to live a life of simplicity. Here I was, madly in love with Pat. Had I lived in another age, I could have taken her without delay or ado Now, because of her career, because of what she wanted to do for the race, because of her probable desire not to settle down into wifely domesticity. I was held off.

Something of my disgruntled feeling must have communicated itself to her. She turned her eyes from the instrument board and the moon kissed waters that tossed below us and looked at me with a half amused expression.

"What's the matter?" she shouted above the roar of the motors. "In love?"

I started and then sank back sheepishly as she enjoyed my confusion.

"You know darn well that I am!" I shouted back.

"Well," she came back at me, "don't give up hope."

Her eyes were sparkling mischievously. Somehow that little exchange, which seems perhaps nothing at all to one reading in cold type what transpired, nevertheless made me buoyant. Perhaps, then, my love for her was not hopeless. Perhaps, in time, I could penetrate that reserve of career and independence into which she seemed to have retired, and make her acknowledge her love for me. At any rate, it was a hopeful thought.

I sank back with a pleasant feeling and fell gradually to sleep with, I believe, a smile on my face as large as that in my heart.

For the next week innumerable conferences with executives followed mysterious meetings in Dr. Belsidus's apartment with important-looking people. His entire store of gold vessels—dishes, vases, platters, knives, forks, spoons, umbrella stands and many other articles—was turned in at the Assay Office at thirty-six dollars an ounce. This act alone convinced me, if such had been necessary. that Dr. Belsidus was planning operations of the first magnitude.

In two days the transaction was completed and the money amounting to two and a half million dollars added to the millions already standing to the Doctor's account in the American National Bank.

On the sixth day after the sailing of the expeditionary forces, the Chief held his final conference with Alex Fletcher, Gaston Nucklett, who flew up from Atlanta, Juan Torlier, Pat and, of course, myself. Rev. Binks was delayed but dropped in just as we had reached the cognac and coffee. It was midnight before full instructions for the conduct of operations had been given and discussed, and the meeting adjourned. We were all a little excited throughout. The Doctor was the coolest of the lot, but even in his expression one could see some of that sense of expectation that pervades the beings of all humans on the eve of great adventure.

It didn't seem that I had slept more than fifteen or twenty minutes when faithful old Jim shook my shoulder until I grumblingly awoke. It was five-thirty. I showered, shaved and dressed quickly. Dr. Belsidus and Pat were already in the big limousine when I got down to the curb. Dr. Matson stood at the window and waved farewell to us as the car pulled away toward Fifth Avenue.

It was seven o'clock when we reached our airport. A huge black and gold transport plane stood in the field near the quarters. It glistened in the rising sun like some huge prehistoric bird with wings spread, pulling a worm from the earth. Jim drove the limousine within about fifty. feet of the air cruiser. We got out of the car, Juan Torlier, seemingly a little sleepy, was taking a final look over the engine.

"How much gas, Juan?" Pat asked as she crawled into the cabin.

"Six hundred," he replied. "Everything's ready, Miss Givens."

Dr. Belsidus greeted the airplane expert with a cordial nod. Two mechanics stood ready to kick the chocks from under each wheel. In back of us the entire group of pilots and mechanicians, designers and engineers stood silhouetted against the rising sun, bidding us adieu. The Chief paused on the steps of the plane and, turning toward them, he spoke slowly and deliberately, a certain note of tenseness in his voice.

"Boys and girls, we are on our way to the supreme test that for which we have striven all these months and years. We have everything we need to succeed. The physical means are in our hands. We have learned how not only to use the instruments the white man uses but also how to make them, and that is of most importance. So long as the Negro

GEORGE S. SCHUYLER

did not make the machinery of modern civilization, so long as there were inner secrets to which he was not privy, just so long was the Negro doomed to remain a slave of the white man. We never lacked courage, we never lacked willingness, what we lacked was knowledge. Now we have acquired knowledge. Now we have accumulated wealth, a point for the spear of knowledge. We are not only the equal of the white man now, we are his superior. I say we are his superior because we know that which he does not know. We know what we are going to do. The white man does *not* know what we are going to do.

"We are leaving now, my comrades, on our great adventure. A week from today we shall be on the shores of Africa. Two weeks from today a new note will be sounded in international affairs. Young men and women, be ready! I shall call upon you. Be sure you are ready to do my bidding."

A great cheer arose from the crowd. The young men and women rushed forward, as he shook the hand of each. Then he went inside and sat by the table that had been installed for him and began to pore over his map and notes as if there were no cheering crowd outside.

I got in and seated myself alongside Pat. In the rear of the compartment a tall black fellow in jaunty blue uniform sat at a table with headphones clamped on and a sending and receiving set before him. I knew he was the navigator.

The engine started with a roar. Pat sent the big plane down the runway for almost a mile before we left the ground and shot over the Hud son River southward. This was no leisurely autogiro. In a half hour we were thundering down to Havana at two hundred and thirty-five miles an hour and cruising at five thousand feet.

WE SPENT SIX HOURS AT Havana and then flew on to Port-au-Prince. where Dr. Belsidus talked quietly with a slender black man for upwards of an hour. Then we hopped over to Jamaica for a few hours' stay. The second evening found us in Port of Spain. There, a Negro, part East Indian drove us through steep, palm-lined avenues to his white house amid a bower of tropical blooms.

The next day, after a brief stop at Georgetown, British Guiana, we hopped off for Recife, where the commandant of the Brazilian cell flew up from Rio de Janeiro for a conference. On the morning of the fourth day, bright and early. Pat sent the giant plane down the runway and leaped off to Africa.

Hudginson, the navigator and radio man, plotted our course with uncanny accuracy. After an uneventful and monotonous nine hours over the south Atlantic, the young man tapped the snoozing Dr. Belsidus on the shoulder and pointing straight ahead said. "Africa, sir!"

XXIII

Belsidus Completes Plans for Surprise Attack on Monrovia

In a few minutes, the cloud-wreathed mountains in back of Freetown, Sierra Leone, loomed straight ahead of us and shortly we were above the pretentious white government buildings from which the Union Jack fluttered. Pat circled until we located the large private field made ready by the Freetown cell of the Black Internationale and described in our reports from Joseph Kalanga. Pat sent the ship over the field and then, turning, came upwind to a perfect three-point landing.

As the plane came to a halt; a little crowd of white-clad black men ran out on the field. I immediately recognized Joseph Kalanga. The others were officials of the organization in Sierra Leone. In accordance with the Doctor's orders, there was no demonstration. We merely shook hands all around. Then the black customs officials and the white British health officer came to do their duty. After a few whispered words between Dr. Belsidus and Kalanga, we all left in several automobiles for the nearby city. In fifteen minutes we were closeted in the library of Kalanga's pretty tropical home. Shortly afterward, Ralph Farley, commander of the Liberian cell, arrived.

"Doctor," began Kalanga, "we have carried out your orders to the letter. A month ago we received the empty grenades and, following the instructions of Sam Hamilton and Rev. Binks, we have filled them with the incendiary chemicals in our workshops underneath our Temples of Love."

"You have made the distribution?" asked the Doctor.

"Yes, sir. Two weeks later—that's a fortnight ago—we sent them by fast couriers. Night before last the drums notified us that the distribution was completed. At a given signal every European shop and home, and every white man, woman and child inside them, will be destroyed. That takes in French Guinea, Portuguese Guinea, Sierra Leone and the French West African hinterland." He was obviously proud of his accomplishment.

"Very good, Kalanga, very good. I have received similar reports from Dakar. Bathurst, Bingerville, Accra, Abomey, Lagos, Libreville,

Stanley ville, the Portuguese Angola and South Africa." Dr. Belsidus announced. Then, turning to the Liberian commander, he inquired, "Mr. Farley, how is the picture in Liberia?"

"Everything is ready, sir." the Monrovian replied. "I have carried out your instructions to the letter. The hinterland chiefs are ready to march to the coast when the signal is given. Most of the Liberian Frontier Force has been concentrated in Monrovia through our machinations. Our men on the Coast, the Krus and Greboes, but not the Vais, are ready with their boats and canoes at the various ports."

"Why not the Vais?" asked the Doctor, obviously somewhat surprised.

"They are not to be trusted, sir. We could take no chances. The incendiary grenades are ready in our Temples of Love. Distribution will be made if and when you give the orders."

"Has everyone been well paid?" inquired the Chief.

"We have distributed the entire cargo of leaf tobacco, salt, rice, canned goods, salt fish and liquor which you sent a fortnight ago. We have also given out over a thousand pounds in 'dash' to the Paramount Chiefs."

"And the airport," continued Dr. Belsidus, "has that been prepared?"

"Yes, sir," replied Farley, smiling, "just as you directed. It is five miles back of Monrovia and not far from the road to the Firestone plantation. The government thinks the land has been cleared for an athletic field for one of our Temples of Love nearby."

The Liberian commander then produced a recent map of Liberia and a smaller one of Monrovia and vicinity on which were indicated the locations of the ten Temples of Love, the airport and various towns from Robertsport to Harper.

"You have done well, comrades," said the physician. "You may go. I counsel you to silence on pain of death. Assemble here tomorrow evening By that time Miss Givens, Slater, Mr. Hudginson and I will be refreshed and we can complete our arrangements."

In another week the troopships would be off Monrovia. We were far from idle in the meantime. Pat and Hudginson flew over Liberia, familiarizing themselves with the location of the airports outside Monrovia and in the vicinity of Robertsport, Harper, Sinoe and Nanna Kru. Dr. Belsidus conferred with numerous close-mouthed Negroes, some in European clothes, others in native robes betokening their rank, met with various steamship agents and otherwise prepared for the momentous campaign.

Freetown is a pretty little city of glistening white buildings that start from the waterfront and march up the green hills. Everywhere black officials were evident, on the streets, in government buildings, in the customs house and in the post office. Kalanga informed us that these black officials were generally more loyal to the British imperialists than King George VI. The only opposition he had encountered had been from them. How little they knew of the changes in store.

When I was not attending the numerous conferences Dr. Belsidus held or getting acquainted with the cell commanders who came in from all over West Africa to meet Dr. Belsidus. I was busy decoding messages. On the last two days these messages came in batches. The evening of the twentieth day following the departure of expeditionary forces from Texas. I closeted myself with Dr. Belsidus and Patricia in Kalanga's library, the day's messages spread out before me. The Chief, in that gay mood he always affected when work had been well done, ordered me to proceed.

"Doctor," I began, "we have the following reports: Gaston Nucklett wires that Jews and Christians staged a pitched battle in Chicago last night, while Catholics and Protestants clashed in Baltimore. Cincinnati, Louisville, Baston and Los Angeles. The White Americans now has a membership of four million and the circulation of *White America* jumped two hundred thousand last week to an all-time high of five million."

"Nucklett is doing fine work. He'll keep the white people so busy fighting themselves that they'll have no time to bother us," observed the Chief.

"Here's a brief dispatch from Alex Fletcher. He says the B.I. farms are showing a profit of one million monthly and the economic enterprises of the Church of Love are running well over three million this month. He says our newest freighter, the S.S. *Kelly Miller*, left day before yesterday with complete machine shop, foundry equipment, smelting plant, sawmills, construction machinery and mining equipment. All technical students left America this week on various steamers following the completion of their courses. Juan Torlier and his entire mechanical staff have flown in to our Texas estate and dismantled the Westchester plant."

"You see," Dr. Belsidus interrupted, "how essential it is that we win."

I continued: "Rev. Binks reports the completion of one hundred more temples in the United States this week and one hundred and fifty by our foreign units in the West Indies and Africa. Negroes are leaving the established churches in droves."

"Well," commented the Doctor, sipping his Scotch and soda, "it is as I expected. The established churches, as they call themselves. have nothing to offer the Negroes except prayers and collection plates. We are giving them an economic foundation and a better show in the bar gain. That makes two hundred temples in the United States and three hundred and twenty-five elsewhere. And that means an equal number of grocery stores, meat markets, beauty parlors, recreation halls and other economic units bringing money into the treasury."

I went on with reading the messages. "Bennie Simpson has dispatched a shipload of cement and mixers on a chartered West African-American freighter to Monrovia, consigned to Farley. It should arrive about the same time as the S.S. *Kelly Miller*."

"And from Capt. Jorre," I continued, "comes word that the entire flees of troopships arrives off Monrovia at midnight tomorrow. General McNeel merely says that the health of the troops is well except for one case of lever, which is not serious."

"Good," he commented. "And now, Miss Givens, turning to the charming brown aviatrix, "what have you to report?"

"We checked the five airports on the Liberian coast and those established in the hinterland of Pandame, Zor Zor, Naama and Sanoquilly. They seem to be adequate. Here are the aerial photos taken by Tom Hudginson."

"Then," observed Dr. Belsidus, "we are all ready for the conquest. Tell Kalanga to get that motorboat ready for tomorrow evening. Tell Ralph Farley to give final instructions to his Kru and Grebo boatmen and guides. Wire Martha Gaskin at the Regal Hotel in London that the time has come."

"What will that mean?" I asked, wondering what tricks he had the beautiful white girl up to now.

"The whole world will hear tomorrow," he remarked, a look of cunning secrecy coming over his handsome black face. "As we have stirred strife among the white people of America, so must we do in Europe, Slater."

The twenty-first day came with the sun burning the earth and men panting helplessly in the African heat. During midday we talked over a long luncheon, but when at three o'clock the heat began to abate. Kalanga drove us down to the waterfront, where we boarded a long, fast, rakish motorboat for our trip to meet the ships off Monrovia at midnight. Pat and Hudginson stayed behind with the big bombing plane until the word should come that we had won. Quickly we stepped aboard and rounding the neck of land that shields the harbor from the outer arm, Kalanga's mechanic opened the throttle wide and we tore down the coast for our epochal rendezvous with General McNeel and Captain Jorre off Monrovia.

"Tomorrow night," shouted Dr. Belsidus over the roar of the motor. "Monrovia should be in our hands. Indeed," he added grimly, almost to himself, "it *must* be."

XXIV

DR. BELSIDUS GETS SECRET MESSAGE
AS OFFENSIVE STARTS

As the sun dipped into the ocean we passed Cape Mount and glimpsed the white residences of Robertsport. The sea was smooth as a lake and the waves from our speeding boat eddied far to right and left. It was so hot even at this hour that we welcomed with relief the coming of darkness.

Until it was too dark to see, Dr. Belsidus sat silently poring over two maps, one of Liberia and another of Monrovia and environs. I don't believe he spoke once during the entire journey.

Pitch darkness came with characteristic tropical suddenness. Kalanga's mechanic pulled farther out to sea to avoid the sandbars that fringe. the Liberian coast. He proceeded more slowly and carefully now, guiding himself by the light on top of distant Cape Mesurado.

At ten o'clock we were three miles off Monrovia. The few lights in the capital clearly indicated our whereabouts even if the big lamp in the lighthouse had not shone so brightly.

Dr. Belsidus got out his night glasses and scanned the horizon. I did likewise. There, off to the right, looming like a ghost and about a half mile away was the freighter. The mechanic turned the nose of our boat toward her and pulled up close to within a few feet.

"Africa!" yelled Kalanga through the megaphone.

"Africa!" came back a voice from the deck. This is the S.S. *Samory*, Captain Jorre speaking."

"This is Dr. Belsidus," said the Chief, rising. "Let down your ladder, captain, we're coming aboard."

"Aye, aye, sir," replied the captain. Then to his men: "Lower away."

With a screeching that carried far in the still night, the ladder came down. Our boat pulled close. A sailor stood at attention on the bottom step with a lantern, Dr. Belsidus ran lightly up to the deck. Kalanga and Allowed him. Captain Jorre and General McNeel greeted us and led the way to the skipper's cabin. The Chief immediately got down to business.

"We'll just have a sandwich and a bottle of beer," he said, when Cap

GEORGE S. SCHUYLER

in Jorre asked him if he wanted to dine. "There's too much to do to bother with dinner. Now, General, are you all ready?"

"All ready, sir, I have carried out your instructions to the letter."

"And how about the other ships, Captain? turning to the skipper. I have just heard from all of them, sir. The *Nat Turner* is two miles off Robertsport, the *Fred Douglass* will be off Cape Palmas in a short while, the *Sojourner Truth* is riding off Sinoe and the *Bessie Coleman* is just outside Nanna Kru."

"Very well. Now, Captain Jorre, signal Ralph Farley to go ahead."

The French Negro stuck his head out the cabin door and shouted an order.

Five minutes passed. A sailor tapped on the side of the open door. He saluted the captain and reported. "We have received the signal from the shore, sir, that all is in readiness. The *Phyllis Wheatley* is almost alongside and Captain Botsona reports all's well."

"Alright, John, you may go," said Captain Jorre. "In another hour, Doctor, the native boats will be alongside. Perhaps even before that."

Dr. Belsidus grunted his approval and munched a sandwich from the pile a steward had brought from the galley. He was the calmest man I've ever seen to be embarking upon such a momentous adventure. Immaculately dressed in tropical whites with neatly manicured fingers. and faultless white shoes and socks, he might well have been preparing to attend some festivity. I felt that he was expecting some word from somewhere. Everytime a sailor reported to Captain Jorre, the chief was at once alert. When the chatter of many strange voices and the bumping against the side of the freighter informed us that the fleet of native boats had arrived, I caught him listening intently for a second, only to as quickly relax. We all sat quietly drinking our beer, waiting for the next word from him.

On the deck below the soldiers were lining up at the low-voiced command of their officers. Squad by squad they descended the ladders and entered the bobbing Kru boats.

At last a tall black officer, a major, entered and saluted McNeel. "Sir," he said, "I have the honor to report that the native boats are loaded and awaiting the command to pull away. Similar word comes from the others."

"Very good, major. Wait for the command. The officers all know their objectives." Then General McNeel turned to the Chief inquiringly.

"No, not yet, McNeel," said Dr. Belsidus. "I'm waiting word from London."

Tense minutes succeeded each other. I consulted my watch. It was eleven-forty. The chief looked at his watch and frowned for the first time since we had left Freetown. General McNeel calmly sipped his beer. Captain Jorre, snapping his fingers and nervously whistling a monotonous little French ditty, kept running out of the cabin to give an order and then bouncing back again.

Midnight! We all consulted our watches again as eight bells sounded on the two ships. Dr. Belsidus scowled more darkly and banged his glass impatiently on the table. He muttered something that I could not understand. But I gathered that his patience was rapidly running out. Outside on the water below and on the deck there was a buzz of subdued voices. Only the command of Dr. Belsidus was awaited and the attack would begin.

Minutes passed and no command came. Twelve-ten. We all furtively consulted our watches. Dr. Belsidus was looking grimmer.

There was a knock at the cabin door. Before anyone could say "enter," the radioman, a young slender mulatto, hurried in and handed Dr. Belsidus a message. It contained but two words, "Yes. Martha."

A broad smile, one of the few I'd ever seen, wreathed the Chief's countenance. He stroked his chin and a light of cruel satisfaction came into his deep-set eyes.

"Alright, McNeel," he commanded. "Let's go. Remember, the cable station first. Then the telephone exchange. And whatever you do, be sure and take charge of the Firestone radio station at Duside before morning. There must be no looting of shops. Sparks," he turned to the radio man, "tell the other ships the time has come."

I was consumed with curiosity about the message and what it meant. When Dr. Belsidus, Kalanga and I were again in the motorboat and following the fleet of war canoes toward the channel in the sandbar, I got up courage to ask him.

"What does it mean?" he boomed good-naturedly. "It means that Martha has succeeded. Before the white world knows of our action here, we shall be established. They will be too busy with their own affairs to bother with us. That message meant that our plans in London have gone well. Prime Minister Baldwin was assassinated this evening by a bomb tossed into 10 Downing Street, where he was holding a conference."

"How do you know the details, sir?"

GEORGE S. SCHUYLER

"Hah, why my lad, the details were worked out long ago," he said. That will crowd everything off tomorrow's newspapers. By the time they hear of our conquest, it will be a fait accompli."

WE APPROACHED CLOSER AND CLOSER to the sandbar. On express orders from General McNeel, there was no sound save the cough of our motor and the squeaking of the oars in their locks as scores of oarsmen bent their bare backs to their tasks. One by one the boats shot through the narrow channel into the placid waters of the shallow harbor. Scarcely ten feet apart now, the long line of craft stealthily approached the shore while helmsmen strained their eyes. It was quite dark with only a few stars overhead. Now the boats took positions several feet apart all along the shore from Kru town to the last warehouse. There was much splashing as the men jumped over the sides and waded ashore in the darkness. Here and there I caught the glint of a rifle or machine gun. Our motor was silenced when we were about one hundred yards from the dark shore. Dr. Belsidus wanted to be in a position where he could command the entire scene. In the native boat next to us. General McNeel sat close to a field radio set getting messages from the shore.

It was positively uncanny. No sound of warfare, no struggle apparently. Not a shot had been fired. It was one-thirty.

The cable station and the telephone exchange are in our hands, Doctor, McNeel shouted gleefully over from his boat. "The city is surrounded. No one will be able to get through. They have just taken the police station and jail. . . The police have surrendered their arms, sir. . . The First Battalion of the First Regiment has left on the double for the Frontier Force barracks."

"It was easier than I thought it would be," commented the Chief. "We'd better go ashore, Kalanga. Tell the boats and the ships to turn on their searchlights, McNeel."

In a few moments scores of searchlights from the bobbing boats augmented by the huge shafts of light from the ships lighted up the entire struggling little city. Black Internationale bayonets were everywhere The mechanic ran our boat to the customs house wharf and we went ashore with the general. Once on land McNeel was busy receiving reports from messenger after messenger.

"There was nothing to it, Doctor," he exclaimed enthusiastically.

Suddenly, the crack of rifles drowned out his voice and the whiz and whistle of bullets forced us to fall flat. There were cries and screams in the darkness beyond the reach of the searchlights and the clash of steel on steel. Had something miscarried? Was there resistance after all?

XXV

Liberia Is Captured Without Opposition; President a Prisoner

You can always tell the caliber of a leader by the manner in which he acts. Dr. Belsidus might have been resting comfortably in his ornate apartment in New York, considering the calmness with which he deported himself.

"Where is that firing, McNeel?" he asked.

"A messenger has just reported, Doctor, that a number of soldiers evidently armed with sub-machine guns are defending President Barclay's residence. We shall silence them, sir. I am going forward now."

"We'll go with you." Dr. Belsidus calmly announced.

"But it's dangerous, sir," General McNeel objected. "We don't know how many there are. It is a surprise even to Farley."

"Come on, let's go," the Chief insisted, a little roughly. "Farley should have known about those special guards."

Motorcycles with sidecars had now arrived from the ships. We jumped in them and, led by McNeel, we raced up the rocky hill; the numerous searchlights from the ships and from the native boats were pretty well lighting up the scene. From the President's private residence came bursts of rifle and machine-gun fire. There must have been twenty or thirty men defending the place. As we stopped to watch the operations from a concealed position. Ralph Farley came up and saluted.

"I'm sorry, sir," he said apologetically. "We tried to find out everything. This must have been a secret guard known only to the President. I know he feared assassination."

"Alright, alright," growled the Chief, a bit irritably. "Next time don't make any mistakes." Meantime, a hot fire was coming from the house, to which our men were answering spiritedly. But it was soon all over. A volley of tear gas brought out the defenders. The last man to emerge with hands over his head and tears streaming from his eyes was the President of Liberia.

It was only three o'clock. Word came that the two companies of the Frontier Force had surrendered at the barracks, Monrovia and environs were completely in our hands.

We went immediately to the Executive Mansion on Ashmun Street. where Dr. Belsidus set up headquarters. He occupied the President's office and I was installed in the adjoining office customarily occupied by Barday's aide de camp.

Messages were coming in thick and fast. At four o'clock came the word that our troops had taken over Robertsport. Harper, Sinoa and Nanna Kru. At four-fifteen our motorcycle detachment reported that it had taken over the wireless station on the Firestone plantation at Duside.

At four-thirty Dr. Belsidus called me. He was sitting at the President's flat top glass-covered desk sipping a cup of black coffee and poring over some papers.

"Now, Slater," he began, "from now on we must be careful. It is at the time of success that we must be most careful. There is much to be done but I think we can get some sleep by ten o'clock at least. First, tell Farley to send a message to the Paramount Chiefs by the drums to assemble at Kakata for a conference three days from now."

"At Kakata, sir?" I asked, rather surprised. "Why, that's nearly fifty miles back in the bush, sir."

"Exactly, Slater, exactly. That's where the new capital is to be. Monrovia is too close to the sea, too close to the white man. We must get back where we'll have time to prepare in case we are attacked, where we can only be attacked by an expeditionary force and not blasted out by the big guns of battleships."

I immediately saw his point. As usual, he seemed to thought out every eventuality.

"Wire Miss Givens to come here immediately," he continued. "Cable Alex Fletcher to charter a fast freighter and send over a shipload of cement. It must be here in fifteen days. That's imperative. . . Cable Hamilton and Fortune to fly immediately to Texas and leave there with the air fleet. Wireless Juan Torlier to hop off with the entire fleet as soon as Hamilton and Fortune arrive. They are to follow instructions and refuel at the secret airport in Venezuela. . . Cable Martha Gaskin the following message: 'Success. Follow schedule.'"

"What does that mean, sir?" I asked.

"It means that she is to strike the second blow. The first blow was the assassination of the Prime Minister of Great Britain. That will drive everything else off the front pages of the world's newspapers for a couple of days. Now we shall blow up the French Chamber of Deputies." He said it all quite calmly, as though it were the most ordinary thing in the world. I must have revealed my surprise. The corners of his mouth went down in a cynical smirk.

"We need plenty of diversions," he said. "We must keep the white world in pandemonium while we are solidifying our position. We must spread terror, secretly of course, until we are strong enough to come out in the open. . . Take this message to Gaston Nucklett: 'Now is the time' . . . Nucklett's done good work but there's not yet enough dissension in America. That message will start a series of floggings and killings of prominent Catholic and foreign-born businessmen and public officials. . . There! With all that going on I believe the white world will be so busy it won't have time to think about what we're doing here. You know, Slater, we shall succeed as long as we are bold. Failure comes only when one hesitates. A little bloodshed, a little destruction, why, that's nothing at all compared to what Negroes have suffered for centuries at the hands of white people. Now, go and get those messages off immediately. And by the way, tell McNeel that as soon as the cement mixers get ashore to start all available men to working on that Kakata road. That's all."

THE NEXT WEEK SAW MORE changes in Liberia than there had ever been in its history, ancient or modern. In three days' time our motorcycle corps had established outposts along the entire boundary. The S.S. *Kelly Miller* had arrived with a machine shop, a foundry, smelting plant, construction machinery, sawmills and mining equipment; all the leading politicians had been arrested and jailed. Pat flew in the morning we captured Monrovia, arriving about nine o'clock from Freetown. Two days later the entire Black Internationale air force was parked on the Monrovia airfield while hundreds of men toiled to erect the temporary hangars.

The most auspicious occasion, of course, was the conference with the Paramount Chiefs at Kakata, on the fourth day following the fall of Monrovia. It was well carried out. In accordance with Farley's directions, each chief had brought a colorful retinue of warriors, wives, court attendants and other functionaries. Some of the warriors had old flintlocks but most of them were armed with spears, bows and arrows.

The conference was held in one of the great palaver kitchens erected for the 1928 conference assembled by former President C.D.B. King.

In the adjoining palaver kitchen there were long tables which groaned under the weight of venison, beef, mutton, strong liquors and good wines. It must have cost a pretty sum.

Dr. Belsidus was determined to make a good impression on these native kings and their warriors because he realized that their allegiance was essential. His huge throne was at the far end of the palaver kitchen on a dais. Comfortable chairs were supplied for the chiefs, chairs which recently had graced the drawing rooms of Liberian aristocrats. At intervals big electric fans on high standards whirled fresh currents of air over the perspiring nobility. The power came from a portable electric light plant. Most of these men had never seen ice or consumed an iced drink. but on this day they were served Tom Collinses and rickeys. Expensive cigars were freely passed around by the box.

New rifles and a hundred rounds of ammunition were distributed to each warrior. All the day previous motor trucks had come up from Monrovia with these small arms. Each chief had received upon arrival at the conference several bolts of cotton cloth, brass kettles, a case of good gin and a hundred pounds of leaf tobacco, along with a complete shaving set including soap, brush and safety razor. Big multi-colored tents had been erected for the chiefs, with smaller surrounding tents for their wives.

It was three o'clock in the afternoon when Farley assembled them in the bang palaver kitchens. Of course, by this time they had received something from the government instead of giving everything to the government. They conversed among themselves with bright eyes and much head-wagging as they waited for the man whom they considered their benefactor.

It was exactly three-thirty when our trumpeters blew a great blast and the saluting pieces rolled up in front of the conference place were fired twenty-one times, as Dr. Belsidus in the black limousine with which I was so familiar drove up to the entrance. He was immaculate as usual in spotless tropical clothes.

Paying no attention whatever to the awed chiefs, he walked to his throne, with General McNeel on one side and I on the other.

XXVI

Native Chiefs Bow Before
Dr. Belsidus After Great Speech

Ralph Farley served as interpreter, since he was well versed in Kpwessi, the lingua franca of Liberia.

Dr. Belsidus spoke without rising from his throne. I have kept a copy of his brief talk, not because it frankly outlined his grandiose plans for the future of Liberia, but because it was cleverly phrased in the idiom of the jungle. He must have given much time and thought to its construction, perhaps being assisted by Farley.

"Great Kings," he began, "today you are greater than you have been in countless moons. Great Kings, today you have the power of the white man in your hands. Great Kings! No longer must you bear oppression and fear the floggers. For you are the brothers and comrades of one who is greater than the white man. White man makes guns. I make guns. White man makes bullets, I make bullets. White man makes hut that runs along the road, I make hut that runs along the road. White man has big palaver kitchen that floats across the sea. I also have big floating palaver kitchen. White man rich, I am also rich.

"A great log has been removed from your path and now you and your warriors will march as you did in the days of the Kumbwa people. I am the great leopard come not to destroy you but to give you life. I am the great elephant that breaks down the trees and jungle in my path. I am the great crocodile that snaps off legs and arms and leaves the body helpless. I am the thunder that strikes the huts in darkness, I am the rain that brings good crops. I am swift as the goat that jumps on the hillside, swift as the pepper bird that calls at dawn. Strong as the ocean that breaks through the sandbar. I am the King of Kings.

"I do not know fear because I am the great leopard. Liberian people would not let you have guns, but I give them to you. Is it not so? Liberian people would not let you have bullets, but I give them to you. Is it not so? Liberian people take food and wine from you, but I give you food and wine. Is it not so?

"When you are strong. I am strong. When you are weak, I am weak. I must be strong and you must be strong. I will send wise men to train your men to shoot the guns that buzz like great bees. I will send to your towns canoes that go by themselves. I will give your warriors clothes like the white man and huts to sleep in at night. I will give your warriors great pans of rice and fish, much chicken and goat, plenty sheep and foufou gourds of palm oil and palm wine. Good will I be to you while you serve me. Like the angry leopard shall I be if you deceive me.

"I am the King of Kings. I have thousands of warriors. I have iron birds that fly across the sea. I have power greater than the white man. You are my comrades. You will have big stone houses like the white man. You will talk over wires. You will eat and grow fat and have rich cloth and many young wives shall occupy your compound.

"You will follow me into the English country and into the French country. Together we shall run the white man into the sea. All the land shall not fight, kill and enslave black men. We shall free black men and for six months' journey to the north, east and south shall be ours. We make them great. But those who oppose us shall die. All Africa will worship in our temples and live in peace and plenty a in the great long ago. our people did

"Eat, drink. laugh, dream of the future because it belongs to you. Today you have nothing to fear, for today, I the King of Kings, rule. You have guns. You have rich cloth. You have boxes of bullets. You have food and hot wine. Is it not so? You have seen how easily I have put the Liberians in stick. So I shall do the white man.

"Return to your homes. Make the drums talk all over Africa. Tell strangers far away what has come to pass. And when I call you and your warriors, you will come running as does the baby elephant to its mother. I have spoken."

Spontaneously, these grave, sedate chiefs jumped up shouting and singing with enthusiasm as Ralph Farley translated the last of the speech of Dr. Belsidus. Then something happened that gave me a queer turn, because it was my first time to witness it. One by one these venerable rulers came forward to the throne, fell flat upon the ground and, grasping the Doctor's highly polished shoe, kissed the toe. Then, rising, each one backed away worshipfully.

On the fourth day Pat flew us down to Sinoe, where Dr. Belsidus addressed another bevy of chiefs. The following day we flew to Harper for the same purpose. Then we returned to Monrovia.

GEORGE S. SCHUYLER

IT WAS TWO WEEKS BEFORE Dr. Belsidus permitted any of the white people, even consular officials, to communicate with the outside. In those two weeks not one word of the conquest of Liberia had gone out, and even if it had, there were so many other seemingly more important items in the news that no one would have bothered reading about what was happening in Liberia. As I have written, the assassination of Prime Minister Baldwin was a sensation. It was only surpassed in the news by the blowing up of the French Chamber of Deputies the following night. These atrocities were followed by increasing anti-Catholic and anti-Semitic riots in the United States, the mysterious sinking of an Italian cruiser following an explosion in her magazine, an attempt to shoot Herr Joseph Goebbels, the German Minister of Propaganda, and similar acts of terror all over the white world. Martha Gaskin had been doing her work well, aided by our cells in various European capitals.

When the news first broke, the report went out that there had been an insurrection of tribesmen, well-armed and well-led. There was no intimation that the expedition had come from abroad. It was not until a moth had transpired that the real story leaked out. Dr. Belsidus had remained much in the background. Pat and I, McNeel, Torlier, Farley and a few others were the only ones who saw him.

It came as a tremendous surprise to the white world that a well gained army of American Negroes had crossed the Atlantic in their own ships without the knowledge of the white man, landed and conquered a country the size of Kentucky or Ohio.

In that month Dr. Belsidus worked swiftly to consolidate his gains.

The road from Monrovia to Kakata was completed and a journey that had taken four hours by automobile before could now be accomplished in a little over an hour. Airfields to the number of nineteen were scattered over the Republic Motorcycle outposts were established every twenty miles along the boundaries between Liberia and Sierra Leone, French Guinea and the Ivory Coast. Non-commissioned officers sent to the headquarters of every Paramount Chief had been busily training native soldiers in the small arms and European military formations. For the first time in its history Liberia had its coast well policed. A fleet of swift motorboats armed with machine guns patrolled from Cape Mount to Cape Palmas, effectively preventing smuggling, through which the previous government had lost much revenue. Twenty sawmills had been flown to as many parts of the land and set up under the management of a young technician trained in America. Two gold mines were already in operation. By flying cement in large quantities to the various districts, the concrete troughs for the chemical farms had been quickly made and some were already in operation. Batteries of sun engines were in operation at Kakata, Naama, Sanoquilly and Harper, where concrete buildings for small arms and ammunition factories had been erected and the machinery was already in place. Gustave Linke, a little black French metallurgist, had already arrived to supervise the making of arms. Under the direction of Ransom Just and with the cooperation of Pat's air fleet, radio towers had been transported and set up in several parts of the country. By this means and the placing of a large radio in every town in Liberia, it was possible for Dr. Belsidus to address the entire population anytime he wished.

The Black Internationale freighters had returned to the United States for more machinery, cement and supplies. Al Fortune, at last doing the thing he so wanted to do, was superintending the building of a coastal road running the length of Liberia from Robertsport to Harper with a thousand workers in five divisions. He swore that it would be completed in three months. In the meantime, dynamite squads were blowing the rocks out of the St. Paul and Loffa rivers to make them navigable by barges far into the inland.

Dr. Belsidus, who was working nineteen hours a day and almost wearing me out, had already moved into the new government building at Kakata. Thousands of cement blocks were being turned out for the other building in course of erection.

As Provisional President, Dr. Belsidus had assured the various foreign governments that merchants, missionaries and foreign planters would not be molested, and he told the fiscal agent of the Firestone Company that he would respect the agreement of 1926 drawn up between it and the Liberian government. Two weeks afterward Dr. Belsidus paid off the two million five hundred thousand dollar loan in full.

We then held a conference and laid out plans for bringing a million Negroes from the United States. It was at this juncture that trouble arose with the French.

XXVII

Pat Admits Her Love for Carl;
Trouble with French Government Looms

The new capitol of Liberia was a two-story, mission-style building of concrete blocks with stucco finish, built around a huge central garden in the center of which was a large cement and tile swimming pool with the latest equipment. Green and yellow chairs and tables shaded by colorful parasols surrounded the pool. And at the end of the garden was a small bandstand, screened by palms. Gorgeous tropical flowers, freshly transplanted, fringed the garden with a riot of color and filled it with exotic perfume. Certainly Kakata had never seen its like before.

As one entered the building, corridors ran to the right and left with offices on each side. Immediately in front was a double staircase curving up to the second floor. Here were the great dining hall where moving pictures could also be shown, the conference room where the staff met, the ballroom and an elaborate apartment for Dr. Belsidus. Around the entire building on both floors extended a wide balcony. On the roof were cleverly concealed water tanks. It was strictly utilitarian, that capitol building.

Nearby, four and six room one-story bungalows were going up in rapid order, as fast, indeed, as concrete blocks could be turned out. I stood at the window of my office, which adjoined that of Dr. Belsidus, and watched the feverish building activities in all directions. Over there, big lumbering trucks loaded with cement, reinforcing iron and factory equipment were coming in on the new improved road from Monrovia, where our freighters were unloading. Over to my right the new airfield, with its concrete runways, control tower and vast expanse cleared in a week by two thousand native workers, was in full operation. Some of the trucks loaded with cement and tools were delivering their loads to big bombing planes, which promptly took off to all parts of the Republic.

Then my heart almost stopped. Reacting to a loud sound, I looked out my office window and saw an old autogiro flutter to the field, skid a few feet and stop. The cowl was pushed back and out jumped Pat. She was dressed as I remembered her on that morning ages ago when we took off from the Westchester County airfield. The same green pilot's cap and jacket, green riding breeches and cordovan boots. She looked my way, saw me standing at the window and waved cheerily. Worn as I was with the terrific grind, the slave-driving of the tireless Dr. Belsidus and the countless details to which, as his secretary, I had to attend, the coming of Pat was a tremendous lift.

We had scarcely seen each other since that afternoon six weeks before when we parted on the dock in Freetown. I waited impatiently for her to come up, fearing that any moment I might be summoned by Dr. Belsidus. I did not have long to wait before she burst in radiant, but seemingly just a little tired.

"Hello, Carl," she said, coming quite close. "It seems ages since we met, doesn't it?"

"Yes, a new world has started, Pat. We have attained our first goal but it's an awful grind. Aren't you worked out?"

"You said it! Why, I don't know how we've managed to do what we have. Do you know that, since I flew down from Freetown, we've been going every minute? Everyday parachuting cement, gasoline and equipment all over the country, trying to keep airfields in shape with native labor you can't understand, scattering pictures of the Chief all over the jungle."

She paused, breathless, and then grinned broadly, revealing her perfect white teeth.

"But I love it!" she exclaimed. "I love it. Carl. Oh, what a privilege to be doing what we are doing. Think what it will mean!"

"Well, what about us?" I interrupted, placing my hands on her shoulders. "What about *our* love? You know I'm mad about you, Pat? Darling, I want you so badly, more than I've ever wanted anything in the world. And now, dear, we've attained those things you said must be attained before we could speak of ourselves. We've both given ourselves unselfishly, Sweet. Can't we go on from here together?

I saw the softness of love mist her eyes and her beautiful lips pant invitingly. They were so close to me. Her faint perfume intoxicated me—the familiar gardenia that had intrigued me that night long ago on the balcony at the New Jersey chemical truck farm. In another moment I had embraced her and pressed those precious lips to mine. Wordless we clung to each other. There was nothing to say. We knew each other's thoughts, knew what we meant to each other, knew what we wanted.

"I just felt this would happen today," she said softly. "I knew it when I looked up and saw you standing at the window. I started not to come in for that reason. I knew I couldn't trust myself once more with you, Prince Charming."

"And I think I should have died if you *hadn't* come in," I whispered, drawing her again to me. "It didn't seem I could stand to see you another time and keep my equilibrium. Busy as I've been in this tremendous undertaking, I've been terribly lonely for you. Just starved. You know what I mean."

"Yes," she said, some of the old mischief returning to her eyes, "I know what you mean."

"I'd be delighted to marry you this minute, Patricia Givens, if you'd have me." I whispered into her ear.

"Well, Carl Slater," she said, grinning, "that's a little sudden. I must exercise the feminine prerogative and think it over."

Dr. Belsidus summoned me over the communicating telephone and tearing myself from Pat's passionate embrace. I hurried in. The Chief was seated at a huge desk in one corner of the vast room whose only other furnishing was a large easy chair alongside his desk. On the wall over his head was a huge map of Liberia. Otherwise there was only the highly polished parquet floor and the great French windows that lighted the office from three sides. He was immaculate, as usual, in cream-colored tropical suit, cream-colored shoes, cream-colored socks with purple clocks, purple shirt and handkerchief, and a purple and cream striped cravat. He looked up as I entered.

"Ah yes, Slater. Sit down. I've ordered other chairs. I'm expecting the French consul and his assistant. It looks as though we're going to have trouble with them. I have learned some interesting things about their plans. They feel it necessary to strike now before it is too late."

This gave me quite a start. I knew that the French had long had designs on Liberia and at various times had been on the verge of taking over the country but were prevented by American diplomatic intervention. Now that they saw a real threat developing, it was probable they were ready to make another stab at us. What chance had we against the might of France? They could take the coast at once, and in a week they could have their Senegalese army at our gates.

"That sounds serious, Chief."

"It is serious," he admitted, without showing emotion. "but I anticipated it."

The door at the far end of the office was swung open and the uniformed doorman announced, Monsieur Rapport, Consul of the Republic of France," and stood aside. The tall, blond, anemic Parisian whom we had met in Monrovia the day after the conquest strode in, followed by the Vice Consul Constaint. Uniformed flunkies brought chairs for the two men. It did not take long for Consul Rapport to get to the reason for his visit.

"Excellency," he said, "my government has viewed the events of the past six weeks not without certain misgivings. Your former government always maintained cordial relations with France, and my government never had occasion to be perturbed over the course events in Liberia. Today, however, my government feels that the unnecessary military display and activity on your boundaries may conceivably dis turb the peace of the tribes in French Guinea and Ivory Coast. Several of your planes have been observed flying over French territory in violation of international law. Incendiary propaganda probably distributed by plane and obviously coming from Liberia has been scattered over the Ivory Coast districts bordering Liberia. This inflammatory material is contributing to the unrest of the natives.

"My government is also alarmed by the speedy construction of concrete machine gun nests all along your boundary, the erection of arm factories and the general evidences of military activity which must obviously be aimed at neighbors. My government also has reason to believe that the so-called Temples of Love which have been widely established throughout our territories have some connection with your movement.

"In view of these facts, my government must view any further such manifestations with alarm and take proper precautionary steps, although it is not, of course, our desire to impair Liberia's sovereignty."

I glanced swiftly at Dr. Belsidus. Consul Rapport meant in plain words that unless we halted our program France would strike swiftly and surely. It was a crucial moment. I wondered how Dr. Belsidus would meet the challenge. Could he defy mighty France?

XXVIII

Belsidus Parries French While He Prepares Armies

D r. Beludus listened gravely to Consul Rapport, occasionally shooting a significant glance at me. When the Frenchman had finished, the Chief spread his manicured fingers on the edge of his glass-topped desk and leaned forward slightly, an expression of great affected sincerity on his finely chiseled face.

"Mr. Rapport" he began, the cordiality in his tone masking the hatred I knew was in his heart, "the government of Liberia is regretful of any action on its part which your government might consider in the slightest degree unfriendly. Some of its aviators in their zeal may have flown over French territory. These young men and women will be warned at once that there must be no repetition of such violations if it is found that any have been guilty. I shall immediately issue strict orders to that effect.

"However," he continued with his snake-like suavity, "we must disdain responsibility for any incendiary literature which may have appeared in your territories. Our desire is to live at peace with all our neighbors. We are much too busy trying to build Liberia to interfere with your natives, and we disavow and condemn the distribution of any propaganda which might disturb the peace of your colonies. We have no connection whatever with the so-called Temples of Love to which you refer. The sect has representatives in Liberia just like the Catholics Episcopalians, Baptists, Methodists, Moslems, and these representatives are welcome. This particular sect has given us no trouble whatever and we regret to hear that the missionaries in your territories are accused of indiscretions. I shall immediately issue a warning to all missionaries against political activities. We wish to do nothing or seem to countenance anything which might give offense to the French Republic, the friend of all black people."

His voice was soft and soothing. He ended with a smile of pretended friendliness and goodwill and leaned back in his chair. I could see that M. Rapport was reassured, that he felt he had frightened Dr. Belsidus by his threat of "proper precautionary steps." He was not quite satisfied, it developed.

"In the name of the French government," he replied, "I am extremely pleased to find the Executive reasonable and conciliatory and shall notify my chief. However, Doctor, there is one more matter, which my government views with misgivings, and that is the military development in Liberia. Your boundary is being fortified, your arms factories are nearing completion, your airplane factory, I understand, is finished, and the natives have been given arms. My government finds it difficult to perceive why such preparations are necessary in view of the notorious peacefulness of West Africa, and indeed all Africa."

Dr. Belsidus beamed upon him in a more ingratiating manner than I had ever seen him affect.

"Permit me to reassure the French government. My government is concerned only with making Liberia impregnable as near as possible. My country, as you know, has suffered in the past because of its military weakness and the division that has existed among our people. We are trying now to initiate a sense of unity and nationalism and we find that military training does this most effectively. Since we have the trained technicians we find it less expensive to make our airplanes and train our aviators here than abroad. Any move of hostility toward our neighbors is farthest from our minds. We want the love and friendship of our neighbors, and we want them to understand that."

Consul Rapport seemed reassured, although I had a suspicion that he was not completely satisfied. However, he affected joviality when he departed. As the great doors were closed behind him I turned to Dr. Belsidus.

He was glowering with rage. I could almost feel his indignation. "White fools!" he hissed. "Do they think they can frighten us? Do they think they can stop us now? Notify everyone of the staff, Slater. There is to be a meeting at once. I don't care where they are or what they are doing they must come at once. Shoot a wire to Martha Gaskin in code to bear down on the French. Giving us orders! Threatening us! I'll show them what black men can do."

"You were very conciliatory," I reminded.

"Of course, I was," he snapped. "I am playing for time. In another month or two I'll talk differently. France is powerful, my boy. It will take the best black brains to beat her. And after her there is an even worse enemy of black people: the British."

I hastened out to radio Martha Gaskin and to send out the call for the conference. By sundown speedy planes were bringing in staff members from all parts of Liberia. After dinner we all met in the conference room around the great oval table. Dr. Belsidus lost no time in getting down to business.

"I had long been expecting some action on the part of the imperialist powers. France is the first that has decided to strike. The French consul was here today. Slater, read them what he said."

Taking out my notebook, I read M. Rapport's words. The others listened attentively. When I had finished Dr. Belsidus spoke again.

"We have come far in the past two months. We are going farther. Al Fortune, how is that road coming from Robertsport to Harper?"

"About seventy-five miles more and we'll be finished, Chief. Everything is working fine. We've got five thousand good men on it, and we're finishing it at the rate of five miles a day. We ought to be completely finished at the latest in three weeks, and perhaps in two weeks. It's flat, sea-level work."

"Get it finished in two weeks," ordered the chief, "even if you have to use a thousand more men. Give them double-time for overtime, give them more food, give them anything but finish in two weeks. Meantime, I want you to get to work on roads from here to Naama, from Naama to Kolahun, and from Naama to Sanoquilly, that will carry trucks. Mr. Farley will get the additional men from the Paramount Chiefs. And now, General McNeel, how goes the training?"

"We've got ten thousand men under arms in each of the five districts, or fifty thousand native troops altogether. They've had six weeks of intensive drills. In another six weeks they'll be ready. What we need is more rifles and ammunition, more equipment of all kinds. There is a shortage of machine guns and we only have two batteries of light artillery. There are no anti-aircraft guns and only one tank. I hardly think we are prepared for an important war, Doctor."

"Well, we'll have to *get* prepared," said Dr. Belsidus, frowning. He turned to the little black metallurgist with the long sweeping mustache. "Mr. Linke, how soon will you be ready to turn out small arms and ammunition? What are the prospects for the artillery General McNeel needs?

"We start," said the French Negro, "to turning out small arms next week. By that time we'll be getting iron from the native mines. In the meantime, however, I am using a boatload of scrap iron we bought from the Belgians. The sunray engines are doing their work well. However, it will be another month before we'll be able to turn out artillery. Some of the equipment is still en route from the States."

Dr. Belsidus then turned to slender, octoroon Alfred Hartman, assistant to Alex Fletcher on financial affairs, who reported steadily mounting revenue from the farms and business enterprises in America, purchase of two more freighters, a fleet of motor trucks and a fast sub marine chaser. Encouraging reports came also from Sanford Mates, the architect, who was busy erecting the industrial plants: from Dr. Matson, who was about to move in a big new hospital at Naama; from Bennie Simpson, whose cement plant and stone crushers were feverishly working to supply the materials for roads and buildings; from Patricia Givens and Juan Torlier, whose plants were at work turning out new planes. But most significant of all, from Rev. Samson Binks, who gave a lengthy report on the five hundred Temples of Love already established throughout Africa and their economic and educational departments.

It was an impressive report of work done, monumental work done in so short a span of time, a brilliant testimonial to the careful preparations made and carried out according to schedule, the start of a new era in Negro progress.

"Two more months," observed Dr. Belsidus, "and we shall be ready for a real showdown with the imperialists. Go back to your respective tasks. Work hard to get through on time. Use every man in Liberia, if you must, but get through on time."

"And at the end of two months?" inquired General McNeel.

"Then," declared Dr. Belsidus gravely, "we shall strike for the conquest of Africa."

XXIX

LADIES AND GENTLEMEN, THE HOUR FOR WHICH WE PREPARED IS HERE

It was around the first of June when we got the ultimatum from the French. Dr. Belsidus, as I have said, had decreed that the conquest of Africa should start in two months, or around the first of August. The ensuing eight or nine weeks were the most hectic Africa has ever seen.

Al Fortune completed the motor truck roads. The great sun-power plants, more huge than any we ever had in the United States, were now completed and functioning. A brand-new cotton mill was turning out cloth in thousands of bales on a twenty-four hour shift, using cotton imported from America until our Liberian plantations could produce. The great chemical vegetable farms which now dotted Liberia were turning out an incredible volume of food. Not only were the Liberian natives better fed than ever before in history, but great truckloads of yams. tobacco and salt fish were sent to our five hundred Temples of Love throughout Africa for free distribution to congregations. Gustave Linke, the little French armament man, was turning out first-class rifles, machine guns and small cannon from the three great factories that drew their power from the sun. Another factory turned out rifle and machine-gun bullets hand grenades and shells. Our fleet of freighters numbered twenty But even then it was apparent by the second week in June that it would be physically impossible to get all we needed in the way of air planes and munitions in time for the great push.

On the fifteenth of June, after our secret agents in Europe under Martha Gaskin had blown up several key buildings and drydocks at the French naval station at Toulon, Dr. Belsidus sent word to her to arrange for immediate purchase of fifty bombing planes according to Patricia's specifications, several thousand rifles and machine guns and millions of rounds of ammunition. In order to effect immediate delivery, he paid cash.

Meantime, young men and women from America, some of the cream of the Negro race, were pouring into Monrovia and immediately being dispatched to key places in Liberia. On the fifth of July and every week thereafter, a thousand arrived, close-packed on freighters chartered for the purpose. It was these youngsters who, as foremen and forewomen, helped to keep production at a peak. Coming in the midst of the rainy season, they found living conditions most unpleasant. Several died from malaria and yellow lever. But most of them adjusted themselves to the new life. In every case they had paid their own money for passage to the new land of opportunity. At that time we were offering the low fare of fifty dollars for passage from America.

By the first of August everything was as near readiness as possible. considering the hectic pace. Working eighteen hours a day, Dr. Belsidus was watching every development. He grew increasingly irritable as the zero hour approached, so great was the nervous strain to which he and the rest of us worked. He snapped and snarled now, where before he had been suave.

Consequently, you can imagine our surprise when at his call we assembled that evening in the huge dining room in the capitol building at Kakata. He was smooth-shaven and immaculate as ever, faultlessly dressed in cream-colored tropical evening clothes. He didn't seem to have a care on his mind.

There was a short table across the width of the dining hall at which sat the entire staff of the Black Internationale, with the exception of Alex Fletcher and Gaston Nucklett, who were in America, and Martha Gaskin, who was in Europe. Down from the cross table ran two long parallel tables the entire length of the hall, which seated nearly five hundred diners. These included all industrial heads, all foremen and superintendents, all field officers of the new Liberian Army, and every important native chieftain in the country.

Outside, a hundred-piece symphony orchestra sent ethereal music up to us, while white-clad, barefoot native workers brought in the heaping bounty of food and drink. It was the first time such a gathering had sat down together and perhaps it would be the last.

It was eleven o'clock when, after several preliminary speakers had their say, Dr. Belsidus rose to speak.

"Ladies and gentlemen," he said. "the hour for which we have prepared is at hand. Whether Africa shall remain slave or free depends upon us. I need not tell you more but I warn you that death shall be the portion of any man or woman who falters. The white man can and will be run out of Africa or exterminated. You all have your orders in detail. Go, and carry them out."

THE ZERO HOUR WAS SET for midnight, August 1st. The heavy tropical rain was falling in torrents, thundering on the roofs and against the window. panes, sloshing into the gutters, almost making the airfield a lake. On that airfield in serried rows of glistening wings and bodies stood the Black Internationale air force. Would they be able to fly tonight? I doubted it. On the well-lighted field I could see Pat in her familiar green gear making her final inspection. I wanted to see her so badly before she took off. It suddenly came to me with a sharp pang that I might not ever see her again. Anything could happen over those trackless jungle wastes. Although we had a long lovers' talk before she went out to the airfield. I was eager for one more word, for one more caress.

But just then came a ring from Dr. Belsidus. I rushed into his office. It had been completely transformed. One wall was completely taken up by a huge map of Africa fifteen feet high and equally as broad. On it every important African town was marked in electric lights set to turn green if in our hands and red if remaining in the hands of the whites. Underneath this map sat a row of telephone operators ready to talk to all parts of Liberia or to transmit messages from the aerial fleet. At the end of the office Dr. Belsidus sat in his accustomed place, garbed in t black and gold pajamas, sipping a cup of black coffee.

"Well, Slater," he said, calmly. "I guess you'd better get yourself into something comfortable because we're going to be right here for a long time. Come right back now, I'll be needing you. Be sure and get things going on the drop of midnight."

"Very good, sir." I turned and left his office and entered mine. There I telephoned downstairs and ordered the beating of the huge tom tom which was to command all Africa to strike.

Boom! Boom-Boom-Boom! Boom! Boom-Boom-Boom!

The great drum roared its message through the slackening rain. Over hill and dale, across swamps and deserts sped the word to strike. To five hundred Temples of Love went the word to exterminate all white people and their black allies. As fast as sound can travel, the message of murder sped.

Dr. Belsidus and I sat at his desk, sipping coffee and smoking as the booming signal went to millions of waiting black men and women, waiting with revenge in their hearts and the joy that comes from striking back persecutors.

The rain suddenly stopped. Shortly afterwards the roar of a hundred airplane motors split the darkness. My heart sank a little. Pat was going up, I might never see her again. A great realization of my deep love for her swept over me and I wished that I might be with her in the cockpit of her plane. But that was impossible. My post was with the Chief.

One by one the bombers and pursuit ships took off. In fifteen minutes they were all winging their way to various destinations within a radius of a thousand miles.

At twelve-fifteen came a laconic but tremendously significant message from Martha Gaskin. Decoded, it informed Dr. Belsidus that in accordance with his instructions the giant British battle cruiser *Hood* had been sunk by a time bomb with a loss of nine hundred sailors in Italian waters.

The Chief rubbed his palms together and chuckled softly. "That ought to start things going," he said. "Nations have gone to war for less. By God, that white girl is doing swell work for us."

"You place great trust in one of another race." I observed.

"I place trust in no one," he growled. "I have arrangements to crush those who deceive me. However, Martha has been faithful and deserves credit."

I was tempted to ask him more about this clever white girl who served him so well, when telephone and radio messages began to pour in. Most of them were laconic but no less encouraging:

Dakar, Senegal Warehouses, railroad shops and barracks destroyed. Two French hangars burned.

Freetown, Sierra Leone: Third squadron successfully bombed white hotels government building. Trading posts, missions and government buildings in interior fired.

Grand Bassam, Ivory Coast: Railroad shops, barracks and warehouses bombed and destroyed.

Nairobi, Kenya: Docks, warehouses, railroad shops burning. Whites fleeing massacre.

So it went, hour after hour. Green lights jumped out all over the huge map. The campaign had been well planned and was being well executed. For weeks and weeks Temples of Love scattered over the Dark Continent had been storing up thermite grenades and bombs for incendiary work. In each colony secret chemical laboratories had been preparing these incendiary bombs. In each community Dr. Binks's followers had been secretly supplied with revolvers, ammunition and long sharp knives. Now the slaughter was proceeding with clocklike precision while the investments of Europeans went up in smoke.

XXX

Fires Flare and Swords Clash as Big Conquest of Africa Nears Climax

With increasing rapidity as the night wore on the green lights on the great map of Africa increased in number while the red lights decreased. It was exciting in the extreme because we knew that each change from red to green meant another community had changed from white control to black.

Reports by wireless and radio telephone continued to pour in. The distribution of incendiary grenades in the five hundred Temples of Love throughout Africa was proving to have been a wise move on the part of Dr. Belsidus. From every part of the continent came shocking reports as mobs of frenzied natives burned churches, warehouses, residences, stores—everything that belonged to the hated white man who had held them down for four hundred years.

By five o'clock, when the first faint suggestion of dawn came out of the cast, the swift night of horror was coming to a close and only a few white strongholds held out. A summary made at that time for Dr. Belsidus showed that every white habitation or business from Morocco to Cape Town had been destroyed and the white people without exception exterminated.

South Africa, Cape Town and Algeria still held out, while white control remained in Nairobi. Asmara, Cairo and the north coast, but everywhere else the blacks were firmly in control.

Taken completely by surprise, the forty thousand or fifty thousand whites in West Africa had been exterminated as quickly by the infuriated natives as had the whites in East Africa and the million whites in South Africa.

Unless the garrisons in Italian East Africa, at Nairobi, Cape Town and Pretoria received reinforcements from abroad, they would be unable to hold out.

But it was evident by noon that there would be no reinforcements from abroad, for Europe itself promised hourly to become a seething cauldron.

The British, with a great empire at stake, had been striving ever since the Italian rape of Ethiopia in defiance of the League of Nations to preserve the peace of the world—a peace based on the subjugation of colored people. The sinking of the battle cruiser *Hood* in Italian waters now made it almost impossible for war to be avoided.

The news of the sinking shocked the white world. The Italians disavowed the act, laying it to Communist sabotage, but it was clear from summaries of press opinion relayed to us by our European agents that the British and French believed the Italians, backed by the Germans, were responsible for the outrage. Martha Gaskin had done her work well. The time aced by her agents had sunk the world's greatest battleship without a trace. In the absence of absolute proof of the cause of the sinking, the finger of suspicion pointed to Italy.

The British cabinet met hurriedly with Premier Chamberlain at 10 Downing Street, while a similar meeting was called by Premier Blum at Quai d'Orsay Masters of conciliation and recognizing the possibility of losing both their empires, the general staffs of these two master imperialist nations sat throughout the hot August afternoon trying to find out what do. The chances are they would have patched up some sort of truce with the Fascist powers in a few days, but all their efforts were in vain against the clever scheming of a black man and the bravery and skill of a black woman.

Dr. Belsidus had anticipated the fright into which the great imperialists would be thrown by the threat of European war and the frantic efforts by the various chancellories to prevent a break. He realized then that an apparent British reprisal for the sinking of the *Hood* would have to be made upon the Italians. It would have to appear that the British were punishing the Italians for sinking their great battle cruiser.

But Dr. Belsidus and Liberia were both a long way from Italy and any of the Italian possessions. While the Black Internationale's secret agents were everywhere in Europe and particularly in Italy and Italian possessions, Dr. Belsidus did not believe they could make the sort of shocking reprisal he wanted.

This was where Pat and her air force came in. Immediately upon completing the conquest of Liberia, arrangements were made for caches of gasoline, oil and parts to be established with as great secrecy as possible at Salaka, in the Gold Coast: Yakoba, in Northern Nigeria;

Yagusi, in the Ubangui country; and near Gore, in western Ethiopia. These caches were approximately seven hundred miles apart, and were in close proximity to Temples of Love. Some of the gas had been transported by truck, some by camel, some by porter and a considerable amount had been parachuted by airplane. A very large consignment had been shipped down the Nile and then transported by motor truck and camel to Gore.

Whatever the means of transportation, by the evening of July 31st, the priests of the Temples concerned reported that all was in readiness. Pat was jubilant because of the successful working out of a plan for whose details she was responsible.

So when the zero hour arrived, a hundred planes took off under Pat's command, loaded down with high explosive and incendiary bombs. Following the West Coast eastward, twenty of the remaining planes bombed in turn Bingerville and Grand Bassam, Sekondi, Accra, Takoradi and Lagos. At the same time a fleet of the same size flew up the coast ho Monrovia and bombed Freetown, Konakry, Bathurst and Dakar.

These operations were completed without accident or interruption before daylight. Long before dawn a dozen towns and cities between Morocco and the Cameroons were in flames.

But it was the brief messages from Pat with her main fleet of a hundred planes that claimed our main attention. Leaving sharply at midnight, she had brought them down on the field ringed with flaming torches at Salaka at three o'clock. There they replenished their supply of gas and oil. Taking off again at three-thirty they arrived at Yakoba, Northern Nigeria, at six-thirty. Refueling again, they made for Yagusi, in the Ubangui country, where the same operation was completed. At ten o'clock they left again with full tanks for the airfield not far from Gore, Ethiopia, where they radioed back at one o'clock that they had arrived.

At the end of each message was the laconic comment, "All whites killed. We knew that meant there was no opposition whatever through the whole section of the continent they had crossed.

At one-twenty Dr. Belsidus radioed Pat to leave at midnight for her objective. By that time the pilots would be completely rested.

About seven-thirty on August 2nd, the terrible reports began to trickle in from the Congo. The wing section under Juan Torlier, which had spread fire and devastation and death from Monrovia to

Lagos, refueled at the latter place from British supplies of gasoline which natives had taken over, and proceeded further south, bombing as they went. Reaching the Belgian Congo, they bombed Banana, Leopoldville, Stanleyville and other settlements. But it was the natives who did the most destructive work.

Not only did they in a few hours destroy what the Belgians had laboriously and cruelly erected in almost fifty years of colonial exploitation, but they slaughtered white men, women and children with great ferocity. You have no idea of the blood-chilling effect of the laconic report from the head of the Black Internationale cell there which read: "Belgian Congo belongs to us. No white person is alive." Later in the day we learned that in many of the principal cities the whites had been beheaded, their hands and feet cut off to be dried as charms, and their bodies thrown to crocodiles. The Belgian Congo was a shambles, indeed, but nothing else could be expected in view of the long series of Belgian atrocities.

At noon we received the report that Cape Town was in flames, fired by the Zulus and other oppressed tribesmen. Surrounded, the white soldiers and native police had fought until lack of ammunition and great clouds of smoke forced them to surrender and plead for their lives. They were promptly murdered, in accordance with Dr. Belsidus's orders that no prisoners were to be taken. At three o'clock came the report that the Boer farmers at Pretoria had been slaughtered.

Sleepless and haggard, Dr. Belsidus was finally induced to retire for a few hours. He took one last look at the great wall map which indicated that only Ethiopia, Eritrea, and French, British and Italian Somaliland remained. He turned and smiled that old enigmatic smile, then walked unsteadily to the door.

"Slater, take care of things," he said, "while I snatch forty winks. Order the air forces to remain where they are at Dakar, Stanleyville and Gore until I order them to move."

Just then a message came in from Europe. It was from Martha. It read:

Mussolini conciliatory, realizing he is not prepared. British and French may postpone war. We must strike now.

Dr. Belsidus handed the message to me. "Well," he remarked as he passed out the door to his room, "I think Miss Givens will take care of that."

XXXI

European Nations Plunge Into War As Africa Is Redeemed

A horrified white world got word of the great African uprising about five o'clock on the morning of August 2nd. Cables and radiograms from our agents conveyed something of the awful shock with which the news was received. From noon onwards we got report after report.

At four o'clock Martha Gaskin radioed in code:

Italians and British about to patch up differences in view of African uprising Must act swiftly if peace is to be averted.

I hated to awaken Dr. Belsidus although I realized the gravity of the situation, Confronted with the loss of all their colonies, the white imperialist powers would stop at nothing to avert war and send punitive expeditions to Africa. Something had to be done at once.

Rather than disturb the Chief, I decided to act for the first time on my own initiative. At four-thirty I radioed in code:

Pat moves at midnight. Cannot get away before. You do what you can.

I signed my name I figured she would understand that Dr. Belsidus was asleep.

At seven o'clock, as I dozed over my umpteenth cup of black coffee, an orderly brought a cable in code from London signed by Martha. It was brief but terrible in its import:

Italian embassy blown up here at forty-fifteen.

I rushed with the message to Dr. Belsidus's room and after some difficulty awakened him.

"What is it, Slater?" he said irritably, lifting himself on one elbow, I handed him the cablegram. He read it, pursed his lips and whistled softly.

"Smart move," he murmured more to himself than to me. "Smart move. That girl really earns her money."

I explained a little hesitatingly how I had taken the authority upon myself to advise her to act.

"Well," he said, "I left you in charge, didn't I?"

I nodded acquiescence. He pondered a moment, gently scratching his head. Then he looked up, scanning my face.

"You must be dead, my boy." he said in a softer tone than was his wont. "Go get some sleep. I'll take over."

And that's how I slept for the first time in almost twenty-four hours.

I felt as if I was in a Turkish bath. I opened my eyes and the brilliant African sun almost blinded me. I was soaking with perspiration, lying across the bed just as I had fallen, fully clothed. My watch informed me that it was eight-fifteen. I had slept twelve hours.

Feeling refreshed but guilty to have slept so long in the midst of momentous events, I hurriedly disrobed, took a lukewarm shower, shaved and was soon striding into the Doctor's office.

He was sitting at his desk, immaculate as usual in freshly laundered tropicals, eating a breakfast of papaya, goat's milk, a slice of smoked meat and scrambled eggs.

"Get a good rest?" he asked cheerfully, flashing his white teeth. He seemed to be in rare good humor.

"I'm afraid I overslept, sir." I apologized. "You see, I'd been up for almost twenty-four hours."

"Quite alright, my boy," he went on, lolling back in his chair and sipping the goat's milk. "Everything has gone as I wanted it to go."

"What happened while I've been asleep?"

"Plenty. Around eleven o'clock our agents in Rome bombed the British embassy, and by a clever ruse got a crowd of those fanatical Fascists to cheer around the building. Of course, it was immediately dispersed by the police but the damage was done. It appeared to be a clear act of reprisal. It was the next to the last straw needed to break the back of white imperialist peace.

"Then," he continued, "came the last straw. Pat took off from Gore at midnight. In accordance with our instructions to Ras Kaner, the signal fires lit by the Ethiopians in the hills directed part of our squadron to Addis Ababa, Diretawa and Djibuti, part to Asmara and the rest to Mogadicio."

"Yes, and what happened?" I interrupted.

"Nothing that surprised me," he said quietly, balancing a forkful of eggs. "They bombed every Italian barracks and supply station. At the same time the Ethiopians attacked. It was a massacre. They didn't have time to make any effective resistance whatever. Those incendiary bombs wreaked havoc. Those that we didn't kill in their beds, the Ethiopians did. With the arms and ammunition they've got, the Italians. will never reconquer them."

"How did that affect the conference at 10 Downing Street?"

"Very badly," he replied, grinning with ill-suppressed satisfaction. "The diplomats reflected the rising tempers of the two peoples. On both there were charges, counter-charges, all sorts of accusations. The Italians charged that British planes from Aden had raided their colonies, spreading fire and death. Before the British government could formulate a reply, we bombed Westminster Abbey and planted a dead Italian inside as 'incriminating' evidence."

I must have visibly recoiled at his cold ruthlessness. He smiled and went on.

"Coming so soon after the loss of their African colonies, the sinking of their biggest warship and the slaying of their ambassador, it was more than the stolid British could stand. The conferences flopped at seven o'clock. Just before you came in I received a radiogram that the Italians had bombed Malta and Gibraltar. The French, acting with England, bombed Genoa and Venice. The war is on, my boy."

WAR HAD BEEN TERRIBLE IN 1914–1918. It was nothing compared to what the world witnessed now. Europe's numerous thickly populated cities were blown to bits as swarms of opposing airplanes dropped their deadly wares. Tanks rumbled to meet tanks and the thunder of big guns made night and day horrible. Nothing like this swift, ruthless, unremittent bloodshed had ever been conceived.

Dr. Belsidus was in high glee. Forgetting that he had not slept for twelve hours or more, he lost himself in his inevitable maps, planning and scheming.

At noon the Germans turned the noses of their planes toward their old enemy, France, and in support of their ally, Italy, and raided Paris. By nightfall every European country was involved and thousands of trucks, tanks and cannons were rumbling toward their respective frontiers.

Dr. Belsidus retired sometime before five o'clock. Every few minutes a new laconic message from our own forces told of the progress of our conquest. It had made all Africa once more the possession of black men. The Near East was seething and watchful India was prepared to strike once more for freedom.

THROUGH INQUIRIES I LEARNED THAT Pat's fleet was waiting at Asmara, Adowa and Mogadicio. I shot through a message to her. I wanted to see her, now that all objectives had been attained, and get firsthand accounts of what had happened on our eastern front.

As I waited for a reply, reports came in from every part of Africa telling of the insane joy of the people at being at last released from the white man's yoke. I could close my eyes and see the happy groups dancing in hot village streets while drums boomed and pulsated. I felt like dancing myself.

Hour after hour dragged by and still no word from Pat. Could she have cracked up after that memorable flight across Africa? It was not like her to remain silent so long when on such an important mission.

At four o'clock Dr. Belsidus emerged fresh as a daisy. I immediately told him of the lack of communication with Pat. He frowned deeply as his eyes ran quickly over the sheaf of radiograms and cablegrams.

In the next three hours he radioed three times. To each message there was no reply.

Where could she be? What had happened? Was there anything wrong? Why her silence?

XXXII

Pat Breaks Silence as European Nations Fight to Bitter End

It was very strange. Pat had always been so punctual, it appeared certain something must be wrong; she had let hours go by without communicating with us. I wondered what Dr. Belsidus would do. Even though the World War we had stimulated was now under way. and the attention of the entire white world was diverted from us, it would be a severe blow, nevertheless, to lose a hundred of our planes.

"We've got to find out what's going on, Slater," he said finally, "and I guess you would be interested in doing the finding, wouldn't you?"

"Why. . . Well. . . yes, of course," I stammered, my cheeks red.

"Oh, I know how you and Pat stand," he said, smiling. "I've known for a long time. Fine girl, Pat. She's the sort of girl I'd like to marry if I was the marrying sort."

"Thank you, Chief. I appreciate that. But tell me, don't you ever intend to marry? You have practically gained all of your objectives now and I should think you would turn to domesticity, if I might be so bold as to suggest it."

The doctor again smiled faintly. "Marriage is for the incomplete," he said disdainfully. "I am complete. Years ago I married myself to the ideal of a free Africa, Slater. That ideal has stayed with and nurtured me, sustained me, and given me the courage to go on. It has done everything that a wife is supposed to do and so seldom does. I need women, Slater and I've taken them wherever and whenever I wanted them. I've used them to serve my ends, to give me pleasure, to help me accomplish what I set out to do, I need no woman to share my defeats or victories. I shall go on alone, Slater, taking my pleasure where I wish without being tied down by female pettiness and possessiveness."

"Aren't you a little harsh, Doctor?"

"Of course. I am harsh. I am always harsh, always have been harsh, always will be harsh," he replied with evident relish. "I am harsh because I tell the truth and act the truth, and do not let scruple or sentimentality interfere with my desires and ambitions. There was a time I might have married had I been able to find a really civilized woman. But even the best of them are incurably sentimental, essentially petty and lacking in true idealism.

"A woman," he proceeded, warming to the subject, "invariably tries to devour her mate as does the female spider. In this she is industrious and persistent. Ultimately she succeeds because of her concentration on that objective. In the end she always has her way. And in the process the man loses much of his individuality and takes on some of the color and characteristics of his wife. That is why civilizations where there is continuous and uninterrupted monogamy inevitably become feminine. And such civilizations finally succumb to newer, cruder ones in which the male is dominant."

This was a Dr. Belsidus I had not known. Perhaps because we never before had discussed women, I could see his point but could not share. it. I could not be complete without the woman I loved, without Pat; I knew I should be completely miserable if I had to go through life without her. I had never felt that one could completely enjoy a woman unless she was one's very own and she shared in ownership. After all, there is much more to the man and wife status than the physical intimacy that seemed to be the extent of the Doctor's interest in women. aside from his use of them to further his diabolical ends.

"Yes, we are quite different, my boy," he said, reading my mind. "There are very few men like me. I spoke in a matter of fact tone without boasting or bragging. If I were not unique, I should have been unable to accomplish what I have."

Dr. Belsidus called in Captain Thomas Hudginson, who had been navigator on Pat's plane when we flew from Texas to Sierra Leone.

"Captain," he said, "I want you to fly Mr. Slater to Ethiopia as quickly as possible. We must find out what has happened to General Givens and the First Air Fleet. Our last message came several hours ago from Asmara How soon can you make it?"

"By using Colonel Torlier's new stratosphere plane, sir, I can do it in eight hours. I can average four hundred miles an hour with that. But the colonel gave strict orders that it was not to be touched. With one of our fast pursuit planes I can reach there in twelve hours."

"Use the stratosphere plane," commanded the Doctor, "by my orders. We must know what is going on. I can't stand this silence from Pat. She has never done this before. Are you ready, Slater?"

"Quite ready, sir."

"Well, get going, then, and whatever you do, keep me advised."

"Very good. Doctor."

The Captain and I turned to go. I was wondering about the stratosphere plane, wondering whether it would be entirely safe up in those rarefied spaces where one's life depends entirely on the oxygen tank, when Dr. Belsidus's telephone rang insistently. He grabbed the instrument and listened eagerly to whoever was talking. I saw his eyes brighten and the smile return to his face.

"Good!" he shouted, hanging up the receiver. He turned beaming toward us. "Nevermind that trip. We've heard from Pat at last!"

A great load lifted from my heart because I had been worried a great deal by her silence. Now she was safe.

"They'll be in tomorrow morning. Then we'll get the details. You may go, Captain. Slater, we'll read over the latest dispatches."

So Pat was on her way back! I was quite buoyant over it, although I wondered about her long silence that had so upset us. But there were other matters to occupy my mind.

THE WAR WAS GROWING MORE devastating by the hour. Every principal city in Europe had been bombed by one or the other of the belligerents, and in every case incendiary and gas bombs had been used. All restrictions were off and human brutality was revealed at its worst. Hospitals, churches, homes of non-combatants, all were blown to bits by the terribly destructive aerial attacks. Millions of armed men hurled themselves against the artillery, machine guns, liquid fire, tanks and bayonets of opposing armies. And as each report came in the grin Dr. Belsidus grew more diabolical. He actually reveled in news of the collapse and destruction of white civilization.

"Magnificent!" he shouted when German bombers blasted a hundred buildings in Brussels.

"Never heard anything better! He exclaimed when Italian submarines sank four British cruisers outside the harbor of Alexandria.

"At this rate, there soon won't be any white people left. Oh, how I've longed for this day!"

The new mechanized warfare was taking a tremendous toll of lives, according to radio and cable advices from our European agents. All through the night Dr. Belsidus gloated over the reports. Between times he issued cryptic orders to his subordinates spread over Africa from Timbuctoo to Cape Town. There was certainly a lot to straighten out, with looting in some places and utter disorganization in others. But thanks to the Temples of Love and their disciplined followers, some semblance of order was beginning to appear.

At daybreak a great roar of motors overhead told us that Pat and her planes had returned. A heavy rain was falling, making the landing field soggy and slippery, but one by one the great ships came down and taxied to their hangars.

Shortly afterward I heard light footsteps on the stairs. The door flew open and there was my Pat, face smeared with grease, but smiling triumphantly, and as pretty as ever.

XXXIII

Dr. Belsidus Finally Establishes African Empire As Story Ends

It was September and the Second World War had been proceeding devastatingly for a little over a month. After the first major battles in which white people both on the fronts and behind them had died like flies, the conflict settled down to a stalemate similar to that of 1914–1918, while pitiless and persistent air attacks reduced the civilian populations further into bestial fear and terror.

Following the swift and terrible conquest of Africa, the Black Internationale had been busily consolidating its gains, restoring order, gaining the allegiance of chiefs and kings in its far-flung empire. Europe was too busy to lift a finger to regain the vast territories from which it had drained so much wealth. Europe had made its death bed and was doomed. We felt safe and jubilant. The longer this new world war lasted, the more time we would have to strengthen our position and bring Africa's diverse peoples securely and definitely under our rule.

Of course, we had to use ruthless methods in some places. There were miseducated Negroes who still favored the rule of white men to the rule of black men. There were still Negroes who had been given a few crumbs from the tables of the exploiters, who now tried to help them by stirring counter-revolution against us. These Dr. Belsidus ruthlessly purged and executed.

The ruthless and expeditious manner in which white rule had been brought to an end had electrified the entire world. Europe had too much on its hands to do anything about it. Australia, New Zealand, Canada and other British dominions and allies were deeply involved in the European mess and likewise could do nothing to save Africa for the whites, A powerful faction in America had talked of intervening to save the prestige of the white race, but Gaston Nucklett's *White Americans* with its constant instigation of civic strife, had so entirely disrupted the country that it was unable to "compose" its internal affairs, let alone composing those of Africa. An uprising in India instigated by our agents there made it exceedingly unlikely that the British would be able to send the expeditionary force to Africa, composed of Indian soldiers

We were all naturally quite jubilant. We had gained an empire at small cost, an empire rich in everything, and were rapidly on the way to unifying it. It was then that our Second World Conference was announced.

By the first of October delegates were assembled from all parts of the world: every part of Africa, Australia, India, the West Indies, South America and the United States. But this time they were not sneaking to a hidden retreat in the New York State hills. This time they were not using the white man's transportation. This time they were being brought from all over the world by our airplanes to the two-story building of concrete blocks at Kakata, Liberia, that in so short a time had grown from a wayside settlement to the capital of the new Empire of Africa.

I shall never forget that great imperial conference, the largest and most significant ever held by black men. There were nearly a thousand delegates present. These included all the heads of Black Internationale cells in the various dark sections of the world, all the chief technical officers responsible for industrial development, all the high military officers and the bishops of the Church of Love from all parts of the earth.

Forming just before dinner outside the capitol building, we marched in twos through the entrance, up the double staircase and into the great dining hall. Uniformed ushers guided the delegates to their re pective places. Across the end of the vast hall was a table which crossed the two long ones at which the delegates were sitting. At that head table were the familiar faces of the Black Internationale staff, the Brain Trust, the wise and courageous men and women who had made all this possible. There were Sam Hamilton, Al Fortune, Gustave Linke, Dr. Matson, Rev. Samson Binks, Ransom Just, Pat, Juan Torlier, Bennie Simpson, Alex Fletcher, Sanford Mates, Gaston Nucklett, Martha Gaskin, General McNeel, myself and many whom I knew through our files and correspondence but had never seen because of their occupation in Europe.

One chair, in the center, was empty. That was the chair of Dr. Belsidus. As I gazed around at the excellent decorations, the gold and black banners, the gorgeously uniformed guards and attendants, I wondered where the Doctor could be.

Then, somewhere a trumpet sounded, to be joined by a chorus of trumpers. The lights in the hall lost their brilliance and grew dimmer and dimmer. Finally, the place was in darkness. There was awed whispering. Then the chorus of trumpets flourished again and the lights came on slowly. We all instinctively looked toward the chair of Dr. Belsidus. He was seated there, expressionless. I recognized the stunt as excellent theater, a characteristic Belsidus gesture.

At a wave of his hand to the major domo, the hundred-piece band below in the sunken garden burst into a new selection, *Caprice Africaine*, written expressly for this occasion. The serving of the dinner began.

It was a little past nine o'clock and the coffee and cordial had just been served when three loud taps from the major domo's staff brought the delegates to attention. Dr. Belsidus, still the stern immaculate figure in faultless tropicals, rose in his place and quietly began to speak:

"Africa belongs once more to the Africans. Africa will remain in the hands of the Africans. Never again shall the white man set his foot in our land, steal our wealth and enslave our sons and daughters.

"Africa is rich. Those riches will remain in Africa. Africa is populous. That populace will remain here and the products of its toil will remain here. From henceforward black men will labor to advance the interests only of black men.

"Africa does not need and does not want the white man. Africa will not have the white man. We will have our own culture, our own religion, our own education, our own army, navy and air fleet. We have the natural resources, the will and the ability to create the greatest civilization the world has seen. While the white man destroys himself with the infernal machines of his invention, we shall prosper and expand.

"This conquest proves that white men are not our superiors. This conquest proves that the white men are definitely our inferiors. They had all the power, all the money, all the machinery of information and communication. We had nothing but our wits. And what happened? How well you know what happened! With nothing but our wits we got money, we assembled men and women of brains, we trained hundreds of technicians, we disrupted white society and under the cover of that disruption we trained and transported a fully equipped army to these shores and fired the shots that have been heard wherever men breathe.

"The white men are tearing at each other's guts. Why? Not because they really want to do it but because we forced them to it. We did it, we brought about suspicion, strife and conflict because we had an objective and we could not attain that objective as long as white men were united.

"But remember this. As we gained an empire through our unity and intelligence, we must maintain it the same way, Negroes for four hundred years were the slaves of white men because they had not learned the lesson of unity, of solidarity, of a common cause. Too often they aided the white man in his nefarious schemes to partition Africa, and always he succeeded because some Negroes, consciously or unconsciously failed us.

"Let us continue to be alert. Let us continue to relentlessly pursue our selfish interests. Let us utilize every ounce of intelligence and knowledge we possess to make Africa impregnable.

"Now that we have ousted the white man from Africa, let us not waste time hating the white man. Let us keep an observant eye on him and profit from his mistakes. Let us stay out of his lands and be sure that he stays out of ours. The world is plenty large enough for both of us. If we properly take care of our part, we shall maintain our independence forever and forever.

"And now, my dear friends and associates," he said, and more emotion crept into his voice, "I would fain give up my leadership. For twenty years I have struggled and striven to free Africa, and I am tired, very tired. But I am not going to quit now. No, there is still much to be done. There is still need of consolidating our power, of making Africa a political and industrial entity while the white nations bleed themselves to death. Until this is accomplished, you need a strong, a ruthless, an intelligent leader. Negroes are not yet used to freedom, and so for a time we must have dictatorship, but that will depend upon you and the manner in which you carry out my orders. For, as you know, I will not tolerate disobedience or inefficiency or laziness.

"So, I am not going to give up my leadership. To be completely safe from white attacks and nearer the center of the continent, we are going to build a new capital at Yakoba, in Northern Nigeria. We are going to build roads. We are going to build factories, operate giant o farms, ranches, mines, mills, become self-sufficient.

"Oh, yes, my friends, there is much to do because Africa is behind. But as we have succeeded in this task, so shall we succeed the others. I shall serve you as I have served you, and you must serve me as you have served me. Together we can build here on this be second largest continent, an empire of black men and women work toward a cooperative civilization unexcelled in this world. And the task, my friends, the Black Internationale rededicates itself. Brains and organization triumphed once. They shall do it again."

There were wet eyes and damp cheeks when Dr. Belsidus ended. I saw Martha Gaskin look longingly at him. She realized she would never possess this black man for whom she had risked so much, and I felt sorry for her.

Pat was almost overcome with emotion. She squeezed my hand tightly and dabbed at the tears on her cheeks. Then she leaned toward me with that softness of the eternal feminine in her brown eyes. I wanted to kiss those pointing lips right there before a thousand pairs of eyes, but I contented myself with one whispered word: "Tomorrow."

She smiled and whispered back: "Yes, love. Tomorrow we, like Africa, shall be united, after so long. United forever."

"Forever!" I repeated reverently. And how I meant it!

PART II

BLACK EMPIRE

AN IMAGINATIVE STORY
OF A GREAT NEW CIVILIZATION
IN MODERN AFRICA

I

DR. HENRY BELSIDUS STARTS DEVELOPING
AN EMPIRE IN AFRICA

The conquest of Africa was history. Moving with a swiftness that amazed the world, Dr. Henry Belsidus, the sinister, suave, inscrutable black man who had once ministered to New York's sick white aristocracy, now sat in his large, almost-bare office in the capitol at Kakata. Liberia, complete master of the second largest continent in the world. Starting with a handful of loyal, brilliant Negroes, he had carefully built up the greatest revolutionary organization the world had ever seen: an organization which in its rise to power had known no law save that of expediency, no mercy except to people of color—an organization so ruthless in attaining its objectives that even I, Carl Slater, who, as the doctor's secretary, knew more about this ruthlessness than anyone except the doctor. . . sometimes even I shivered at the memory of the past.

When the delegates from fifty countries had secretly assembled in rural New York for the First World Conference of the Black Internationale, there had been elaborate preparations to conceal the meeting from the police and the agents of colonial countries. That had been five years ago. Now, a thousand delegates from every country where dark men and women dwelt were assembled at the new African capital at Kakata, Liberia, to listen to the reports of the technical and military officers. Last night they had heard Dr. Belsidus conclude his memorable address with the long-remembered words:

"There is much to do because Africa is still far behind. But as we have succeeded in this task, so shall we succeed in the others. I *shall* serve you as I *have* served you, and you *must* serve me as you *have* served me. Together we can build her on this the black continent, an empire. of black men and women working toward a co-operative civilization unexcelled in this world. And to that task, my friends, the Black Internationale rededicates itself. Brains and organization triumphed on They shall do so again."

It seemed a tremendous program, almost an impossible one. Here was a continent, almost wholly agricultural, with several hundred verse nations speaking a hall thousand languages. The European nations, whose colonies we had taken in the recent short campaign of blood and terror, were now locked in a light to the death which our agents had instigated. But how long would that wat last? And when it was over, would the victors ignore Africa? Would they let us go ahead and grow powerful before they attacked us? If they attacked, how could we hope to hold off their mighty battle fleets and their swarms of airplanes? Our technical staff was driving ahead feverishly to prepare for the inevitable struggle, but our progress was maddeningly slow. Here in a few months we had conquered a whole world and in a few short months we might lose it.

I dismissed the gloomy thoughts and concentrated on our honeymoon. Patricia Givens, whom I had loved from the first moment I met her in Dr. Belsidus's office in New York, was now Mrs. Carl Slater. In a few moments we would be winging our way to Ziggeta, high in the Liberian mountains where the Black Internationale's chief architect, Sanford Mates, had built a beautiful resort for staff members.

The door opened and she came striding in, brown, slender and beautiful, looking trim as usual in her green helmet, green jacket and riding breeches of the same shade which disappeared into highly polished cordovan boots.

"Ready, Sweet?"

"Sure, I have gassed the plane and all our luggage is packed inside. The Doctor has given us a month off. Isn't that swell? He said he guessed airplane production could continue without me for a month."

"I guess it can, too." I said, "but let's get away from here. You know, I'm jealous. I want you all to myself."

"For how long?" She was holding her head on one side, smiling with a twinkle in her eyes.

"Forever, Pat." I replied, drawing her to me. The look in her eyes told me better than words that she knew how much I meant it.

A few minutes later we climbed into one of the Black Internationale's black and gold pursuit planes, and were soon hurtling through the cloudless sky on the happiest trip of our lives.

It brought back memories of the first time I had gone aloft with Pat a time that seemed ages ago but which only was really a little over four short years. Then we were flying from the Black Internationale's private airfield and factory in Westchester County, New York, with its big hangars and machine shops presided over by Juan Torlier, the dull

GEORGE S. SCHUYLER

black giant airplane designer from Spanish Guinea who had received his training in the airplane factory in Barcelona. I recalled how we had flown first to the Black Internationale's great cement factory near Poughkeepsie, where Bennie Simpson, the freckled mulatto, superintended production and supplied the material for the hundreds of Temples of Love where Rev. Samson Binks schooled Negroes in the new black man's religion. And then had come the amazing chemical farm in New Jersey where gigantic vegetables grew in giant trays filled with chemical solutions that made soil unnecessary. But no less wonderful had been the batteries of steam engines operated by sunshine and efficiently maintained by their inventor, short, reddish brown engineer Alton Fortune, just as tall, studious chemist Sam Hamilton operated the amazing farm.

Today all these marvelous technical innovations and inventions of black scientists had been multiplied a hundred-fold in little Liberia. They would soon be multiplied a thousand-fold throughout all Africa.

Three-quarters of an hour later, Pat brought the little fighting plane down in a perfect three-point landing on the spacious field at Ziggeta. A staff car was waiting to drive us to the hotel, perched high on the side of a verdure-clad mountain whose summit was crowned with mist.

There was quite a number of the staff week-ending at the hotel. On our way to our suite we met Gustave Linke, the black French metallurgist in charge of our armament factories: Ransom Just, the short fat mulatto radio engineer, Martha Gaskin, the slender blonde in charge of our espionage in Europe; and General Barton McNeel, the burly, gray-haired World War veteran who had led our expeditionary force to Liberia, after training it in a remote section of Texas, and conducted the recent conquest of Africa. It seemed as though all the important officials had decided to come to Ziggeta to rest up after the strenuous round of activities at the Second World Conference.

We dined that evening with Dr. Andrew Matson, the handsome Young Howard graduate, once Dr. Belsidus's medical assistant, but now Surgeon General of Africa. He was a striking figure in his white tuxedo and black trousers, as impeccable but not as sardonic as his boss.

"A mighty fine-looking couple. I'll say," he remarked, making no effort to conceal his admiration for Pat. I didn't blame him. She was indeed lovely in her tight-fitting rose-colored evening dress.

He said a number of other nice things, and then the talk inevitably got around to shop.

"How long do you think it will take to build enough hospitals for all Africa?" I asked. "About ten years?"

"We shall have very few hospitals," he said calmly, then smiled at our visible surprise. "We are going to do new things in medicine in this country," he went on. "We are going to abandon Christian ethics and deal with the problem of health and sickness rationally."

Pat leaned forward, intrigued. "What do you propose to do?"

"Yes" I added, "there's a lot of disease in Africa: sleeping sickness, yellow lever, yaws, elephantiasis, malaria, syphilis, blindness. . . how can you treat all this disease without hospitals?"

"Before the white man came to Africa," he said, unperturbed, a smile twitching at the corners of his mouth, "there were no hospitals, and yet the Bantu peoples had lived here for fifty thousand years. How do you suppose they managed to flourish and develop such fine physical types? I'll tell you: In one way or the other they eliminated the unfit. That's what we shall do. That's what we *are* doing."

"You mean you are killing the sick!?" I was shocked in spite of myself. It seemed so monstrous.

He threw back his head and exposed his fine teeth in a hearty laugh when he saw the revulsion in our faces.

"I see you are still soft in spite of everything," he jeered. "Meet me tomorrow morning at ten o'clock on the verandah and I'll show you what the Black Internationale health service is doing for the health of Africa."

II

SURGEON GENERAL OF AFRICA REVEALS
HOW SICKNESS IS HANDLED

We arose early for newlyweds, but the brilliant African sun was well above the eastern hills when we came down to breakfast. The dining room was already filled with uniformed officials. Dr. Matson, immaculate as usual in his white uniform with gold buttons and epaulets, had already breakfasted and was engaged in earnest conversation with Ransom Just, a short, fat, light-brown man who had accomplished wonders as the radio technician of the Black Internationale. At Pat's suggestion we joined them. The two men rose, greeted us pleasantly and resumed their seats.

"We were just talking about the new installations," said Just, his round face reflecting his enthusiasm.

"What installations!" It was becoming bewildering, this matter of installations. Since the day we had taken control of Liberia there had been a continuous and feverish succession of installations: tray farms, sun power plants, airplane factories, new roads, lumber mills, mines, cotton mills, temples, steel mills and the thousand and one technical assets needed for the building of a great empire. Now Dr. Belsidus and his Black Brain Trust were driving ahead with the same program for all Africa.

"Better to show you than to tell you," said Rannie. "When you finish, we'll go over to the temple. You've got to go there anyway to see Andy's clinic."

"Who ever heard of a clinic in a church?" asked Pat, incredulous.

"Well, you know, I reminded her, "we're following the same system here that we did in America. The Temples of Love are the center of everything—schools, stores, recreation halls, beauty parlors, radio stations, and now, clinics. It's the Doctor's idea that religion being the most basic thing in life, the church should be the center of all activities."

"Let's go," said Andy. "I don't think you two have seen our temple here. I know you didn't get up in time for mass this morning."

"Mass? When did that start?" I hadn't heard about that."

"It's another one of Binks's ideas," he explained. "Sort of taking a leaf from the ancient Egyptians. Every temple now has services at sunrise and sunset, to greet the rising and sinking of the sun. Quite impressive ceremonies, too. Atheist that I am, I was really moved by the first mass I attended. It beats the Catholic ceremony all hollow. . . Well, let's get going."

We rose and walked out of the high-ceilinged room to the tiled corridor.

"We'll go this way." said Andy, pointing to a stairway by the underground passage. "I understand that every temple and surrounding buildings are connected by a labyrinth of underground passages. This one goes deep underground."

"What for, I can't see." Rannie remarked.

"You'll see quickly enough if there's ever an air raid," said Pat. "It's protection for our people in case of war. And you know we're likely to have to use them anytime."

We walked down the cement stairway two flights and found ourselves in another corridor which led to an elevator door. Andy pressed the button and the car came up. The door slid open and we entered. The car descended perhaps fifty feet, the door slid open and we found ourselves in a musty-smelling cement passageway, brilliantly lighted and scrupulously clean. We walked along this for about a thousand feet until we came to a heavy wooden door. Rannie pushed it open and we found ourselves in an immense room no less than six hundred feet square. The ceiling was about twenty feet high with a row of cement pillars every two hundred feet on which rested big long teakwood beams supporting the ceiling. The floor was smooth cement and the place was indirectly lighted. On the floor were six or eight pursuit planes and a big bombing plane, among them Pat's little black and gold pursuit plane in which we had flown up from Kakata. In the rear of the vast room was a well-appointed machine shop and several gasoline and oil pumps. In the front was a series of steel doors that rolled upward, permitting the planes to be rolled out to the big elevators that carried them to the airfield above. Several young men and women in overalls were huriedly at work on two big engines.

We walked across the room to a small elevator which automatically lifted us about forty feet.

"You see," said Pat a little proudly, for the underground hangars were her idea to protect our planes from bombing in case of air raids, "it will be almost impossible to destroy our ships from the air. The temples are always built immediately above the underground hangars. If a bomb strikes the temple it will of course collapse, but that will only further protect the hanger underneath."

"That's a clever wife you've got, Carl," said Andy.

"Humph! You telling me?"

The elevator came to a stop, the door slid open and we found ourselves in the retail service department unit, immediately under the temple and just above. Corridors ran in two directions with shops and offices opening on each. The hole place being air-conditioned was as cool as if it had been in Canada. Tropical clothing such as we wore made us positively chilly. The corridors were crowded with natives: Buzis, G'Bandes and Mandingoes wrapped in their striped cloths and gowns, waiting amid much jabbering to get into the big clinic that ran along one side of the main corridor next to the Turkish bath and tonsorial parlor.

"Come right on in folks," Andy invited. A stalwart black policeman opened the door of his office and we entered. It was plain, efficient, dean, with not a superfluous article. We sat down on a modernistic cream leather sofa while Dr. Matson changed to his surgeon's white duck uniform.

"This clinic," he explained, "is almost exactly like the thousands we are building throughout Africa. We have a staff of four or five specialists and six or eight nurses. Every person in the district is given a rigid physical examination. No one can refuse. They bathe in the shower room there before examination. If examination shows them to be incurable we give them something to end their sufferings."

Pat gasped audibly. Andy smiled.

"It seems so brutal," she complained.

"No, on the contrary, it's quite sensible and altogether humane. Incurable people are not only a drain on our all-too-meagre resources but they are a worry and strain on their relatives, and besides, they are often in constant pain. It is better to end it all and devote our time to those whom we can help."

He was ready now. An attendant gave each of us a long white cape and Andy led the way first into a long chamber lined on both sides with booths seven feet square, each with a small window. "Here is where we permanently cure arthritis, malaria, asthma. St Vitus dance, gonorrhea and syphilis. We are also getting pretty good results with certain mental diseases. I worked it out. We call it the leve box. Take a look inside."

We looked in the first booth. A young girl was lying completely nude on a low operating table sweating profusely.

"What's the idea?"

"Well, we blow in humid air, increasing its temperature until the patient's body is raised to fever heat, where we sustain it for a given period. We repeat it as long as necessary but after a few treatments the patient is cured. As you can see, we can handle fifty people at a time. Formerly we used short-wave radiation, but we found this method more effective and economical."

We walked through the long room peering here and there through the window of a booth. The nurses were hurrying about consulting thermometers. Doctors were busy in one end of the room with their examinations.

"We're working on an entirely new theory of medicine." Andy explained. "We never use drugs of any kind except when necessary, and that is seldom. Most physical disabilities are due to the inability of the body to throw off poisons or to combat deleterious germs because it has been improperly nourished and accordingly weakened. This is true of most dental, eye, lung and stomach trouble. Patients suffering from pellagra or other nutritional deficiency diseases are placed on a rigid diet of fresh, raw food tastily prepared. We permit no liquors; we have outlawed flour, rice, hominy and white sugar. Our dieticians have discovered ways of preparing uncooked foods quite as attractive and palatable as the old methods of preparation. Nothing that we ate at the hotel was cooked, and you notice that neither tea, coffee, liquor nor beer was served. This is now the rule in every district in the empire and is incorporated into the tenets of our religion. Of course, it is too soon to be able to say what the effect of this will be throughout Africa, but here in Liberia, where we've had much longer to work, we have virtually done away with sickness, with the result that the people are happier, more industrious and more productive, as our Department of Labor will testify."

"Well" said Pat, a little wistfully, "I like my pork chops occasionally, what harm does a good stew or baked ham do?"

"Application of fire to the delicate membrane and cell structure of plant and animal life destroys most if not all its nutritional value," the physician explained, "reducing its nutritional value from fifty to eighty-five percent. Introduction of this dead matter into the system imposes a burden upon the body which it is unable to perform, deprives the human cells of needed material for replacement, with the result that what we call sickness results. The weakened organism is unable to resist malignant germs and we have all the maladies with which we are familiar. Dr. Belsidus is in agreement that disease must be banished from Africa and that this drastic means is the best. Now come into the model diet kitchen and I'll show you how food is prepared by the new method."

We passed through an opaque glass door and entered the strangest kitchen I had ever seen.

III

Model Diet Kitchen Explained;
Dr. Matson Tells of Advantages

There was not a stove in the kitchen. Along one side was a long row of heavy wooden tables, each equipped with a number of electrical appliances. Along the other side were glass cases with coils of frost pipes inside, keeping the great pans of prepared food chilled. Men and women in spotless white were busily engaged preparing vegetables, meats and fruits for the next meal. The place was perfectly air-conditioned. with figured linoleum on the floor and occasional chairs and setters down the center of the room.

"We do not call these people cooks." Andy explained with a smile, "because they don't cook. We call them dietitians. As you know, this is where the students get their initial training before being assigned to other kitchens. Eventually we are hoping to have one of these kitchens in every district in Africa, utilizing the available supply of food."

We walked over to the nearest worktable. A young dark girl was cleaning and slicing some large fish. As she cut each slice she placed it in a large enamel pan where it was just covered with some liquid. Then she would dip into a big yellow bowl near at hand, take out a couple of slices of onion and place them on top of the fish. Then she would cut another slice.

"This is our method of preparing fish. Andy explained, nodding to the girl. "It is soaked overnight in lemon juice and onion. In the morning it will flake apart as if it had been cooked because the sharp acid of the lemon has that effect on the ligaments. In the morning she will take it out of the refrigerating room, place it in a squeezer to remove all the lemon juice, mix it with mayonnaise dressing and serve it on lettuce leaf. The soaking takes out the sharp fishy taste. We prepare most of our fish that way, although some is preserved in honey."

We moved on down the room. Next was a young man preparing fresh beef. We watched him with much interest. He put the meat in an electric grinder along with an occasional onion and green pepper. Then he poured into it a large cup of sauce made of lemon juice, honey, black pepper, chili powder, olive oil, cinnamon, nutmeg and sage in definite

GEORGE S. SCHUYLER

proportions, mixed it in a nearby electric dough mixer and then turned it into an oblong white enamel pan. It was pressed down securely with the hand until the pan was full. It was then turned upside down on a very large platter. Slices of tomato were placed along the side, with a row across the top lengthwise. Then he poured mayonnaise dressing into a canvas bag with a spout and made geometric designs across the dish of meat, the yellow contrasting pleasantly with the red and the occasional bits of green pepper. Chopped parsley was sprinkled over the top and the whole was ready for the chilling table.

"A dish like that is allowed to set for three or four hours," said Andy. "while the rich sauce permeates it. Then, as you will see at lunch, it is delicious."

At the next table was a young woman making layer cakes. She dumped raw cashew nuts into a grinder and they came out as a fine flour. This was mixed with honey, spices, cherry juice and flaked coconut to form a dough. It was rolled out to a thickness of a half inch, placed in a wooden platter and set in a nearby electric dryer which removed the excess moisture.

"Sometimes it is dried in the sun." the Surgeon General explained. "We use whichever method is most convenient, although sunshine is obviously superior since it adds to the nutritional value of the dish."

The young woman now ran washed raisins through a peanut butter machine and they came out as a paste. Whole wheat flour was added and a workable dough was secured. This was sprinkled with various spices and grated lemon peel and thoroughly mixed with powdered dried olive. It was rolled out and also put to dry. This operation was soon completed. She took the two layers out of the dryer and placed them one on the other with a layer of finely sliced mango alternating between slices until the whole was about five inches high. Then whipped cream was spread on top and the girl defily placed halves of large sliced strawberries in an attractive design. She bore the cake away proudly to the pantry in the rear.

"Well, Doc," I said, after we had inspected a number of tables and watched preparation of salads, ice cream, desserts, fowl and refreshing drinks, "this is all very interesting, but you know very well that efficacious as all this may be, you cannot expect people to change the dietary habits of a lifetime."

"Ah, but they will, Carl," he replied. "It is always much easier to eat food that is prepared for you than to prepare it yourself. The whole plan of African life of the future will center around the temple. Here will not only be the recreation of the community but the dining hall as well. This will relieve women from the drudgery of cookery and free them to take up other pursuits if they wish. Then, too, we are giving the people something unknown in modern civilization."

"What's that?" asked Pat, suddenly breaking a long silence.

"Through our educational system which also centers in the temples we are disseminating the truth about disease. You know that in the past, doctors have made the matter of life and death rather more mysterious than it really is. We are simplifying the whole thing by telling the truth as we see and know it, and showing them the relation of diet to health. This is something new. We can do it because we have no cliques with a vested interest in selling injurious food and drugs to the people. We can do it because we who have Africa's health in our care find it more profitable to keep people well than sick. We are building here a rational society."

"Well," said Ransom Just, "the folks down at Kakata are eating pretty much as they please."

"The officials, yes." Andy admitted, "but that won't be for long. Dr. Belsidus is in agreement with me on this program. As we establish our setups in each locality and erect a temple, there we shall have a clinic, a kitchen and all the things you see here. And we shall feed the people in our communal kitchens. The marvelous physique of the Africa where they have not come into contact with white people is due large to their superior nutrition. Even where and when they cooked their food, it was fresh food, not preserved food. We in the Western world have preserved food. We in the Western world have been reared dead food, embalmed food. Here we are going to feed our population on fresh food."

"But, Doctor," said my wife. "how are you going to keep food without canning it or something?"

"Canning is really old fashioned and unnecessary today. Let's go in the rear. I'll show you what we do." He led the way out of the stoveless kitchen. We entered a corridor which we crossed with the doctor in the van and came to an elevator which dropped us perhaps live or six stories farther under the ground.

We stepped out into a small room. Dr. Matson pointed to a window in a door opposite the elevator. We walked over and looked in. It was an extensive warehouse. In crates, bins and boxes were a profusion of the fruits, vegetables and meats of Liberia. A gray haze seemed to hang over the place. I mentioned it to Andy.

"You see," he explained. "it has been recently discovered that by quickly freezing food seventy-five or one hundred degrees below zero, it can be kept fresh indefinitely. Under the circumstances, it is unnecessary to rid it of three-quarters of its value by canning or otherwise preserving it. There will soon be one of these storehouses far beneath every temple. And as you've probably guessed, we're even down beneath the underground hangar. Our food supply is well protected. With one of these in every district and the natural fertility of the soil, we shall have sufficient food to withstand any drought or siege. We're building for the centuries here, Slater."

"Yes, so I see and I'm mighty glad, Doc, to get this close-up of what you are doing. Down there at Kakata we've been so busy we haven't had much time to keep track of your achievements. But tell me, what are these installations you and Just were talking about before we came out of the dining room?"

"It's about time I had a chance to show you what I'm doing." said the radio engineer. "Get back on this car. I want to show you something up above that is making educational systems as we have known them unnecessary and ditto for the newspapers. We're not ushing up with the white man anymore, we're surpassing him. Come on!"

We piled into the elevator again. The Surgeon General pressed a button and we were on our way to the Ziggeta radio and television station designed to make Africa a cultural unit.

IV

BLACK EMPIRE HAS RADIO AND TELEVISION STATION WHICH IS FINEST IN THE WORLD

We got out of the elevator on the clinic level and, with Rannie fest in the lead, we walked down the broad corridor to a small door. The radio engineer unlocked it and we entered. Dr. Matson switched on the light. We were on the platform at the beginning of a small tunnel in which was laid a narrow-gauge track. Nearby was a small electric car with four rows of seats but no top.

"Get in," said Rannie, waving to the vehicle. "We're going to give you something to lift your eyebrows about."

"Where are we going?"

"Right under the mountain," said Dr. Matson, seating himself in the from seat alongside the engineer. When we were all placed comfortably in the upholstered seats, Rannie Just pulled the lever and the little car sped straight ahead into the well-lighted tunnel which was only about eight feet in diameter. At intervals there were recesses in the cement wall where, Dr. Matson explained, workmen could stand out of the way of the car when they heard it approaching.

When we had gone about a half mile, we came to the end of the line and piled out on a cement platform. Rannie Just pressed a button alongside a heavy wooden door. In about fifteen seconds the door slid aside and we entered a small cage. The door closed, a button was pressed and we shot upward for about three minutes without a pause. Then the elevator stopped, the door slid open and we walked out into bright sun light. We were standing on a curved balcony of cement work with broad windows through which the hot Liberian sun poured relentlessly, and yet we immediately noted that it was much cooler here than it had been at the hotel.

"Where in the world are we?" asked Pat, as we walked over to the windows. For answer Dr. Matson merely pointed out and down.

It was a magnificent view. We could see for the more than one hundred and fifty miles to the ocean across the great expanse of hills and jungles, a vast carpet. of tropic green. Here and there a column of smoke issuing from the verdure marked a village. Far below us on the side of the mountain stood the trim little hotel and to one side and at the foot of the mountain stood the great Temple of Love with its gray domed roof with a broad balustraded ledge. In front of it a great expanse had been cleared as an airfield, and even as we watched a little black and gold pursuit plane came zooming out of a yawning opening in the ground, catapulted from the platform above the subterranean hangar, and flew off in the direction of the sea.

Near the temple we noted many other buildings we had not yet visited and about ten miles away we could see the gray roof of our new electric steel plant which Al Fortune, our engineer, Sanford Mates, our architect, and Gustave Linke, our metallurgist, had rushed to completion just the week previously.

"We're nine thousand feet up." said Dr. Matson, lighting up a cigarette, "and approximately four thousand feet above the temple."

"Well, what's the idea? Observation post?" I was curious.

It seemed a waste of valuable material to go to the trouble and expense of building a tunnel, an elevator shaft and this formidable structure on the peak of the mountain merely for such a purpose.

Little Rannie Just's rotund face took on a look of outraged astonishment.

"Why, this is our radio and television station!" he almost shouted. "We get excellent results here because we're so high. This is probably the highest station in the world. We can send and receive to and from the ends of the earth by short wave. Come on, I'll show you a thing or two."

We followed him down the balcony, enjoying his enthusiasm amazed by curiosity also. Television to us was but a name. We knew nothing about it, had never seen it, but we knew that even in England and America it was in its swaddling clothes. My respect for Rannie knowledge rose higher than ever when I realized that this Negro was doubtless in advance of all the white radio engineers in the world.

Finally we walked off the to a flat yard leveled right on the up of the mountain next to the concrete radio station, whose two lofty steel towers pointed like gaunt fingers into the blue. The level space covered about three acres. An acre was taken up with a small house, in which dynamos hummed. This place had a flat roof on such were scores of Al Fortune's unique sun-power machines. They wondered the entire roof of perhaps fifty by one hundred feet, and resembled futuristic anti-aircraft guns or Brobdingnagian mosquitoes. they were troughs about five inches deep and ten feet long, lined with polished aluminum and set on legs so that they inclined at an angle of forty-five degrees. In back of the higher end was a cylindrical water pump, and at the lower end, a small engine. From the engines steam pipes ran into the powerhouse, where the steam power was converted into electricity. Two young black engineers in faded overalls were moving among the machines, checking their performance.

"You're probably more familiar with how these things work than I Carl," said Rannie, "and if you don't know everything, ask those beys over there. They're Al's proteges."

They were almost exactly like the machines I had studied at the chemical farm in New Jersey. The sunlight was caught on the highly ped surface of the aluminum, which was so curved as to focus the rays on a long tube resembling a thermos bottle, made of Pyrex glass with an inside diameter of one-half inch and an outside diameter of one and one-quarter inches, and called the "focus" tube. Within the focus tube was a miniature flash boiler of the type used in old-fashioned steam automobiles. It was a steel tube one-half inch in diameter made of the highest-grade steel, thin-walled but strong enough to resist pressure of steam up to two hundred pounds per square inch. The steel tube slipped into the Pyrex glass tube, which was jacketed by vacuum and was painted with lampblack so as to absorb ninety-five percent of the sun's rays that fell upon it after passing the focus tube. Inside the steel tube was third tube known as the water tube, only an eighth of an inch in diameter, and joined along its entire length by four copper wings, fastened with high-melting point solder to the inside of the steel tube The supply of water to the tube was automatically regulated by the meter in the rear.

The four copper wings were fine conductors of heat, enabling the heat produced by the absorption of solar rays in the lampblack on the outer surface of the steel tube to penetrate with the utmost facility to vaporize the water. In this way it was possible to get power for nothing beyond the cost of manufacturing the engines. Each produced steam: at the desired pressure of one hundred and seventy-five pounds to the square inch. Each machine produced four horsepower and there were one hundred machines on the roof.

Next to the powerhouse stood three big silos insulated with "glass wool and filled with sand. As the sun machine could only function while the sun was shining, these silos were used to store up heat at extremely high temperatures and could retain it almost without loss for years. Thus, whether some days were short or cloudy did not matter,

GEORGE S. SCHUYLER

Steam was always available, and thus electricity was always available I noticed there were a score of the machines on top of the radio station.

"The sun is our greatest asset," observed Dr. Matson, pointing to the burning disk in the cloudless blue sky.

"Yes, I agreed, "it frees us from dependence upon coal and oil, and without those two products no modern nation can become great. There's no place in the world that has more sunshine than Africa and the supply is inexhaustible and eternal."

THE REMAINING SPACE ATOP THE mountain was laid out with lawn, shrubbery and benches, but two canvas-covered anti-aircraft guns added a grim note which quickly brought one's mind back to hard reality. We followed Rannie and Andy to the balcony from whence we had issued and entered a room of strange, gleaming, futuristic camera-like machines. The place was hung with black velvet draperies and was powerfully lighted from every direction.

"Sit over there, all of you," Just directed, bustling with importance. We went over to a long sofa on a slightly raised platform. Just went over and spoke to his three assistants manning the apparatus. Then he took his position nearby at an instrument board.

"Now," he said, "we'll get in touch with the Chief. Watch that mirror." He pointed to a glass screen four feet square which was set in the all about four yards from us.

Switches were turned and machinery began to hum. The powerful point of cold light played over us like sunshine pouring through the lattice work of forest leaves. Just's voice droned, "Calling ZXQ2R, calling ZXQ2R. Dr. Belsidus, please. Calling ZXQ2R, Dr. Belsidus, please. Yes MXQ2R calling Ransom Just. Yes, yes. Come in, ZXQ2R. Alright. Go ahead!"

V

IT's WAR AGAIN! ITALY AND FRANCE
STRIKE TO DESTROY BLACK EMPIRE

There was a click and a hum. An image began to take form on the glass screen in front of us. Gradually it grew more distinct.

"More juice," yelled Rannie, frowning and waving his hand at his assistants, who leaped to obey.

Now we could plainly see Dr. Belsidus, in spotless white, seated at his broad flat desk in the capitol at Kakata. He looked up and gave one of his rare smiles.

"Well, are you newlyweds enjoying your honeymoon?" he asked. His voice came to us as clearly as if he had been sitting in the room.

"Oh, yes," said Pat, pressing my hand as she spoke.

"That's good," he remarked. "Have a good time because I'm likely to be calling you back any day."

"Is that so?" The news gave me a sinking feeling. I had hoped to get a long and happy rest.

"What's wrong, Chief?"

"The white nations have patched up their differences," he said, gravely. "We may expect an attack at anytime. I know we'll lose North Africa and probably Egypt, but we must hold the rest. At any rate they haven't attacked yet. There is still a breathing spell to get ready. I don't need you two now, but maybe pretty soon. I know you'll come when I call."

"We'll come right now, Doctor," said Pat, "if you want us."

"No have your fun," he insisted with a faint preoccupied smile, "probably the last you'll have in a long time. Goodbye."

"Goodbye Chief."

There was another click. The current died and the image vanished.

"Well, what do you think of it?" asked Rannie, eager for compliments. We both assured him it was wonderful, and we weren't being untruthful.

"The best they can do in America." he boasted, "is to send about twenty miles. We can send and receive from any point between Cairo and the Cape. Boy, we're teaching the white folks something. We've got twenty of these machines placed already. All I've got to do is turn the knob and I can talk to our men in Dakar, Takoradi, Lourenco Marques,

Tananarive, Cairo, Casablanca, Zanzibar, Stanleyville, Addis Ababa Nairobi and a number of other points. Later we're going to send over plays and concerts and lectures. All Africa will soon be able to not only hear but see us."

"How did you get it set up so quickly?"

"Why don't you ask your wife?" he chided. "Her boys flew the parts and the mechanics to the various points. The stuff was delivered inside of two days."

"Yes," Pat interrupted, "and it would have been delivered in one day if you'd had all of it at the airfield like you promised."

"Alright. Alright." he said. "I'll do better next time."

"You're making pretty good progress on these communications, Rannie." I said.

"Pretty good?" he echoed. "Say, brother, there's nothing like this been done before. And what you saw isn't all. We have a sending and receiving station in everyone of our five hundred temples, and it's some job keeping them in running order, especially when we're working often with green hands. But just give us another month and we'll be delivering newspapers every morning to every part of the continent."

"How? With airplanes?"

"No, by wireless," he said, enjoying my incredulity. "Let's show him something, boys

He walked over to the other side of the studio and we followed him wondering what was up. He stopped in front of a large cabinet radio on top of which sat a large box with a slit in it like a mailbox.

"This is the receiver," he explained, "through which we receive the facsimile newspaper. Inside is a photoelectric cell. The basis of the system is the impulses similar to those that make possible the sending of dots and dashes of the Morse code. The receiver is connected to the wires of the loud speaker. The attachment is set in operation by the electrical energy supplied by the receiver and is connected to the wires that change that energy into mechanical energy, which prints the reproduction of the picture or reading matter broadcast. Watch closely, now and you'll see. Alright, boys. Call Kakata."

Switches were thrown and again the machinery hummed. Rannie stood in front of the glass screen, the points of light playing over his figure. The assistant's voice droned out the call letters. A figure on the screen took form. It was one of the radio engineers I had seen about the capitol building at Kakata.

"Hello, Jake," said Rannie.

"Goodmorning. Mr. Just. Do you want something?"

"Yes. I wish you'd send over the first page of some pamphlet. I'm showing Mr. Slater how the machine works."

"Yes sir. Right away, sir."

The image faded. Rannie came over to the radio set again.

"Now, watch that slit," he directed.

A light flashed on the inside of the box and wheels began to turn. Suddenly the edge of a piece of white paper protruded from the slit. Then more and more came out, seemingly a sixteenth of an inch at a time. There was printing on it. In five minutes a large nine-by-twelve inch section was torn off and presented to us, as Rannie stopped the machine. It was one of the propaganda pamphlets we had scattered over Africa, an exact facsimile.

"We've just started experimenting on this," he explained, "and it's working perfectly. I'm already arranging for mass production of these, and as soon as they come out of the factory we'll fly them to the various temples. You know the Chief is nuts about communication."

"Yes, and about everything else, if you ask me." Andy added, speaking for the first time. "But let's get going. I've got to fly down to Kakata."

He led the way out of the radio-television station to the balcony. After one look at the magnificent panorama from the nine thousand-foot level, we entered the elevator, descended to the tunnel, boarded the electric car and were soon back under the temple. From there we walked back through the underground passage to the hotel. As we strode along, Dr. Mason talked.

"You know," he said, "our aim is to have a duplicate of this setup in each one of the live hundred departments into which Dr. Belsidus is dividing the continent. Each department will just be about the right size twenty thousand square miles, twice the size of the American state of Maryland."

"They won't all have the same number of people, though, will they?" asked Pat who had flown over so much of Africa during the recent campaign.

"No, of course not, Andy continued. "Some of them will almost be without population, especially in the desert areas, but Alton Fortune and Sanford Mates were telling me of a plan they're working out to place surplus population in the Sahara."

"But that would be suicidal," I objected. "There's absolutely nothing up there but sand."

"Nevertheless, they've already established one artificial oasis, as they call in. Al is at the hotel now. Why don't you have him show you what they're doing up there. It's right near Timbuctoo. You can get there in five hours in Pat's plane."

"Maybe we shall."

We entered an elevator and a minute later stepped out in the corridor of the hotel. We had gone a mile from the place and a mile up in the air, yet had only been above ground once, when we visited with Al Fortune.

We had lunch, as Andy suggested, with Al Fortune. Power and authority hadn't changed the short, plump, reddish brown engineer very much. He was still the bitter anti-white fellow he'd been when he was directing Dr. Besidus's robber band at night and experimenting with chemical farming in New Jersey by day.

"Sure, I be glad to have you come up tomorrow," he said, as we sat down to the meal of strange but tasty and nutritious dishes, "but we haven't any suitable quarters yet. Sam Hamilton spends a lot of time up there puttering around. It's going to be a bigger farm than we had in New Jersey. We struck plenty of water when we got down two thousand feet."

"Water in the desert? Come, come, Al." It seemed incredible.

A gong sounded insistently. A hundred conversations died. Then the familiar voice of Dr. Belsidus came over the loudspeaker.

"I want all executives to return to Kakata this evening. Conference at five o'clock. Europe has started its war to recapture Africa. The Italians bombed and took Tripoli an hour ago. A French air squadron has flown over Tunis demanding surrender and we may expect the British to strike at anytime. Patricia Givens, General McNeel and Carl Slater return immediately. That is all."

We sat in stunned silence for a full half minute before chairs scraped ed the buzz of voices filled the dining room.

"Well," said Pat, rising, her face grim, "let's go."

VI

Dr. Belsidus Undisturbed as White Nations Sweep Forward to Recapture Black Empire; Has Plan to Make Enemy Fight His Way!

There was a rush for the door. Pat and I hurried to our suite, threw our clothing into our bags and ran downstairs to the underground corridor that led to the hangar. Close behind us was General Barton McNeel, tall, gray-haired and very dark, a distinguished. thoughtful man, veteran of two American wars who had led our forces to victory in the recent campaign which cleared the white people out of Africa. I had never seen him excited, even under fire that night when we landed in Monrovia. But now it seemed that he had lost just a little of his calm. He was more grim and tense than I had ever seen him.

The motor was already roaring as we entered the subterranean hangar, and hurriedly climbed in. I sat next to Pat while General McNeel took the remaining seat in the rear. Pat gave the mechanic the signal, the blocks were taken from under the wheels, and the ground men pushed the little fighter slowly forward until it was clear of the hangar and on the catapult outside. The door of the hangar rolled shut and the steel cover over the catapult was rolled swiftly aside. Then, with the motor making a deafening noise, we were suddenly flung upward like a jack-in-the-box, out into the sunshine and sent tearing through the hot afternoon to Kakata.

I glanced back at General McNeel. He was looking thoughtfully at the gray roof of the electric steel plant, operated by sun power, which had only last week been completed. I knew exactly how he felt because I felt the same way. We had schemed, sacrificed, risked our lives to free Africa and build a powerful empire that would make black men and women forever honored and respected. We had tasted the cup of victory. We had seen the white men run off the continent and black men triumphant from Cairo to the Cape. We had hope for peace, for time to build here on the bosom of Mother Africa a great united land—one people, one soul, one destiny. We had hoped to build here a haven for all those wearing the burnished livery of the sun, who wearied of battling discrimination and segregation, disfranchisement and perpetual insult in alien lands and yearned for a place of rest. We had hoped, now that we were able to hold up our heads with the free people of the earth, to be able to demonstrate here the genius of the black people in the pursuits of peace.

But we all knew now that it had been but a dream, an ambitious hope, an idle fancy. Yes, we all knew it. I could see it in the look of tired resignation in McNeel's face, in the grim intensity of Pat, as she strained her eyes for the towers and smoking chimneys of the new capital of Kakata.

I looked below me at the verdant land glistening with numerous little square patches of water that indicated the chemical farms already feeding half of Africa. All this might be destroyed, I thought. And then, strangely enough, I thought of Dr. Belsidus. What would he do now?

Pat brought us down without a jar in a perfect three-point landing on the great airfield at Kakata. The three of us hurried over to the two-story, mission-style concrete block with stucco finish where the business of the African empire was transacted. We went up the wide double staircase that curved to the second floor and made our way hastily to the Doctor's spacious office. A uniformed attendant halted us respectfully, bowing.

"The Doctor says to come to his apartment, sir," the man told us.

That in itself was unusual. In New York Dr. Belsidus has almost always received those of us who were very close to him in the privacy of bis apartment to talk over matters of state. But since establishing the Kakata capital, he had taken to meeting with us in the conference room, due to the vast increase in the number of executives.

Another uniformed attendant stood outside the apartment door. He bowed low as we approached, then saluted General McNeel. Turning to one side, he spoke into the mouthpiece of the communicating telephone at his side.

"Pardon me, sir." he said, "but General McNeel, Mr. Slater, and Commander Givens have arrived."

"Let them in," said a familiar voice.

The man swung the door open and we entered the Doctor's black and gold apartment. The floor was of red glass. The walls and ceiling were dull black. A great chandelier of gold and cut glass and ornamental wall lamps fashioned into exotic gold figures shed illumination upon the scene of somber magnificence.

In the exact center of the long wall opposite the door was the spacious regal bed. It was around eighteen inches high with a gorgeous cloth of gold spread on it. At the head a startling canopy of highly polished mahogany enginged with gold curved over the bed like a protective shell. In the ceiling of this canopy were mirrors that showed the bed below. At intervals along the walls were fragile-looking gilded chairs with yellow satin seats. On the wall on each side of the bed were life-size paintings of beautifully formed nude girls. The picture to the right depicted a dark reddish brown African girl, an incomparable figure against a background of exotic green jungle. On the left was a young white girl reclining invitingly on a large red couch. On the wall opposite were three other life-size paintings showing Chinese, Navajo and Hawaiian beauties. The five beautiful paintings were illuminated by indirect floodlights. There were no windows in the apartment. It was air-conditioned like the entire building and Dr. Belsidus considered windows distracting and unnecessary in a chamber to which he repaired only when he was through temporarily with the outside world and sought absolute privacy.

We saw him as soon as we entered, lying high up in the bed, dressed in purple and white pajamas and nonchalantly smoking one of his special cigarettes six inches in length in a holder equally as long. He didn't seem at all perturbed.

"You made good time," he said, waving us to the chairs an attendant had brought and ordering refreshments. As the man walked away on his errand, the Doctor shouted after him, "Tell Portabla to come in." The attendant bowed assent.

I looked at Pat, frankly puzzled. I knew of no one by that name with whom Dr. Belsidus was intimate enough to call to his private apartment. I could see that she knew nothing about him either. Nor did General McNeel, from the looks of his face.

We didn't have long to wait. In a few moments the door opened and the flunky bowed and brought in a skinny black man with an ungainly stride, long arms and eyes that seemed sunk far into his head but which glowed like those of a person possessed.

"You call for me, Doktor?" he asked with heavy Latin pronunciation.

"Yes, Vincente, I want you to meet Commander Patricia Givens, head of our air force, General McNeel, Commander-in-Chief of our armed forces, and Carl Slater, my secretary. Friends, this is Vincente Portabla, formerly professor of physics at the University of Rio de Janeiro and exchange professor at the Lenin Institute in Moscow. He has come down to help us."

Prof. Portabla bowed low. It made him seem comical because of his awkwardness. He mumbled a few words and then lapsed into silence, brooding with a vacant stare like some zombie. I wondered what on earth Dr. Belsidus was going to do with this fellow. It wasn't professors we needed now, it was munitions of war.

We all sipped our drinks in silence. Once or twice I stole a glance at the Doctor. He was resting as easily as though he hadn't a care in the whole world. Although I knew his inactivity belied his inner feelings. personally I couldn't help but fume within. Precious moments, minutes, hours were being lost while he dawdled.

Tripoli had fallen. French war planes had demanded the surrender of Tunis. Doubtless the British fleet was even now plowing the sea to its African colonies and protectorates. And what did we have to combat such a mighty force? Four or five hundred planes, a hundred pieces of field artillery, a few score anti-aircraft guns, a few thousand veterans and millions of black men and women who were willing enough to fight for Africa but for whom we had not nearly enough firearms. We had done our best but we hadn't had time to prepare properly. The whites knew this, I supposed, which was why they were attacking now, before we became strong.

"We can only be defeated," said Dr. Belsidus, "if we fight the white people their way, and with all the advantages on their side. I intend to make them fight my way, with all the advantages on my side."

"And may I ask, Doctor." I inquired, "how that is to be done?"

"In just a few moments," he said, "you will see, my boy, you will see."

VII

Dr. Belsidus Prepares to Meet Invading Forces of England, France, Germany and Italy with a Strange and Deadly Army

P at," he asked turning to my wife, "how many of those new stratosphere planes have we now?"

"Torlier had fifteen just before I left for Ziggeta, Chief."

"What is their non-stop range?"

"Six thousand miles. You see, once we get to the ten-mile level, our consumption of gasoline is cut almost in half. But of course we'd need almost all our space for gas, Chief. We wouldn't be able to carry any bombs."

He smiled that cruel, sardonic smile that I had seen so many times before when some devilish idea intrigued him.

"I do not want you to carry any bombs," he said. "I want you to carry something much lighter but much more dangerous."

"More dangerous than a bomb?" she asked surprise in her tone.

"Much more dangerous," he said. "After all, air bombs do not win wars. Look at the examples of Madrid and Shanghai. They continued to be held even after repeated heavy attacks from the air. No, my dear, what I have in mind is far more dangerous than bombs."

The Doctor sat up and spread out on the table a large map of Africa which had been rolled up alongside his bed.

"The effective enemies of Africa," he said, "are England, Italy, France and Germany. Our job is to prevent them from taking Africa. McNeel what have you mapped out to combat this invasion?"

The General's solemn face grew stemmer. He looked down into his drink, then turned the glass around two or three times in his large capable hands.

Finally he spoke in his usual slow measured tones. "We have our strategy for such an eventuality as this, of course, but frankly I doubt that it can be very effective. At the moment I cannot see how we can prevent them from taking the entire coast. We have less than five hundred planes. And any one of the airplane carriers of England, France, Italy or Germany carries that many. We have an insufficient supply of gasoline to last through a long war, and our South African plant for extracting gasoline out of coal will not be completed for a few months. We have only a hundred field guns of various sizes, and that is nothing to use against even a second-rate power. We have a million rifles, ample stores of small arms ammunition and thousands of machine guns. That's a wonderful showing for the short time we have had our plants in operation. But frankly, Chief, it couldn't last long in the face of such opposition as we have now. We can bomb battleships, troopships, and landing parties, but we can only do it as long as we have control of the air."

"And that won't be long," added Pat. "I'm afraid we couldn't take it long, Chief."

All the time Dr. Belsidus was poring over the map, using an architect's compass to measure distances. It was plain that he was paying very little attention to General Barton McNeel. Finally he looked up with the same sardonic smirk on his handsome

"So you think we're washed up, eh?" he inquired, cutting his eye at the General.

"Well," McNeel hesitated, "of course, Africa's a big place. We have the advantage of tremendous distances. They could only take the coast. We could really last for years in the interior, especially now that we've armed the masses. But we are woefully deficient, sir, in the things with which war is made, and while we are acquiring rapidly the means of supplying them, we just haven't got time, what with the enemy already in possession of Tripoli and on his way to take the rest."

"Yes, I understand. It's not your fault or anybody's fault. We just didn't have time. But in spite of that we have a good chance to stop them."

The three of us could not conceal our surprise, but Prof. Portabla remained imperturbable, as if nothing in the world mattered.

"Stop them how, Chief?" I asked, eager to learn what he had in mind.

"By the same means that we conquered this continent, Carl," he replied grimly, "by using our brains. No matter what the white man's got, black men have the brains to duplicate it, improve upon it or originate mething entirely different. The latter, my friends, must be our course."

"Yes," objected the General, "but we haven't time to originate an thing now, Chief. The enemy is upon us."

"That's alright," he scoffed. "They'll soon get off us. I have not been idle. I anticipated this move of the white powers. That is why I sent for Professor Portabla."

He clapped his hands and a flunky hurried to the bedside. "Bring my clothes, boy," he ordered. Then, turning to Pat, "Commander, I want you to prepare your fifteen stratosphere planes at once with your best pilots, navigators and radio men. We cannot have any mistakes. McNeel, you and Slater and Portabla come with me."

Pat hurried out to get ready. We lingered while Dr. Belsidus dressed. Finally he was ready. We all went down to the entrance of the building where we got into an official car and were whirled to an obscure. concrete building about a mile away. The building was not over twelve feet high. It was completely surrounded by a ten-foot moat filled with water, and around the moat was a fifteen-foot, close-mesh wire fence. A sign on it read, "Danger. Charged wire." I had never had much curiosity about the building. There were hundreds of such structures scattered found Kakata. One couldn't keep track of all of them. Yet it struck me that I remembered seeing Dr. Belsidus entering the place once or twice.

We got out of the car. Dr. Belsidus warned the uniformed chauffeur to wait. We walked to the gate. An attendant admitted us. He pressed a button and a drawbridge lowered from in front of the door of the concrete building. With Dr. Belsidus in the lead, we walked across. He pressed a button alongside the door. It creaked open swloly and a pair of inquisitive eyes studied us from the dark interior. Then the door was swung open and we all entered as the uniformed attendant stood to one side.

"This is my experiment room," the Chief explained, turning to the right and walking up a flight of six steps. We went through a short hallway to a thick glass door that looked over the entire floor below, with the exception of one corner which was partitioned off with shatter-proof glass. Around the sides of the long room ran a balcony about six feet below the low ceiling.

"Come on out," the Doctor invited. We followed him and there below us on the floor of the vast room were at least fifty large cages about ten feet square and two feet high. Each cage was swarming with rats. We gazed at the scene amazed, incredulous.

What new madness was this? Here with the enemy upon us, Dr. Belsidus was taking us to see his rats. Was the man mad?

"There are close to a thousand in each cage. They shall serve us well, the little dears." He chuckled diabolically. Then he stepped back, turned and shouted to the attendant at the door. "Hey, Kandie! Telephone the garage for fifteen open trucks at once, a derrick and about ten men."

For the first time now Prof. Portabla opened his mouth. "What ees thees rats for? Why do you keep them?"

"For an emergency like this," said the Chief. "I knew this would be forthcoming. I prepared. I told no one, not even you, Carl. You will observe that each cage has a large sign attached to it. It seems meaningless because the letters don't seem to make sense. But don't be fooled. I have been preparing for this for a long time. That sign marked C means cholera. The one marked ST means spotted typhus. The one marked BP means bubonic plague, and so on. It has taken hard work, doing this in spare time with almost no assistance, but now we are practically ready."

"I don't follow you, Chief," I said.

"Ah, but you will, my boy, you will." Then, hearing the sound of the trucks outside the most, he roared. "Good," and began to direct the men.

"Open that front door wide enough to get those cages out, hear? And be sure and don't let one of those rats bite you or it will be your finish."

We went downstairs and out front to watch the operations. The front had been swung back until the doorway was about twelve feet wide. Soon the laborers were bringing the cages out and placing them on the trucks with much growling and cursing. One by one they came out until the fifteen trucks were loaded and the last had chugged away. Then Dr. Belsidus led us back to our limousine and we were sped to the airfield.

Already lined up on the field were the torpedo-like stratosphere planes. Piled on one side of each plane were a score of wire cages about two feet square. Alongside each pile of cages stood one of the trucks from the laboratory with its strange squealing burden.

The attendants grouped around each plane stood at attention as the Doctor hurried over, shouting orders. "Get those rats in those smaller cages. Be careful now. Don't let any get away and don't let any of them bite you."

It took about an hour to get the rats from the huge cages to the little ones, and then to transfer the little cages to the airplanes. We all watched the operation with great curiosity. We didn't yet know what Dr. Belsidus had up his sleeve. Then he called to Pat.

"While you were gone," he told her. "I increased the supply of gasoline at Fez one hundred percent. You will fly your planes there at once, as soon as those cages of rats have been loaded on, and refuel. Here are sealed instructions. Get going. I expect you to succeed. It means everything."

VIII

BLACK EMPIRE'S NEW STRATOSPHERE PLANES TAKE OFF ON EPOCHAL FLIGHT, SET TO INVADE EUROPEAN COUNTRIES

Pat paused a moment as if undecided, looking first at me and then at Dr. Belsidus.

"Well, what's the matter?" he snapped, frowning, "Hadn't you better get going?

"Chief," she began, her eyes softening. "I know it's a silly request when there is so much to be done and so few of us to direct it, but cannot Carl go along with me as. . . er. . . well, as a sort of observer. We haven't been together much you know, and. . ."

"It's no time for sentiment," he snapped, "but I suppose I'll have to let you do it. Go ahead, Slater, if you want to go, but hurry up. Every minute counts. Return immediately to Fez when you have completed your task. I'll wire you special instructions to Fez, Slater."

Pat was radiant. As for me. I was much surprised because I had not dreamed of accompanying the raiders. She took her place at the controls and I got in beside her. I looked back in the cabin and there was young Tom Hudginson, black and handsome as ever, who had been our navigator on the flight from Texas to Sierra Leone. I felt sure we would reach whatever destination we were directed to with him doing the navigating.

We closed our cowling, sealed all openings and were ready for the flight. It was a magnificent sight to see the fifteen bullet-like trimotor. planes lined up with their propellers whirring for the getaway. It was three-fifteen exactly.

"Alright, Number One," Pat shouted into her mouthpiece.

The huge black and gold ship on the extreme right streaked down the field; climbing rapidly into the blue. The other ships followed one by one until we were all aloft. Although I had been in many planes, I had never seen any climb so rapidly and at such a steep angle. Our altitude meter registered in succession: one thousand, two thousand, three thousand and four thousand feet. But this seemed only a beginning. We went on and on. At twenty thousand feet we were far above the clouds in a lonely, spaceless world accompanied only by our fourteen companions now in perfect "V" formation. Hudginson was kept busy correcting our course.

"Turn on your oxygen." commanded Pat. "The air's getting thin." She turned from her mouthpiece and glanced at me, then she pointed at the valve she had previously indicated. I turned it.

A hiss of air penetrated the thunder of the motors. I immediately began to feel better, more refreshed, more buoyant as the precious air filled the cabin. I had begun to feel dull and sleepy as the air became thinner.

We continued to climb. We were up fifty thousand feet before Pat gave the command to flatten out. Our speed in this rarefied atmosphere was three hundred and twenty-five miles an hour, but because of the thinness of the air, gasoline consumption was far less than an uninformed person would have imagined. The rareness of the atmosphere made the air resistance negligible.

I looked at the clock in the instrument board. It was exactly six-forty-five. We had gone one thousand of the sixteen hundred miles from Kakata to Pez. Tom Hudginson corrected our course again and Pat shouted orders for the dive for Fez when she gave the signal.

On we went, literally flashing through the air now, ten miles above the earth. The sun had disappeared; it was almost black dark. Pat watched carefully now for the wing lights of neighboring planes, while she shouted cryptic orders over the radio. It was ticklish business, this blind flying ten miles aloft with no earth in view, but the first brilliant stars were appearing out of the void above.

In another hour we had covered nearly four hundred miles. Pat called to the other ships. We had two hundred miles to go. "Down to forty thousand," she commanded. We could see the lights of the other ships dip as they dove for the new level. Ten minutes later she cried, "Down to thirty thousand. After a similar interval, she gave the command, "Down to twenty." Then, turning to the intercommunicating telephone, she called Hudginson: "How are we doing, Tom?"

The navigator paused and consulted his instruments for a moment; I listened in to the conversation with my headset.

"We're due to be about ten miles due south of the Fez airfield," he said.

"Prepare to land," she commanded the others, switching to the radio mouthpiece. "In order: Number One first on the extreme right of the field."

In a second or two she began calling the airport. "Hello, Fez! Hello, Fez! B.I. Stratosphere Squadron landing. Yes, alright. Fez. Coming down."

We dipped sharply. Below, a square of brilliant light shone where floodlights played on the airfield. It shot up to meet us. We were landing fast. There were already four of our planes on the ground with another descending. We crossed the field twice before it was our turn, then came down to a perfect three-point landing. The other planes followed suit.

The field was surrounded by mounted troops keeping the Moorish populace back. A black official drove up with eight limousines to take us to headquarters. He and the others saluted admiringly as Pat stepped down from the cockpit. Negro mechanics swarmed over the giant machines while great gasoline trucks drew up alongside them to fill up the tanks and replenish the supply of oil.

At the airport headquarters a half mile away where the black, green and gold of the New Africa had displaced the tricolor of France, we gathered around a long table in an inner room with Pat at the head and the airport commander at the foot. There were forty-six of us in all.

We had rare steak, salad, tomato juice and fruit. Pat permitted each man a small glass of wine. When we had finished, the commander of the airport switched on the television machine. There was a hum, a cloudiness on the mirror and then the image of Dr. Belsidus at his desk in Kakata appeared. His voice was clear and firm.

"Hello, Sandu, he said. "So the squadron has arrived safely! Well, Pat you've done a good job. Follow your instructions to the best of your ability Slater, instructions in code have been sent to you. Do not open them until you are aloft again. That is all."

The image faded and in a moment was gone.

Pat drew out the heavy manila envelope containing her instructions:

Attention, everyone Commander Sandu will issue you at
once as many small parachutes as you have cages of rats.
I think you will each need about twenty. Attach them
immediately to your cages but be sure none of the rats bite
you.

Ships Numbers 1, 2, 3, 4 and 5 will constitute the First
Flight. Ship No. 1 will fly immediately to Rome, Italy. There

you will drop half of your cages. You will then proceed to Naples and Palermo, dropping half of the remainder over each city. You will then return here and await further orders.

Ship No. 2 will proceed to Genoa and Turin, dropping hall your cages on each city, and then promptly return to Fez.

Ship No. 3 will deal similarly with Milan and Venice. Ship No. 4 will take as its targets Munich and Vienna, while Ship No. 5 will take Budapest and Trieste.

Ships Numbers 6, 7, 8, 9 and 10 will constitute the Second Flight, No. 6 will proceed directly to Glasgow to drop half its load and then will drop the other cages at Liverpool. No. 7 will proceed to London and Plymouth, dropping fifteen cages on the former and five on the latter, thence returning to Fez. No. 8 will go to Lisbon and Cardiff, dropping half its cages over each city, and returning here. No. 9 will drop its cages at Hordeaux and Brest, while No. 10 will proceed for the same purpose to Birmingham and Manchester, returning to Fez.

Ships Numbers 11, 12, 13, 14, 15 will constitute the Third Flight No. 11 will go to Marseilles and Lyons, No. 12 to Paris and Lisle, No. 11 to Bessels and Amsterdam, No. 14 in Antwerp and Hamburg and No. 15 to Berlin and Leiprig, all returning to Fez.

The dropping of the cages should be completed before daybreak and all planes should be back in Fez as soon as possible. This whole opera non is be conducted in the utmost secrecy, In case of forced landing the plane is to be immediately destroyed.

It is now nine o'clock. Our farthest objectives are Berlin and Glasgow, only fifteen hundred miles. That, at most, is a five-hour trip unless you run into a storm, which is unlikely at the altitude at which you will travel. You should be back here by seven-thirty tomorrow morning at the latest. If you all understand, let's get going.

The pilots and navigators filed out of the room, each pilot telling Commander Sandu the number of small parachutes he wanted Sandu noted this on a piece of paper which he handed to a sergeant orderly. We piled into the limousines and were whisked back to our ships. Another great adventure was about to begin.

IX

CARL ACCOMPANIES PAT ON STRATOSPHERE FLIGHT TO LONDON; DR. BELSIDUS ORDERS HIM TO "BAIL OUT"; FOLLOWS ORDERS AND IS ATTACKED

I was about to follow Pat into the ship when a lanky black soldier hurried up on a motorcycle. He saluted, handed me a sealed envelope and saluted again. I knew what it was and could scarcely contain myself until we were in the ship and had finished tying the parachutes to the cages of the rats, a job that required about ten minutes.

One by one the big planes left the ground and disappeared into the blackness of the Moroccan night. At last it was the turn of our No. 7. Pat gave her the gun, we raced down the field like a shot and then began climbing steeply. Every so often Hodginson corrected the course. This was blind flying with a vengeance. We seemed to be soaring aloft into nothingness. I looked at Pat, so cool and calm at the controls, and I felt more proud of her than ever.

When we were beyond the three thousand-foot level and still climbing steeply, I pulled out the envelope and tore it open. Then, turning on a nearby light, I got out my code book to decipher the message. In a few minutes I had it. It was from Dr. Belsidus and read:

> After London errand proceed north twenty miles until you
> see four red lights going on and off simultaneously. Bail out.
> You will be picked up by friends. The word is "Kakata," Go to
> London headquarters. Further instructions there.
>
> THE CHIEF

I re-read it and silently passed it to Pat She was apparently as puzzled as I.

There was no plumbing the mind of Dr. Belsidus. Schemes of the most amazing complexity and subtlety sprang from his mind like corn from a popper. He had said nothing to me previously about going to London. Why could he not have told me before? Why all the secrecy?

And why should I go to London when Martha Gaskin, his chief white European agent, had been doing such a swell job there disrupting the international picture?

I slowly tore up the message and tossed it out of the window. We were now four miles up. We sealed the cabin and turned on the oxygen. Higher and higher we went until we flattened out at fifty thousand feet to a speed of close to three hundred and fifty miles an hour.

Eleven o'clock. Hudginson gave Pat our position. We were not far from Plymouth. The big ship dipped for the dive toward our first target. I went back to aid Hudginson. We both hung on desperately as Pat sent the plane down at an angle of forty-five degrees. We strained our eyes for the first glimpse of the English city.

We hadn't long to wait. When we broke through the last belt of clouds, there a few miles ahead were the myriad lights of the ancient shipping center. In a few moments we would be above it. Pat dropped down to about three thousand feet.

Hudginson opened the trap door in the floor of the plane. Pat throttled her motor and we idled over the city. I handed Hudginson the first cage of rats, taking care that my hands were not bitten. He tossed it out, pulling the string of the small parachute, which immediately opened, Swaying from side to side, the parachute and its sinister burden floated slowly to the roof tops below. Four more cages followed it within the next minute. The navigator closed the trap door, Pat gave the motor the gun and we were off to London.

London from the air! A spectacle not easily forgotten: a faery tracery of light against a background of black velvet! The metropolis, the brain. the heart and soul of the world's greatest empire!

After all, what could we hope to accomplish against the might of Britain? And how much less than that could we accomplish against Britain combined with the rest of the white world? Still, Britain hadn't always been big, and had there not been a time when Africa was powerful and looked down upon puny European countries? If this had happened before, could it not happen now? And yet how inadequate were our resources compared to those of England, France, Italy. Belgium. Portugal and Holland.

We were high above the British metropolis now. Pat circled over the densely populated poorer sections as indicated on her map. Again we opened the trap door and one by one sent the fifteen remaining cages floating with sinister leisureliness toward the earth.

GEORGE S. SCHUYLER

I went back to my seat while Hudginson returned to his instruments. Pat looked at me and I looked at her. We were both thinking of being separated again when only a couple of days before we had been wed. But Pat was a good trouper. Not a sign of her real feeling appeared on her face. She just looked at me and her eyes told everything.

We were moving off toward the north now. We both watched for the four mysterious red lights. The thickening fog made observation difficult. We were over the place now, cruising at three thousand feet.

"I can't see anything," Pat shouted, "and I'm afraid to go any lower. This soup is awful." She looked over and smiled through her annoyance, one of those heartening smiles that sends men away to high ad venture with singing hearts.

At last there they were: four tiny red dots just below us. Pat looked at me again with eyes that said. "Be careful." I got up, adjusted my parachute, and then leaning over gave my wife a parting kiss.

Hudginson opened the side door. We shook hands and I dived out head first. When I was clear of the ship, I pulled the cord and in a few seconds was floating gently earthward. The four red lights were a little to my left now and the breeze was carrying me still farther away. But there was nothing I could do about it.

Suppose I should miss them? Suppose something should happen before they could reach me? It was certainly not a pleasing prospect. England was spy crazy after the ruthless activities of our espionage. Every stranger was suspect.

I was only three or four hundred feet up now. The pattern of things below me was quite plain. Evidently, I was coming down on a golf links or an estate just outside of London, for not far away was a row of houses. I could see nothing of the four red dots. Would they be able to see me?

The damp earth rushed up to meet me and I was dragged several feet before I could get out my knife and cut myself loose. A little stunned, I stood up, stretched and looked about me. I was definitely and absolutely alone in a field as still as a grave at midnight.

It was a little more than I had bargained for. After all, I had no relish for a firing squad, and how could I explain my presence in England without a passport or landing permit?

I decided finally to walk toward the row of houses and get on a main road where it might be easier for our men to find me. To think was to act. At one o'clock in the morning in a spy-mad country one is apt to get the jitters.

I had walked not more than a hundred feet toward the row of houses, feeling my way through the thick grass, when I heard a sudden movement just a few feet to my right. I stopped dead still, my heart thumping like a trip hammer, my automatic pistol gripped in my hand.

There was no sound. Again I proceeded, more cautiously this time. trying to peer through the Stygian darkness. Again came the sound, closer now, It was unmistakable.

I could feel my hair rising. Here I was in a strange country, one o'clock in the morning, ignorant of my whereabouts except in a very general way, and being stalked by someone.

I decided to wait and watch. Accustomed now to the blackness. I was able to discern objects a few feet away. I turned around and around. pistol gripped tensely, awaiting attack, from what direction I did not know.

In the distance to the south I could see the glow of the myriad lights of London. Although I knew that in that direction lay grave danger if unaccompanied by one of our agents, it seemed eminently inviting in comparison to this desolate heath.

Another sound. More definite: closer. I waited tensely, peering fearfully into the blackness. I thought I saw something blacker than the night moving along the ground. My heart leaped as I whirled and leveled my pistol.

Suddenly I was leaped upon from behind and knocked down by a heavy body, my pistol lost in the scuffle. Dazed by the impact. I threw up one arm. There was a low snarl, a guttural blood-curdling snarl, that chilled the blood and conjured fearful emotions. The arm I had lifted to ward off a blow was seized by a gigantic mouth with terrible teeth. I felt a huge paw at the back of my neck. Surely no dog in the world was so large or strong. What manner of beast could it be?

X

SLATER ARRIVES IN LONDON ON SPECIAL MISSION FOR BELSIDUS

I struggled but in vain: and yet the beast made no effort to touch me beyond holding me down to the ground. Then out of the Stygian darkness came a peculiar two-toned whistle, repeated twice. The beast stiffened to attention at the first sound. At the second he released my arm, jumped off my back and stood to one side. Again the peculiar whistle sounded, nearer this time. The strange animal now emitted a crying sound similar to that of a small woman in distress. I stood rooted to the ground, fascinated by this singular experience, but not without the foresight to get out my pistol for use in case the beast decided to attack again.

Once more the peculiar whistle sounded. It was quite near now, I looked expectantly, pistol ready, in the direction from which it came. Again the beast cried in reply, and a moment later two figures emerged from the gloom to my left and were immediately beside me. I pointed my gun and stepped backward.

"Get away or I'll shoot." I threatened

"Kakata," muttered the other.

"Kakata!" I replied joyfully, as I recognized the password. "I was looking for you fellows. I didn't know what happened.

"We saw you come down," said the taller of the two, "but then lost you in the darkness. We had to send Mira to find you." His voice was definitely English.

"Mira? Who is Mira?"

"Mira is our leopard over there," he said, turning toward the beast now standing at a respectful distance. "Come here, Mira."

The big beast padded over close to where we were standing. The man turned a flashlight on her. She was a magnificent animal, entirely black and with as wicked an expression as I've ever seen on a beast.

"Let's get on," growled the smaller of the two men.

"Righto," said the other.

He snapped on his flashlight, turned its beam toward the row of houses, made several mysterious signals, and shut it off.

"Come on, we'll go this way." With one of my strange companions on either side and the black beast following close behind, we strode along over the field toward the houses.

Finally we reached a paved road. The tall man signaled a halt. We had not long to wait. Two headlights leapt out of the darkness and raced toward us. In another moment a huge black limousine jerked to a stop beside us.

"Get in, Mr. Slater," the short man invited.

I stepped in and they followed me. The black leopard jumped in the seat next to the chauffeur. The big car started and moved with high speed toward the metropolis. As we entered the city we slowed down considerably and were soon barely creeping through the crooked old streets of a miserable tenement section. Billows of fog shrouded the sorry buildings bordering the stinking streets while bleary lamps blinked feebly through the murk.

I could see my two companions now for the first time. One was tall, raw-boned and grim. The shorter man had a little more flesh on him but also had the thin bony features of the London Cockney. Both were very light mulattoes and were well dressed. As we lurched past a flickering streetlamp again, the little fellow caught me studying him. He smiled faintly.

"Aye, Mister Slater," he said. "I guess you find all this rather mysterious: parachuting, trained leopards, and the like."

"It's a bit out of the ordinary," I conceded, "but I've got to the point where nothing the Black Internationale does is very surprising."

"My name's Stradford," he said, and then gesturing toward his associate, "and this lad's Wilbern. We've heard a lot about you. Mister Slater, and all the other great men surrounding Dr. Belsidus. Miss Gaskin has told us much."

Martha Gaskin! The mention of the name conjured up the vision of the pretty blonde, hopelessly in love with Dr. Belsidus, who headed his European espionage corps. It was she who had been responsible for the terroristic acts that had precipitated the short-lived European war. What was she planning now? And what part was I supposed to play?

We were getting downtown More people, more lights, more traffic. The big car rounded a sharp corner into a side street and after proceeding a few yards turned into a driveway leading to a warehouse. The limousine kept on toward the closed door. As we neared it, the door suddenly opened from top and bottom like a mouth and we crept inside.

The door closed with a thud behind us. Lights turned on, brilliantly illuminating a large garage. There were four other cars in the place and equipment for all sorts of emergency repairs.

Stradford and Wilbern got out and I followed. The leopard jumped down from the front seat. Then for the first time I noticed the chauffeur was a black giant close to seven feet tall, a powerful man strong enough to fell an ox with his fist. Cut into his forehead just above the bridge of his long cruel nose were three vertical African caste marks. He reminded me very much of Jim, the gigantic, dumb chauffeur-valet of Dr. Belsidus.

Wilbern, as tall as he was just came to the chauffeur's shoulder. He and Stradford grinned when they noticed the awe with which I was looking at the giant.

"That's K'bamgi, Mister Slater. K'bamgi, shake hands with Mister Carl Slater."

The giant extended his ham-like paw, which enveloped mine like a blanket. His wicked little eyes were dancing with pleasure

"K'bamgi is glad. K'bamgi has heard all," he boomed. "K'bamgi is glad, indeed." He bowed low and then straightened like a ramrod.

"Come on," growled Wilbern, his eyelids half drooping over hazel eyes. "She's waiting for us."

He led the way to the back of the garage where a brick wall barred the way. He walked to the wall and pressed against it. The brick touched by his hand sank inward about an inch. To our left a square section of the floor turned upright, revealing a flight of metal stairs. The short man motioned to me to descend. They followed: Wilbern, Stradford, Mira and K'bamgi, in that order behind me. As I reached the floor below I looked back in time to see the trap door above fall into place.

"We've always got to take the utmost precautions," said Stradford, noticing my glance. "London is a nest of spies, informers and police. We take nothing for granted."

The giant Negro nodded his head affirmatively. Wilbern simply grunted, and handed me the key to a small iron door. I walked to it and turned the key. The door opened easily enough but there was another door beyond it, a door of armor steel, shining dull gray in the dim light of the lone electric light bulb. I pulled the knob but the door wouldn't budge.

I looked back at the others. With the exception of the big slinky black cat, they all were enjoying my discomfiture.

"You see, Mister Slater," said Stradford proudly, "we have taken the utmost precautions." Then he brought a little pipe about four inches long out of his inside coat pocket. It would be better to describe it as a twin pipe because there were really two pipes fastened together but with a single mouthpiece. He put it to his mouth and blew. Again I heard the peculiar two-toned whistle that had called Mira away from me out in the suburbs. And again Mira emitted that crying sound similar to a small woman in distress.

There was a rattle of bolts from the other side of the door and in a moment it opened slowly outward. One by one we stepped inside a narrow, dimly lighted hall carpeted with a heavy-pile runner. Black velvet drapes hung from ceiling to floor, killing every superfluous sound. The hall was all of fifteen feet long and about five feet wide. Halfway was a small table at which sat a tow-headed little man: a hunchbacked mulatto sitting before a wide instrument board with radio earphones damped over his misshapen head.

As we entered the hallway, I saw him press a button. The steel door behind us closed with a bang. He then inserted a plug in a hole. A light sprang up.

"They have come," I heard him mumble into the receiver on his chest. He listened to the voice on the other end, nodding his head up and down, then pulled out the plug. Now he turned his narrow yellow face to us and grinned an expanse of discolored fangs.

"You may enter," he said, bowing to me. "The others are waiting."

He pressed a button. The black velvet drapes at the other end of the hall parted and a heavy vault-like steel door slowly opened outward.

GEORGE S. SCHUYLER

XI

Martha Gaskin Demonstrates How Spies Are Dealt with as Carl Attends Secret Meeting; Dr. Belsidus Speaks from Africa

"Wait," ordered Wilbern, pulling me back. "Put this on."

He thrust a black mask into my hand. I fastened it on, and then was permitted to enter the chamber beyond. I noticed that Stradford and K'bamgi were also masked. Mira, the leopard, brought up the rear.

The long rectangular chamber was completely hung with black velvet drapes and the same material obscured the ceiling. At the far end was a life-size painting of Dr. Belsidus in surgeon's uniform with scalpel in hand, Down the center of the room was a long mahogany table at which sat twenty masked men, ten on each side. At the far end sat Martha Gaskin, pretty as ever and without a mask, her golden hair in sharp contrast to the black background.

"Hello, Carl," she said, smiling. "Just sit anywhere. We've been waiting for you."

"Yes, Martha, I know. We got here as soon as we could. The boys had a time finding me out there in that miserable blackness. I don't suppose you people in London ever see either the sun or the stars."

"The fog is a great help sometimes, Carl," she replied, a significant tone in her voice. "I just don't know what we would do without the fog to help some of our operations."

All the time the others sitting around the long table looked in my direction but said nothing Some toyed with pencils or fountain pens. Others sat with folded hands, waiting.

"Comrades," said Martha, "Carl Slater is now here and we can proceed." She picked up a communicating telephone and spoke into the receiver: "Ezekiel! We are almost ready."

She hung up the receiver and turned again to us. "Sit down," she said, indicating the vacant chairs. We took seats, all except K'bamgi who took his post behind Martha's chair. I sat at the foot of the table.

She clapped her hands twice. From behind the drapes to the rear of her came a dark brownskin girl with a small box and a sheet of papers. She was a tall, handsome girl with delicate features that spoke of royal blood and an air that betokened acquaintance with refinement and leisure.

"Alright, Della," Martha directed.

The colored girl opened the box, which was revealed as a fingerprinting plate. She went to the first masked figure, sat the box before him and laid one of the sheets of paper on the edge of the table.

"Who are you?" she asked.

"I am Number One," he replied.

"And the password is. . . ?

"Kakata."

"Very well. Place the fingers of your right hand on the inked surface and then place it here." She indicated the square on the paper. The masked figure obeyed her. She picked up the sheet and handed him the towel on her arm with which to wipe his hand. Then she passed on to the next person and so on around the table. Martha Gaskin was the only one she did not fingerprint.

In about ten minutes she was finished, departing as quietly as she came, and in the same direction.

Ten minutes more passed, during which the utmost silence obtained, except for the tap-tap of occasional pencils, pens and fingertips on the polished surface of the rich mahogany table.

At last Della returned, an implacably grim expression on her face. She handed a slip of paper to Martha Gaskin and then retired.

Martha read the slip in the midst of almost painful silence. Not even a pencil tapped now. She patted her blonde hair with one slender, delicately manicured hand. K'bamgi moved nonchalantly from behind her chair and sauntered along behind the masked figures on that side until he was about halfway. He was taut, as if about to spring. I saw Martha's right hand slip under the edge of the table. I watched the scene fascinated, curious, terrified.

Martha's right hand came back to rest on the edge of the table. looked up now for the first time and smiled sweetly.

"Number Eighteen," she purred, her voice and expression suspiciously soft, "even I cannot leave this place unless permitted by Ezekiel, the little hunchback in the corridor. What chance, then, have you? Will you talk willingly and tell us what your masters know about us, or must we make you?"

At the mention of "Number Eighteen," K'bamgi had moved as stealthily as a cat to a position immediately behind the masked figure that had boldly called out his number to the beautiful Della a few minutes before.

The accused moved suddenly and his hand shot to his mouth, but K'bamgi was faster. His great hands closed about the man's wrist and twisted it cruelly until the small vial the handheld fell with a tinkle to the table.

The masked figure next to the culprit reached over and snatched off the black mask of the accused. Before us was revealed a young white man, ghostly pale. K'bamgi held the man's hands behind him with one of his tremendous paws and looked toward Martha for further instructions.

"Search him, Number Seventeen," she ordered.

Deft fingers expertly frisked the man, bringing forth a small pistol cleverly concealed in a secret pocket and three vials of poison.

"Are you ready to talk freely?" asked Martha.

"I have nothing to say," he muttered, and then closed up like a clam.

"Take him away, K'bamgi," she directed, "and make him talk."

"Ah, yes," chuckled K'bamgi, "I make him talk."

He yanked the young man out of his chair and hustled him through the drapes behind Martha in the direction the girl Della had gone.

"Now you may unmask," she said.

The unmasking revealed such an assortment of humanity as it would be to find gathered in a chamber anywhere in the world. Some were black, others were varying shades from brown to white, and some were white. Again Martha telephoned to the hunchback in the hall:

"We're ready now, Ezekiel."

There was a crackling of radio static, a buzzing and blurring. Then distinctly we heard the sound of a distant voice: "This is Kakata, Super Short Wave. You may go ahead. London." Martha picked up a microphone from the table in front of her and began speaking.

"Gaskin talking. All well for Slater. Cargo sale everywhere. No planes reported down We await the voice."

"Attention, London," came over the air through the concealed radio set. "The Voice talking. This is the Chief. Carl, remain with friends. More later. That is all."

"Well, that's once the Doctor had no orders," said Martha. "He must be in mighty good spirits in spite of the invasion."

"But what's the idea of dropping the rats over London?" asked Sam Wilbern. "What help will that be?"

Martha smiled grimly. "Dr. Belsidus is carrying the war to the white man and he is doing it in a new way. More people are killed during wars by cholera, spotted typhus and bubonic plague than are destroyed by bullets. Is that not so?"

"Sure, but I. . ." Wilbern wrinkled his brow.

"Remember," Martha went on, "each of those diseases is best transmitted by rats. Each one of those rats our planes dropped tonight is in ested with one or the other of these dread diseases. Each plane, I am informed, carried twenty crates of rats with one hundred and sixty odd to a crate. Eight hundred in Plymouth. Twenty-five hundred in London. How long do you think it will be before the plague sweeps all England? And mind, fifty thousand of these agents of death roam European cities tonight."

There were swift intakes of breath as she spoke so calmly of the devilish warfare of Dr. Belsidus.

"But what about us?" asked Wilbern. "Won't we get it, too?"

"When it gets bad, we'll leave," she said, fixing him with her cold blue eyes, "but we'll not leave until our work is done. Do you understand, Sam Wilbern?"

XII

Martha Gaskin Reveals the First Step
Black Internationale's Espionage Group
Will Make to Attack Enemy by
Way of "Back Door"

K'bamgi returned to his place behind Martha's chair. Della Crambull, the pretty brownskin girl, came out and took a seat near me.

"Who was he?" asked Martha without turning her head.

"Him Reginald Duncanson, British secret service."

"Did he talk?

"Oh, yes," the black giant grinned cruelly and the vertical caste marks in his forehead came together. "Him talk plenty when we make."

"What do they know?"

Now the colored girl, Della, spoke up. "Very little, Martha. He was working on a personal hunch. He trailed Number Six here, he said."

Martha's blue eyes grew hard. "He must know more. How did he come into possession of the whistle? How did he know the password? He must tell us that. We must know at once. Use the acid. We must know. Too much is involved. It means our lives."

Della rose and disappeared beyond the velvet drapes. K'bamgi followed her.

"What is this about acid?" I whispered to the rat-faced Stradford, who sat next to me.

He grimaced faintly, then whispered: "A very corrosive acid is dropped on various tender parts of the body and permitted to eat its way to vital organs. If the man talks, the drops cease. If not, well. . ." He shrugged his shoulders and tapped gently on the smooth surface of the mahogany table, just the suggestion of a sardonic smile twisting one side of his face. My shudder must have been perceptible.

Was there no end to this cruelty, this ruthlessness, this cold and calculating killing? But then what omelet was ever made without breaking eggs? How had Africa been enslaved except through murder? Even at the moment this clean-cut Englishman was being tortured to death countless thousands of black men and women in Africa were nursing the wounds inflicted upon them by ruthless white masters before the genius of Dr. Belsidus had freed our race.

"Now," said Martha, "let's get down to business. Our plan to involve Europe in war was a success, as you all only too well know, but self-interest, the fear of mutual destruction, brought on an early armistice, and now, with white ships and armies converging on Africa, our whole program is imperiled.

"Dr. Belsidus is depending on us to attack from the rear, to demoralize and disorganize the enemy so that his whole program will be undermined and destroyed. He has approved our Plan No. One for England. You see, we cannot depend upon the plague alone. Some means of combatting it successfully may be found. Besides, it will take some weeks for it to get going to epidemic proportions. In the meantime we must strike an effective blow.

"That effective blow is Plan No. One." Her voice fell to a whisper.

"What is Plan No. One?" asked a handsome brownskin man in evening dress.

"It is without a doubt the most effective we could use," she said, "and is characteristic of Dr. Belsidus."

What new scheme was this from the brain of the Chief, I wondered? The man seemed to fairly sweat devilishness.

"In a way," continued Martha, "our civilization is like an inverted pyramid standing on its small end. The swarming billions get their goods from several million stores, but these stores get their goods only about a half million factories. Of this half million factories scattered over the modern industrial world, less than forty thousand make industrial machinery which the other factories use. Of these forty thousand machine shops, less than twelve hundred make the machine tools, the machines which make all other machines, including their own.

"Now imagine what would happen if some superhuman power were to destroy all the machine tools in the modern industrial world? And suppose we were prevented from making anymore? We could not make automobiles, electrical devices, household conveniences, plumbing fixtures, railroad equipment, airplanes, steel ships, movies, no more machinery of any kind."

"And," interjected Stradford, "no more cannons, machine guns, rifles, pistols, nothing."

Martha nodded her blonde head. "Exactly, Jake. Now, of those twelve hundred tool factories. Three hundred and fifty are in the United

States, one hundred and fifty are in Asia, fifty are in Australia, twenty-five in South America, twenty in Canada and the rest are in Europe. Of these six hundred and five European tool factories, three hundred are here in England."

"And all we got to do is destroy them?" a light brown man eagerly asked.

"Yes," she continued, "if possible, but Dr. Belsidus's idea is that tool factories can be rather rapidly rebuilt, although it will naturally take time to build hundreds. But that would only be a matter of a few months in an emergency where the fate of the British Empire was at sake."

The velvet drapes parted behind her and Della and K'bamgi came out. The black giant took his position behind Martha while Della went to her seat. I saw K'bamgi lean down and whisper at length in the white woman's ear. Then he sauntered down the room. When he reached Number Six, a real black, evil-looking fellow, he suddenly grabbed the man's arms and, whipping out a pair of handcuffs, snapped them on the Negro's wrists. It all happened so suddenly that the swift execution left us breathless.

"You see, Fancher." said Martha, looking straight at the man who cowered in his seat with the giant K'bamgi towering above him, "the young Englishman did talk. He told us everything. Understand? You let a pretty white woman get information from you that might mean the death of all of us, and you never got a cent for it. Now you are in for it, my man. Britain with all its might cannot save you. You must die. Fancher, a victim of your lust, but before you die you will talk— K'bamgi see that Fancher talks, for we must know everything."

The giant grinned cruelly. "He will talk," he boomed, yanking the ashen-faced Negro from his chair and hustling him out of the room. This time Della did not go with K'bamgi.

"Now," said Martha, as if dismissing an unpleasant but not very important subject, "let us go on. Oh yes, I was saying that these three hundred tool factories in England, these three hundred key factories of British industrialism, could be rebuilt in a few months in an emergency. The World War showed us what can be done in speedy construction. Dr. Belsidus realizes this. But he realizes also that it takes many years to produce a tool maker. There are sixty-five thousand of these tool makers in Great Britain. At least six thousand of these are key men. Remove them and the industry is severely handicapped. Remove the entire sixty-five thousand and British industry is destroyed for a generation."

"And that means forever," growled hazel-eyed Sam Wilbern.

"Exactly, Sam," Martha went on "We know the location of every single one of these key tool factories. Moreover, we know the name and address of every foreman, superintendent and manager. We must act at once. Our first job is to remove them. This must be accomplished before the week is out. We shall start with the men in direct charge of operations. There are only a few hundred of them. Della will give you whatever you need in the way of money and supplies. Wherever possible for safety's sake use only white assistants. You are to proceed carefully Remember, the whole future of the African Empire depends. upon it. Della, the lists, please."

The dark girl got up and disappeared into the other room. Almost immediately she returned with a big pile of typewritten sheets and began handing batches of forty or fifty sheets to each operative. I looked at one of Sam Wilbern's sheets. On it was typed a long list of names with street address and city typed alongside each one. Opposite some few names were red stars.

"You will notice," Della explained, "that several names in your group are marked with red stars. They are to be removed first. K'bamgi will give you additional pistols with silencers and as many boxes of poisoned darts as you wish."

All eyes now turned to Martha for final word. "I have nothing to add," she said. "You know that if you fail, Africa may be lost. All over the white world our operatives are working on similar projects. See that you do your part. Dr. Belsidus will countenance no less."

As she finished speaking the steel door to the hallway opened and little hunchbacked Ezekiel shambled in like some grotesque nightmare, propelling his dwarfed and twisted body toward me, a yellow sheet of paper in his outstretched hand, "For you, Mister Slater," he said, "From the Chief."

I read the few words on the paper that made my heart skip a beat.

XIII

CARL ORDERED TO REMAIN IN LONDON AND EXPEDITE EXECUTION OF "PLAN NO. ONE"; MARTHA GASKIN'S IDENTITY REVEALED

R emain as a personal representative," the message from Dr. Besidus read, "and work with Gaskin. Your newspaper experience will come in handy. Expedite execution of Plan No. One. Time is short. Situation critical. Speed absolutely essential. Ample funds transferred to Bank of England from New York. All planes safe."

What could I do here in London, unacquainted as I was with the city? Martha Gaskin knew far more than I about it. How could I help this woman who was an expert in espionage and terroristic tactics? I had not thought that I would have to remain in London. What of the plague which would soon be sweeping the city unless the calculations of Dr. Belsidus were all wrong? Would I ever see Pat again? I frowned involuntarily. Certainly the prospect was not a pleasing one. And yet, dead or alive, one had to go ahead. There was no backing down now even if I had wanted to do so.

I glanced up and caught Martha's keen gaze. I knew she was curious about the note, so I carried it to her. The others waited in silence.

The white woman looked up from the message, a thoughtful expression on her face.

"We shall have to change our plans somewhat," she announced to the gathering. "Mr. Slater, please come with me. You, too, Della, Jake and Sam. The others will wait here until we return."

She rose, and we followed her behind the black velvet drapes. through a door and into a small sitting room like thousands of others in apartment houses throughout the world. There were etchings on the walls, a radio, two easy chairs, a library table, an overstuffed couch and two small Chinese rugs. Martha waved us to seats.

Somewhere near at hand I could hear low groans. Suddenly there was a pitiful shriek. Then silence. I looked around uneasily. Martha, noting my perturbation, smiled indulgently.

"K'bamgi is making our friend Fancher do some talking," she observed a sinister mocking in her tone. She lit a long Russian cigarette and leaned back on the couch, eyes half closed.

"We can't get rid of them quick enough by the usual methods," she snapped. "We've got to think of something else. These key men of British industry must die immediately."

"You can't eliminate six thousand people in a flash," I objected, "unless you're going to get them all in one place and gas them. Otherwise we'll have to do it through assassinations, as you originally planned."

The other three nodded their heads in agreement and waited for the white woman to speak.

"Well," she said finally, "why not get them all in one place?"

"That's impossible, snorted little Jake Stradford, contorting his little rat face.

"I thought we had agreed to drop that word," she rebuked. "Listen—"

For upwards of an hour she talked rapidly, outlining the most devilishly ingenious plan I have ever heard. We went over it in every detail, checking and re-checking, changing and altering until we had polished the scheme to what seemed perfection.

"It will cost an awful lot of money." observed Della.

"Yes," observed Martha enthusiastically, "but think of the results!"

When we returned to the conference room, Martha dismissed the agents with a warning to do nothing until further orders. As they were filing out of the room into the corridor beyond, K'bamgi came in.

"Well, what did Fancher have to say?" asked Martha looking up at the solemn black giant.

"Him talk when K'bamgi ask him," guffawed the savage, rubbing his sardonic countenance with a huge paw, evidently well satisfied with the results of his efforts. Then he leaned over and whispered to her earnestly. She nodded her golden head and the blood drained from her face

"Number Six and Number Seventeen, wait," she cried, running out into the corridor to get the two men.

They came back hurriedly and she whispered to each one in turn. They nodded and hastened out.

When we were alone at last, except for Della, Jake, Sam, K'bamgi and the hunchback Ezekiel. I asked her what Fancher had revealed.

"He was crazy about a white girl," she explained. "I don't think he was really disloyal but he got to boasting as men will when they are drinking and with a girl who fascinates them. He cannot remember all he told her but admits he was indiscreet."

"What will you do with him?" I asked.

"K'bamgi done take care of him," said the giant. "He gone."

"Gone? Gone where?"

"Do you remember the acid bath we used at our first conference?" asked Martha, smiling sweetly.

"Oh, yes. . . My memory flitted back to that horrible scene years before when a traitor had been dumped in a vat of acid that consumed him like paper in a flame.

"Well, we have one here, too," she observed, archly.

The others snickered diabolically.

I DON'T KNOW HOW MANY hours I had been sleeping in one of the spacious underground bed chambers when I felt the tap of a clammy hand on my bare arm. I woke with a start and recoiled from the gnome-like face of Ezekiel.

"Day has broken," he announced. "Your tub and breakfast await you, sir."

Struck by the efficiency with which everything seemed to be run, I hurried through bath and a light breakfast. K'bamgi came in with underwear, a tweed suit, shirt, socks, cravat, shoes and overcoat, and while I dressed, he brought in a small trunk and a suitcase which he informed me were packed with other clothes.

"How did you get these things so quickly?" I asked.

"Ha! Black Internationale have everything. Tailor, laundry, everything. . ."

"In this building?"

"In many buildings. Black Internationale have great organization. Change face, change nose, change hair, change fingertips, do everything necessary."

He grinned broadly at my wonder and the vertical caste marks in his massive forehead came close together.

It was now around ten o'clock in the morning. I went out into the little sitting room, Della and Martha, fully dressed, were awaiting me.

We made our way upstairs to the garage, K'bamgi in his chauffeur's uniform preceding us and blowing one of the peculiar whistles whose blast opened the way through steel doors.

He opened the door of the big black limousine and we piled in. Sam and Jake, looking very genteel in morning clothes, were already seated inside.

K'bamgi started the big car and drove toward the closed garage door. When we had almost reached it, the door flew open and we passed through. I looked about to see who had opened it, remembering a similar occurrence the night before, but we were the only persons in sight. Martha noted my puzzled expression and laughed.

"It's the photoelectric eye," she explained. "Whenever the tiny stream of light is broke either inside or outside, the door opens, but not otherwise. It is most important when you are being pursued. We have to be prepared for every eventuality."

"Where, Miss Gaskin?" asked K'bamgi.

"To the townhouse."

"Townhouse?!" I echoed.

"I neglected to tell you, Carl," she explained, "that socially in London I am the Countess Maritza Jerzi. It is very convenient when you want to hobnob with the British nobility and perhaps pick up some useful information. It will be helpful in carrying out Plan No. One, too."

"But how did you manage it?"

"Well," she said, "the Count was of an excellent Polish family but he didn't have a shilling to his name. He was fortune hunting and was glad to marry into what he thought was wealth. We had quite an elaborate wedding, really. Dukes, Barons, Counts, Princesses. . . Oh, everybody was there. . . But, alas, three weeks later he died!"

"How?" I asked, curious.

"Oh, he just died suddenly," she said, as the others guffawed.

XIV

MARTHA, AS COUNTESS JERZI, COMPLETES DETAILS FOR COMPLETION OF BLACK INTERNATIONALE'S "PLAN NO. ONE"; DREAD DISEASE STRIKES IN LONDON

That day and the next two days were hectic, indeed. Martha, as Countess Jerzi, flitted around town, contacting the best people for the sponsorship of a great dance recital by Della Crambull, who had gained flattering notices for her dancing at the Palm Leaf Club. This was an exclusive Mayfair cabaret, owned by Martha, where the beautiful dark girl appeared twice nightly, at nine and eleven o'clock, supported by a troupe of African dancers, all in the pay of the Black Internationale.

In the meantime, I was kept busy as the press representative of the Countess, sending out numerous news releases to the metropolitan and provincial press accompanied by photographs and mats. On the second day we began mailing out the invitations to the six thousand key technicians. These read as follows:

The Countess Maritza Jerzi has the rare privilege of announcing an elaborate and exclusive dance recital by DELLA CRAMBULL, the incomparable African dancer of the Palm Leaf Club, supported by her native African dancers, in honor of the Master Technicians of Great Britain, whose genius and efficiency assure British world supremacy, Friday, January 7, at 8:30 P.M. The Great Delphane Hall, the London Symphony Orchestra. Please present invitation at door.

CHAIRMAN: H.R.H. LORD DESBOROUGH

Then followed a long list of distinguished sponsors, the cream of British nobility, several of whom were listed as speakers.

Coming at a time when British industrial, political, and military supremacy was threatened by ambitious rival powers, there was a generous response from those who realized all too well their debt to British technical genius. Names that loomed big in *Who's Who* lent the project its support. The gay Countess Jerzi was promising a series of such performances as a token of appreciation of the part played by science in British world supremacy.

What particularly amused us was the willingness of many wealthy persons to contribute substantial sums toward meeting the expense of bringing the technicians from all parts of England and Scotland to London free of charge. We had planned to bear the entire expense.

It was well that we had decided to launch our No. 1 immediately. On the morning of the third day after my arrival, the London papers reported:

RARE DISEASES STRIKE DOWN MANY

London physicians are puzzled and disturbed by the number of deaths from rare diseases in the past two days. Almost every hospital in the city is reporting a sudden increase in the number of cases of spotted typhus, cholera, yellow fever and smallpox in most virulent stages There have been several deaths, and the medical profession has launched an investigation to determine the source of this alarming visitation. If the incidence of these diseases continues to increase, it will say some doctors, be necessary to institute a quarantine in affected areas. At present, however, such a step is not considered necessary but medical authorities are not relaxing their vigilance.

We were just sitting down to breakfast in the stately dining room of the mansion on Berkeley Square at which Martha, as the Countess Jerzi, had had so many social triumphs.

K'bamgi entered the room dressed in his chauffeur's uniform. We nodded to the big black. He hurried to Martha's side, leaned over and whispered into her ear.

"Was it clean?" she asked aloud.

"It was as you wished," he replied, straightening up.

"Good," she exclaimed, visibly pleased. "There'll be no more interference with our plans now."

Della, Jake, Sam and I looked up curiously, expecting an explanation. K'bamgi left the room.

"What was it?" asked Della.

Martha leaned forward and lowered her voice to a whisper. "Six and Seventeen have reported. Sir Robert Von Humpstead is dead."

"The head of Scotland Yard?" asked Jake, awe and satisfaction struggling for supremacy.

"Exactly," said Martha, firmly. "Fancher talked to the English girl and she talked to Duncanson, who communicated his suspicions to Sir Robert Von Humpstead. He had little to go on but it is certain that he would have followed up Duncarson's absence. Nothing must interfere with our plans now. We're working against time as it is, what with the plague spreading."

"From them damn rats?" asked Sam, in a voice indicating that he knew the affirmative answer.

"Yes," observed Della, "and it's going to spread like everything. They may quarantine the town in a couple of days when they get real panicky."

"Aye, that they will," agreed Jake, "and then what a time we'd have getting away."

"Shut up," snapped Martha. "We'll all be cleared out before then. I hope." She was irritable under the terrific strain as, indeed, were all of us. There were a thousand and one angles to Plan No. One.

The rest of the day I stayed close to the telephone in Martha's townhouse receiving reports from all parts of England, giving directions for the smashing conclusion of Plan No. One.

By three o'clock the entire group of Black Internationale operatives had received their final instructions and were at their stations wherever there was a key machine shop in England and Scotland. It was white men who were to do the actual work of destruction. It was our black agents who directed them.

At four o'clock Ezekiel, the hunchback, telephoned that the stratosphere planes had left Fez. Shortly afterward I heard from Jake and Sam that all preparations had been completed for the dance recital at Great Delphane Hall.

I met with the gentlemen of the press for the Countess Jerzi in her drawing room. Martha was too busy checking on final arrangements to see them.

When we all gathered at the dinner that evening, an air of suppressed excitement was in the atmosphere. I am sure none of us ate very much. Della seemed the most composed of all. The white woman was the most jittery. This surprised me because Martha had always been so calm. But then, when before had we launched upon such an ambitious project?

She looked at her wristwatch at seven-thirty, and then glanced around the table. There were Della, Jake, Sam, K'bamgi and me.

"K'bamgi," she began, "you will drive us to the hall immediately. That will take fifteen minutes on the outside. You will immediately come back here and burn everything that might be incriminating in the fire place. You will then go to the rendezvous and get Ezekiel. He has his instructions to destroy the place when he leaves.

"Jake, have you and Sam attended to everything? There mustn't be any mistakes tonight, you know."

"It's perfect," he assured her. "If we can keep the doors closed five minutes we'll be successful."

"Good," she exclaimed. "Now, remember, when the signal is given. Jake and Sam will let loose with everything they have, then immediately go to the roof. I will leave my box exactly five minutes before and go to the roof to await. Della, when your buzzer sounds, you join me. They've already taken your clothing to the roof and you can change in a minute. Carl, you will stay at the periscope as long as you safely can do so.

"K'bamgi, you and Ezekiel motor immediately to our country place as soon as the rendezvous is destroyed."

"And what of our operatives?" I interposed. Were they to be left to their fate?

"They have their orders to assemble at the country place at midnight."

"And their white assistants. . . ?"

"They'll have to do the best they can," she snapped. "We can't save everybody."

She rose and along with the rest of us went out to the long black limousine. In a moment we were away and threading through the fog bound traffic, to carry out the most astonishing and diabolical plot man has yet conceived.

XV

PLAN NO. ONE WORKS AS FIFTEEN THOUSAND PEOPLE DIE IN DELPHANE HALL; LONDON FOG CLOSES DOWN TO TRAP MARTHA AND CARL AS PLANE CRASHES

K'bamgi let us out at the stage entrance of the Great Delphane Hall and immediately sped away. We went immediately to Della's dressing room. It was exactly seven-forty-five.

"Now," Martha reminded Jake and Sam. "as soon as I leave my box you are to go to work. Have you arranged for the front doors?"

Sam nodded. "Yes, we'll have them barred right after the bell for the second act."

"Good," she said, "the police have been instructed to let no one in or out after that time. We've got clear sailing."

"And I've told my troupe," said Della, "to go immediately to the roof as soon as the curtain falls on the first act."

"Then we understand everything perfectly," Martha remarked.

"Take your posts."

Jake, Sam and I left and went downstairs. In the basement was the giant fan that blew fresh warm air into the vast auditorium. Nearby were several huge steel drums attached to a pipe which ended in front of the fan and could be turned on and off. Sam demonstrated how it worked while we stood by. Then I went to another part of the basement nearby, from where I could view the audience through a periscope.

It was exactly eight o'clock but already the auditorium was half filled. White shirt fronts and studs gleamed out of the semi-darkness, Martha was in a front box with Lord Desborough, Lady Desborough and several other nobles. She was fascinating in shimmering white, nodding and smiling graciously, an accomplished coquette. It was a marvel how she could appear so nonchalant at the verge of such a terrible crime.

At eight-fifteen, the London Symphony Orchestra filed in. At eight-twenty-five Roberto Cacceli, the conductor walked in hurriedly, bowed gracefully to the deafening applause. At eight-thirty he raised his baton for the opening bars of the Congo Ballet overture. The lights dimmed and the house was in darkness At eight-thirty-five the curtain was raised on the West African village scene and the great ballet began.

I could see nothing of this from my periscopic outpost, but the generous applause indicated that it was being well received.

Finally, after almost an hour the final curtain dropped on the first act and the last strains of the exotic music died. The lights sprang up, followed by a great buzzing of voices as the multitude rose to stretch legs and go to the salon.

The fifteen minute intermission was scarcely half over when the seats began filling again with the talkative audience. Having a good opportunity to count them now, I estimated the crowd at no less than fifteen thousand. There was no doubt that the technical brains of England were assembled and that everybody was pleased with what they had seen.

How little they knew about their immediate future! Not a soul there suspected he was catching his last glimpse of earthly joys.

Three more minutes and the orchestra would begin the overture for the second and last act. The musicians were already taking their places.

Suddenly I heard in the distance a dull boom. I knew the hunchback Ezekiel had destroyed the secret underground chambers of the Black Internationale. How much had been plotted there beneath the streets. of London: bombings, arson, assassinations, espionage, every fiendish scheme for the overthrow of white supremacy had been mapped there with devilish cunning and carried out with consummate skill. Only one more plot awaited completion before our work would be done.

I kept my eyes glued to the periscope, At nine-thirty Conductor Cacceli tapped with his baton and the lights dimmed. I saw Martha gracefully rise and excuse herself, and hurry backstage. In the pause before the crash of music I heard very faintly the hiss of escaping gas. I hurriedly donned my gas mask. This was not a gas to take chances with. Studious brown Sam Hamilton, the Black Internationale chemist-in-chief, had invented it. Odorless and colorless, heavy and lethal, it surpassed anything the white chemists had been able to produce for speedy asphyxiation. One died from it with never a suspicion that anything was amiss.

The overture was scheduled for five minutes. One minute passed and I noticed several people wiping their faces. Two minutes passed and during a pause in the music I could hear the hum of the great fan as it speeded the vapor of death. Three minutes passed. A number of people slumped forward in their seats. As Conductor Cacceli lifted his baton be fell forward, prostrate. The musicians rose panic-stricken, but one by one they fell back into their seats or to the floor. One or two gained the door under the stage but that was securely barred, in accordance with our plan. There was screaming and running about.

Four minutes passed. There were a few faint shouts, mostly from the balconies, but the majority of the audience sat lifeless. The place was still in the darkness. It was all too tragically evident that Plan No. One had been a success.

It was time for me to go. I noticed that Jake and Sam had preceded me. I raced up the iron staircase and tapped on the penthouse door, which was immediately pulled open. I stepped out on the roof and took off my mask. The fresh air smelled mighty good.

In the center of the roof stood an autogiro, or windmill plane, into which the dancing troupe was piling. Soon the door slammed shut and with a short run the autogiro rose almost straight up and disappeared in the fog.

It had scarcely gone when another autogiro landed and took off with Della and the remainder of the dancers. This plane also threshed away into the foggy darkness.

We waited five minutes. I was getting nervous. Suppose someone should break into the hall and discover that vast concourse of people asleep for eternity. The police would search the roof as a matter of course. The others were as nervous as I.

"Why doesn't he come?" Martha complained. "I told him to be here at nine-forty sharp and to cruise overhead until the other planes had cleared."

"I hope nothing's happened, lady," said Jake, apprehensively, "or we'll be in the soup, sure."

"Aye," said Sam. "That we will, but I fancy we've at least an hour. If nobody breaks in and finds the mess."

The four of us paced back and forth. Down below in the streets we could hear the motor horns and see the lights of the long line of parked cars. Several times the whistle of the traffic policeman at the intersection floated up to us through the thick fog. I thought about Pat and wondered would I ever see her again; thought about Harlem and the good times I'd had there; thought about Dr. Belsidus and the future of Africa. It was Martha's voice that brought me back to the present.

"I hear it!" she cried, in ecstatic relief.

Sure enough, there was the sound of an airplane motor in the distance. It came nearer every second, but we could see nothing through the opaque fog. The plane circled around and around.

"He can't see the roof," cried Jake. "That's the trouble. I'll get in the center and turn on my flashlight."

Suiting action to word, Jake ran to the center of the broad roof and turned the beam of the flashlight into the sky. The autogiro was still circling around. The pilot still could not see where to land. Every second the fog was getting thicker.

"We're done for, mates, if he can't land," mumbled Sam. "It's nine-forty-five now. Somebody'll smell a rat pretty soon and then we'll be done for, I'm tellin' you."

The autogiro settled again, lower this time, yet we were unable to see it as doubtless, he was unable to see us. Lower and lower he came, circling around and around in our vicinity.

We felt once more buoyant as rescue seemed near. Yet the inexorable minutes ticked their way into eternity and still we remained on that broad roof. The autogiro came lower. It was sure to land now. The sound of the motor was almost deafening.

It came lower. We could see it at last! It was scarcely twenty yards above our heads and settling rapidly. As it neared, my spirits rose. After all, we were going to get away with it. We moved over to the edge of the roof so as not to be struck by the plane in landing. The motor died.

Suddenly a gust of air from the street cavern below shot up and caught the plane at the edge of the roof. It side-slipped, dipped drunkenly and plunged into the street below where it struck with a resounding crash.

I looked at my watch and I noticed that my hand was shaking. It was nine-fifty. Rescue was now out the question, it seemed. We all looked at each other wondering what we should do next.

XVI

Martha and Aides Escape from London after Asphyxiation of Vast Assemblage, But Are Stopped, Arrested on Highway

We looked at each other hopelessly. We had told the other autogiro pilots *not* to return. Would they disobey our orders when we didn't show up? And if they returned, would they return soon enough? At anytime now the terrible tragedy in the great hall below might be discovered. There are always slips like that. Once discovered, how could we hope to escape from London? We no longer had a secret place in which to hide, either, even if we got off the roof.

"Let's get out of this!" snapped Martha. "They won't get back in time, even if they do return. We can't stay here and be caught like rats in a trap. Come on!"

"Aye," Sam agreed, "let's get out of this."

"But how?"

"Down the fire escape." Martha directed. "Quick!"

Jake led the way. Fortunately, the fog remained dense. That was our protection from prying eyes. Down we climbed, one, two, three, four flights of slippery iron steps, until we were on the last platform above the alley. We would have to reach ground by a weighted ladder. Scarcely twenty paces away stood a stalwart London bobby, his broad back turned to us. Could we get down without detection?

Again Jake led the way. He stepped gingerly upon the rounds of the ladder. It slowly began to swing to the ground. He began climbing down Martha followed him, gathering up the train of her evening dress with her left hand. I came behind her and Sam brought up the rear.

The end of the ladder was now more than two feet from the slimy cobblestones of the alley. Fortunately for us it had been well oiled and not a squeak had come out of it. The big bobby still stood with his back to us with his hands clasped behind him looking out at the passing traffic.

One by one we stepped off the iron ladder and moved into the shadow. Sam was the last to step off. As he did so, the ladder, free of his weight, swung easily upward and struck against the lower platform of the fire escape with a resounding bang.

We shrank against the wall in the deep shadows, but Sam wasn't fast enough. The bobby turned around as if on a pivot and saw him.

"Oo's there!" he challenged, walking back in our direction. "Come out of there. Hi saw ye."

We stood perfectly still as he approached us. A chill of apprehension possessed me. Had we fulfilled so much of our mission only to be caught now? I saw Sam and Jake pull out their silencer-equipped pistols, but Martha restrained them with a gesture. She stepped out into the light.

"Officer," she called sweetly, "I wonder, would you help us."

He hesitated, looking past her at the three of us standing in the shadow, and then returning his gaze to her smiling countenance."

Wot is it, Ma'am?" He was frankly suspicious, but with masculine chivalry ready to serve a lady in distress.

"We've got to get some costumes from the warehouse very quickly. These fellows are part of the troupe who are going with me to get them. In the rush of getting ready we forgot them. Will you get us a taxi and go with us to clear the traffic? We're in a terrific hurry."

"But Hi cawn't leave my post, Ma'am." he objected.

"Oh, please," she pleaded. "We must have those costumes for the last act. It won't take long." Then lowering her voice to almost a whisper. "There's five pounds in it for you, sergeant."

"Five quid?" He gasped in awe and avarice. "Ow long will hit take, Ma'am?" He looked behind him to see if he was observed.

"Just about fifteen minutes if we hurry. Just call a cab and tell the chauffeur to speed!"

"And 'oo are you, Ma'am?" There was still just a trace of suspicion in his voice.

"I am the Countess Maritza Jerzil!"

"O! Well, ma'am, w'y didn't ye tell me before? W'y yore givin' th bloornin' affair, ain't ye?"

"Of course, officer."

"Come on!" he hurried out of the alley to the curb and whistled for a taxicab. Martha stayed close beside him. We followed, proud of the manner in which she had saved the situation but wondering how we would get rid of the fellow once we were out of the neighborhood.

We hurried into the old-fashioned taxi that trundled up to the curb.

The four of us sat in the rear seat while the bobby stood on the running board. Martha gave an address about a half mile away. We pulled out from the curb and roared down the street, making traffic lights and traffic signs with ease.

Out of the bright-lights district, we turned down a side street and entered a mean quarter. Martha motioned for Sam's pistol, a gleaming black, stubby weapon with a silencer attached. We three Negroes watched her, fascinated. Then we turned a corner into a shabby, dimly lighted, crooked street and as the dense fog rolled about us, she brought up the pistol.

Schicck! Schicck! Schicck!

Three shots that sounded like the breaking of the mainspring of a watch. The big officer plunged forward into the gutter with three holes drilled in the back of his head.

The chauffeur, surprised by the officer's fall and ignorant of its cause, stopped the taxicab with a lurch, got out and ran to the sprawling body. As he bent over, Martha's pistol rose again.

Schicck! Schicck! Schicck!

Three lead bullets buried themselves in his back and he fell across the body of the bobby.

"Get out, Jake," she ordered, "and be sure they're dead. Sam, you drive. Take that fellow's cap."

The two men did as ordered. Sam took the chauffeur's cap and got in the front seat. Jake carefully but swiftly examined the bodies, then jumped back into the cab.

"They're stone dead," he reported. "Alright. Now drive to the estate."

The tall mulatto nodded and, starting the motor, tore through the narrow street. Rat-faced Jake Stradford leaned back in the seat, a diabolical smirk on his reddish yellow face.

"That was mighty neat, lass," he complimented Martha. "I thought we'd have to drill that bobby right in the alley. We'd probably not have got away with it, what with all them other flatfoots away."

"Well, we made it anyway." she sighed with relief. "Now if we can only get to the plane everything will be fine."

"How far is it?" I asked.

"About a hundred miles. We can make it in three hours at the outside, counting all stops for traffic. We ought to be there now."

"Righto," said Jake. lighting a cigarette, "because they'll sure send out the alarm when they discover what's happened at Delphane Hall. England will damn well be too small for us."

We were rushing through the suburbs now, making fifty miles an hour, Traffic was scarce and we were outstripping all there was. The miles reeled off and as we put more and more distance behind us, our hope rose high. Just a little farther and we'd be safe. I looked at my watch.

"What time is it?" Jake growled. "Eleven o'clock exactly."

"Well, the dirt's out by now," he exclaimed. Then he shouted to Sam, "Speed her up, old man."

Sam nodded.

We were going down a straight black stretch through the black and silent countryside, making about sixty miles an hour. Suddenly we spied a waving red light ahead and coming closer we noticed three con stables standing in the middle of the road. They were pointing rifles. Sam slowed down upon Martha's advice.

"What's the matter, sergeant?" asked Martha in her most sugary tone. "We're in a dreadful hurry."

"I'll bet ye are," the sergeant growled grimly. And then, "Come on, pile out of there."

"What for, officer?"

"Ye're under arrest!"

XVII

Martha and Her Group Shoot Their Way Out of Police Trap and Arrive at Rendezvous; London Bombed as Return Air Trip Begins

What do you mean. . . under arrest?" asked Martha, summoning her most haughty tone. "Are you mad? Come, stand aside, constable. I'm in a terrible hurry."

"Ye're under arrest, I tell ye," insisted the beefy police sergeant.

"For what?" she asked aloud, but under her breath she said, "shoot out!" Jake Stradford looked at me, his evil eyes almost closed.

"Orders, ma'am," boomed the officer. "We've got orders to let no cars pass, especially not this taxicab."

"But why not? I hired this cab in London to take me to my estate."

"Aye, but the driver of this cab, the man who owns it, was murdered a little while ago in London, and a policeman along with him. Ye're in the taxicab, so we'll have to hold ye 'til the Hinspector comes. Besides, there's been somethin' terrible happened in London."

"Oh, what happened?" asked Martha, seemingly all excited. At the same time she nudged both Jake and me.

"Lottsa people killed at Delphane Hall, ma'am. They think hit's spies done it. So we gotta arrest everyone on the road that can't prove who they are. We gotta be sure. So you'll have to get out and come inside an let th' Hinspector take a look at ye."

"Very well, Sergeant, if you insist, but it's a great nuisance." Then turning to us, she said very loudly. "Alright, gentlemen, I suppose we'll have to get out," then, softly, she told us. "Now!"

Martha opened the door of the taxi and held out her hand. The police sergeant took his rifle in one hand and extended the other to help her. At the same instant, Jake and I lifted our pistols simultaneously and drilled the other two constables. They yelled and sprawled forward. The sergeant turned in alarm. As he did so Jake, who was closest to him, reached his pistol past Martha and shot him in the side of his head.

At the hissing sound of the silencers, Sam Wilbern, who had kept his motor running started the car and we went forward with a lurch, soon attaining a high speed. We breathed freer as we left the site of our narrow escape behind, but we were all visibly shaken by the ordeal. My respect for Martha grew. It was only her casual manner that had thrown the constables off their guard and enabled us to drop them.

Twenty minutes later we gratefully left the road and turned into the gate of an estate. For a couple of miles, we drove through dark and silent woods, and then we came into open country, a great closely cut meadow, elaborately flood-lighted like an airfield. Four huge planes stood in the center.

"Well, here we are," said Martha. "Drive up close to the planes, Sam."

The mulatto followed her directions. I immediately recognized the ships as our stratosphere planes. We piled out of the cab. The first person to meet us was K'bamgi. He nodded his huge head and grinned. Around us were the assembled Black Internationale secret agents, Della Crambull and her troupe of African dancers, and several other Negroes from the Liverpool and Glasgow offices.

Hunchbacked little Ezekiel Maxton shambled his way through the group, carrying a sheaf of papers in his yellow claw.

"Are we all here?" asked Martha.

"All except No. 4," reported the hunchback. "He got caught in the explosion in Manchester."

"What are the reports on the working of the plan?"

"Of the three hundred key factories, continued Ezekiel, "we completely destroyed two hundred and forty-three by explosion, thirty-two were partially destroyed, and fires are still burning in twenty-five."

"Very good, although not as good as it might have been," she commented. "Now what about London? Have you picked up anything out of the air?"

"They discovered the bodies in Delphane Hall just before eleven of dock. A wireless was immediately broadcast to stop all cars coming from London. And then a second warning to especially watch for a taxicab with three men and a woman I don't see how you got through, Miss Martha."

"We had to shoot our way out of a trap," said Martha, casually. "It was a narrow squeak. Now, what's the latest report of the plague?"

"Cases increased five-fold during the night. The same story from Plymouth, too. Reports from Europe also tell of the spread of the epidemic Paris, Marseilles, Rome and Vienna have the most alarming conditions."

"Good! Another week and they'll be too busy to think about Africa." Then, turning to K'bamgi she asked, "K'bamgi, what about our headquarters and the town house?"

"K'bamgi and Ezekiel do good, good, very good job. Nothing left." He revealed his beautiful white teeth.

"Fine! Now we've got to get going. This place is too hot for us. Scotland Yard may be here any minute. Who's commanding those planes?"

People moved aside for the flight commander to come through for his orders. Since I knew most of the important officers in the air service. I looked with no little curiosity to see who had directed the flight of the squadron from Fez. As he came closer, my heart leaped as I recognized that it was not a man, but my Patricia.

I snatched her to me and we embraced hungrily while the others looked on, all smiles.

"You didn't expect me, did you?" she asked, laughing mischievously.

"No, darling," and I pressed her to my heart again.

"Hello, Martha," she said, recognizing the others at last.

"Hello, Pat. It's good to see you. Is everything ready to go?"

"We're all ready to take to the air. We filled our tanks while we were waiting for you to come. Another hour and we'd have been gone. We didn't know what had happened to you."

"We'd better go on, then."

"Okeh!"

I followed Pat to her plane and hopped in beside her. Martha, Della, Jake, Sam, Ezekiel, K'bamgi and two others piled into the big ship with us. Where on my last flight there had been crates of rats piled high. there were now ten seats fastened to the floor. In the back of the compartment were piled up a dozen heavy opaque glass cylinders about a foot in diameter and four feet long on a special rack. It was not until we were on our way that I found out what they were for.

We left the ground quickly. I was sitting next to Pat. Right in back of us with his instruments on a small metal table, sat Tom Hudginion, the big black handsome fellow who had been navigator on the memorable flight from our secret Texas training camp to Freetown, Sietra Leone, on the evening of our conquest of Liberia.

The powerful engines sent us up fast. We circled high above the fog and the clouds until we were above the sprawling metropolis of London. The altimeter read seven thousand feet. The other three planes were to the right and left rear and straight behind to form a spearhead.

Pat turned around and signaled to Hudginson. He leaned down and turned a small wheel. The narrow trap door in the floor of the plane opened downward. He pulled a lever and one of the opaque glass cylinders slid out of its rack and into space. Another and another and another followed it in obedience to each pull of the lever until a dozen had hurtled downward.

A few seconds later a blinding light flared up from below. We watched the conflagration, fascinated. At short intervals of five or ten seconds the other planes successively dropped their death-dealing cylinders.

"Thermite!" yelled Pat above the roar of the engines. "Incendiary bombs!"

I learned later that Sam Hamilton had designed the glass cylinders especially for this secret bombing. The only sound they made was the crash when they struck the earth. This enabled attack planes to deposit their death loads, wrap the city in flames and escape before the source of the attack was accurately determined.

With a great section of London in flames, it was time to get fairly away. Pat turned the nose of her big plane upward and southward. The air grew rarer. We sealed the cabin and turned on the oxygen tanks as we flattened out at fifty thousand feet. The speedometer read three hundred and fifty miles an hour.

Weary from the exciting events of the evening and not having slept since six o'clock the previous morning. I began to nod and was soon lost in slumber.

Suddenly I fell forward, banging my head against the shatterproof glass window. I woke up with a start, gazing wildly about me, fear clutching at my throat as I saw that we were descending at great speed and at a precarious angle in the midst of a heavy rainstorm that shook the ship with its intensity.

GEORGE S. SCHUYLER

XVIII

Black Empire's Squadron Lands at Fez Only to Hear That French Air Fleet Is Attacking; Two Planes Lost in Air Raid; Pat's Ship Pursued

Visibility was nil as we hurtled straight down. The altimeter needle moved steadily from fifty thousand feet to forty thousand to thirty thousand to twenty thousand. Then at last we faintly observed the great airfield at Fez. Only a few pilot lights were on this time instead of the bright illuminations with which the field had been previously flooded. At two thousand feet Pat straightened out and gave landing orders. One by one we descended through: the driving rain to the muddy field, Pat talking to the ground all the time.

As we landed, switched off the motor and lifted the cowling. Commander Sandu hurried up in a motorcycle sidecar, with several big gasoline and oil trucks in his wake. The first streaks of dawn were showing in the East.

Sandu ran up, saluted Patricia and greeted the rest of us with his usual unfailing courtesy.

"I have the honor to report," he told her, "that the squadron is to leave as soon as the ships are refueled, by order of Dr. Belsidus. The other ships left here two hours ago for Kakata. I have brought breakfast for all of you. It will be wise to leave before daylight."

I noticed the haste with which the ground crews were going over the engines and refueling the planes. Every so often one of the subalterns would look anxiously at the sky. One man was seated at a huge wheeled sound detector nearby. There was an air of suppressed excitement hovering over the place. Around the airport headquarters I noticed, as the dawn came, a battery of formidable anti-aircraft guns pointing menacingly into the still-dark skies. Ever and anon a huge searchlight tore a column of light through the driving rain.

"Are you expecting an attack?" I asked Commander Sandu.

"Yes, if it clears. They may even bomb us in this weather."

"Who?"

"The French. Four days ago they occupied Casablanca, and day before yesterday they bombed us, but we drove them off after quite a dog fight. We got two of their bombers but they got one of our pursuit planes. We're expecting them to attack again at anytime. That's why you must leave as quickly as you can. We had more planes than they had yesterday, so they didn't get a chance to bomb us, but our spies in Algiers and Tunis report the entire North African French air fleet will visit us either today or tomorrow. It won't be safe here after sunrise."

"Suppose they destroy the field, what then?"

"We'll put up the best fight we can, of course. But if they are too strong for us, we'll go underground."

"Underground? You mean you have an underground hangar like the one at Ziggeta?"

"Exactly. We can put every plane underground in five minutes. That will save a lot of ships but it won't give us mastery of the air."

"And without controlling the air." Pat added, "we can't control anything, and it will be only a matter of time before we'll be driven back into the jungle like the pygmies."

We fell silent, reflecting gloomily upon this possibility. To have accomplished so much and then have to accept defeat was maddening. A black non-commissioned officer strode up to Sandu and saluted.

"All ready, sir." he said, and retired.

Sandu looked at the rapidly lightening sky and pulled nervously at his cigarette. The rain had lessened considerably and seemed about to stop altogether. Already the motors of the three other stratosphere planes were thundering. We shook hands with Sandu and went inside to start the last leg of our journey to Kakata, the Imperial capital.

THE FIRST PLANE RACED ACROSS the field and after a run of half the length took to the air. The other two planes followed. We were just starting our run when all hell broke loose. Out of the north swooped squadron after squadron of big French bombers at two thousand feet. Above them raced a cloud of fast little pursuit planes. Sirens screamed. Anti-aircraft guns crashed.

Boom! A geyser of earth shot up in the center of the field and instantaneously a great chasm loomed. Another and another and another.

The airdrome collapsed like a house of cards, a great sheet of flame shooting out as gasoline tanks exploded.

I was proud of Pat in that critical moment. The yawning holes across the airfield made it impossible for us to complete our run. Taking in the situation at a glance, she turned the big plane completely around and ran back the other way. I wondered at the maneuver because it seemed that any place on that field was dangerous. But there I was wrong.

As we sped along, a strip of earth much wider than our plane opened up as if by command, revealing a wide ramp. Down we went, deeper. deeper, ever deeper into the earth. The earth closed behind us. We finally came to a level, cemented subterranean field about one hundred feet underground. Here there were several large and small planes.

Pat came to a halt, cut off the motor, and we all piled out. Far above could hear ever so faintly the detonation of the big aerial bombs far overhead.

"My!" exclaimed Martha. "That was close."

"Aye," said big Sam Wilbern, "and that it was."

It was a new experience for him and Jake Stradford, for Della Crambull and little Ezekiel, but the black giant K'bamgi had gone through worse during the world war.

While we were discussing what we should do, a telephone bell rang somewhere. After running around a bit in the dimly lighted cellar, we found the instrument over near the wall. Pat answered it. "Yes, we're safe, Sandu, but what of the others? Did they get away? . . . Oh! Too bad." She turned away from the telephone to speak to us: "They downed two of our ships. The other, being the first off the ground, was able to reach the safety of the stratosphere, I hope." Turning again to the mouthpiece, she said: "Tell us as soon as they are gone."

From a nearby periscope I got a view of the field above. The French had certainly made a thorough job of bombing. Every building was razed and the airfield was pitted with shell holes. It was deserted except for the anti-aircraft guns and their crews.

But now an unusual thing happened. Nearby, great motorized snow shovels came crawling up ramps out of the earth. There were a half dozen in all, followed by two steam rollers. The shovels quickly pushed the dirt back into the shell holes and the rollers followed to level it all down. In less than fifteen minutes there was a straight runway down the field.

We received the signal to come out. Our ramp was lowered. Our engine hummed and we ran up to the field. Sandu, standing on the sideline waved as we passed.

After a good half-mile run we took the air and promptly curved southward, gaining altitude momentarily. Pat had no intention of being caught as the other ships had. Up we went. At two thousand feet we broke through the cloud belt into the sunny sky. We all felt considerably easier. Pat telephoned Sandu that we were safe and on our way. Hudginson checked our direction.

We had climbed five thousand feet and were going higher when Hudginson came forward and, touching Pat on the shoulder, pointed to our left rear. There, less than a mile away, were six pursuit planes bearing down rapidly upon us. Probably they had lain in wait above the clouds for just such an opportunity as this.

K'bamgi ran to one of the two machine guns, and Jake Stradford rushed to the other. Hudginson worked like mad radioing Fez, Kakata and nearby airfields of our predicament. No ship of our size could possibly hold out against these mosquito-like pursuit planes, which made as much speed at low levels as we did in the stratosphere.

On they came. Up we went. They could only follow us to a certain height, but would they get to us before we attained that height? Already they were eating up the space between us. Soon their machine guns would be strafing us fore and aft. One such plane we might fight. To drive off six was out of the question.

I looked over at Pat. She was grim as I had ever seen her. The others watched in terrible fascination as destruction approached.

XIX

Black Internationale Plane Shot Down in Flames Following Cat and Dog Fight over Fez: Pat and Carl Forced to "Bail Out" in Parachutes

Now we could hear the rattle of the machine guns as K'bamgi and Stradford bent to their work. The giant black was in his element. Cap off and sleeves rolled up, he leaned over, squinting along the barrel of the machine gun, pouring a steady stream of bullets behind us. On the other side of the plane Stradford was doing the same.

The pursuers came on. A minute before they had been mere pin heads, but now they were quite close. Pat sent the nose of our ship upward at a steeper angle. The altimeter read ten thousand and nine hundred feet. The super charger was put to work to aid our climb.

I went back to help with the ammunition. The two machine guns were eating it up. But how long could we last? What would happen when we had to change guns when the present barrels were worn out?

On came the pursuers, slower now as they struggled to make the altitude Big raw-boned Sam Wilbern, grim as an executioner, got out a sub-machine gun and took my seat next to Pat in order to deal with anything that attacked us from in front.

The pursuers were less than four hundred yards behind now but on a consider ably lower level. They came up shooting. A row of neat bullet holes appeared in the door. One of the African dancers slumped forward with the blood gushing out of his mouth. One of the mulatto secret agents fell into the aisle, a neat hole drilled in his head.

"Parachutes," yelled Tom Hudginson. hitching his own on his back. The others followed his example. There were a score of holes that had appeared in the floor and the walls of the plane.

The gnat-like pursuit planes were circling us now. K'bamgi swung his gun in a wide arc, spraying death as the weapon turned. The leading plane burst into flames and with a sickening lurch to one side slipped down, down, down below the cloud belt to certain death below.

We were climbing higher and higher. The little planes followed relentlessly. K'bamgi and Jake swept the sky in unison. Another plane went down over and over, its pilot fortunate enough to get loose with his parachute.

The other four planes closed in desperately. It was now or never and they knew it. We were up over fifteen thousand feet and already the air was becoming difficult to breathe. They wouldn't be able to follow us much longer. Wary now of the devastating fire from the tail of our ship, the four pursuers divided their forces, two attacking on each side.

Bullet holes appeared like magic in the walls, in the floor, in the wings. We gave as good as we received, but four of our crew were dead or mortally wounded.

Pat seemed to bear a charmed life. The windows around her had been struck several times but the gas tanks, oil lines and engines were so far intact.

Hudginson handed around oxygen helmets as the numerous bullet holes made our big oxygen tank ineffective despite the fact that the plane was sealed.

Now the pursuing planes were falling behind as we surpassed them in our ability to climb. Converging in formation, they made one final effort to down us. Through a glass I could see that their pilots had also donned oxygen helmets. That was discouraging, even though it was obvious that they could not follow us much longer. We were up at nineteen thousand feet.

Suddenly, dropping far below us, the four converged their fire from underneath. Sam Wilbern, who was leaning far out the front window firing at them, dropped his gun and pitched forward. In the rear Jake Stradford's little rat-like face was grim in death. Handsome Della, now grotesque in oxygen mask, grabbed his gun to carry on. K'bamgi, shooting through the trap door in the floor, clasped his stomach, his weapon hurtled to earth and he toppled out behind it.

Grimly, Tom Budginson dragged the other bodies to the trap door and cast them out. Considerably lightened, the plane climbed inexorably upward.

Della and I poured our last belt of cartridges into the machine guns and sprayed our pursuers with one last desperate volley. Coming up head-on, they made a very small target.

Then, one of them stalled, fell backward, and slipped far, far, down into the sea of clouds, to the earth below.

GEORGE S. SCHUYLER

Only three left now. Della and I grinned at each other. There was some hope perhaps. Then another burst from the converged machine guns below perforated the plane at all angles.

The big ship lurched sickeningly. The blood was streaming from underneath Pat's helmet. Hudginson, rushing forward, caught her as she swayed to one side. I was right behind him. He handed her to me and took the controls.

"Jump!" he screamed. "I'll follow!"

Della fired the last of her cartridges. I signaled to her to go first. With great courage she dived out of the trap door and fell like a plummet.

But her courage was matched by Pat's. She tried to smile as I stuffed a piece of gauze under her helmet. Hudginson was shouting for us to jump. But the problem was not easy. I wasn't sure that Pat could remain conscious long enough to pull the cord of her parachute. No, I couldn't chance that.

There was no time to ponder. Another burst from the planes below might finish all of us. They were falling behind us but not far enough to enable us to escape. Besides, the bullets had perforated our tanks.

I held Pat firmly in my arms and closing my eyes jumped with her into emptiness.

We shot down, turning over and over. As we passed our relentless pursuers, a bullet tore through my shirt sleeve.

Down we went, with me clutching desperately to my beloved and her holding to me as best she could.

I had wanted to pull our cords as soon as we were free of the ship but that would have made us a clear target. How long should I wait? One's brain works with amazing clarity and speed when one is dropping like a meteor toward the earth.

At last the clouds! Holding on tight with my left hand. I managed to reach over and pull Pat's cord. My heart sank for a breathless second. The pilot parachute checked our fall. I let loose my embrace and prayed that God would protect her—my first prayer in a long time, perhaps my first since I had joined the Black Internationale.

I shot down past her as her big parachute bellied out and she floated gently through the mist. Then I pulled my own cord, and in a moment I, too, was meandering through the ozone, descending like a wrath or feather through the clouds to the earth below. Above me several hundred feet I could faintly see Pat. She reassured me with a feeble wave.

Safe, at least for the moment. I wondered about Hudginson and the ship. Even as I speculated as to his fate, there was a roar above. I glanced up apprehensively. There, hurtling down in a mass of flames came the ship falling directly toward Pat and me.

There was no time to do anything. There was nothing we could do. I closed my eyes in agonizing suspense.

XX

Pat, Carl and Tom Hudginson Land on Desert and Learn They Are on the Direct Air Route Between Fez and Kakata

Roaring like a meteor, the great machine came down, swirled past so closely that the flames almost scorched my clothing, then disappeared. I certainly heaved a grateful sigh when that peril was past.

And yet, had not our troubles just begun? Where were we? Where would we land? It had been impossible to follow any direction except upward during the battle. We had gone this way and that trying to shake off our pursuers. Suppose we were over the Mediterranean or over the Atlantic? Supposed we landed in the Sahara, the most desolate spot in the world? Without means of transportation or communication, we would die of privation.

I looked upward, partly to take my mind off those unpleasant thoughts. Pat was floating about a quarter mile above me. I wondered about Tom. Had he been in that plane or had he jumped in time? Even then, had he escaped the machine guns of the French pursuit planes?

Well, it was now time to consider other things. I was through the clouds and could see the earth below, I tore off my gas mask and threw away. I wouldn't need that any more. As I came closer to earth my worst fears were confirmed. To be sure, I was landing on terra firma instead of on sea, but far as I could see, which was not very far, there was nothing but a barren waste of sand.

I struck ground easily and was only dragged a little way before I palled in my parachute and came to a halt. Yes, there was no doubt about it, it was the desert, and neither food nor water in sight. About half mile away were the smoking embers of the stratosphere plane that was to have borne us safely to Kakata. I made a mental reservation to rummage through the ruins and see what could be found of any value to us.

But now I had to think of Pat. I looked up. There she was, coming down easily. I got loose from my chute and, going as rapidly as I could through the shifting sand, followed her course.

When at last she struck the ground. I was there to aid her, so that she was not dragged more than ten or fifteen feet. It was lucky I was there. too. I tore off her mask. Her green helmet underneath was drenched with blood from her head wound. She was quite unconscious.

Frantically I felt her pulse, tore loose her collar and massaged her hands and arms like someone possessed. This vigorous treatment brought a little steadier pulse and a flicker to her eye lashes.

Somewhat reassured now, I cut strips from her parachute, bound up the nasty scalp wound and made a pillow out of the rest of the chute.

After what seemed an eternity her eyes flickered open. She looked up. recognized me and smiled faintly.

"Oh, Pat!" I cried. "Darling, I was so frightened. Speak to me, dear. How do you feel?"

After several seconds she slowly murmured, ". . . I'm. . . all. . . right. . . Just dizzy. Sweetheart. . . Where are we?"

"I don't know. I can't see anything but sand in all directions."

"Della, Tom. . . where are they?"

"I don't know. I haven't seen Della. Tom may have been able to bail out but I haven't seen him yet either. The plane's not far off. You rest easy and I'll run over and see if there's anything worth salvaging."

"Yes," she replied. "I'll wait right here." She smiled grimly at her jest.

DISTANCES IN THE DESERT ARE deceiving. It took me fifteen minutes to reach the wreckage of the ship. It was a mass of bent and twisted wreckage.

half buried in the sand, but the rear part of the cabin could be used protect us from the elements.

I looked for traces of Tom Hudginson but there were none. For one or two things I was extremely grateful. The compass was uninjured and Tom's instruments were intact. Best of all, the metal box of emergency rations was almost as we had left it except for considerable bulleting. In it was tomato juice, grapefruit juice, chocolate bars, crackers and several cans of sardines. Nearby was Jake Stradford's automatic, loaded.

Taking a can of tomato juice for Pat, I hastened to return to her. If it would be better for us to stay near the plane, where we could be more easily seen by possible rescuers. So after having her drink the tomato juice, I planned to carry her to the wreck if she was unable to walk. The gun I shoved in my belt.

As I topped a small sand hill from which I could see where she was lying, I noticed to my amazement that someone was standing over her. My heart jumped and I redoubled my pace. I had heard of wild desert marauders that lay in wait for hapless travelers, robbing and murdering them. I pulled out the silencer-equipped automatic and hurried through the loose sand to her side.

The man standing over her turned as I hailed him from behind and then my surprise was ten times greater than it had been before. It was Tom Hudginson!

We both grinned and Pat smiled through her pain.

"By George!" the big fellow exclaimed. "I thought I was going to be all alone on this man's desert, and here I find you two as snug as a bug in a rug."

"It's certainly good to see you, Tom. I thought you were a goner. You should have seen me search the plane for you just now."

"Well, I thought I *was* a goner. After you and Pat bailed out I saw the old ship couldn't last much longer. Just as I got ready to jump they set the crate on fire and then I knew I had to go, or else. I landed about two miles from here,"

"Alright. Now let's carry Pat over to the plane. There's room enough for the three of us in what's left of the cabin. Besides, I found the compass and your instruments okeh. Maybe you can find out where we are."

"Okeh," he laughed, "but a whole lot of good it will do us. I'm sure we're a month's walk from anywhere."

"Well, I jested, "at least we'll have the satisfaction of knowing where we starved to death."

We made a crude swing out of Pat's parachute and as gently as we could carried her over to the wreck. While I went back after my parachute. Tom got out his instruments and tried to ascertain our location. with rare presence of mind he had shoved his maps in his blouse just before taking over the stick from Pat.

Fortunately the sun was quite high now. By the time we had eaten and smoked a cigarette, it was much higher and calculations were easier Pat lay quietly, breathing easily. I felt sanguine about her recovery. After all, the machine gun had just grazed her skull, and while she had lost considerable blood, I felt that she would pull through alright even. without proper medical attention. She was young and healthy.

An exclamation from Tom aroused me from my thoughts.

"What is it? You're not going to tell me we're only five minutes from the coast, are you?" I jeered.

"Oh, nothing that good." he replied, evidently pleased, "but not much worse. We never got off our course. We're about four hundred miles south of Fez on the direct route to Kakata

"Yes." I sneered, "and right in the heart of the desert."

"Of course," he agreed. "but we're right on the course and that means it will be easier for the others to find us."

"But how do they even know we're down?"

"I told them. I called them as soon as we were attacked. They may be here before night."

"Very comforting, Tom. But suppose they *don't* find us. What then?"

"Oh, well," he said, laughingly, "the chocolate bars and tomato juice will keep us going for a while."

We both laughed with nervous heartiness. I looked over at Pat sleeping peacefully. Suppose, indeed, that they didn't find us?

XXI

Della Crambull Appears Out of the Night at Desert Camp of Stranded Fliers; Has Two Frenchmen in Tow; Tom, Carl, Inspect Plan

It was in mid-afternoon before anything happened to brighten our ill-concealed gloom. A swift plane passed overhead flying very high. Being without glasses, we were unable to tell whether it was one of our ships or not, but it certainly lifted our hopes.

"You know Carl," Tom suggested, "I think we ought to spread that chute of yours on the ground. Maybe they'll see us better."

It was a good idea, but I improved on it by suggested we tear it into strips and make letters on the land. The result was that in about an hour we had a big "B.I." spread out, the strips weighted down by pieces of the wreckage.

But no more planes passed over. The sun sank lower in the west, sunset became twilight and twilight sank into darkness. As it got darker the temperature fell. By nine o'clock it was really chilly.

Tom and I rummaged around through the wreckage and collected a few odds and ends of wood, paper and cloth. With some difficulty, we managed to get this refuse to smoldering and finally burning. We knew it wouldn't last very long, but it was better than lying there almost freezing in Stygian darkness.

Pat was coming around rather nicely, getting over her loss of blood. We made her eat a rather hearty dinner, according to our meagre standards, and she was now sleeping peacefully.

Then we were both startled by a wail out of the darkness!

I thought immediately of those desert marauders who, by crying like a woman, lure travelers away from their campfires to robbery and death. I got out my automatic. Tom took his pistol out of its holster.

"Shall I answer?"

"No!" I commanded sharply. "How do we know who or what it is? Let's just keep quiet and—"

Again came the wail. It was nearer now, definitely a human voice. For certainly there could be no other life in this desert waste.

"Suppose we get away from this fire?" said Tom. "We can move a bit into the dark and when whoever it is approaches the fire we can see them better."

"And leave Pat?"

"We'll not go far. Just a few yards, enough to get out of the light." He explained.

I threw onto the fire a thick magazine I'd fished out of the wreckage and we withdrew into the shadows beyond the ring of light. As the fire flared up on its new fare, there came again that cry out of the darkness.

It was eerie, mysterious, bloodcurdling, coming out of the blackness of the night in this desolate place. Was it someone in distress calling for aid? Or was it some devilish trap set by merciless thieves of the desert?

Again came the cry. It was much nearer, much plainer.

"We ought to answer," Tom argued. "Whether friend or enemy, they can't see us, but they can certainly see the fire and they know there is somebody here. I think we ought to answer. Suppose somebody really needs us?"

"Alright, alright. Go ahead. Maybe you're right. But if they can see the fire and are undoubtedly coming toward it. I can't see any use in announcing our presence until we find out who they are."

"You win," said Tom, "we'll wait."

We did wait. Five minutes, ten minutes passed. The cry did not come again. We put our ears to the ground.

"I hear somebody coming." Tom whispered.

"Me, too."

The footsteps, whooshing in the sand, came closer and closer. We froze to the ground in the outer darkness and waited, pistols ready.

It was nerve-tingling suspense, lying there under the starless black vault of heaven, awaiting we knew not what.

Finally we heard voices approaching with the footsteps. We drew further into the shadows. Here was no one person approaching but apparently several. We steeled ourselves for the ordeal.

At last figures loomed out of the darkness into the circle of light.

There were two white men in French uniforms, each loaded down with a big white bundle. There was another or others behind them in the darkness.

A voice out of the night shouted a sharp command in French. The two men put down their bundles. We waited breathlessly for the third person evidently the one in command, to put in an appearance before we played our hand. We didn't have long to wait.

Out of the darkness behind the two Frenchmen came, of all people, Della Crambull, bareheaded, a pistol held firmly in her hand.

"Hello, Della!" called Tom. She whirled as the big fellow approached with me close behind him.

"Hello, boys. My, but it's good to see you. I just figured this was your fire. Came over here on a hunch." Her voice sounded tired

"Where did you get these fellows? And what's that they're carrying? Where did they come from?"

"Now wait a minute," she laughed. "Not all at once."

She sat down close to us and opposite the two Frenchmen. She gratefully emptied a can of grapefruit juice, and then, lighting one of our few remaining cigarettes, she blew out a column of smoke and began.

"These two fellows are from that last plane we downed before we had to bail out. One of our bullets broke their feed line. They had to come down in a hurry but their plane was intact when it landed.

"Well, I floated down not far away. They didn't see me because they were busy trying to mend the break. I had my pistol. I sneaked up and surprised them. When they saw I was a woman. they tried to rush me and I had to part one fellow's hair. Ever since then they've done just what I told them.

"I saw our plane when it fell and I figured out you couldn't be so far away from it. So I made these fellows bring their parachutes along. I figured we could use the cords to tie them up and use the cloth for covering. It's mighty cold out here even if it is Africa.

"I think there is a chance to use their plane if we can repair that feed line. They've got quite a lot of gasoline."

She paused. The two young Frenchmen kept watching her and us. "Let's tie those two frogs up." Tom proposed, "before they go lamming out on us."

"Where to?" asked Della. "This place seems to be about the center of nowhere. They'd pass out before they got fifty miles. Their best bet is to stick with us, but we've got to fix them so they can't start anything."

Following her advice, we tied up the Frenchmen securely but not painfully, covered ourselves with sections of their parachutes, and taking regular turns at watching, we all managed to get considerable sleep before daylight. Pat was certainly pleased when she woke up and found Della at her side. The two talked animatedly while Tom and I parceled out the rations, giving the two French pilots a chocolate bar apiece, which they ate without being untied.

Then, leaving Della and Pat to watch the prisoners, Tom and I trudged off the five or six miles to the French plane, carrying only a roll of bicycle tape he had salvaged from our wreckage.

After what seemed an interminable walk. me upon the little snub-nosed fighter in a level place between two sand ridges. It was indeed in good condition but the feed line was cleanly severed, with one of the broken ends stuffed to prevent the loss of gasoline. Nevertheless, it was apparent that a lot had escaped.

"Think we can do anything with it, Tom?"

"It's a gamble, Carl," he said, emerging from his inspection, "but it's the only chance we've got unless one of our planes sees our signal."

"What's a gamble? What are you talking about?"

"This!" He held up the roll of bicycle tape. My heart sank.

"You must be crazy." I growled.

"Yes," he came back, "and I may be smart."

XXII

Carl and Tom Repair Plane, Return to Desert Camp and Take Off with Pat, Della; But Gas Gives Out and Party Is Captured by Cannibals

In less than ten minutes Tom had repaired the broken feed line as good as possible with bicycle tape. He admiringly surveyed his handiwork.

"Now, let's get out of here," he suggested, quite needlessly.

Soon the engine was roaring. We let it run for several minutes to see how our repair work held. It seemed to be doing very well. But I wondered what we would do if something happened while we were aloft, especially since we now had no parachutes. And yet, anything was better than dying in that barren place.

Tom taxied the little plane around until we found a fairly level place, then he took it off the ground and in about two minutes sat it down close to our little camp of the night before.

Even the two Frenchmen were pleased. But they soon realized that there was little reason for them to rejoice. The plane was much too small to accommodate all of us. A two-seater, it would be a tight fit to get four of us into it. To carry six persons was out of the question.

"Why not leave them here?" Della inquired, harshly. "This is war, and our first duty is to ourselves. They can make it to the coast, and if they can't, it's just too bad."

"Couldn't we come back after them?" suggested Tom. I could see his sense of humanity was greater than Della's.

"What? Risk our ships to rescue a couple of punks?" Della's lip curled disdainfully. "Don't you know the French are controlling the air in this section? No, let's leave them here with what little food we've got and let them shift for themselves. They wouldn't do as much for us."

Brutal as it was, Della's suggestion was best. We certainly could not carry the Frenchmen and, as she pointed out, it would be dangerous to return for them with the Moroccan skies dominated by French planes.

Pat voiced a mild protest, but she could see that we had no other alternative. So we untied the two pilots and turned over our little camp to them. Of course, they excitedly demanded that we take them along, but quickly subsided when they saw the futility of their appeals.

Once more Tom started the plane's engine. We were wedged in like sardines. Pat was strapped in the rear seat. Della and I managed somehow to wedge ourselves into the pilot's cabin with Tom.

We were off the ground and flashing southward in a few seconds. I took one last glance below where the two Frenchmen stood forlornly watching us amid the wreckage that had been our camp. The day before our plight had seemed helpless. Now we were winging our way straight south to safety.

IT WAS WITH A SIGH of relief that we saw the sinister desert disappear behind us as we winged over Senegal and then approached the savannahs and the virgin forests of French Guinea. In three hours the speedy little fighter was carrying us over the sluggish Niger.

We were making close to three hundred miles an hour, but we were worried as we watched the gasoline slowly disappear. We had had one hundred and sixty gallons. When we started, and now, with only a little more than half our journey behind us, the tanks were rapidly emptying. We began looking for suitable landing places in the wilderness of primeval forest.

Tom shouted his position into his mouthpiece in the hope that some of our planes or stations would pick up the message.

Our map told us we were now approaching Northern Sierra Leone, only a few hundred miles from Kakata. And yet how far that would be if we landed in the trackless jungle!

We were now down to twenty gallons. Tom dropped down to five hundred feet so that we might better see any possible landing place. There was none in sight. We rose to a thousand feet and circled about.

We were down to eleven gallons. To land was imperative, but there was no place to land.

In desperation Tom opened the throttle wide. We shot ahead while the gas gauge shot down to zero.

I looked back at Pat. Her face told me that she was aware of our plight, but she smiled reassuringly.

GEORGE S. SCHUYLER

Suddenly the motor went dead! The gasoline was gone. We were coasting at seven hundred feet gliding down to what?

"There!" shouted Della, pointing excitedly to our right. Sure enough there was a break in the carpet of forest, revealing a tiny village of not more than fifty huts grouped around the usual square.

Tom quickly steered the little ship toward the opening between two huge cotton trees. Our wings brushed through the branches as we shot through.

The square was wide enough for the plane, but it was scarcely a hundred yards long. We all held our breath as the ground leaped up to meet us. We owed our lives that day to Tom Hudginson's great skill.

The little ship was equipped with retractable landing gear. Instead of letting the wheels down for the landing, Tom plumped down and skidded on the belly of the plane. With chickens, goats and naked children running and screaming with terror, we sledded down the little square, rapidly losing speed, to our great relief.

But we couldn't lose enough speed. At the end of the square stood the palaver kitchen, a large, thatched, bandstand-like structure, the pride of the village.

We demolished the front of it and bent our propeller, but we came to a halt with all aboard safe and sound.

We piled out and stretched our cramped legs. The village was still as death, but we could feel eyes watching us. We stood there, just a little ridiculous and somewhat ashamed for having damaged these humble folks palaver kitchen.

I was about to help Pat out of her seat when the maniacal screams issued from the forest in all directions. We were soon surrounded by angry brown men, naked except for breech cloths, and brandishing bush knives, spears and old rusty rifles. Their teeth were filed to sharp points and their cruel eyes regarded us appraisingly.

A horrible suspicion chilled me. Della removed any doubts I might have had. "Good God!" she cried. "Cannibals!"

Rough hands quickly secured us. It would have been futile to resist There were too many against us. We were shoved into a dark hut and the door fastened.

I shuddered at the thought of what might happen. Had we escaped from the desert only to be eaten?

XXIII

Black Internationale Group, Captured by Cannibals, Fail to Convince Chief That They Are Not French; Prepare to be Sacrificed

The heat was oppressive; the air was stifling. Hour after hour we waited, alternately fearful and hopeful. I was terribly afraid for Patricia. Her head wound badly needed dressing and she was slightly feverish.

Outside was the drone of voices as the life of the little black village went the even tenor of its way. Several times I beat on the heavy wooden door but no one seemed to pay any attention to it.

"We're in a spot, alright," said Tom, striding around the circular hut, his hands thrust deep in his pockets. "This is a cannibal tribe as sure as you're born. I can tell by their teeth. They'll probably tear us to pieces before morning, especially if it's a moonlit night."

"What's the moon got to do with it?"

"Plenty. Their orgies usually take place on moonlight nights. If you hear a drum in about three hours, just prepare for the worst."

"If there was just some way of making them know who we are. . ." mused Della, who sat holding Patricia's hand. "They must have heard of the Black Internationale. Bishop Binks once told me that there was a Church of Love in every district in Africa, so there must be one in this district. And if there is, they must know about the Black Internationale. I wish we could see the chief."

"You'll probably see him soon enough," I remarked, "but don't forget that we came down in a French plane, and that every native in this part knows and hates the tri-color."

"But they can see we're not white," Tom objected.

"Well, don't you know that most of the French soldiers and aviators in these parts are black men? Oh no, color can't save us now. We've got to dope out something else."

"And we'd better be quick about it, too." Della added.

But minutes slipped into hours, the temperature gradually lowered and the crickets started their evening chorus, and yet we had thought of no scheme to cope with our dangerous situation.

Boom! Boom! Boom! Boom-bup-bup-bup! Boom-bup-bup-bup! Boom-Boom!

The initial flourish of the drums froze the words in our throats. I felt a chill creeping over my body. It was a moonlight night. There *would* be a dance. The worst *might* happen.

It was maddening to wait like rats in a trap in this stinking hut hundreds of miles from succor while men like beasts paced outside ready to deal out horrible death. I had heard of these terrible orgies in districts deep in the primeval forests, far from any authority.

The naked victims were crucified, head down, while flames leaped about them. And when their pitiful screams had been mercifully stilled by death, they were set upon by these hordes of demons and literally rended limb from limb with those horrible teeth.

Even in one's sitting room in Harlem one shuddered at the thought of such a fate. Here in the heart of the jungle, imprisoned in a hut with the booming of the drums deafening one, the sense of terror was almost paralyzing.

We sought relief in talking airily of many things and once or twice Tom or I tried to manage a witticism, but it just wouldn't come off. We were all deucedly scared and that's all there was to it.

The tempo of the drums now grew steadily faster and louder. Soon we heard wild music of harps and pipes interspersed with savage choruses. The pandemonium grew until it was almost ear-splitting. Then suddenly, all was quiet. It was a creepy quietness, like a cemetery.

We heard low voices outside the hut. A hand fumbled with the bar. The heavy wooden door was flung wide open revealing a semi-circle of giant, almost-nude warriors bearing streaming torches.

Two of them entered the hut authoritatively and indicated that we were to follow them. The savage sternness of their caste-marked faces brooked no refusal.

With Pat leaning heavily on my arm and Tom and Della following, we marched out into the clean, fresh air, grateful to escape from the evil-smelling hut but by no means sanguine over the immediate future.

The golden moon hung low over the conical huts like a great disc of burnished copper, shedding its effulgent light upon a mighty concourse of native men, women, and children packed around the central square. It looked like every native for twenty miles around had showed up for the feast.

In the exact center of the square stood four freshly hewn crosses describing a rough square, their crossbars close to the ground. Around them were several piles of kindling wood and logs and two or three gourds evidently filled with palm oil.

"I guess we're in for it, alright." muttered Tom.

As we marched up the square we were greeted with shouts and jeers. At the far end, just in front of our plane, we were ordered to halt.

Before us, in a low carved chair inlaid with gold and ivory, sat an old wrinkled black man, swathed in an elaborate blue and gray striped gown, his bony feet in colored leather sandals, his gray hair braided and tied with tiny red ribbons. On top of his old head sat a yellow fez. The entire assemblage had grown quiet.

He sat motionless, except for his right hand, which toyed with a leather fly switch. His old eyes studied us closely but his ancient face betrayed no emotion. When he was satisfied with his inspection, he suddenly shouted a command.

A little man detached himself from the small group standing behind the chief. Approaching him, he bowed low and, grabbing the old fellow's foot, held it affectionately in his hand.

The old chief was expressionless. The man nodded his head several times in assent. Then he rose, backed respectfully away from the old man and then, when almost upon us, he turned, straightened up and addressed us in miserable French of which I could make neither head. nor tail. Fortunately, Della understood him.

"He says the chief wants to know why the French have visited him?"

"Tell him," I said, "that we are not French, that we had a great battle in the sky and that when one of the French planes landed we sneaked up on the French, captured it and made our escape. Tell him that we want to go home to Kakata, to the great black chief whose brave armies have run the white men into the seas."

Della told the interpreter in French and he translated it into the language of the chief. The old man's eyebrows went up in surprise. Stroking his chin slowly, he looked at first one and then the other of us. Then he spoke animatedly to the interpreter who turned and disappeared into the darkness.

GEORGE S. SCHUYLER

The old chief was expressionless once more. He waved his bony let hand. There was a crash of drums in response.

Out from the shadows now moved grotesque masked figures garbed in rice straw, their bare arms streaked with clay. Numbering a dozen or more, they moved to each side of us, swaying rhythmically with the barbaric music.

Then a huge figure bounded out from behind the palaver kitchen man with a hideous mask, with necklaces of bones and teeth rattling around his neck and with bracelets of the same gruesome objects gracing his wrists and ankles. Above each knee was a circlet of straw. On his fingers were fastened cruel iron claws. His naked black body was striped with white ashes or clay. His teeth were sharpened to a point like a leopard's.

Around and around us he danced wildly, grotesquely, obscenely, while his chorus of straw-clad figures formed a circle and gyrated in perfect time. More and more the populace joined in as the drums and pipes rumbled and screamed their savage hymns of hate.

It was evident the old chief had not believed us. We prepared for the worst, though whispering reassuringly to each other. It certainly couldn't last much longer. The grotesque figures were moving closer and closer, sniffing, groaning and screaming I took Pat's hand and awaited the inevitable.

XXIV

SQUADRON OF BLACK EMPIRE AIRPLANES RESCUES QUARTET LED BY CARL SLATER, JUST AS NATIVES PREPARE TO LIGHT FIRE AND ROAST THEM

Tom and Della stood bravely and unmoved as the devil men danced closer. The giant witch doctor whirled before us, brushing our faces rhythmically with a horse's tail and screaming imprecations. It was certainly our end.

"Look at me, Carl," whispered Pat, squeezing my hand.

There in the shadow of death, we silently pledged our undying love. anew. What irony, what bitter irony that we, who had risked so much for the liberation of black people, should come to our death at the hands of black people!

The sweating dancers were now almost touching us. I knew our horrible death could only be a few seconds off.

Sure enough, in another moment eager hands seized us and bore us to the upside down crucifixes. We were tied securely while volunteers began stacking the faggots around our heads.

Then developments followed each other in such speedy order that it is difficult to give the right impression in writing.

Palm oil had been poured over the faggots and a native woman was running up with a blazing torch. Suddenly overhead there was a drone of many motors. Now from the sky came a dozen vari-colored flares. We could see easily from our position that the low-lying planes silhouetted against the bright moon were the familiar black and gold fighters of the Black Empire. Sixteen in all.

As the red, green, blue and white lights fell into the square and flared brightly, the savage audience fell back in panic, screaming and pushing. The wrinkled old chief forgot his dignity and ran.

The squadron circled back and dropped a shower of tear gas bombs which splattered around us like hail. In a half minute what had been, a few moments before, a cheering, singing, shouting assemblage was turned into a crying, coughing, gesticulating mob running is circles, screaming in strange gibberish. We also were in tears, but our heads being so low, our suffering was not so intense, as the gas rose quickly.

The planes flew over again. This time from each came two parachutes puffing out in the breeze. With uncanny accuracy that attested to long training, the men brought their chutes down in the village square, detached themselves and, clutching their automatic rifles rushed to our rescue.

In a few seconds we were on our feet again, surrounded by our men The lieutenant commanding them explained everything.

"We received your last message, sir," he said, "but atmospheric conditions prevented us from getting your positions clearly. Dr. Belsidus immediately sent up several squadrons and we have been combing the entire district between Kakata and Senegal. The country is so thickly forested that we despaired of finding you. Then, a few minutes ago, we saw the big gathering of natives in this square and knew something extraordinary was going on. So we took a chance, dropped a few flares and gas bombs to frighten them off and came down to investigate."

"You came just in time. They were about to light the fire under us."

"This is rather out-of-the-way country, sir," the lieutenant went on. Then he added, "Cannibal country, sir."

"Don't we control this district?"

"Yes, after a fashion. You see, this is a long way from the nearest Temple of Love. Besides, as in days of old, each chief controls his own district. They probably mistook you for French and wouldn't believe you belonged to the Black Empire. Thousands of French and British officials were killed by the natives in similar manner during the conquest."

THE SOLDIERS ROUNDED UP ALL the villagers they could, including the chief and explained who we were. The old chief was terror stricken and would have prostrated himself at our feet if we had not restrained him. We were given two big guest huts, one for Tom and me and one for Pat and Della. After an excellent native meal, we turned in for the night. The soldiers talked to headquarters over their field radio set, which had been parachuted from the skies when they dropped.

At daybreak next morning the lieutenant came to my hut and announced that everything was in readiness for our forty-mile trek to the nearest road through the jungle. The old chief willingly supplied hammocks and carriers, and naked porters laden with palm oil live dickens and turtles, rice, cassava roots, yams, plantains, limes, palm wine and honey. With the twenty-four soldiers, this made quite a sizeable company.

We made twenty miles the first day, stopping at a much larger village named Kanda. The following day, about one o'clock in the afternoon. we reached the junction of the forest trail with the motor road. We "dashed" the carriers and sent them back home.

Four big Black Empire trucks commanded by a sergeant were waiting for us. The soldiers piled into two of the trucks. In the other two trucks, which were covered, were two army cots each for our comfort during the rough journey over the bumpy roads to Falaba, which we reached about three o'clock.

At the airfield outside that large town were three big black and gold transport planes awaiting our arrival. After a good meal at the airfield headquarters with the officers on duty, we boarded the big planes and were soon winging our way southward on the last leg of our journey. The twenty-four soldiers and the lieutenant were in two of the planes while Pat, Della, Tom and I were in the third.

An hour and a half later we landed at the big airfield at Kakata. As the wheels of the big ships touched the ground a great opening yawned ahead of us, disclosing a ramp leading down into the bowels of the earth. One by one the big planes approached the ramp, throttled down to about 30 miles an hour and disappeared into the ground. I noticed that big anti-aircraft guns bristled around the field. At the far end of the field a gang of laborers was busy filling up a couple of craters.

A staff car was awaiting us. We were whisked to our bungalow. It was now about six o'clock. Everything seemed about the same as when we had left Kakata several days before on our mission of destruction, and yet there was a difference.

Where before at night the capital had been brilliantly lighted, it was now in darkness except for an occasional searchlight sweeping the African sky. No light showed even in the capitol building itself. I noticed that our servants kept the shades carefully drawn. There was a tense ness, an air of sinister expectancy pervading everything.

"What's been going on, Pameta?" I asked the maid as she serves dinner about eight o'clock.

"Boom Boom from sky," she explained. "Kill many peoples yesterday. Big house go 'squawah.' Airplane come from ship by Monrovia. Maybe come back pretty soon. Maybe tonight. Maybe tomorrow." She rolled her eyes in terror and almost dropped her tray.

Pat was in her room resting after having her wound dressed by of the surgeons. It proved less dangerous than it had seemed and be prophesied that she would be able to return to duty in a few days le her to get a goodnight's rest and went over to my office.

The capitol building was shrouded in darkness. At the entrance a sentry hailed me and then with a salute permitted me to enter the great doorway. Inside, the place was brightly lighted. As I started to enter my office, a uniformed page hurried down the corridor.

"Pardon, sir, Dr. Belsidus wishes to see you at once in his apartment. It is very important."

I followed him down the hallway until we went to the Doctor's door. The flunky spoke into the mouthpiece announcing me.

"Have him come right in," said the all-too-familiar voice.

The man swung the door open and I entered the regal chamber where, as I expected, Dr. Belsidus was not alone.

XXV

DR. BELSIDUS CALLS COUNCIL OF WAR AND INFORMS CABINET OF INVENTION OF NEW DEVICE THAT WILL REVOLUTIONIZE WORLD

I t was a resplendently regal place, this apartment of Dr. Belsidus, done in black, red and gold. The Doctor himself, in his purple and white pajamas, was sitting propped up in bed, surrounded by members of the Supreme Council reclining in the fragile-looking gilded chairs with red satin upholstered seats. Sitting on the side of the bed in a seagreen satin hostess gown was pretty Martha Gaskin, head of our espionage service. Her blue eyes were bright and full of love as she glanced periodically at Dr. Belsidus. Her spun-gold hair was caught up behind in the Grecian manner, like some goddess just descended from Olympus.

The Doctor was far more nonchalant than I had expected to find him with his capital just bombed, enemy ships riding outside of Monrovia fifty miles away and another raid imminent. He nodded not unkindly to me as I entered.

"Glad to see you back, Slater. How is Pat?" he asked considerately.

I explained our whole adventure and the superficial nature of Pat's wound. The others congratulated us on our escape while a servant brought me a chair and a slender, cooling drink. When I was settled. Dr. Belsidus began speaking.

"Gentlemen," he said. "I have received and digested the very detailed reports you submitted upon my order. I don't suppose you have anything new to add, have you?"

The others nodded negatively. It was certainly a brilliant group of men. There was Sam Hamilton, the studious brownskin chemist who had developed the revolutionary aquiculture: Alton Fortune, the great engineer who had developed our sun-power machines; Gustave Linke, the black metallurgist who headed our armament works: Dr. Andrew Matson, head of our medical service: Bishop Samson Binks, head of our Church of Love with its temples in every part of the world where Negroes lived; Ransom Just, the short, fat, yellow man who had done wonders in radio and television: Juan Torlier, the airplane designer and builder: Bennie Simpson, Director of Public Works; Alex Fletcher.

GEORGE S. SCHUYLER

shrewd financial expert who handled the Black Empire's money, San ford Mates, the architect: General Barton McNeel, head of the African Armies; and finally Prof. Vincente Portabla, the tall, lean. awkward black scholar who had once headed the department of physics at the University of Rio de Janeiro. Only the absence of Pat, head of the Air Force, prevented us from having a full attendance.

"Well, then," proceeded Dr. Belsidus, "we shall have summation and critique. Briefly, here is the situation at the moment. The Italians have taken the Libyan coast cities and are sending troops to Eritrea. They have already bombed Massawa. The Australian fleet is moving a large body of troops toward South Africa. The British, under cover of their vessels have occupied Bathurst, Freetown, Accra and other cities along the West Coast. The French have taken the coast towns of Algeria Morocco, Senegal, French Guinea and the Ivory Coast.

"The white air fleets dominate the skies above Northern Africa and our ships have had to stay on the ground, or under the ground, for the past two or three days. The British, based on Aden, have raided our centers in East Africa, and these raids will increase. We are still in control of the air in central and western Africa, but this cannot apparently last long." He paused, sipped his drink and glanced at the circle of grave laces surrounding him.

It certainly didn't look good for the Black Empire. With control of the air and the sea, Europe would soon again control Africa. We had neither the arms nor the munitions nor the men to hold back trained hordes of Europeans.

"However," he went on, "I do not regard the situation as seriously as you probably do. We are going to win, gentlemen, no matter how dark the future may seem at the moment. And we are going to win because black brains are as good or better than white brains. We have proved this before and we are going to prove it again."

Gray-haired General McNeel asked, "How?"

"By a new product of our scientific knowledge that is far ahead of anything the white man has so far invented. Dr. Belsidus quietly replied. "For this remarkable machine we have to thank Prof. Portabla and our old comrade, Ransom Just. But equally important in the equation is the effect of what we have accomplished in Europe itself."

A diabolical smile came over his dark face. He toyed with Martha's golden hair as he proceeded, as if that action symbolized his subjugation of the white race. Then he spoke again.

"Even if I did think of it myself," he went on jestingly, "the bombing of the European centers with plague-ridden rats was a stroke of genius. In less than two weeks of this activity we have completely terrorized the population of Western Europe. Death creeps over the continent. The medical services have bogged down. White people are dying like flies in the great cities and the survivors are fleeing to the isolated countryside. It is just like the Black Plague of the Middle Ages. This is a new kind of warfare, my friends, and we are practically immune. It is unlikely that the plague will cross the Mediterranean. And if it does, the Sahara will stop it as it did the last one.

"This situation, coupled with the destruction of hundreds of key factories by incendiarism, makes it exceedingly unlikely that we shall long be bothered with the white people. It will take them many years to recover to the place where they can again invade Africa."

"But, Chief," objected Alton Fortune. "What about the enemy right here literally at our gates? Those battleships and troop-laden transports are not in Europe. They are right here. How are we going to stop them? And if we don't stop them, isn't it a cinch that we're goners?"

Dr. Belsidus turned slightly on his pillows and pressed a button.

"Look!" he commanded, pointing to the wall directly in front of him. "I am now going to show you the machine which will change the history of warfare and of mankind. Alright, Sanders!"

There was a loud mixture of whirrs and hisses, a light appeared on the wall and a blurred figure began to take form Finally it stood out distinctly. At first it looked like a champagne bottle on wheels, two huge wheels. Then one could see that it had a great network wires strung all over its surface, stretched on slender steel spines. At the back a great cable descended, disappearing off the screen.

"Move it up and down, Sanders," he ordered into the microphone.

The nozzle lifted slowly until it was in a vertical position. Then the great machine moved backward and forward by itself, turned around and the nozzle went down to horizontal position.

"That machine is right nearby, gentlemen," said the Chief, enjoying out astonishment. "We shall use it when we have to use it, and when we do warfare will be changed. We have several others at strategic points. We are now as far ahead of the white man in armaments as he was ahead of black men in the past when we fought his cannon with spears. I shall not explain how this machine works until you see it in action.

That will probably be tomorrow morning. In the meantime, we haven't as much to worry about as you thought. I am sure. . ."

A shrill siren cut his sentence short. Whistles and bells outside sounded stridently. We all jumped up, grim-faced. It was an air raid "Sit down!" boomed Dr. Belsidus. He had never shifted his position. His capable black hand still fondled the golden hair of Martha Gaskin. We shamefacedly resumed our seats, but with misgivings in our hearts.

"Alright, Sanders," the Chief commanded. "Let us have a look outside."

In a flash we were shown the screen the action outside the building. A great battery of flashlights searched the skies. Dimly, we could see the crews around the anti-aircraft batteries.

Then, far above, there was the drone of motors. The guns began to bark and pulls of light dotted the blackness of night. Now the sky seemed filled with hostile planes, scores of them. Great bombs fell and resoundingly burst. It looked like the end of Kakata, the Black Empire and us.

XXVI

WAR COUNCIL SITS IN STUNNED AND
AWED AMAZEMENT AS "INFERNAL MACHINE"
WIPES OUT AIR FLEETS OF BRITISH
AND FRENCH NAVY

Awkward, lean Prof. Vincente Portabla galvanized into activity. Excitement made his smouldering eyes blaze behind the gold-rimmed spectacles. His bony black hand grasped the microphone near Dr. Belsidus.

"Alright," he shouted. "Stand by, everyone. One million volts. Open the hatch! Sixty degrees. Two million volts. . . Move forward. Quickly now!"

We saw a square of light appear in the center of the airfield. It grew larger and larger. Then out of it slowly moved the giant contraption whose workings we had just seen demonstrated on the screen a few moments before.

"Very well," continued the Professor. "Breeng eet up! . . . Quick!"

The drone of oncoming ships was plain now, plainer than before. The sky to the south, now moonlit saw hundreds of glistening bodies thundering toward Kakata.

Now we could see the great infernal machine of Prof. Portabla rolling up the ramp onto the airfield. It was glowing with some unearthly light. The spines of steel and copper were radiant and sparkling.

"Three million volts!" cried the Brazilian. "Now get your direction."

The nozzle of the great machine swung around slowly as the wheels turned, apparently by remote control. "Four million volts!" yelled the Professor, growing more and more excited.

This infernal machine was glowing now to a dull red color.

We watched intently, hardly a breath escaping us as we waited to see what this machine, which was not much larger than a bombing plane or a Pullman car, would be able to do against the combined air fleets of the British and French navy.

A deafening roar shook the capitol building as the first of the great serial bombs streaked to earth. We were thrown to the floor. We scrambled up again, dazed by the force of the explosion.

Dr. Portabla shouted into the microphone which he still clutched in his bony black hands. But there was a diabolical tone to his voice now. Gone was the excitement.

"Very well," he ordered. "Go to work. Act quickly. Swing across the southern sky between forty-five and sixty. Proceed."

We watched the machine with bated breath. As it swung slowly without the touch of human hand, bombs were falling all about us with resounding crashes that split the eardrums.

Dr. Belsidus was quite calm. Dr. Portabla had become almost Teutonically stolid.

Now the nozzle of the machine, pointed upward toward the onrushing planes, waved slowly back and forth like an iridescent finger. Our numerous searchlights lit up the night sky. revealing every plane.

Suddenly, an incredibly amazing thing happened, something I would have never in the world believed if I had not seen it with my own eyes.

One by one the propellers of the swarm of planes fell silent, and one by one the great ships plunged like flaming plummets to the earth. crashing resoundingly.

The huge nozzle waved slowly back and forth, a giant orange ray darting out on its message of death into the blue.

Squadron after squadron crashed to the earth. Panic-stricken, the remaining planes, many of which had already dropped their cargoes of bombs, turned to flee back to the coast from whence they had come.

"Thirty-five to forty-five!" yelled Portabla, grimly stroking his chin. "Five million volts!"

The infernal machine glowed to a bright orange. The nozzle lowered One by one the fleeing bombers and pursuit planes fell like stricken flies.

Soon the southern sky was empty of everything except the moon and stars.

We looked at each other for a full minute before anybody spoke Then the first one to speak was the Brazilian physicist giving orders to his unseen men.

"Breeng eet down to zero," he commanded, "and put eet away. That ees all."

The machine gradually turned from a bright orange to a red, then from red to black. Slowly a square of light appeared near it again. Uncannily, the great thing moved down the ramp and into the ground.

The square of light grew smaller and disappeared as the bomb-proof cover closed over the entrance to the underground chamber.

Dr. Belsidus was as pleased as a boy with a new bag of marbles. The grim smile was gone. In its place was a broad grin.

"Well, Portabla," he said, extending his well-manicured hand to grasp that of the Brazilian. "It worked. You and Just did a swell job. Couldn't have been better. How many of these machines have we ready?"

"There ees ten now." Portabla replied. "Each day Senhor Linke turns out one."

"How many can we use at once?"

"Ze meenimum powar ees four million volts for each. Eef we suspend many other acteevities, we can use all ze machines at once."

"Do we generate that much power here?" Dr. Belsidus continued.

"Not here, but in many other places, We send ze powar by wire."

General McNeel interrupted at this point. "This is a life saver, alright," he conceded enthusiastically. "It gives us air control again, and with air control we can hold off invasion for a long time."

"Eet also geeves us other control," insisted the Brazilian.

"I don't understand," said the General.

"Seet down, all of you. I wael explain wiz ze 'elp of Senhor Just."

The others took their seats while Professor Portabla paced back and forth, giving us a course in physics applied to modern warfare.

"Ze machine which you see ees in reality two machines in one. Ect ees first of all an atom smasher, a huge cyclotron, which generates an atomic or proton beam which can disintegrate any metal. Secondly, it ees a developer of a radio beam which possesses the faculty of stopping the propellers of machines and rendering batteries and connections useless.

"Ze machine, as you noticed, was not moved by ze human hand. No, gentlemen, no human could approach zees machine. Eet ees moved by radio remote control. Ze beeg cable you see in ze rear furnishes ze electric power. When zees beams turn on any machine, he perish."

"You mean it will stop *any* machine?" cried McNeel. thoroughly excited.

"Certainement, Senhor McNeel." the Brazilian assured him. "Ze machine is ze machine no matter what you call heem. Eeef iss metal,

GEORGE S. SCHUYLER

oet mus go. First we stop heem, zen we destroy heem. Come, we shall go out. I weel show you."

Even Dr. Belsidus went with us as soon as he had thrown on some clothes. We did little talking too awed by the awful potentialities of this machine to say much.

Preceded by an armed guard front and rear, our little party got into automobiles and proceeded to go about Kakata to see what damage had been done by the planes and to them.

One giant bomber had come to grief in the very center of the airfield. We drove close and examined it. It was almost unrecognizable. It had been scorched and melted like slag, its parts fused together as if it had been dipped into a volcano filled with molten lava.

All over the countryside were scattered these blobs of slag which had once been death-destroying bombers piloted by white men who believed themselves all-conquering.

There had been considerable damage done by the bombs. Several buildings were razed and there were a dozen huge craters about the own. Over a hundred persons had been killed and several hundred wounded when one bomb hit a big barracks filled with soldiers. But considering the number of machines participating in the raid, we got off lightly, much lighter than did the attacking fleet. It was reported to Dr. Belsidus that of the three hundred planes participating in the raid, only twelve had escaped and returned to the plane carriers off Monrovia.

"Tomorrow," mused Dr. Belsidus, lowering his eyelids and smiling grimly, "we shall move our machines to Monrovia."

XXXVII

Dr. Belsidus and His Huge Cyclotrons Roll into Monrovia and Destroy Navies of France and England in Uncanny Manner

I hurried back to the bungalow. Pat, who should have be asleep, was sitting up bright-eyed when I entered the room.

"Oh, it was wonderful!" she cried. "I wouldn't have believed it possible. I really wouldn't. It's. . . well, it's unbelievable!"

"It's certainly uncanny, alright," I agreed. "That fellow Portabla was a find, wasn't he?"

"Well, Carl, it just shows that we've got enough brains in the colored race to beat the white race doing anything if we can only assemble those brains. Dr. Belsidus realized this and acted upon it. Therein lies his greatness. Other Negroes were merely concerned in protesting that they were not inferior, that they were capable of doing anything that the white man did, and that therefore black men should be given the same chance as white men in a white man's world. But there was one thing plainer than any other and that was that if in truth black men were the equals of white men in all things, white men who controlled the world were not going to willingly give black men the opportunity to demonstrate their equality or superiority. It just doesn't fit in with the laws of survival.

"The first thing that was necessary," she continued, her face a deeper reddish brown with her excitement, "was to find out what we had in the way of brains and achievement. Dr. Belsidus did that. The next thing was to get these men and women catalogued and card-tiled. Then came the job of getting them into one secret worldwide organization. After that it was only a matter of time before we had money, and from thence we conquered. I knew from the beginning, darling that we couldn't tail."

"Well, you'll fall if you don't get back into bed," I warned laughingly. "And if you don't, I'm going to put a pillow over my ears because I've got to get up early,"

"What for? You need rest after all that's happened."

"I know, I know, but we've got to start out early tomorrow morning before daylight. We're attacking the fleet off Monrovia!"

IT SEEMED AS THOUGH I had scarcely touched the pillow when the telephone rang insistently, again and again. I reached over and grabbed it cursing sleepily.

"It is three-forty-five," announced the operator. "The chief commands that you report at the capitol at once."

I hurriedly performed my morning ablutions, threw on my uniform, swallowed a glass of orange juice and, kissing Pat goodbye, dashed out of the house and over to the capitol building.

Dr. Belsidus was dressed as usual in his immaculate tropicals and sitting at his low flat-top desk watching the giant map of Africa on the wall, where tiny red and green lights showed where enemy forces and ours were located, which ports were still in the hands of the whites, etc. On the opposite wall was a giant television mirror which brought at intervals pictures of the situation in different parts of the continent.

He looked up as I entered. There was a deadly calm and assurance about him that I don't believe I had seen since the white Powers moved to the attack. He sipped a tall glass of chilled orange juice, I waited respectfully until he had finished.

"Alright, Slater," he said finally. "We'll be going."

I telephoned that the Chief was ready to go. As we stepped into the corridor, a guard of four heavily armed, handsome black giants in black and gold uniforms fell in behind us. Downstairs, the Doctor's familiar bulletproof black limousine awaited with the gigantic Jim, his mute chauffeur, at the wheel.

I followed the Doctor inside. It brought back to me the first night I had ridden in that big car through the streets of Harlem to the Chief's headquarters in the East Seventies. We had certainly gone a long way since those days.

We were driven rapidly to the airfield, our bodyguard standing on the running boards.

Already the huge cyclotrons, ten in all, were lined up, swathed in dun-colored cloth, their huge wheels rising ten feet in the air Prof. Portabla and Ransom Just were ordering about a swarm of mech and electricians as searchlights illumined the scene.

Soon they reported to General McNeel that all was ready. One the other the cyclotrons wheeled down the paved road that led Monrovia less than fifty miles away. Behind each of the machines we several truckloads of machinists, electricians and equipment, and altery of multiple anti-aircraft guns with a giant searchlight.

IT WAS FIVE O'CLOCK WHEN we arrived on the outskirts of Monrovia. Dead and dying men were lying everywhere and the cries of the wounded were a strange accompaniment to the rumble of our giant machines a they passed through the narrow streets like great ghosts of dinosaurs seeking prey in the darkness. Many buildings along the way had been destroyed and several were still smouldering. An orderly explained that the defense forces had beaten off a landing force from the fleet just two hours before. Later General McNeel drove up and told how his men had regained control of the city, after the air fleet had been destroyed over Kakata, only to be attacked two hours later.

"We're expecting another attack in a few minutes," he said, "just as soon as it gets light enough. That barrage they laid down the last time almost wiped out the town."

As he was speaking, Prof. Portabla hurried up and reported that the cyclotrons were in position and cables supplying them with juice would soon be attached.

Dawn was coming up out of the jungle. The fog was heavy over the miasmic swamps and lowlands. We could not see the long lines of enemy ships two miles away. Then, with the typical dramatic suddenness of the tropics, the sun came up, dispelling the fog as if by magic, and there, just a bit offshore, stood the long lines of gray battleships, cruisers and destroyers.

The covers were off the cyclotrons now. Lined up at intervals of about five hundred yards, they looked like huge prehistoric monsters. At a wave of Dr. Belidus's hand. Prof. Portabla shouted his orders into his radio telephone

There was a love hum all along the line. It grew louder and louder. The crews retreated a couple of hundred feet from the machines. Gradually they grew red, then orange, and the voltage was stepped up. The myriad spines that made them resemble some sort of futuristic porcupines were like livid hairs. The proton rays darted out of the nozzles toward the lines of ships a scarce two miles away

GEORGE S. SCHUYLER

"We are taking the first line," announced Ransom Just.

For a minute nothing happened except the low hum as the great machines ate up all the electric power which the ingenuity of the electricians had brought down from the interior.

Another minute passed. We all waited, watching intently through our field glasses. Sailors were running frantically about the decks of the proud battleships of the white Powers.

Suddenly explosion followed explosion in uncanny procession. Before our eyes we were seeing the national pride of England and France going sky high and dropping back in fragments into the water. Most of the white men never had a chance to escape, although we did see a few floundering in the heavy sea.

The rumble of the cyclotrons continued. Raising their nozzles a bit. they attacked the second line of ships. In two minutes and ten seconds after Prof. Portabla gave the command, there was a second series of deafening explosions.

Inexorably, the great machines sent their devastating proton rays seaward. It was an ignominious death the whites fleet died, for not a single shot was sent in reply.

Prof. Portable explained that, "Ze radio beam he stop all batteries and dynamos. Zay cannot operate ze beeg guns. Zay cannot operate ze am munition conveyors. Zay cannot signal because zay cannot use tele phone or radio. We blot zem out completely. Zay can only lay zere an be destroyed."

At seven o'clock the Brazilian gave the command to cut off the power. The great combined navy that had threatened the very existence of the Black Empire was scattered over the bottom of the sea.

XXVIII

Battle of Monrovia Stuns Europe; Dr. Belsidus Prepares to Wipe Out Foreign Armies in Africa by Use of Latest Electric Ray Machines

News of the great victory was promptly broadcast to the world It was a greater sensation than the fall of the Roman Empire, the defeat of Russia by Japan or the Bolshevist revolution.

The reaction of the white world was one of profound fear, but great exultation filled the air wherever men and women of color gathered Throughout Africa, black people danced and sang with joy. In America and the West Indies and Malaysia, colored folk shouted the glad tidings.

We ordered a celebration in everyone of the three thousand districts into which Dr. Belsidus had divided Africa.

At high noon the black air fleet took off for Dakar, where four cruisers, remnants of the French fleet, were at anchor. With the loss of only one plane, we sent the craft to the bottom of the harbor.

The entire air fleet, preceded by stratosphere planes, left the following morning for Fez to clear the North African air of enemies.

The outlook seemed more promising now than ever, but victory had by no means been achieved. While a considerable number of units of the British and French fleets had been sunk at the Battle of Monrovia there were still a number of ships to be reckoned with. Powerful squadrons were at Cape Town, Alexandria, Tunis and Tripoli. As long as they remained, the Black Empire would not be safe because we had no battleships at all, and it is an axiom of warfare that he who controls the sea controls the situation.

That evening Dr. Belsidus called me into the office, along with General McNeel, Prof. Portabla, Juan Torlier and Gustave Linke. Attendants brought chairs and we seated ourselves. The doctor lost no time in getting down to business. A few seconds later, Martha Gaskin and Della Crambull came in. Both bore piles of papers.

"Miss Gaskin," the Doctor began when she was seated, "let us have the reports from Europe."

The white girl remained seated and swiftly read the reports from our various agents in England, France and elsewhere. The plague is sweeping Europe with unprecedented virulence. Millions are sick or dying. The situation in this respect is worse in the congested cities than elsewhere. All who can leave are fleeing the towns for the countryside. In the highly industrial areas like Manchester, Birmingham, the Ruhr Valley, the manufacturing areas of Belgium and Northern France, production is virtually at a standstill."

Dr. Belsidus's eyes twinkled at the news.

"Go on," he commanded.

"Agents report that typhus is sweeping all central Europe and the Balkans, while smallpox has gripped Italy. Everywhere there is a great increase in the number of influenza cases."

"What the prospect of them supplying fleets and armies abroad?" asked the Chief, leaning forward slightly, his brow wrinkled in concentration.

Now Della Crambull, the beautiful dark girl, spoke up. "I have been checking the reports from the seaports," she began. "Most of them are doing very little. Passenger service seems to have taken precedence. The rich and influential are getting away as soon as possible, because it is now obvious to everyone that the medical services have broken down. The troops sent on African service will probably not be ordered back home because of the plague, according to our latest information."

"Then they'll be virtually isolated," said the Chief. "Now is our time to annihilate them. McNeel, what is the total strength of the white invaders and where are they located in force?"

The gray-haired soldier reached into his inside pocket and brought out a small card covered with figures.

"There is a large British garrison at Cairo numbering about fifteen thousand men. The French have a total of about twenty-five thousand men in Tunis and Algeria, while the Italian army in Libya reached twenty thousand yesterday. The other garrisons do not count. These troops are mostly infantry, artillery. anti-aircraft batteries and cavalry. There are about a thousand planes in all. It is still a formidable force, sir."

"Yes, I know," said the Chief, scowling darkly. Then, turning to Prof. Portabla, he asked, "I suppose taking the cyclotrons up there would be out of the question?"

"It would take weeks," replied the Brazilian, "in the state of African roads, and even then there is the question of power. Mr. Fortune says most of the sun-power stations near the north coast have be bombed."

The Chief pondered this for a moment. Then he turned to Juan Tolier, Gustave Linke and Ransom Just, who had come in while Portabla was talking.

The cyclotrons are our best bet," he said, more to himself than to them. "but they weigh ten tons. It is impossible to use them to drive these white armies out of Northern Africa. We shall have to use our troops and that will take a long time. Is there anything you gentlemen can suggest? The quicker we finish the job the better."

"We still have the electric radio ray," suggested Just. "We have been using it in conjunction with the proton ray. The former will halt airplane and automobile engines; in fact, it will halt all electric transmissions and batteries, but only the proton ray will destroy."

"But have you anyway to project this electric ray except through the cyclotron?" asked Dr. Belsidus.

"Not now," Just admitted. "You see, Linke and Portabla have been so busy getting the cyclotrons into shape that we haven't been able to give much time to developing a machine to carry the other equipment."

"Why couldn't we mount it in one of our stratosphere planes?" asked Torlier. "The machine probably wouldn't weigh over five hundred pounds. And even if it weighed a ton we could carry it."

General McNeel, who had been listening carefully, now spoke up. "If we can get something like that we'll have the advantage. They'll have nothing to stop us. It will be a decisive weapon."

Dr. Belsidus straightened with sudden decision. "Alright, boys, we'll try that. Just, you get together with Linke, Torlier and Portabla and work out something as soon as you possibly can. Victory must be complete."

ORDERS WERE GIVEN TO HAVE the air fleet return immediately. The following morning, the black and gold ships flew in early and swarms of mechanics began preparing the bombers and stratosphere planes for the new equipment. Pursuit planes stood ready for protection.

Over at the great fabricating steel plant there was great noise and bustle as machinery hammered out the new equipment. At the electric equipment plant, Ransom Just was busy with the powerful cells, bulbs and other accessories for the new infernal machines. At the order of Dr. Belsidus, my wife remained in the house, but she nevertheless directed the preparation of the Black Empire Air Corps for the final battle and selected the pilots for the planes.

Summaries of news stories appearing in the world press were sent in daily by our representatives. To say that the white world was stunned by our great victory would be putting it mildly. As the decisiveness of the conflict dawned upon them, the white countries became panic stricken. Gone was the old haughty sureness that had come with long possession of superior arms. Black men had the superior arms now, and Europeans knew that black men had good cause for vengeance.

The exodus from the great European industrial centers continued in panicky haste as the plague grew in intensity. Dissatisfied with the speed of the plague, Dr. Belsidus sent at least one great bomber loaded with germ-laden rats nightly to be dumped over some big city. This continued for a week. Meantime, the three principal white armies remaining on African soil held their positions, perhaps wondering what to do. Their numbers were increased during the week as more units were sent out from home countries to save them from the ravages of disease. But our spies informed us that food and equipment and ammunition were scarce because the working classes at home ports and industrial centers were the hardest hit by the plague.

Seven days after the Battle of Monrovia, our factories had turned out sixteen of the electric ray machines, sufficient to equip nearly all our stratosphere planes.

On the morning of the eighth day, with Tommy Hudginson in command, the huge squadron took off in the early morning mist, surrounded by a swarm of pursuit planes. A fleet of big bombers followed later in the day, each loaded with huge incendiary and contact bombs. All that day and far into the night Pat sat up getting reports and issuing instructions.

XXIX

Italy, France, England Beaten in Final Battle as "Black Empire" Takes Its Place among Leading Nations of the World to Remain Forever Free

I was torn between two desires, I wanted to stay behind with Pat and I wanted to go along and see this last decisive battle for the Dark Continent. Dr. Belsidus decided the question for me. Shortly after the stratosphere planes left with their infernal cargo, my telephone rang. It was the Chief.

"Get ready to go with me, Carl," he commanded. "I guess we might as well be in at the kill. We'll leave at noon. If Patricia's well enough to go with us she can come along."

So that's how it happened that Dr. Belsidus, Martha Gaskin, Pat and I found ourselves winging northward in the Chief's speedy private plane which Jim, his giant bodyguard and chauffeur, had learned so well how to pilot.

We flew immediately to our secret air base near Murzuk in southern Libya, where the entire air fleet was gathered, arriving there about twilight. Like the airport at Fez, the hangars were underground. There was room enough for the stratosphere ships and bombers, but the pursuit planes had to remain outside.

We went to the rest rooms while the planes were refueling and enjoyed an excellent dinner. After dinner Pat and Tom Hudginson and General McNeel held a conference of war with the pilots, while Dr. Belsidus, Martha Gaskin and I took a stroll on the desert sands under the bright moonlight. Then we all took a bit of a nap in preparation for the ordeal to come.

An orderly awakened us at two o'dock. We hurriedly performed our ablutions and after a swallow of orange juice all around we went to our plane. We ran up the ramp to the field above and parked nearby the entrance In a few moments, four of the huge stratosphere planes in rapid succession rolled out of the ground and took to the air for the thousand-mile trip to Alexandria. Close behind them came eight big bombers and a dozen pursuit planes.

When they had disappeared to the northeast, a similar fleet left on the six hundred-mile journey to Benghazi, the great Italian air base near the Libya-Egypt border. We followed closely in the wake of this contingent. leaving the other planes to go on the four hundred and fifty-mile trip to Tripoli and the seven hundred-mile journey to Tunis.

At about four-thirty we were thirty miles from Benghazi, where we knew the bulk of Mussolini's air fleet to be stationed. The stratosphere planes landed with about a mile interval between them. We came down just behind them. The bombers and pursuit planes proceeded to their goal. Dr. Belsidus ordered Jim to take to the air again, as he wanted to see the attack. In about six minutes we were high over the air base. The eight bombers scattered and dived down upon the hangars and bar racks. At one thousand feet they released their messengers of death. There was a terrific roar. The buildings' planes, machinery, everything disintegrated into a million pieces. The bombers wheeled, dived and released their remaining bombs. Gasoline tanks burst into flames. Terrified men ran wildly in all directions. Now the little pursuit planes dived to within a few feet of the ground, their machine guns spitting death pellets at the frantically fleeing Italians. In a few moments the place was a shambles, a field of bloody desolation. Not an Italian plane remained.

A few minutes later a similar report came from Tripoli, to be followed by as favorable news from Tunis. At both places several Italian and French warships and transports had been sunk. And finally, about six-thirty, the fleet that had gone to Alexandria reported the destruction of the British base and the sinking of a cruiser and a destroyer.

But now was to come the test. We knew that in a few hours, British planes from Baghdad and Quetta would be seeking revenge, and that Italian planes from Sicily and French planes from Marseilles would be on similar missions. We had only to wait. The bombers returned to Marzuk for more bombs. We and the pursuit planes remained a couple of miles behind the parked stratosphere planes, while a couple of the little wasps patrolled the seashore on the lookout for the enemy.

Just before eight o'clock, the patrols radioed the approach of the avenging Italian air fleet. In a few moments we could hear the drone of hundreds of motors, like a swarm of gigantic bees Jim shot our plane into the air and sped a few miles to the rear, just for safety's sake. The dozen pursuit planes followed us. The motors of the stratosphere planes hummed but they did not leave the ground. Instead, their roofs were shoved back, revealing the glistening, infernal radio machines inside, with short ugly aluminum snouts pointed toward the enemy.

The sky was soon blackened by the great fleet, twice as numerous as that which had bombed Kakata. I admit that I had considerable misgivings. Suppose our radio machines didn't work! Jim must have had the same thought because he went so high that we had to turn on the oxygen

On came the Italian air fleet. But now an amazing thing happened. On plane after plane, the propellers suddenly went dead and the machines glided to the earth. Several crashed out of control. Again and again this happened, until the earth was covered with grounded ships. A score that were too far back to be affected turned and scooted for Sicily.

Now, at a signal from Pat, our dozen pursuit planes dived out of the skies, strafing the helpless grounded planes with incendiary bullets and small thermite bombs. In a few moments the whole plain seemed to be ablaze. Relentlessly, the little black and gold ships passed back and forth over the helpless Italian planes, reducing them and their pilots to cinders. And what happened at Benghazi was repeated at Tunis, Tripoli and Alexandria. Our bombers later blew up the remaining Italian planes.

After a leisurely reconnaissance flight over the field of victory, stratosphere planes and the rest followed in our wake to Murzuk. There we rested during the heat of the day. At five o'clock we speeded back to Kakata.

THREE DAYS PASSED, THREE DAYS in which the world marveled at the rise of a new world power, in which black people everywhere rejoiced, in which delegates in their colorful uniforms arrived by plane from outlying districts of the Black Empire, from America, from Malaysia and from India. They flooded the streets of Kakata and taxed the capacity of our two skyscraper hotels.

On the evening of the fourth day the delegates assembled in the great conference hall hung with black and gold streamers. Gorgeous music came from the Imperial Band in the sunken garden below the open windows Microphones were banked in front of the Doctor's lectern to carry his every word to the ends of the earth. At nine o'clock the music died. Then a flourish of trumpets brought the vast assemblage to attention. Suddenly the Doctor, in immaculate tropical whites, stepped from behind his high-backed chair and, saluting the audience, seated himself.

After the customary preliminaries he rose to speak. Only a few words they were, but I have preserved them for posterity.

"My dear friends and comrades and colleagues," he said, "we are gathered here this evening to celebrate the liberation of Africa and the emancipation of the black race. We who were once the lowest are now the highest. We who were once despised and slandered are now honored and feared. We who were said to have no future except to hew and haul for the white race have created a future more glorious than the white man ever imagined.

"It was no easy task. We had been miseducated. We had been kept ignorant. We had been kept poor. We were in the main awkward and unskilled. It seemed that only a miracle could save us. But the days of miracles, if they ever existed, are now passed. A few of us realized that no one would or could help the Negro except himself, that no brain except his own could devise a means of extricating him from his dilemma. All we had was our brains, my comrades, and all too often they were twisted by the white man's education.

"But there were a few of us who had hopes and dreams, a few of us who tossed aside the white man's morals and scruples which we had been taught, along with his religion, and made a new philosophy for ourselves, a philosophy of courage, singleness of purpose, of loyalty, of intelligence. We imbued the black people of the world with a new ideal, a new vision, a dream of conquest and nobility. We used every instrument in our power to achieve success, and we have achieved success.

"And now, a word of warning to the black people of the world. You have a great empire created out of black brains and strength. You can only keep it intact by continuing to work and think and plan. You must not make the mistake of the white man and try to enslave others, for that is the beginning of every people's fall. You must banish race hatred from your hearts, now that you have your own land, but you must remain ever vigilant to defend this continent which is rightfully ours.

"I have led you to victory, with your cooperation. Now I shall lead you to a higher civilization than Europe has ever seen, with your cossent. The glory that was once Egypt's and Ethiopia's and Benin's and Timbuctoo's and Songhoy's and Morocco's shall again make Africa first in the family of nations.

"Through your brains, your labors and your sacrifices. Africa has been redeemed. The shackles have been struck off. We are free and one children shall be free forever. Go forth, my comrades, and imbue your followers with the determination to remain forever free!"

He sat back, looking somewhat weary, I thought, and passed his slender hand over his face and sighed. A storm of applause swept the conference hall

Pat gently squeezed my hand, communicating some of her intense feeling.

I looked down the front row to where Martha Gaskin sat, her blonde hair looking odd among those Negroes. She was twisting her tiny hand kerchief in her hands, while a pair of tears coursed unnoticed down her cheeks.

THE END

A Note About the Author

George S. Schuyler (1895–1977) was an author, journalist, social commentator and somewhat controversial figure. Born in Providence, Rhode Island, Schuyler's formative years were shaped by his time in the U.S. military. Enlisting at age 17, Schuyler rose to the title of First Lieutenant before going AWOL due to a racist encounter with a Greek immigrant. Sentenced to five years for the abandonment, Schuyler was released after less than a year for being a model prisoner. In the aftermath of his release, he lived at the Phillis Wheatley Hotel in New York City, coming to learn the teachings of Black nationalist, Marcus Garvey. Not fully convinced of Garvey's teachings, Schuyler would separate himself from both Garveyism and socialism, contributing articles to the *American Mercury* and embracing capitalism. Embarking on a career in journalism, Schuyler would find success and acknowledgement for his editorial skills as he took on the role of Chief Editorial Writer at the *Courier* in 1926. That same year he would pen a controversial piece, "The Negro-Art Hokum" for *The Nation* which—combined with his advocacy for capitalism—further alienated himself from his contemporaries. The article, which argued that art should not be segregated by race and that Black artist had no true style of their own, would inspire Langston Hughes' famous, "The Negro and The Racial Mountain." Five years after this, Schuyler would try his hand at a long fiction form, producing notable novels such as *Slaves Today* (1931), *Black No More* (1931), and *Black Empire* (1936–1938); and while Schuyler would continue to produce work up until the point of his death, it was his public and explicit conservatism and opposition to the Civil Rights Movement of the 1960s–70s that would push both he and his literary work into obscurity. At the time of his death, his legacy and talent as a writer were so overshadowed by his politics that no one within Black circles wanted to interact with his work at all. Despite this, Schuyler produced some of the first satires by a Black writer and addressed intra-community issues at a time when most Black authors appealed solely to the middle-class.

A Note from the Publisher

Spanning many genres, from non-fiction essays to literature classics to children's books and lyric poetry, Mint Edition books showcase the master works of our time in a modern new package. The text is freshly typeset, is clean and easy to read, and features a new note about the author in each volume. Many books also include exclusive new introductory material. Every book boasts a striking new cover, which makes it as appropriate for collecting as it is for gift giving. Mint Edition books are only printed when a reader orders them, so natural resources are not wasted. We're proud that our books are never manufactured in excess and exist only in the exact quantity they need to be read and enjoyed. To learn more and view our library, go to minteditionbooks.com

bookfinity & MINT EDITIONS

Enjoy more of your favorite classics with Bookfinity,
a new search and discovery experience for readers.
With Bookfinity, you can discover more vintage
literature for your collection, find your Reader Type,
track books you've read or want to read,
and add reviews to your favorite books.
Visit www.bookfinity.com, and click on
Take the Quiz to get started.

Don't forget to follow us
@bookfinityofficial and @mint_editions